The

IRON
CIRCLET

Chronicles of the Black Gate: 4

PHIL TUCKER

-2017-

Nous

Agerastos

Bythos

THE IRON CIRCLET
Phil Tucker

First Edition. First printed in the United States of America

10   9   8   7   6   5   4   3   2

Chapter 1

E xhaustion clutched at Kethe, sought with ragged futility to drag her down into a few hours of oblivion. To sleep. To rest. To put an end to her turmoil and pain. Yet all she could do was sit there on the rocky scree beside Asho, watching him breathe deeply, studying his gaunt face. He was lying on his side, arm curled under his head, knees raised to his chest. Even in sleep, he looked wounded, as if some crucial part of his soul had been deeply and irrevocably torn.

And she was helpless to comfort him.

All it would take would be to lie behind him, hold him close, fit her knees behind his own, interlock with him, share warmth, her presence, her concern.

Yet she couldn't.

She felt as if she were trapped in stone. A gulf had opened between them, one that she thought she'd managed to hide from him while they'd conversed in low tones, but which now, with his having fallen asleep, yawned wide and kept her from going to his side.

He'd spoken fervently for an hour about what he'd been trying to accomplish in Bythos. The rallies, the struggles, his identification with the Bythians and his final pulling away from that inclusion. How he was only more convinced that the Empire had to fall. He'd complained bitterly about Iskra's decision to work with the Ascendant, taking for granted that Kethe was still the girl he'd fought beside on the ramparts of Mythgraefen.

Taking for granted that she'd not changed.

Kethe closed her eyes, and from deep within her core arose the White Song. A single, quavering note of such beauty that she felt tears brim in her eyes. Somewhere beyond this vast and dismal cavern floated Aletheia, and at its peak was the White Gate, glorious, transcendent, mystical, and refuting every belief that Asho clung to.

How could she hold him tight when she no longer doubted Ascendancy?

She felt hollowed out. Gutted. Who was she?

Kethe? Or Makaria?

Sitting up straight, she looked over the low wall of rocks behind which they were resting and at the remnants of the imperial army. A few hundred Ennoian soldiers and guards. A handful of Consecrated, amongst them Khoussan and Dalitha. All of them knowing to their bones who she was. All of them waiting for her to lead them against Tharok. To be the hammer against the Abythian forces' anvil.

She reached down and curled an errant lock of white hair behind Asho's ear. Her heart ached for him. He'd suffered down here. Suffered terribly, and the lines of pain etched into his face spoke volumes about his ordeals. Before falling asleep, he'd said something about his father, but the subject had been too painful for him to pursue. He'd fallen asleep with tears running down his cheeks, and she'd hated herself for not being able to comfort him.

Hated herself still.

With a sigh, she rose to her feet. She stretched, feeling the aches and deep bruising from yesterday's ferocious fighting, and then picked up her scabbarded blade. It was a hand-and-a-half blade, short and wickedly sharp, but while her other sword had been masterfully forged by Elon, this weapon was in a different category altogether; it was a work of art, its hilt gilded, its edge straight and unmarked despite having been used brutally in battle. Unlike her sword, her green enameled armor was battered and dented, covered in dust and dried blood, and her cloak was tattered. She felt just as worn, just as poorly used.

Kethe closed her eyes. *Gather yourself. You need to be Makaria now, if only for a little longer.* She inhaled deeply, held the breath, sought the White Song and found comfort in its clarity, its purity. Held her breath, allowed that white glow to suffuse her mind's eye, then exhaled and walked around the rocks to her soldiers.

Ser Cunad rose to his feet, bowed with lithe grace, and removed his bascinet helm, revealing a shock of golden hair. "Virtue."

"How long till the Solar Portals open?"

He glanced up at where the *aurora infernalis* was roiling, obscuring the cavern roof in a swirling mass of refulgent hues. Streaks of dusty green flowed into cobalt yellows, and plumes of deep blue rose and then spread out, transforming into glowing purples. The winged silhouettes of agony vultures spiraled overhead, vast and ominous.

"Soon," he said. "Very soon. Shall I form up the men?"

"Do so," she said. "I want to be in position to strike the moment the Abythian Portal lights up."

He bowed once more, then hesitated. "Virtue, please forgive me if I go too far, but it is an honor to serve under you."

"Why would that be going too far?"

His smile grew vulpine. "Because I can't help but recall fighting you before Kyferin Castle's walls during your mother's tourney. If I had known then what you would become, I wouldn't have striven to dash your brains out with such vigor."

Kethe snorted. "If I recall correctly, I stove in your cuirass and stepped over you on my way to defeating Kitan."

Cunad gave a wry half-bow. "Precisely. It pleases me that my defeat was a portent of your coming greatness. Excuse me." With that, he strode away, smiling smugly, and began barking out orders to men who quickly began to scramble into formation.

Kethe shook her head and walked over to where the Consecrated were sitting in a loose circle. Khoussan was standing there tiredly, a dirty bandage wrapped around the cruel cut that ran down the left side of his face, held in place by a strip of cotton that wound over the bridge of his nose. His dreadlocks were matted with blood, and even his great muscular frame looked worn down; his shoulders were bowed, his eyes bloodshot.

"How are you holding up?" She touched his arm, aware of the other Consecrated as they also stood. The remnants of Henosis' and Ainos' cohorts, men and women she'd never had the chance to speak with.

"I'm fine," he said, his voice a deep rumble, and, somehow, hearing the steady strength in his voice, she believed him.

"I can't tell you how glad I am that you're here," she said quietly. She fought the urge to hug herself. "How are you so calm?"

"How?" He smiled, and for the first time she saw pain in his expression. "You helped me die, Virtue. You helped me let go of the man I used to be. Now? I'm but a tool for the Ascendant. I only hope to be worthy."

She searched his face and saw that he had spoken without any trace of sarcasm. He believed it, and she felt chilled at the realization; this was her doing, her work, her pushing him till he' reached his breaking point and evolved. Why did the same equanimity evade her?

Kethe pushed those thoughts aside. "Any sign of Ainos?"

The Virtue had left at dusk to send reinforcements from the Blade Towers; though men had streamed across the badlands to flesh out their numbers, Kethe hadn't seen any sign of Ainos since.

"No," said Khoussan. "She might still be searching for soldiers."

Dalitha seemed to emerge from Khoussan's shadow. Blood and vomit had dried down her front, but she'd avoided injury; still, her eyes were shining fever-bright, and she looked as delicate and flighty as a sparrow. "Should we wait for her?"

"No," said Kethe, biting her lip. "No, we can't wait. We must be ready. When Akinetos, Mixis and Synesis punch through the Portal below, at the front of five thousand soldiers, we have to be in place to prevent Tharok's escape into the labyrinth."

The other Consecrated were listening intently. Kethe spoke a little louder to include them all. "He dies within the next hour. His invasion stops here. I'll admit he did well, surprising us all with innovative tactics, but he pushed too fast, too hard. He's stranded and without support. Now, he'll face the fury of the Empire. Now, he'll learn what happens when he arouses the righteous wrath of the Ascendant's finest warriors."

Heads were nodding, shoulders going back, confidence returning to the expressions around her.

"We're going to lead the host down. Prepare yourselves. We descend soon."

Kethe felt someone watching her, and, turning, saw Asho. His face was inscrutable.

"I'll be right back," she said to Khoussan, and walked over to meet him halfway. "You're awake." *You're awake. Brilliant. What else can you point out to him?*

"Did you think I could sleep through a speech like that?" His smile was wry. "You've gotten good at this whole leadership thing."

"What, those three sentences?"

"However many there were. Last I saw you, you couldn't talk to a crowd without getting flustered. Now? You're a natural."

She smiled. "You want to hear inspiring, you should try standing on the training ground in Aletheia while Theletos speaks to hundreds of Consecrated as the sun rises behind him. That'll get your blood flowing."

Asho frowned, and Kethe immediately felt her cheeks burn. "I mean, he's, ah, much better at this than I am. That's all."

"I'm sure," said Asho. He was looking at her differently, as if evaluating her, seeing her for the first time, or perhaps in a new light. "Last night, I never got to ask you about your own experiences." His voice was quiet. "And for that, I'm sorry. I was so eager to share with you that I only talked about myself. But I see you've gone through your own share of changes."

"Asho," said Kethe. She wanted to take his hand. Wanted to take him aside, tell the world to wait, to find a quiet corner and explain, to walk him through all she had lived through. To try to share the impossible beauty of the White Gate.

But she couldn't.

There simply wasn't time.

That, and she didn't think she could find the words while looking into his eyes.

"Asho, we're about to head down. Do – do you want to march down beside me?"

"Beside you?" He arched a pale brow. "Of course. Why wouldn't I?"

"You're without your powers..." She faltered. "My Consecrated and I are going to be at the very front..."

"I still know how to wield a blade," he said. "Unless there's some other reason you'd rather I not be there?"

"What? No. Of course not. Good. Come over. I'll introduce you to everyone."

"No, that's all right." He looked past her to where the Consecrated were standing. "I'll fight beside them, but I don't need to meet them. Even if they are... yours."

"You don't...?"

He took her hand. "Kethe. They're the enemy. They're the pillars of the Empire. The ones who will one day become Virtues and continue the oppression and injustice." He spoke softly, reasonably, as if reminding her of core truths. "I don't want to meet them, to become their friend. All right?"

Kethe felt as if she were being twisted apart. She couldn't meet his eyes. "Right," she whispered.

"Kethe," he said, his voice insistent. He leaned forward. "You remember your words outside Mythgraefen, don't you? What you said to Ser Wyland?"

"Of course I do." She pulled her hand free. They were being watched. Tears came to her eyes again, and she took a shuddering breath, feeling the fool. Why did he make her feel so young, so unsure of herself? "This isn't the time, Asho. We're about to fight *Tharok*. Everything is on the line. We'll talk after he's dead."

"Yes," he said, stepping back. "I agree. Everything is on the line."

He said it as if he meant something else, but before she could ask, Ser Cunad approached. "Virtue Makaria, the men are ready. Do you wish to address them?"

"Yes," she said shakily. She followed him, feeling ashamed of her sense of relief. She could feel Asho's gaze on her back.

So saying, she stepped to the mouth of the ramp that descended into the labyrinth, its depths lit by soft green buglights, and turned to face the assembled soldiers. A sense of calm descended on her. This was what mattered. Regardless of what came after, this mission, this moment, this was what she was born to handle.

"We're going down to kill a monster who seeks to destroy our Empire," said Kethe, pitching her voice to carry. "Tharok is below with some fifty kragh and four trolls. He gambled everything on getting through the Gate last night, but now he's stranded. Our forces in Abythos will be the anvil. We'll be the hammer. When the Portal opens, we'll crush him between us and end his damned invasion once and for all."

A series of grunts and affirmations rose from the ranks. She saw Asho look about him. He'd never seen her address troops like this before, had never seen so many grimly determined to follow her into battle. They weren't about to cry out their support, to roar their anger; instead, they were quietly and fiercely focused on the task at hand.

"Follow me below, and then hold till I give the signal. We'll not engage Tharok till after the Portal opens and our forces have come through to fight him. When I give the command, we'll split into three groups. I'll lead the main attack. Three Consecrated will lead each of the other two groups in guarding our flanks to prevent the kragh from swinging around and attacking us from behind. Clear?"

More grunts, and several soldiers clanged their swords on their shields. She drew her own blade.

"All right." Kethe's eyes roved over the crowd, meeting people's gazes, her expression solemn and focused. "This one is for the Ascendant. Let's go kill in his name."

With that, she turned and strode down the ramp, letting Asho fall in step with Khoussan and Dalitha, the other Consecrated moving alongside them, and soon they were below ground, the tramp of boots and the jangle of armor echoing off the rough walls.

The ramp circled down and down into the depths of the labyrinth. Passageways opened here and there in its sides, leading off into the darkness. They walked over discarded supplies, bodies, and around abandoned wagons and carts. Kethe's heart thudded powerfully as they marched ever deeper.

She never looked back. She led them all down, ever down. The ramp leveled out, the buglight growing brighter as they reached the vast Portal chamber. Their sentries stepped out of their niches in the walls and moved over to Kethe, whispering reports to her and then heading back to join the ranks of soldiers. All was quiet. Kethe stepped forward into the chamber and saw for herself: Tharok's forces were clustered before the huge Portal that rose in the central island which was surrounded by ravines that plummeted into the depths. Causeways linked the central island to circular pathways that ringed it, the broadest of which ran directly from the ramp to the Portal's base.

The trolls were guarding the causeways. As one, they rose to their feet, looming massively in the green light, their batwing ears twitching and their hands tightening around their gore-splattered warhammers. Each stood about thirteen feet tall, and their alien visages were implacable as they stared out across the ravines at her.

Kethe looked past them and found Tharok himself amongst his kragh. He was easily the largest of them, black-skinned and powerfully muscled, a great scimitar held in one hand, a dull circlet of iron marking him as the warlord. Radiating authority and power, he moved to the fore of his forces and grinned, his heavy tusks making the expression predatory. Despite his size, Kethe knew firsthand that he could move as fast as the wind; the evening before, Tharok had done the impossible and fought off three Virtues, combining raw savagery and strength with an almost impossible speed.

Kethe wished for a company of archers. Spearmen. Anything that would allow them to strike the warlord down from a distance.

The other fifty or so kragh had risen to their feet. They moved to the edge of the island, a wall of broad shoulders, green flesh, heavy weapons and bestial ferocity. Just one of those kragh was a match for three trained men; she'd seen them keep fighting the evening before, long after a man would have fallen to blood loss and wounds.

Silence filled the vast chamber. Both sides stared at each other, waiting. Kethe's pulse pounded in her ears. She could sense the assembled men behind her, the ranks upon ranks of soldiers ready to do battle, breathing in sharp, shallow breaths, knowing that at any moment she would give the order to charge and they might die. She felt the tension curdle her belly, tighten her throat. She was no longer a stranger to battle, but facing those trolls, staring down at Tharok himself, she knew that the causeways would soon be awash with blood.

Any moment now.

The Portal rose high behind the kragh, its interior empty. No glimmer yet of its impending activation. But soon, soon, it would fill with black ink and then the battle would be joined.

A hundred throats let out a hiss of anticipation as the first stirrings of magic appeared in the center of the Portal. Filaments of black undulated across its surface, connecting one side of the arch to the other, and then, in a flash, they spread out and flooded the space completely, forming a choppy surface like ocean waves stirred by a fitful wind. Kethe saw the kragh turn to look up at the Portal's surface, saw them lift their weapons in anticipation.

Everyone stared at the Portal but the trolls and Tharok. He alone of the kragh was gazing out at them. Waiting. Confident somehow that events were going to go his way.

"Get ready," said Kethe, raising her sword as if to salute their enemy. White fire raced up its length, startlingly bright in the subdued green glow. "Wait for my mark!" The soldiers behind her growled and groaned. The ranks sounded like a bar of metal being warped by too much stress. "Steady!"

The first figure stepped out through the black ink of the Portal. A kragh. Not stumbling back as if in a fighting retreat. Not hurried or in alarm. Cautious. Wary. A mountain kragh, mace held in both broad hands. It blinked, saw Tharok and his forces, and its mouth split into a wide grin as it moved forward.

Kethe stood frozen. The silence coming from the ranks behind her ached.

More kragh came through. Five. Ten. Twenty. They were marching forth in rough ranks, a steady stream that quickly began to fill the central island.

Without a word, the two trolls guarding the central causeway advanced, and Tharok came behind them, leading his kragh forward.

"Makaria?" It was Dalitha, her voice little more than a croak. "What do we do?"

Kethe's arm shook. Where were Akinetos, Mixis, Synesis? Their Consecrated, their thousands of soldiers? She tightened her grip on the hilt of her blade until her knuckles ached. Fury flooded through her, matched only by denial and confusion.

Still, the kragh came through the Portal. Each footstep of the trolls was accompanied by an audible *crunch*. They'd reach her within thirty seconds.

Asho stepped up to her side. She didn't look at him. She stared instead at the Portal, willing with all her being for the flood of kragh to be suddenly cut off, for men in bright armor to pour though, for this nightmare to come to an end.

She could end it. She could dive forward, between the trolls, and spear Tharok through the chest.

"Kethe," whispered Asho. "We have to retreat."

"Retreat?" Her voice was rasp. "To what? This is the final line. Behind us, the Empire stands open."

The kragh were a flood that showed no sign of abating. The trolls were nearly upon them. Asho touched her arm. "Our death here does nothing. We must go back. To Iskra. To the Ascendant. Kethe, come on!"

Tears were running down her cheeks. Her bright, fierce, irrational defiance broke, and she released her death wish, her futile desire to hurl herself at the grinning warlord. Kethe lowered her sword. When its white fire extinguished, a collective moan came from the soldiers.

"Retreat," said Kethe. Her voice sounded hollowed out, strange even to her own ears. Gathering herself, she called out with greater volume, "Back up the ramp. Retreat!"

The men scrambled away, turning and shoving at each other as they raced back up into the gloom. The Consecrated pulled back in a more controlled manner, not taking their eyes off the trolls.

In a matter of moments, Asho and Kethe were left before the approaching enemy by themselves.

The closest of the trolls raised its hammer.

"Damn it, Kethe, come on!" Asho yanked her back.

She stumbled backwards, refusing to tear her eyes away from Tharok, who raised his great black blade, eyes gleaming as he prepared to charge, but he never got the chance. With a grip of iron, Asho hauled her around and into a stumbling run.

Numbness. She ran as if within a dream, dazed and following Asho's lead. They'd failed. Up they ran, ever up, until they spilled out into the great cavern once more, under the glowing aurora, out into a huge mass of milling soldiers who were yelling out questions and oaths as panic seized them by the throat.

Kethe stumbled to a stop. She didn't know what to say to them. She couldn't meet their eyes. Her earlier words mocked her, played over in her mind even as she recalled the kragh coming through the Portal.

"Kethe?" Asho gave her arm a shake. "You have to take control. You have to get these men away from here."

"I can't – I don't understand," she said. Her mind felt mired in mud. "Mixis. Akinetos. There were *five thousand soldiers* left in Abythos. How could this have happened?"

Asho cursed and leaped up onto an outcropping of stone. "Listen up!" He pitched his voice to carry, a battlefield bark that drew the soldiers' reluctant attention. "Fall into ranks, damn you! March! March to the Solar Portals!"

Ennoians gaped up at him, but then Ser Cunad moved to the fore, shoving at men as he bellowed his own commands. "You heard the man! Move! You want to die here today? Form up! Double march!"

Slowly, sluggishly, the soldiers stepped back into some semblance of order, moving quicker with each passing moment, and within moments the first regiment was hustling out onto the broad trail that cut across the huge plain of sharp rocks toward the distant towers. The others soon followed, and when the first troll emerged, the entire force was hurrying away, casting terrified looks behind them.

Asho stayed by her side. She'd been ready to die for the Empire; now, here she was, jogging like a coward toward the Portals. She ran in a boneless, rough manner, occasionally slowing as she thought of turning, of facing the enemy. Always, Asho pulled her on.

It was a fair distance to the towers and the pale cubes that were the homes of the Bythian slaves. Halfway there, Asho leaned in close. "Kethe. What are we going to do?"

"Do?" She shook her head, trying to clear it of muddled thoughts. "I — I don't know."

"We need to think, and think fast. The towers are a deathtrap. The cubes... we could fight a retreat through them, but to what end?"

"The Ascendant," said Kethe. "We need to warn him. Theletos. Tell them what's happened."

"All right," he said. "That makes sense." He blew out his cheeks. "We've lost Bythos, at any rate. No sense in trying to hold on to it."

Kethe nodded numbly, then forced herself to think. To get her act together. "Bythos is lost. Yes. The Bythians — they'll have to fend for themselves."

"Maybe Shaya will be able to protect them," said Asho. "She swore that Tharok meant them no harm. We'll have to trust that she swayed him. The Ennoians and Sigeans within the towers, though — we'll have to send word. Get them to evacuate."

Kethe fought the bleak despair that sought to swamp her. "I'll send some of Ainos' Consecrated to find her so that she can organize the evacuation." She took a deep breath and stood straighter. "For now, though, our main priority is to alert Aletheia."

She looked back over her shoulder. The kragh were spilling out from the ramp like blood pooling from a mortal wound. "We need to tell them that Abythos has fallen. That Tharok is coming." Tears brimmed in her eyes once more. "And may the Ascendant have mercy on our souls."

Chapter 2

The humans fled before him, and Tharok knew that it was right; it was proper that they should quit the field of battle without offering him resistance. He had known that the odds were in his favor, that the winds of war were firmly at his back, yet it had been delicious — nearly exquisite — to see the fire of rebellion in their leader's green eyes, that hope and fiery anger, quench itself as she realized how futile her chances had been. That she had fought well the evening before made her defeat — no, her *breaking* — all the richer to savor.

Tharok walked up the last of the ramp and out into an airy vastness. At first, he had the disorienting sensation that he had emerged into some nightscape, but no; it was a cavern, he realized, one so immense that its far reaches were hidden from sight, so large that it housed an entire collection of towers in the distance. A wonder.

Above him swirled mad colors, an ocean of delirious fog that hid the cavern's roof. He stood still, uncaring that he was blocking the passage of his army, that hundreds upon hundreds stood packed on the ramp, waiting respectfully for him to move. Instead, hands on hips, he stared up musingly at the aurora, and for the first time wished that one of the old shamans was by his side. Someone wise in the way of the spirits who could explain this phenomenon to him, untangle its import so that he could disregard it if it was safe, or plan to defend himself from it if it was not.

But the shamans were gone.

Brooding, he walked on, and out onto a fan of crushed rock that served as a loading area. To the far right stood countless wagons laden with barrels, crates, supplies and foodstuffs. *To stock the fortress*, he thought. *An endless supply of goods with which to resist any siege. Mine now.*

In the near distance, he saw the last of the human force retreating toward the settlement. Narrowing his eyes, he looked past them toward a jumble of white boxes, hundreds of them tumbled upon each other like scattered die, a morass of nonsensical geometry. A village? Mineral agglomerations?

Beyond them, the towers.

Each a weapon, rusted and cruel, reaching high toward the aurora with improbable delicacy, vast swords that surely no mortal hand had erected. Or if they had, then they must have been geniuses. Who built with metal?

Bestirring himself, he turned to his kragh. Order was needed, and so he gave it, barking out commands to his medusa-kissed chieftains, who in turn began to direct and position the kragh in great masses upon the plains.

Tharok, desiring height, moved to an outcropping of rock and leaped to its summit. With one boot on its peak, he leaned forward to rest an elbow across his thigh and studied the plain before him. It was littered with sharp, cruel rock formations, a demonic landscape that would lacerate any army to pieces if it tried to march across. There were dozens of trails cleared through the rocks, however, broad enough for ten kragh to march across, all of them leading back toward the human settlements.

"Kyrrasthasa has entered Bythos, warlord." The words were softly spoken by his knee, and, looking down, Tharok saw Death's Raven gazing out over the badlands. "She bade me warn you of her approach."

"Warn?" Tharok tested the word. "You imply I should be concerned?"

Death's Raven looked up at him. His wrinkled skin was the same dull, sooty black as Tharok's, and a crimson glow emanated faintly from the cracks and recesses of his hide. That eerie glow made his smile all the more unnatural. "The answer to your question, warlord, depends upon your wisdom. I shall leave it for you to determine."

Tharok grunted in annoyance and looked back to the ramp. His kragh were still emerging at a steady rate. Already, over a thousand of them had gathered, spilling out across the plain. His chieftains, obeying his orders, had begun to lead groups of one hundred toward distant paths, moving slowly and carefully so that the kragh did not injure themselves.

When Tharok finally gave the order to approach the towers and those strange white blocks, his kragh would close upon the humans down myriad pathways, like fingers closing into a fist.

Arid. Barren. There was no way to feed his horde here in Bythos. Tharok cast his eye upon the supply wagons. Those would sustain them for a few days, but little more. He would have to move fast, and keep moving. His horde was not meant for sieges or waiting. Always they would clamor to attack.

The flood of kragh emerging from below was cut off, the last casting worried glances behind them as they hurried to join the others at the edge of the clearing. The kragh, his kragh, turned to gaze at the ramp's mouth, their animation and boastful cries stilling as they awaited the emergence of a goddess.

Kyrra's arrival was presaged by faintest of glows, lurid crimsons, metallic yellows and poisonous oranges challenging the aurora above mere moments before she slithered up and into view.

Tharok clenched his jaw and tightened his grip on his scimitar, World Breaker. The very sight of Kyrra stirred his most primal depths, urged him to drop to one knee, to pay obeisance to her, to do worship unto her glory.

She was sinuous, muscled, predatory, her upper body statuesque while her serpentine coils were graceful and brilliantly colored, eye-stinging yellow along her belly, blending into the fieriest of crimsons up her sides and giving way to pitch black on the overlapping carapace running down her spine.

Yet it was her upper body that commanded his attention, sculpted into a vision of female perfection, her skin the color of darkening coals, smoldering, dusty red with a fan of soft yellow scales rising across her abdomen and between her breasts. A mass of snakes wreathed her face, hissing and undulating, and her eyes — even at this remove, they seared him, their gaze as pitiless as the sun, a glaring nullity that burned his vision.

Kyrrasthasa, the last medusa, who could recall being worshipped like a goddess by Tharok's most distant ancestors and yearned to be worshipped in like manner once more.

She made her way toward him, and Tharok forced himself to stand tall, shoulders back, lifting World Breaker and resting it over one shoulder so that it drew the eye. Inwardly, he gave thanks to having chosen this outcropping on which to stand; it allowed him to face her as an equal.

"Greetings, warlord." Her voice was soft, intimate. Almost a caress. "No matter what the future holds, your current successes have ensured that your name will go down in history."

A threat? "The future is golden, Kyrra," said Tharok. "This is but my first major victory. Many more shall follow, till there is nothing left to be won."

"Indeed," said Kyrra. "And I shall be by your side to celebrate that very moment."

"I am sure you shall," he said. "The situation in Abythos?"

"Well in hand." Her upper body moved back as she circled her coils beneath her, the great rattle at the tip of her tail emerging from the center. "The humans and their champions stand entombed within stone, trapped for eternity by my gaze. Those who escaped like rats into the walls were hunted down by your kragh and slaughtered. The citadel is ours."

Tharok nodded. It was good to hear confirmation. He turned to regard the distant towers. "Have you visited this cavern before, Kyrra?"

"Never," said the medusa, following his gaze. "But I find it much to my liking. I can sense... mysteries and wonders beyond my ken, waiting to be divulged by the rock. This is an ancient space. It stirs long-forgotten memories. There is much to be gained here."

Tharok grunted. "Such as the Solar Gates. We shall take the towers, claim those cubes, then turn our attention upon the remainder of the human empire. How many of your shamans survived the onslaught?"

Kyrra's eyes narrowed a fraction. "A dozen. It would have been far more had you not let the remaining shamans slip free while you were at Gold."

"I told you," said Tharok carelessly, looking away. "They escaped of their own volition. Shamans. You can't trust them." He looked down and grinned at Death's Raven. "Regardless. A dozen. That's still something. They will be instrumental in our attack on Aletheia."

"I think not," said Kyrra. "I agreed to their usage in Abythos due to how crucial a role they would play in blasting open the citadel's doors. Now, however, you face no such obstruction. Numbers shall tell the day, and numbers you have."

Tharok fought to keep his voice steady. Calm, even. "You are not the warlord, Kyrra. Slither carefully."

"Agreed," said Kyrra, bowing her head with mocking respect. "Yet you have ever shown yourself amenable to heeding good advice, so listen: I sense mysteries within the Abythian complex through which we just emerged. There is something ancient and powerful here that we could bend to our will. Give me and mine time to study, to draw it forth. It will prove to your great benefit down the road."

Tharok looked past Kyrra at the ramp. He had not been oblivious to the myriad tunnels and passageways that had extended in every direction. An ancient power. One that Kyrra could wield against him? Did he trust her to summon it forth?

"Tell me more."

"It is hard to explain to one without stonesense," said Kyrra, but her voice was not mocking. "Your trolls would have a better understanding of it. There is in the complex a hint of intelligent design, of something organic. The curves, the radial tunnels, the very shape of it speaks to me. The very walls are saturated in power. It can be no coincidence that this cavern houses the humans' dread Black Gate."

"Black Gate?" Tharok frowned at her, but even as he said its name, information began to pour into his mind, a wealth of knowledge that caused him to rock back on his heels.

He saw it within his mind's eye: a floating diamond, a prism of the purest night, lofty and fey. Closed, he intimated, shut in some irrevocable manner that precluded its proper usage. A massive weight strained against those restraints, yet, despite the enormity of the pressure, it was for naught. The Black Gate was shut, and its closure had denied this world a fundamental element that had once underpinned its existence.

Kyrra watched him, eyes half-lidded, and a smile curved up one corner of her mouth. "It seems you know more than you let on."

Tharok fought the urge to press his palm to his temple. There was more, much more, but he could make no sense of it. Reams of knowledge so abstruse and theoretical that their import escaped his grasp. "Yes. The Black Gate. I — I know something of it."

More, he felt a growing desire to gaze upon its ebon might. To draw closer to it. To bask in its darkness.

"Not nearly enough," rasped Death's Raven. "It is of vital importance to the humans' theology. They consider it a portal to their own personal abyss, the entrance through which their damned souls are flung into eternal perdition. Much of their actions, their history, their culture and society can only be understood in light of their fear of it."

"And, are they right?" Tharok looked from the corrupted shaman to Kyrra. "Is this Portal truly a gateway to their hell?"

Kyrra shrugged languorously. "It is not for me to know such things. But I will say this much: the Black Gate precedes the existence of humanity. Make of that what you will."

Tharok nodded and turned back to the blade-like towers. "And now it falls under my dominion. I wonder, is there anything to be gained in opening it?"

Death's Raven laughed, a rusted, grating sound. "Who knows what you might let through, warlord? It is a gamble, to be sure. But if the humans were to learn that you had broken the chains that held their hell locked, I am sure they would not be pleased."

"No," said Tharok. "Terrified, more like." He frowned and then leaped down from his perch. "We march. Now. To the towers. I would see this Black Gate. I will make my decision when we reach it. Then, I will turn my attention to securing the Solar Gates. It is unlikely that the humans will seek to hold them from this side, but one should not underestimate their stupidity."

Kyrra made no response.

Tharok strode forward, raising his arm as he did so, and let forth a roar as he pointed at the distant towers. Over a thousand kragh roared back and began to march, following the numerous trails they had reached, closing in upon the distant human settlement as one.

Tharok marched at their fore. He found himself missing his wyvern, missing, even, his mountain goat, but no matter. He set a brisk pace. The remnants of the human force had disappeared into the distance. The only sign of their passage was a thin haze of dust.

He was of two minds as he drew closer to the tumbled white cubes. Part of him exulted in the very fact that he was in Bythos, marveled at his accomplishments, felt a wild and reckless joy at leading his horde into the human empire. Yet over that, like a layer of frost, rested a calm and calculated control, an awareness of the factors at play, the forces he had to balance, the strategies he had to execute to maintain his momentum.

The cubes were a city, he saw, a sprawling conglomeration of dwellings. Pale-haired humans were standing atop the cubes and crowding the streets between them, staring wide-eyed at the approaching kragh. Thousands of them, the Bythians of which Shaya had spoken, their wretched condition giving truth to her words.

He didn't have time for this. For niceties. The Solar Portals were open, and the humans were fleeing back to their superiors, preparing, planning for his assault. He should sweep past these cubes, leave these slaves behind for now, move on to greater and more important matters.

And yet. He thought of Shaya's eyes when she confronted him the night before, of her pain and sense of betrayal over how his kragh has attacked her Bythians. Then he thought of Nok's own dark gaze, heavy with consideration and doubt. Something stirred within him, a reluctance, a sense of obligation, and he raised his fist before realizing he meant to, and the thousands behind him ground to a halt.

Alone, he walked forward. *Madness*, he thought to himself. *Exposing yourself like this to danger. One spear, one lucky arrow...*

He killed that thought.

Hundreds of Bythians stood shoulder to shoulder, plugging the entrance to the broadest street, while hundreds more watched from vantage points. He could sense their fear.

Shaya had no doubt already returned to Abythos, which meant he had no means of communicating with the humans. He wanted to curse himself for his shortsightedness. He had cast away an invaluable tool.

The silence was palpable. The Bythians were slowly drawing back. *Damn you,* he thought at the circlet. *Prove your worth.*

The circlet began to burn on his brow, the heat sudden and vicious. He startled, head snapping back like that of a rearing mountain goat, and the Bythians as one let out a murmur of fear and cowered. The pain grew, as if the circlet were forcing thorns into his skull, and Tharok fought to stand still, to not grimace or put his hands to his head. His kragh were watching, Kyrra was watching. He had to stand still. Be strong.

The pain receded. Was gone.

Liquid was trickling from his nose. He put his fingers to his upper lip and saw that their tips were red. And yet, a new layer of understanding had settled over his mind. Blood was both blood and *blood*, a second word he had never known before. His eyes traveled over the world before him: *cube, people, cavern, dirt, towers.*

Alien words. Human words. Simple nouns. He tried for more and found *honor.* It wasn't a perfect fit. One word that failed to reflect the degrees of mastery a warlord might have, the variations of valor and honesty that powerful mountain kragh sought to personify. His mind sought to reflect these variations, but kept stumbling back to the one word: *honor.*

His heart was racing. Here was a subtle insight into humanity that he had never imagined. How they thought. How they saw the world, as expressed by their words. He thought of the ardor he had felt for Maur: *lust*. No, too simple. It lacked the overtones of admiration and the desire to propagate. *Love* slipped into his mind, and he almost snorted. *Devotion, admiration, respect, desire* — the words tumbled through his mind, trying to fit themselves to his understanding of his ardor for her, but did not seem to fit completely, perfectly, to capture the complexities of his desire.

The Bythians were staring at him. He could feel the weight of his horde's gaze upon his back. Now was not the time to delve into the grammatical and lexicological subtleties of human-to-kragh translations.

"People of Bythos," he called out in the human tongue. The words, so clear and simple in his mind, came out abused and rough through his lips. It felt like trying to pick up a clay cup full of water with two heavy rocks.

Yet the Bythians understood him. Understood him enough to hesitate, to arrest their flight.

"I am Tharok, warlord of the kragh." Human words were so soft, like ropes of velvet, sibilant like the wind whispering through a gorge. "Bring me your chieftains. I would talk."

The Bythians whispered amongst themselves, and a handful of them stepped nervously forward. Older men, for the most part, their faces carved by a life of hard labor, their hands gnarled claws, their backs curved by time and abuse. Yet there was a light in their eyes, a firmness to their expressions, that marked them indeed as the leaders.

They approached. Four of them. It was hard to tell them apart, but one was slightly taller, and it was to this bigger male that Tharok addressed himself. "I made a promise — a vow? No. An oath." He struggled to find the right word. "To Shaya, daughter of Zekko. To protect — adopt? Bythians. Her help has made my coming possible." Again, he paused, not liking the connotations. "I value her help. So, I shall free the Bythians as I promised." He paused, then said loudly, "You are free, and under kragh protection."

The Bythian chieftains stared at him. Had they not understood his words? Their eyes were wide; their mouths were open as if to display the tusks they did not have.

Tharok could sense his horde piling up behind him, massing and desiring release. There was no time for this. "My kragh will move around your settlement. Stay here for now. In time, we will talk more. Decide your future. But you are safe. This I swear. Understand?"

The Bythians nodded, looking even more afraid than ever, and Tharok felt his patience slipping. He turned and looked back across the plain. His kragh had choked every path, extending all the way back to the Abythian Gate. Thousands of them. It was inconvenient that they could not take the white cubes as their camp, but he would make that sacrifice.

He searched out and found Uthok, warlord of the Falling Stones tribe. The old mountain kragh's black hide spoke of his Kiss, and he was leading one of the ten great blocks of a thousand warriors. Tharok pointed at the old kragh, then pointed at the blade towers. Uthok nodded and bellowed his orders. Half of the forces on the plain began to move sluggishly toward their new target.

Looking to his right, he caught the eyes of Jojan of the Black Clouds. He, too, had been Kissed by Kyrra and placed in charge of another huge agglomeration of tribes, though most of his forces were yet to pass into Bythos. Though Jojan was standing a good distance away, the kragh chieftain's eyes were locked on Tharok, so he saw Tharok's pointed command and began to lead his kragh in turn toward the Solar Portals.

Tharok then turned to the dozens of attendants, messengers and subservients who stood gathered behind him. None were medusa-Kissed, but all were ready, eager, even, to serve. "Put the word out. No kragh is to enter the white cube city. The penalty for doing so is death. Make it known, and fast."

The small group scattered, racing out to find chieftains and warlords, to spread the word. They would find him again once they were done and would await his next command. An inefficient system, but the best he could improvise.

"Kyrra," said Tharok, abandoning the human tongue with relief and turning to regard the medusa where she rose amidst her shamans and most dedicated of worshippers. "Come. We go to examine the Black Gate."

Instinct guided him. Or perhaps something — some force — drew him. He marched around the circumference of the Bythian cubes, Kyrra and his honor guard just behind. His eyes kept climbing the heights of the towers as he approached them. They were cylindrical for the first two-thirds of their height, he saw, tapering only at the last into cruel blades which no kragh or human could inhabit. Their exteriors were black metal streaked with great swaths of rust, and thin, slitted windows perforated their walls. Massive vultures circled their tops, and he found in their grim appearance something that satisfied his desire for cruel grandeur.

Yet his path led him not to their base, but rather to a great crater off to their side, situated between the cubes and the towers. Cresting a rise of shattered rock, he gazed down upon the center of the bowl-like depression, and there he saw it, hovering and glittering with otherworldly power: the Black Gate.

He had not expected it to be so large. It rose some thirty yards high, swelling at the center and tapering to points at the tips. It deceived the eye. For a moment, it resembled a prism, geometric and with depth, and then it seemed but two-dimensional, a clean cut in the fabric of reality, only for edges to appear once more as if it were slowly revolving in place.

Energy crackled around it, bolts of black and purple lightning that sparked into existence only to disappear just as quickly. Even from the top of the rise, he could scent how charged the air, making it redolent of that same flat, burnt smell that came after a powerful thunderstorm.

He could see no chains. No shackles. No lock or other form of barring the Gate. Whatever means the humans had used to close the way to their hell was not apparent to his eye.

A platform had been built, centuries ago, to one side. Massive blocks of black stone had been elegantly set atop each other to form a broad stage that faced the area before the Gate. A space from which a warlord could address a crowd? On the far side, opposite the platform, rose a cruel scaffold from which hung numerous ropes. A handful of withered corpses were strung up by their necks there, their bodies torn and rent by savage wounds.

Tharok glanced up at the great vultures that circled endlessly above.

Kyrra slithered up to his side, her arms crossed over her chest, and gazed down at the Gate. Tharok glanced up at her. "What do you sense?"

"Familiarity," she said softly. "On some level. There are pockets beneath the earth akin to this Gate. But nothing so grand. Pebbles compared to this boulder. *Isthrikhan,* we call them. When my kind searches for a lair in which to sleep, to while away the centuries, we make them around such gates. There was one," she said, looking down at him at last, "in the lair in which you found me."

Tharok grunted. "So. Not portals to humanity's private hell." Kyrra swayed from side to side and did not immediately agree. Tharok frowned. "What?"

She shrugged, a sinuous rise and fall of her shoulders. "I've never seen an *Isthrikhan* large enough to pass through. Who knows what lies on the other side?"

The four trolls stepped up onto the lip of the crater's rise and, as one, hunkered down, fists planted on the rock, to stare morosely down at the Black Gate. Tharok looked past Kyrra at the closest one, a crusty old female, more bone than flesh, the rock formations along her shoulders and the backs of her arms deeply riven by cracks. He could feel her through the circlet, could sense her burning blue flame in the dark, but her attention was wholly fixed on the Gate. If he tried, he knew he could wrest her obedience, but it would be a struggle.

He let her be.

Then, as one, the four trolls lifted their heads and let forth a low, mournful howl, akin perhaps to a twisting, violent wind issuing up from the very bowels of the earth. It caused the hairs to prickle down the back of Tharok's neck and along his arms, and he fought the urge to fall into a fighting stance, to draw World Breaker and prepare to defend himself.

Draw closer, said a voice in the depths of his mind.

Tharok stiffened, and now he did grip World Breaker with both hands. Sweat beaded his brow. The urge to take a single step down into the crater grew suddenly to an almost unbearable pressure.

The trolls' dirge rose in volume. It threatened to drown his thoughts, the sorrow and pain in the sound making it harder with each passing moment to concentrate.

The Black Gate loomed in sight. What harm would there be in taking a closer look? He began to descend.

A hand took hold of his shoulder, and heat from its palm sank into his flesh. Startled, Tharok looked up and into Kyrra's bronze, slitted eyes. A modicum of clarity returned to him, and with great effort he reached out with his power and seized control of the trolls. Their howls were cut off. Under his command, they drew back from the lip of the crater and shambled away. His ability to control them grew easier with each step they took.

"What," he rasped, "was that?"

Kyrra had also turned to watch the trolls descend. "The rock children are more primal than we medusa. They sense and understand the world in ways that are beyond words, beyond concepts, even. They are channels, if you will, for the energies that course through the stone."

He thought of confiding in her the words he had heard. Of asking her for advice, for greater understanding of that which he wore on his brow. Yet she was not his ally. She was not his friend, for all that she had saved him from taking those fateful steps forward. So, instead, he reached up, hands shaking, and pulled the circlet from his brow.

A rushing roar as of the world being torn apart clamored within his head, and he struggled to stand, his knees buckling. A huge pressure that had been engulfing him fell away, leaving him with a sensation of lightness as he took in breath in sharp, shallow pants, the scope of his thoughts at once reduced and clarified.

He looked down at the circlet. Tightened his grip on the metal band, then thought for a moment of trying to warp it, bend it and ruin its perfect form. No. Without it, he might as well bend knee to Kyrra.

Inhaling slowly through his nose, he wiped the back of his forearm across his brow. He couldn't keep it off for long — the trolls needed his guidance.

Kyrra was watching him with inscrutable eyes. Would she strike at him? He fought the urge to back away, to raise World Breaker. He was off-balance, unsure of himself. He needed distance from the Gate.

"Come," he said. "There is much to do. The Gate can wait."

He hurried down the far side of the crater's rim, trying to hide how his hands were shaking. Trying not to think about why the circlet had sought to compel him closer to the Black Gate.

The four trolls stood still, watching him. One raised its hammer. He immediately slipped his circlet on.

Confidence fell upon him like a cloak. He stood straighter, marched with more determination. He didn't look back to Kyrra, but knew that she could hear him. "Attend to the battle of the towers. Make your base there. I shall return soon."

"Where are you going, warlord?" Her voice was soft, sibilant. Mocking? Perhaps.

"To the Solar Gates," he said. "To Aletheia."

Chapter 3

Tiron had begun to think the tunnel was interminable. Torch held aloft, he'd hurried down its narrow throat, shoulders brushing the raw rock walls, the sound of his companions' boots echoing from behind him. At last it curved to the right, dipped, and then rose suddenly to culminate in a narrow doorway.

Soft evening light flooded the last segment of the tunnel, pouring in through a vertical slit where the door had been left ajar. Tiron wanted to shoulder it open and stagger out into the fresh air, but caution and years of experience caused him to stop, one hand held up to arrest the others, and move slowly to the crack to peer outside.

The air was fresh, delicious, and clean, free of the odors of civilization. He looked out onto a verdant slope. Knee-high bushes grew in profusion along with elegant, tall trees with smooth gray trunks. He closed his eyes and listened. Nothing. Some distant birdsong, though he'd never heard the like before. The sound of the wind in the canopy.

"Stay cautious," he said to the others, and pushed the door all the way open.

They weren't the only ones to have used this tunnel; several marshals had fled minutes before, their passage made evident in the scraped earth over which the door now opened easily. They'd had to force their way out.

Moving out onto the small hillside, sword in hand, Tiron turned in small circles, searching for a sign of those others. Nothing. It wasn't much of a hill, either. More of a forested hump on the plains outside the Abythian walls. The others spilled out quietly behind him, but Tiron didn't pay them mind; instead, he moved carefully through the bushes, around a few trees, and then stopped at the sight of the distant citadel.

They'd come nearly a mile underground, but even at this remove, Abythos was massive. Curlicues of smoke were rising from the town outside its walls where kragh were making a crude camp, their hundreds of fires already twinkling in the gloaming. The size of the horde was greatly diminished, however; most of them had entered the castle.

Lord Ramswold stepped up by his side. "I still can't believe it has fallen."

"Believe it," said Tiron. He couldn't make out the hundreds of statues that had choked the main gate. The frozen forms of the Virtues and Consecrated, the knights and soldiers who had fallen prey to the medusa's gaze. "The Empire's lost."

"Lost?" The elderly marshal who had shown them the tunnel and accompanied them out — Marcus — sounded a note of indignation. "This was a grave defeat, assuredly, but the Empire isn't finished quite yet."

"No?" Tiron leveled a flat stare at the old man. He felt almost grateful for being given someone to focus his frustration on. "We just lost five thousand knights and soldiers. An army that we barely scraped together after our terrible defeat by the Agerastians only a few months ago."

Nobody spoke. The marshal refused to look away, however. "The Ascendant still rules in Aletheia."

"Not for long," said Tiron with a smile. "Tharok's entire horde is entering Bythos. He'll overrun it in a matter of hours, meaning he'll have access to the Solar Portals. Direct access to Aletheia. Nous. Sige. Zoe. Ennoia. The entire Empire." He shook his head. "There isn't time to gather an army. There isn't time to mount a new defense. He's gained a terrible mobility. Stymie him in Nous? He'll take Sige and attack from the flank. It's over." He turned back to survey the columns of smoke rising over the plain. "Three days. That's how long it will take him to conquer the entirety of the Empire."

Lord Ramswold bestirred himself. He was slender, with golden curls, an aquiline nose and a high brow; at Tiron's words, twin spots of color appeared on his cheeks even as purple exhaustion ringed his eyes. "There is always hope as long as good men survive. We are beaten, yes, but only for now. We must make a plan. Find a way back to the Empire, and there fight to defend it."

The others murmured their agreement. Of the original glittering Order of the Star that had left Ramswold's Red Keep, only three had survived Abythos, and all were badly battered and bloodied. Ulein, stocky like a young bear, with thick brown hair like dirty hay, square-chinned and far too young for this madness; Isentrud, tall, raw-boned, her braided blonde hair having fallen across one shoulder when she'd lost her helm, her mouth wide and generous, her eyes without guile; and Leuthold, the captain of Ramswold's guard, tall, lean, and hand-some in a hard, unforgiving way.

"Perhaps we could sneak back into Abythos through the tunnel," said one of Marcus' two attendant advisors, a Noussian woman with generous curves and a sharp gaze. She was addressing Ramswold. "Time our return carefully, then sprint through the Gate?"

Tiron snorted. "Sprint through a kragh horde?"

She rounded on him. "Well, offer a better plan, then!"

Ulein was rotating his arm carefully, hand on his shoulder. "I remember a story my nan used to tell me, about the brigands who snuck into a castle disguised as washerwomen—"

"Oh, for fuck's sake," said Tiron. "Washerwomen?"

"We — we could dust ourselves in gray powder, perhaps," said Isentrud, eying Tiron nervously. "Pretend to be statues frozen by the medusa whenever the kragh walk by. And when left alone, make our way slowly toward the gate...?"

Tiron rubbed his face vigorously and then grimaced. "No. This is life, girl. Not some damn minstrel's tale."

"You seem more adept at mocking than offering your own solutions," said Marcus dryly. "Have you nothing in all your great sagacity to offer?"

Tiron felt his anger fall away. Into its place stole exhaustion and pain. Aches from the battle, strains and lacerations. "No, Marshal. I don't. Because there is nothing we can do. We're five warriors and three useless scholars. There's thousands of kragh bottled up in that citadel. Anything we try to get back in will get us killed."

Ramswold raised his chin. "I refuse to believe that our cause is lost. There must be something we can do."

"We wait," said Tiron. "And watch. The way things are, we've no options. But the Ascendant knows, miracles bloody happen. Or so I'm told. Maybe the medusa's spell will wear off, and the statues will come back to life. Maybe all of the kragh will go through, leaving nobody behind to guard the Portal. I don't know. But we camp, we rest, and we watch. And should an opportunity present itself? We'll take it."

"That's inspiring," said Leuthold. "Wait and hope for a miracle."

"I'm not here to inspire you," said Tiron. "I'm here to keep you alive. You want inspiration? Talk to your lord."

With that, he walked off and leaned against a large tree, leaving the group before he could spill more of his bile. Dull fury pounded at his temples in time with his pulse; everything he'd said had been true, but, somehow, he still felt as if he'd failed them.

"All right," he heard Ramswold say softly. "Let's make camp. Come. Those bushes might provide us with some form of bedding. Let's make the most of what's left of the day, and then I'll lead us in prayer. We need the Ascendant's blessings now more than ever."

Tiron jutted out his lower jaw and watched the distant Abythos. They'd been humiliated. Defeated with ease. Manipulated with so fine a degree of control that he was still struggling to piece the flow of battle together in his mind. Just how much of it had been their obeying the enemy's master plan?

All of it, as far as he could tell. Tiron scowled. Never had he faced so resourceful and brilliant an opponent. Grudging admiration arose within him, but he moved swiftly to crush it. Kragh. Outwitted by blasted kragh. Unthinkable.

Tiron stared at the distant citadel long after the fall of dusk had made the details opaque.

Morning found him sitting against the largest gray-barked tree, knife in hand, slowly whittling a thick branch into a spear point. Curled strips of wood lay about his lap, and his hands moved smoothly, the strokes lifting fine curls of pale wood. His eyes, however, were trained on the distant citadel. Abythos. Never in a hundred years would he have imagined that the siege would end with his being outside it with no options and no hopes. A helpless spectator to the Empire's demise.

The kragh were on the move. The vast camp that had engulfed the settlement outside the walls was being abandoned. Columns of kragh were flowing in through the broad Gate. In the morning light, Tiron could make out how callously the kragh treated the petrified statues that blocked their way. He'd almost cut off his thumb when he saw them smash the first statue to shards, then shove the rest onto their sides to clear a path into the courtyard within.

He was helpless. It brought back memories of his time beneath the Wolf Tower in Kyferin Castle, the years he'd spent trapped in that hole, pacing and unable to exact revenge, limited to giving vent to his grief through mad howls.

A group of some hundred kragh emerged through the front gate, moving against the flow. The others, the common grunts and soldiers, moved aside with obvious respect.

Tiron lowered his knife and watched carefully. The group was composed mostly of warriors, but in their center was a small group in black robes mounted on massive goats. Scholars? Priests?

The group marched ahead, cutting through the ruined human settlement and emerging onto the broad road that had been nearly obliterated by the arrival of the kragh only a day ago.

Tiron sat back. Conveying news of their victory to another contingent of kragh? Summoning reserves? Impossible to tell. But a hundred kragh was far too many for them to waylay. Tiron rose, knees protesting, and faded back into the undergrowth. The odds of being seen were slim, but the road drew close to their hill, and there was no sense in risking it.

"Ramswold," he called softly to where the others were resting in their makeshift camp. "Silence."

The chatter came to an abrupt stop, and then he heard the rustling of someone approaching. The young lord scooted up cautiously and crouched beside Tiron, peering through the bushes at the road below.

To his credit, he didn't immediately ask senseless questions. In silence, he observed the approaching group. Good. He was learning.

"Any use in following them?" asked Ramswold. "Attacking their camp at night? We could attempt to capture a sentry to interrogate. Learn what's happening."

"No," said Tiron. "A good idea, but none of us speak kragh. And I doubt even I could intimidate one. We let them go."

Ramswold nodded. The kragh marched past the hill, oblivious to their observers. When they were past, Ramswold reached out and touched Tiron's shoulder, stopping him from moving back to his post.

"Ser Tiron," said the young lord. "A moment."

Ser Tiron. He's being formal on purpose. Prefacing something he knows I won't want to hear. Tiron eyed him sidelong. "What?"

"Your attitude. You need to change it." Color came to Ramswold's cheeks, but he kept his gaze steadfast. "Our morale is brutally low. Ulein is barely responding to questions. Isentrud — well. Even she, eternal optimist that she is, has become morose. We need to keep our spirits up, regardless of our predicament. They all look to you. Your negativity is damaging us badly."

Tiron bit back a bitter retort. To be lectured by one so young, and worse, to know the man was right — it made him want to lash out.

Instead, he forced himself to nod slowly. "You're right." He pinched the brow of his nose. "You're right."

"You don't need to lie to me," said Ramswold. "I can take the truth. But the others – give them hope."

"Hope," said Tiron. The word sounded alien on his tongue. "Hope will get us killed out here. We need to be smart and keep our heads down. We need to stay alive."

"I disagree," said Ramswold. "But if you cannot find anything uplifting to say to them, then please refrain from actively cutting their confidence down. Will you agree to that much?"

"Yes," said Tiron. "I'll let you coddle them. Now, here's some practical advice: keep them busy. Have them remove their armor and set to cleaning it. Have the marshal and his advisors search for berries, roots, nuts or the like. See if they can find any pools of water we can cleanse by lowering a cloth into it to filter out the sediment and dirt."

"I thought it dangerous to drink standing water," said Ramswold.

"Yes, but I'll take dysentery over dying of thirst. Just keep them busy, no matter how menial the task. Keep their minds engaged. I'll watch the citadel, and come midday I'll return to the camp with some plans."

Ramswold nodded. "That makes sense. Thank you."

"Don't thank me, you blasted fool. I'm the last person you should be thanking."

"Not true," said Ramswold. "You warned us, back at the Red Keep. Right at the outset of this adventure. You told us what to expect, and you were right. Your experience has kept the few of us who survived alive. You will always have my gratitude for that."

Tiron scowled and turned away. "Thank me when we're back at the Red Keep. Now, go. Enough of this prattling."

He moved back to his vantage point and sat amidst the shavings, taking up the crude spear once more. He placed the edge of his knife at the point's base, but didn't cut. *Hope.* Delusion, more like. Yet, what was the harm in it? He knew well enough. False hope could mislead you, cause you to take lethal risks. It was better to be grimly realistic. Harder, yes, but the odds of surviving were higher for it.

Ramswold would learn. Was learning. Hadn't he expressed gratitude for Tiron's bitter wisdom? His dream of a magical Order had crashed into the cold, hard reality of warfare. It wouldn't be long now before he started to adopt Tiron's own approach to campaigning.

Tiron began to shave at the spear head again, feeling better. If there was one thing he'd learned amongst the Black Wolves, it was that there was no room for naivete in battle. No room for dreams and puerile aspirations. Cynical calculation, clear-minded assessments, the ability to make the hard decisions, to inspire your men through your actions and not your words: those were the hallmarks of a great knight.

The Order of the Star. Tiron snorted and cut hard through the grain. There was a reason such things existed only in court tales.

Tiron glanced up and froze. Another group was emerging from the citadel. No, not a group; merely a pair. Even at this remove, he was impressed by how huge the kragh was. Massive, dark-skinned, with a hammer so ponderously massive slung over his back that Tiron doubted he'd be able to lift it. The kragh dwarfed the human female at his side, her pale hair marking her as a Bythian.

Interesting. A kragh and his slave? Where were they headed? They seemed intent on following the road like the first party. Tiron tapped his lips with the tip of his knife, then set the rough spear down and crept back to camp.

"… that's the very meaning of faith," Ramswold was saying. "To believe in the Ascendant's goodness even when the world tells you to despair. In a truly perverse way, we are being blessed. How often are we given the chance to truly test our resolve?"

Ramswold's gentle smile took on a wry edge when he turned to Tiron as if anticipating a rejoinder. The others looked up at him warily, almost as if expecting a blow. Their surprise when Tiron grinned was evident.

"Good news. The Ascendant has provided. Looks like a very minor miracle is making its way toward us. Who here's ready for a fight?"

The group stirred. Ulein looked up from where he was sitting. Leuthold pushed away from the tree he'd been leaning against. Marcus put on his glasses and stared at Tiron.

"A minor miracle?" Isentrud's smile was hesitant, but there. "As in, one Virtue coming to our rescue instead of five?"

Tiron hesitated. "Yes? Perhaps not quite so overt. It's a chance to strike a small blow for the Empire and gain some information. There's a kragh with his human slave coming our way. They should reach us in about fifteen minutes. We'll strike them when they round the curve that takes them out of sight of the walls. Kill the kragh, free the Bythian, and then learn from her what's happened since the Solar Gates opened this morning."

"Oh," said Isentrud. "I thought..."

"Good," said Ramswold, his tone firm. "We need information, and freeing a lady from a kragh is a worthy quest. Let's don our armor and prepare."

Leuthold extended his hand to Ulein, then helped the young man rise to his feet.

Marcus and his two advisors approached. "How can we help?"

"Your names?" Tiron looked to the Noussian woman and the pale-skinned youth at Marcus' side. "That would be a start."

"Olina," said the Noussian defiantly, hands on her hips. She was short and plump, with a rounded nose and full lips. Despite her evident softness, Tiron found himself appreciating the fire in her eyes.

"Garvis," said the youth. Taller than Tiron, but weighing perhaps half as much, he stood in a permanent stoop as if trying to disguise his stature. His skin was flecked with freckles, his eyes were a watery blue, and his nails were bloody and bitten to the quick.

"Olina, Garvis. You three will remain out of sight. We might sustain wounds killing this kragh, however — he's as large as a bull, and we have no ranged weapons. Be ready to tend to our injuries once the battle is open. See if you can find clean cloth for bandages, pool the water together, and so forth."

Marcus nodded. "A makeshift infirmary. I once studied under Alacar of Elsberry fame. Our resources are few, but I'll see what we can do."

"Good," said Tiron.

He clapped the old man on the shoulder as he strode over to the other four. They were busy buckling on their scabbards, checking the straps of their armor. Isentrud was examining her badly dented cuirass with a glum expression, as if resigning herself to not wearing it.

"Listen up. We're going to lose the element of surprise the moment we emerge into view. The road doesn't come close enough to the hill for us to launch a true ambush, so instead we'll split up. Two groups. The first will emerge behind the kragh at some distance to block his retreat to the castle. Ramswold, you and I will then move out to block his advance. Once we're in place, we'll close in and cut him down before he can gather his wits. Questions?"

They all shook their heads. Tiron saw new purpose in their expressions, a focus and determination that had been missing only moments ago. The promise of action. Of taking control of the situation, even if only for a brief skirmish. Good.

When they were ready, Tiron led the small group around the hill toward the far side that overlooked the road. The kragh would pass within fifty yards of them. Tiron crouched behind a bush and bit his lower lip. A sizeable distance.

"Leuthold, your group will move first. Move at a diagonal so that you hit the road a good fifty paces behind the kragh. The distance will prevent him from becoming too alarmed — he should spend some time simply watching you, trying to divine your goals. Once you're in place, Ramswold and I will emerge. By the time he realizes he's encircled, it will be too late."

Leuthold nodded again, and then Ulein and Isentrud moved along the base of the hill to a different hiding spot. Of the four of them, he was the calmest. No surprise there; he was older than the three knights by some five years and had spent his life as a professional soldier.

The kragh and his Bythian slave came into view. Tiron felt himself relax. Violence, he understood. Violence was transformative. It promised change. An end, a beginning. New information, an outlet for his frustration.

As the pair drew closer, Tiron began to appreciate just how large this kragh truly was. Not large – huge. It stood over six feet tall, almost seven, and was as broad across the shoulders as a cart. Its tusks were fearsome; its hair was bound back in a complex braid. It was lightly armored, with a broad leather belt sporting a bronze full-moon buckle, and a single shoulder guard strapped across its chest. Its tunic and leggings were of plain black wool.

Something was off, however. While the Bythian woman wasn't bound or manacled in any way, neither did she look subservient, afraid, or depressed. Instead, she was talking animatedly with the kragh, walking alongside it with a pack of her own over her shoulder, dressed in good clothing and with a staff in hand.

"A traitor?" asked Ramswold, echoing his thoughts.

"Perhaps," said Tiron. "It won't matter, however. She'll tell us what she knows, regardless."

"No torture," said Ramswold.

"No. It won't come to that."

The pair walked along the road, and Tiron was disconcerted to hear the kragh laugh, a deep chuckle that obviously pleased the woman, who was watching him with evident delight. Her smile curdled Tiron's anger. He had no sympathy for anyone who could be light of spirit after walking through thousands of petrified dead.

Leuthold broke cover when the pair drew abreast of Tiron. The trio ran at a diagonal to cut off the kragh's retreat.

Just as Tiron had surmised, the kragh and the Bythian turned around, alerted by the movement, but the distance prevented them from reacting violently; they simply stood still, staring in confusion at the three humans. The kragh was quick-witted, however; a moment later, he turned back to examine the hill.

"No need to run," said Tiron, rising to his feet and stepping forward. He suppressed a shiver of excitement. His heart was beating powerfully, his aches forgotten, his sword light in his hand. "He expects us."

Ramswold followed him out into the open.

The kragh dropped his pack to the ground and unshouldered his hammer. Even Elon would have had trouble lifting that weapon, much less wielding it. One blow would stave in a wall. Fold a horse in two. There'd be no blocking it, no way to parry. Speed, then. Distraction.

"Who are you?" The Bythian woman placed a hand on the kragh's arm as it began to growl low in its chest.

"Ser Ramswold of Ennoia," said the young lord, taking charge. "We're here to rescue you, my lady. Though it seems you might not welcome the attempt."

Leuthold and the others were moving up the road quietly. The kragh shifted his feet so that he could keep both parties in view.

"Rescue?" The woman frowned. "You're correct. I don't need saving. I'm here of my own volition."

"You're a traitor, then?" Ulein's voice was tight with anger.

The kragh rumbled something in its crude language. The woman nodded but didn't respond. Instead, she hesitated and then chose to address Ramswold. "Please, my lord. There's no need for bloodshed."

"This is war, my lady, and he is the enemy. I'm afraid, therefore, that you are wrong on that count."

Leuthold and the others fanned out to encircle the kragh. Tiron stepped off the far side of the road to do the same.

"But we're not your enemy." Tension had entered the woman's voice. She spoke more quickly. "You were part of the Abythian defense? Then — then you wish to help the Empire, do you not?"

Ramswold gave a wary nod of agreement.

"Then you would set back your cause if you killed Nok. Please, I swear it by the Ascendant. Don't do this. You need him to stay alive."

"I do?" Ramswold's voice was growing cold. "Unlikely. And you blaspheme by taking the Ascendant's name in vain."

"I swear it." The woman touched the kragh's arm again, reassuring the brute, and then stepped away, approaching Ramswold with the same strange blend of determination and hesitation that one might show when approaching a rabid dog. Good; it would be easier to fight the kragh if she wasn't by his side. "Please. You saw the group that passed by only a short while ago? A hundred or so kragh?"

Ramswold nodded.

"We're following them. Tracking them. They're hunting down a group of rebels. Rebels we wish to join."

"Rebels," said Ramswold, making no attempt to hide his skepticism.

"Yes," said the woman, orienting on him now. "Again, I swear it. A tribe that split away from Tharok when they saw the direction he was taking. We don't know where they are, but the shamans — the kragh in black robes? They do. We're using them to lead us to the rebels so we can warn them. Help them survive the coming attack."

Ramswold was clearly out of his depth. He gave Tiron a worried glance. Tiron ached to leap forward and attack, to hear the kragh roar, to clash and bring it down.

The woman spoke a series of harsh syllables, and the kragh stiffened. She repeated them, and the kragh grunted with obvious reluctance. It stared down at its hammer, then cast it to the ground. The corner of its head embedded itself in the dirt, so that its haft remained sticking up at an oblique angle. The kragh then stepped away from it.

Tiron straightened. That, he hadn't expected.

"Please," said the woman. "We aren't your enemies."

"Who are you?" asked Tiron.

"Shaya. Daughter of Zekko. This is Nok. We must find the rebels. Only they can help free the one kragh capable of stopping this madness."

"And who might that be?" asked Tiron.

Shaya closed her eyes as if summoning the strength to respond, to speak a name that might incite them to violence. "Tharok. The warlord of the kragh."

Chapter 4

The Ascendant had summoned key individuals from across Aletheia to his personal reflection chamber to deliberate the future
of the Empire. Iskra watched from one side as the circular chamber
slowly filled with men and women whose obvious sense of their own
importance had been confirmed by their being invited. They were in
a muddied state of fear and surprise, hope and concern.

They all did their best to ignore her, but when they shot glances her
way, unable to resist, they stared at her as if she were a demon born.

The Ascendant's presence stilled their tongues. A few were clearly
overwhelmed to simply be in his company. He stood beside a tall
window, hands linked behind his back, watching as dawn broke over
the cloudscape outside the floating stonecloud. Slender, head shaved,
robed in simple white and with a self-possession far beyond his fourteen years, he dominated the room and the gathered nobles without
even looking at them.

It was a small, domed chamber, high-roofed and gorgeously dec-
orated. Frescoes depicting the divine acts of the first Ascendant had
been painted in meticulous detail across the walls and ceiling, gilt
with subtle touches of gold, eyes brought out by the pasting of precious jewels. The marble floor was covered with a thick carpet stitched

with complex geometries, and a circular table of fiery red wood was surrounded by ornate chairs that looked distinctly uncomfortable to sit upon.

An Agerastian courier entered the chamber, his appearance provoking a stiffening of Aletheian expressions, and hurried to her side. He was the third within the last ten minutes, and he pitched his voice softly so that only she could hear.

"Your Imperial Majesty, General Pethar bids me convey that two-thirds of our forces are now gathered at the Solar Gates as requested. The other third, including the wounded, are setting up camp outside the Ascendant's palace. Token forces are spread throughout the levels to impress upon the populace that we are in control."

Iskra gave a slight nod, dismissing the youth, who bowed deeply, shuffled three steps back, and departed. She ignored the stares. Her claim to the title of empress in the presence of the Ascendant was no doubt heresy of the worst kind, but she was too tired, too preoccupied, to care.

The door opened, and a striking woman in her late forties entered, clad in a sumptuous robe of crimson and black, her composure impressive. She took three steps and then lowered herself to one knee. "Heavenly Ascendant, I came as quickly as I could. You do me too much honor with your summons."

The Ascendant turned from the window at last, a slight smile on his youthful face. "Rise, Red Rowan. With your arrival, our numbers are complete. Please, all, be seated."

There was a soft shuffling as chairs were pulled back, and soon all seven of them were seated. The Ascendant remained standing. He looked from one person to the next, each an august figure of great importance in the Empire, and finally at Iskra before addressing them all.

"Much has changed. Aletheia is occupied by an Agerastian army. They were brought here by Lady Iskra Kyferin, Empress of Agerastos, who made this show of force due to concern for my Empire. She came so as to effect change. Needed change."

Such was the awe that the Ascendant commanded that nobody spoke. Iskra saw faces pale, however, lips thin.

"The Fujiwaras are no more. The Minister of Perfection, the Minister of the Moon, and all other appointees from their clan have been relieved of their duties, and that ancient family is forever banished from Aletheia."

Now, people did gasp and stir. One old man let out a croak of disbelief, while the Red Rowan seemed to thrill, hands clasped together as her eyes shone.

"I will no longer remain cloistered within my palace as I have done, but shall henceforth take a direct hand in overseeing my Empire. My primary goal is the cleansing and ascension of all souls contained within it, and toward that end, I aim to reform the Empire in any and all ways that will further that divine goal."

Iskra fought to not smile. The nobles and ministers looked as if they were being dealt one blow after another.

"Empress Iskra is thus to be made welcome. She is my guest, and her army will serve our interests in all things."

All eyes slid over to her. Speculation, hatred, amazement — she saw a full spectrum of emotions. She met them with equanimity born as much from exhaustion as anything else.

"The Solar Gates should be opening even now," said the Ascendant softly. "We shall soon have word of how the siege of Abythos is faring. Depending on that news, Empress Iskra has agreed to send reinforcements from her own army if needed. If not, then they shall soon return to Agerastos, leaving a token force here as an honor guard as we set about the task of reforming the Empire."

"Your Imperial Highness," said a gruff-looking lord. He had a bushy white mustache, a florid face, strong features and large, heavily veined hands that emerged from his conservatively cut robes. "Reform the Empire? Please forgive me for speaking so frankly, but, if I may dare to ask, whatever do you mean?"

The Ascendant smiled. "Reform, Minster of the Sun. To change, and for the better. For too long have the Fujiwara held sway, molding the Empire as they saw fit. No longer. Henceforth, the Ascendant will decree how the Empire will be structured and run. I will make no proclamations yet; instead, I will study the Empire, learn how it operates, and, after taking counsel, I will begin to make my changes."

"Counsel?" The Minister of the Sun looked greatly relieved. "Of course, Your Holiness. May I presume that those summoned here today will be members of that august company?"

The Ascendant nodded.

The door opened, and a young man entered. He was tall, clad in an elegant crimson robe, his pale gold hair unruly and crowning a handsome face. Wicked burns marred his cheeks, and his eyes were hollowed by pain, but his smile was wry, and he carried himself with a casual authority.

Theletos the Longed-For.

Iskra rose to her feet. "How—?" Only hours ago, he had been carried away by attendants, on the verge of death, charred and wracked by the Vothak's fell magic. That he was standing, that he could smile — impossible.

He ignored her, closing the door and looking instead to the Ascendant. "Your Holiness. Is all well?"

He was wearing new swords at his hips. His last set had been partially melted by the Vothak's black fire.

"No, dear Theletos, but we are endeavoring to make it so. You should not be on your feet."

The Virtue relaxed a fraction, and his smile returned. "Being bedridden bores me to tears. And I heard that the fate of the Empire was being decided. Forgive me for being curious."

The Ascendant inclined his head. "Very well. We were just beginning. I was informing the new imperial council as to my intentions."

"I am sure that they were delighted to hear them," said Theletos, crossing his arms and leaning his shoulder against the wall.

A severe, ascetic-looking Sigean with a hooked nose and slitted eyes leaned forward, both hands placed flat on the table. "Your Holiness, I am your humble subject in all matters, and I look forward to placing the resources of my clan in your service. The removal of the Fujiwara, however, and the presence of the, ah, Agerastians, will cause alarm amongst the people of Aletheia. May I suggest that the critical voids in the government structure be filled immediately with pro-tem appointments, and that a message of reassurance be sent out to ease the city's collective worries?"

"Elegantly put," said the Minister of the Sun. "The Minister of the Palace cuts to the heart of the matter. As the highest-ranked appointee present, Your Holiness, I would be honored to advise you in how best to fill these vacancies."

The Minister of the Palace stiffened.

The Red Rowan's gaze flitted back and forth, and she opened her mouth to speak but was cut off by another.

"You presume too much," said a wiry elder, his face long and dolorous, his iron hair shorn close to his scalp. He was wearing a robe of faded violet with red tints over a profusion of other colors, and sat with such a stiff posture that it appeared almost unnatural. "It is for the Ascendant to decide when and how to fill these appointments. As perhaps the only official completely removed from all Fujiwara influence, I, Grand Controller, would find it more than understandable if he wished to seek guidance from sources untainted by their proximity to that fallen family."

Theletos snorted, drawing quick glances from those seated. Iskra stirred. She could sense the vast mechanism of the Aletheian government creaking into motion. She turned to the Ascendant, whose expression was serene. He raised a hand to speak, cutting off any responses, but just then a knock sounded on the door.

"Enter," he said.

The door opened, and Iskra felt a shock as if her spirit had been plunged into a bath of ice water.

"Kethe!" She rose to her feet.

Her daughter was standing in the doorway, clad in ornate green plate, its surface marred by countless dents and splattered with dried blood. Her face was gaunt with exhaustion and concern, and for a moment she met Iskra's eyes, her own lighting up with emotion before she tore her gaze away and fell to one knee before the Ascendant.

"Your Holiness." Her voice trembled.

"Speak, Makaria." The Ascendant rounded the table to stand before her.

Theletos pushed away from the wall as Asho appeared in the doorway behind her.

"Your Holiness." Kethe's voice broke. She struggled to swallow, her gaze fixed on the carpet. "The citadel has fallen. Our army is lost. The kragh have taken Bythos."

Nobody spoke. One of the nobles — a svelte older man with rakishly arranged robes of clashing colors — let out a whimper and slid off his chair to fall bonelessly to the floor.

Theletos was the first to react. "Empress Iskra, you must move the entirety of your army to the Solar Portals."

"Yes!" roared the Minister of the Sun, rising to his feet. "The Portals must be defended!"

"More information," said the Grand Controller. "We cannot make decisions without knowing exactly what has happened. Virtue Makaria—"

"We have all the information we need," barked the Minister of the Sun. "The Empire lies open to these beasts. We must defend Aletheia!"

"Defend?" The Red Rowan also rose to her feet. "My husband always said that defense was an attempt to delay defeat. We must attack! Now, with the thousands of Agerastians and what remains of our forces, punching into the kragh's underbelly while they carouse and celebrate their victory—"

Everyone was on their feet, speaking over each other, faces flushed. Iskra looked to the Ascendant. He was frowning and staring down at the table's surface, eyes moving from side to side as if he were following the erratic course of an invisible fish.

Asho moved to her side and bowed. "My lady."

He seemed to have aged ten years since she'd seen him last. "Tell me, quickly. What do I need to know?"

"Tharok, their leader, is a tactical genius. He punched through into Bythos just before the Portal closed, then guarded it while his forces overwhelmed our own and conquered the citadel. He has perhaps ten thousand or more kragh in his army. Trolls. Wyverns. Complete control over them."

The nobles were still arguing. Theletos, Iskra noted, had drawn Kethe aside and was interrogating her quietly. She quelled the desire to go to her daughter, fought down her disappointment over not being approached first. She turned her attention back to Asho.

"We have two thousand Agerastian soldiers, and perhaps five hundred more personal guards scattered throughout the city. Can we hold him off? Can we defend Aletheia?"

"I wish I could say yes, my lady." Asho's voice was soft, and she saw that he was trembling. "But I don't think so."

At that point, the Ascendant placed a hand on the table's surface, a simple gesture, but it was as if he had drawn a blade. The nobles fell silent and turned to him.

"The Agerastian soldiers are not ours to command," he said simply. "They are Empress Iskra's." He looked at her. "Will you command your men to face the kragh?"

All eyes turned to her.

"Of course, your holiness," she replied. "But I would urge you to consider abandoning Aletheia. We are but two thousand. They are five times—"

Iskra was drowned out by outraged shouts. She ignored them and kept her eyes on the Ascendant, who raised a hand, and again the silence fell, but this time it quivered with barely suppressed anger.

"It is a grave discourtesy to interrupt an empress," he said softly. "Please, show greater decorum."

With great effort, the nobles managed to look abashed.

"We are but two thousand, Your Holiness," she continued. "They are five times that number or more. If we make a last stand here, we will be defeated."

The Ascendant nodded slowly. "Theletos?"

The Virtue stepped forward. The news had awakened something within him, had lit a flame where only embers had smoldered before. Gone was his pain, his weary mockery. He gazed fervently at the Ascendant.

"The Portal to Bythos is wide enough for fifteen, perhaps twenty kragh to come through at once. We won't be fighting ten thousand of them. We'll be fighting at most twenty at a time. If we arrange our forces correctly, we can kill them as they enter. This is a bottleneck that favors us. We may never have such an opportunity to massacre his forces again."

Asho's smile was bitter. "You haven't seen these kragh fight. You didn't see the trolls bludgeoning knights aside as if they were toys. Worse, you're leaving out their most fundamental advantage: their warlord's genius for battle. He won't just march his kragh into a trap." He looked over at Kethe. "Right?"

Kethe hesitated. She looked from Asho to Theletos, then away. "We'll have to be careful. But if Theletos thinks we can hold the line, I'm willing to trust him."

"Beyond that," said the Minister of the Sun, "beyond any of that, we can't *retreat* from Aletheia! What madness is this? Give up the pinnacle of the Empire? Allow the White Gate to fall into the hands of *kragh*?" That brought about a murmur of agreement from around the table. The Minister of the Sun looked to the Ascendant. "Your Holiness, Aletheia has never fallen. Not even to Ogri! Let him come. Your guidance, your wisdom, your compassion and power shall see us through to victory! If we have faith, we cannot be defeated."

Again, people murmured their agreement, and Iskra saw Theletos give a decisive nod. The Ascendant's face was inscrutable.

Asho slammed his hand down on the table. "The White Gate can survive without us for a few days. We can't survive a frontal assault. We need to retreat! We need to go back to Starkadr and await the arrival of further forces from the edges of the Empire. Evacuate Aletheia! Save its citizens while we can!"

Theletos' smile oozed scorn. "Flee? If we flee now, we will never rally. We are more than just an army, Bythian. We are the hope and soul of the Empire. We cannot recover from a defeat here. If we abandon Aletheia, if we surrender the White Gate, the Empire dies."

"Then let it die, if it means saving thousands of lives—" began Asho, but he was quickly drowned out by more yells of outrage. Everyone stood again, and Theletos lowered his hands to the hilts of his swords.

"Enough," said the Ascendant. Despite his speaking softly, it was as if a bowl of glass had suddenly dropped over the shouting, cutting it off immediately. "We shall fight the kragh. It is our duty to protect the people of the Empire. If we cede Aletheia, this Tharok will turn his attentions to Zoe, to Sige, to Nous and Ennoia. We cannot allow that to happen. Thus, we shall take advantage of this bottleneck, this moment, and we shall stand firm. With the White Gates at our back, we shall repel the kragh."

Was that a tremor in his voice at the end? Despite his title, he was still but a fourteen-year-old boy; though his face showed no hesitation or doubt, she could sense it, could feel the weight of responsibility crushing down on him. Again, she wondered: was he divine? Or was he but flesh and blood? She didn't know, but in that moment, she felt nothing but admiration for a young man attempting to lead an Empire in what could prove its final hours.

"However, we shall not do so recklessly," he continued. "I shall order that our court and notables begin evacuating immediately. If we repel the kragh, they may easily return. If we fail, we will not be caught unprepared. Lady Iskra? Will you assist us in this?"

"Very well," she said. "I won't abandon you. I will direct my forces to move to the Solar Portals under General Pethar's command. Virtue Theletos, you are welcome to advise him in this coming engagement. I will send word that your counsel is to be heeded, and for the Vothaks to assist in moving your people to Starkadr."

"We must act swiftly," said Theletos. "Makaria, come. The kragh may attack at any moment. Your Holiness." He bowed deeply and strode from the room.

Kethe hurried over to where Iskra was standing and hugged her. For one precious moment, Iskra held her tight, squeezing her as hard as she could, breathing in her scent and burying her face in her daughter's hair, and then Kethe pulled away, tears bright in her eyes.

She hesitated as she looked at Asho, then turned and hurried after Theletos.

"Come, ser knight," said Iskra, taking Asho by the arm. "Please."

Asho allowed her to guide him outside the council chamber and stood mutely by as she gave commands to several Agerastian couriers, who raced off in an all-out sprint. Her commands given, she turned back to him.

"What are we doing?" he asked.

"We're fighting for our survival."

"No, we're sacrificing the Agerastian army to protect the White Gate," said Asho in a low hiss.

"The Ascendant has welcomed change," said Iskra. "You've missed a lot while you were in Bythos. He was controlled by the Fujiwaras, whom we drove off, and is now free to act for the first time. He said he wants to listen to my advice. That he wants us to work together."

"It didn't sound like it in there," said Asho, jabbing his finger at the council room. "It sounded more like he was politely ordering you to send your men to their deaths to defend Ascendancy."

"This kragh invasion is bigger than our argument with Ascension, Asho." Iskra had to fight to keep her voice calm. "If we lose Aletheia, if we lose this war, then there will be nothing to remodel, to fix. We need the Empire in place to fight them off. We need to help them defeat Tharok. Unless you think we can do that on our own?"

"No. Fine." Asho paused, fighting for calm. "But their religious beliefs are crippling our ability to think strategically. We cannot hold off ten thousand kragh. We need to fight Tharok on our terms, not his. You think he didn't plan for this next phase?"

"Asho." Iskra pinched the brow of her nose and closed her eyes. "I hear you. But there are realities in play I cannot control." She dropped her hand. "I cannot fight Tharok alone. I cannot convince the people of the Empire to abandon their religion. I cannot fight Ascendancy and Tharok at the same time. I must help if I am to be given scope later on to effect change. The Ascendant has decided to stay. Would you have me abandon him and Aletheia to Tharok?"

"If you withdrew your armies, they would have no choice but to evacuate. You're enabling their madness with the deaths of your men."

"No." This time several people looked in their direction, but she ignored them. "If I abandoned them now, I would never be anything but an enemy and a traitor to the millions of people who comprise the Empire. I have no choice."

Asho pursed his lips and bowed his head. His body was stiff with tension. "As you will, my lady." Each word was bitten off. "How would you have me serve you?"

"Go to the Solar Portals. If you're correct, we're going to need every man and woman who can swing a sword below. Report to General Pethar. I will stay with the Ascendant and safeguard our interests."

Asho's eyes were flat, his face, expressionless. He bowed again. "As you command." And with that, he strode past her and down the hall.

Iskra watched him go. How much of that anger, she wondered, had been sparked by Kethe's following Theletos' lead? She closed her eyes and recalled the hug. She inhaled as if she was smelling her daughter anew, savoring the memory, the strength in her arms, the vitality that had burned in Kethe's eyes. She had passed her Consecration. She had been made a Virtue. She was alive. Those were the most important facts. Everything else could be worked out.

Smoothing down her clothing, Iskra turned back to the council room. She had lost her first argument with the forces influencing the Ascendant, had failed to move him, to convince him to abandon Aletheia. Fixing as calm and regal an expression on her face as she could manage, she stepped back inside.

She would not lose the next.

Chapter 5

Asho strode through Aletheia, sword in hand. Once, in a different lifetime, he might have been awestruck. Now, he simply didn't care. Didn't care that he was making his way through the sacred heart of the Empire. That around him were the supposedly most pure people in existence. He didn't care for the peerless artwork, the elegance of the stoneshaping, the stunning views of cloudscapes he glimpsed through the windows.

The entirety of the stonecloud was gripped with fear. The circular avenue that spiraled down toward the Solar Portals was deserted but for soldiers and men bearing weapons. The few citizens whom Asho saw were pallid, shrinking back from the awfulness unfolding before them, hurrying to hide. To find safety.

Knowing, Asho felt, that on some level nothing and nowhere would ever be safe again.

Agerastian troops were hurrying past him, peeling away from the positions they had been sent to guard. Nobody recognized him. Nobody addressed him. He didn't care.

Down he went. Down to fight the kragh, and with each step, he was aware of the absence at his side. Kethe. Where was she? Leading her Consecrated, he supposed, ready to fight beside Theletos, ready to be what the Empire needed her to be, apparently: a Virtue.

Asho felt his anger curdle. No matter that he knew her better. That they'd saved each other's lives countless times. That on one dark and distant night, they had stood atop the ruined walls of Mythgraefen and had defied the forces of the Black Gate together, alone.

And won.

He could almost see the why of it. How she could believe that she was now more than simply Kethe. She'd become a symbol as much as the White Gate. A rallying point. A source of strength and faith. Her presence at Theletos' side would reassure the guards of Aletheia that the Ascendant was with them.

Yet, wherever Asho looked, he saw only the forces of Agerastos. Saw men who wouldn't care if Kethe fought beside Theletos. Saw men who worshipped, if anything, a fabricated medusa goddess. And if such was the case, whom was Kethe trying to impress with her fidelity?

A broad tunnel opened off the side of the descending spiral, a tunnel down which all the Agerastians were running. It had to be the way. Asho turned down it, but he wouldn't run. He wouldn't rush. The battle that was coming would be there when he arrived. It wouldn't matter if he was on the front line or at the back. There would be kragh enough for all.

Glorious carvings adorned the length of the tunnel. Tapestries. Globes of golden light were ensconced in the walls. Mosaics were underfoot. Everywhere, there was beauty. Asho studied it with cold disinterest as he walked on. How much of this would survive the invasion?

He could hear thousands of men preparing to die up ahead: the cries and barks of sergeants, the susurrus of men in ranks talking, checking weapons, hammering shields, nerving themselves up to face monsters.

The tunnel widened, and then he stepped out into the great chamber itself.

Half an hour ago, Asho had followed Kethe out of this very hall at a sprint; entering at a walk, he finally took in the full scope of it. Its roof disappeared high above. Its walls extended away on both sides like those of a castle. The majestic Portals rose in the center, each fifteen yards high and all but one carved from the purest white stone. Myriad roads were marked on the floor by colored mosaics, meant to guide traffic to each Portal in an orderly manner, but nobody paid them any heed. This was a staging ground now. These stones, hallowed and sacred, were about to be washed in blood.

The entrance to the great Portal chamber was slightly higher than the ground floor, affording Asho a view of the army. The Agerastians were formed up before the Bythian Gate. The others were ignored, their surfaces shimmering with white energy. Some soldiers were coming in from Nous and Ennoia, but for the most part, those Gates were still.

A slight space was open before the Portal, perhaps five yards. Beyond that were packed the Agerastians, with the Aletheian private guards on the flanks.

Spearmen were on the front ranks, a bristling phalanx that would impale anything that emerged from the Gates. Behind them were hundreds upon hundreds of swordsmen, and then the archers.

Theletos and General Pethar were standing atop a makeshift plat-form, directing the positioning with calls and the sound of horns. The killing ground was ten yards wide and five yards deep. Every eye was turned upon it. Only a few would be able to fight at a time, but the rest were ready to step in at a moment's notice.

Despite himself, Asho felt heartened. The Portal chamber was massive, but even so, the two thousand men filled the area before the Bythian Gate right back to the wall. There was no way Tharok could fight his way through that many men, no way his kragh could create enough of a bridgehead before they were crushed. Could they?

Asho descended to the level of the others and lost sight of the killing ground. Theletos and General Pethar were still easily visible atop their platform perhaps twenty yards back and to the right of the Bythian Portal. But where was Kethe?

Asho insinuated his way through the pressed ranks, finding avenues of approach between the units. He had a vague idea of finding Kethe when a cry torn from a thousand throats caused him to look up.

A boulder was sailing through the air, turning slowly as if in no rush. Easily as large as a cart wheel, it fell amongst the massed soldiers, eliciting screams and bellows of pain and anger as it carved a bloody furrow through the men.

The shock of the impact rippled through the men gathered around Asho as if the rock had been dropped into a lake. Men braced themselves, clutched at each other, raised onto their tiptoes to stare up front.

Asho was watching this time. He saw the next boulder emerge from the top of the massive Solar Portal. It trailed white smoke behind it for only a second before it was clear, spinning faster than the last, only to crash down with a reverberating crunch and plow through the ranks once more.

"The trolls," gasped Asho.

There was nothing he could do. The men around him were pushing at each other, heaving like an ocean lashed by the storm. People were shoving from behind; others were pushing back from in front. General Pethar was bellowing commands, but more boulders were sailing through the Portal.

One. Two — three — four. Their impact elicited heart-rending screams. How many men was each stone killing? Dozens?

The rocks kept coming, a constant barrage, some sailing almost twenty yards over the soldiers before crashing down and shattering limbs, crushing heads, snuffing out the lives of men trapped in the tight ranks.

A voice rose above the chaos. "Charge the Gate!"

"No!" screamed Theletos. "Hold you ground, the Black Gate take your souls!"

But fear and panic caused too many men to latch on to whomever was leading the charge. Asho felt another shiver run through the ranks, this one of anticipation, and by leaping up he saw a mob of men race toward the Gate, swords held high.

More boulders came careening through. One was particularly massive, almost the size of a pony, rough and oblong. It flew over the charge and crashed down right in front of Asho, who ducked down into a crouch as it bounced overhead and tore into the ranks behind him.

Asho looked up and saw Theletos gripping the railing of the platform, his whole body tensed as he watched their forces hit the Portal and race through. An endless tide of men, unnerved by the sheer amount of carnage that was mowing them down, unable to stand helpless, unable to wait to be obliterated. The Agerastians and Aletheians ran into the white fire of the Portal, their screams cutting off as they disappeared.

Fools. Madmen. Right into Tharok's army.

Asho began to elbow his way forward. People cursed him, and some shoved him back, but he paid no heed. He was without his magic. Without a demon blade. He had nothing but his ire and determination to see him through, but in the face of confusion and vacillation, that was enough.

One name echoed in his mind: *Kethe*. He had to find her. He had to protect her.

The charge slackened, faltered, then stalled. Men were shoving at the white fire, trying to pass through, only to be shoved back. Boulders were still flying overhead, with catastrophic results. Soldiers began to appear, passing back into Aletheia, retreating with grievous wounds. Men with limbs hacked off, great bloody wounds in their chests, their faces opened up and their jaws shattered.

Theletos let out a cry that pierced the madness and raised his blades. White fire engulfed his swords, and he boomed out a single word with such power and volume that even amid the madness, soldiers looked up and paid heed: "Back!"

Asho found his progress arrested. He was close, though. Only fifteen yards to the front line. He saw one of the boulders resting to his left and wished he hadn't. It was smeared with blood, and bodies were crushed beneath it. The ranks had closed around its glistening bulk, but he could imagine the trail of dead that it had left behind.

"Here they come!"

The yell caused Asho to snap his gaze forward just in time to see the kragh come charging through the Portal, axes and hammers raised high. Their roars were inhuman, reverberating through the air; their maws were open, spittle flying. Twenty came through all at once, another twenty right behind them.

"Loose!" screamed Theletos.

Arrows flew. But it was not an orderly flight. The archers' ranks had been wrecked by the boulders, their morale shaken. Many overshot. Shafts punched into kragh shoulders and chests. Some stumbled. A few went down. But the bulk smashed into the Agerastian frontline with a roar.

Still the boulders were flying through the Portal. This more than anything was ruining Theletos' plan. Soldiers couldn't focus on the battle ahead. Too many were watching the massive rocks, tensed and ready to dive aside. Yet they couldn't. There was no room. Screams of despair would briefly turn into screams of mortal agony and then were cut off altogether.

How many boulders had come through? Twenty? The men in front of Asho were shoving forward, blades held at the ready. Asho could see the kragh in snatches between shoulders and helms. Axes raised. He caught brief flashes of their bestial visages, their tusks. He'd fought in armies before, was becoming wise to the feel of the ranks, the solidity of the men around him. And, as the boulders continued to rain down, he felt the Agerastians ready to break.

"For the White Gate!" Theletos leaped up onto the railing of the platform. He balanced with impossible grace on the slender wooden bannister, twin swords flaming so bright, they burned the eye. "For the Ascendant! For death!" Then he leaped down into the maelstrom and was gone.

Asho growled and shoved forward again. Men parted. Instinct caused him to look just in time to see a boulder falling toward him. He could make out the cracks and crevices on its face as it spun. Asho screamed and surged forward. The base instinct to live overwhelmed him. He squirmed and dove, and managed to hoist himself up between the shoulders of the two men in front of him and fall forward just as the boulder crashed down a foot behind him.

He fell to the ground. A forest of legs shifted around him. Someone stepped on his calf; someone else tripped and sat on his back. Asho grunted, got his feet under him, and forced himself upright. The man in front of him moved away, disappeared suddenly. Relieved, Asho straightened and saw why.

Kragh.

Blood was spattered thickly across its face. Its tusks gleamed crimson. Heavily muscled arms were cast to one side, holding on to the massive hammer that had just demolished the man who had been standing in front of Asho in a sideways swing.

Instinctively, Asho raised his blade and speared it into the kragh's throat. Cut through the tendons and windpipe.

Blood fountained. The kragh's eyes widened, and it brought its hammer back around, a backhanded blow that it shouldn't have been able to execute.

Asho went to parry, and at the last second regained his senses. He threw himself backward instead, into the arms of the soldiers behind him. They caught him, surprised, then hurled him forward as the hammer swung past.

Asho used the momentum to plunge his blade into the kragh's armpit. The blade sank in two inches, then stuck. The kragh screamed, spraying blood, and dropped its hammer. Asho reared back, placed his foot on the monster's thigh, and shoved. The kragh fell away, bleeding profusely, freeing his blade.

There was no time to recover his breath. Kragh to the right. To the left. Then a massive one loomed in front of him. *Nok*, thought Asho, frozen as he gaped up. *No — it's not...*

He thought no more.

The mountain kragh stood a full seven feet tall, and it was wielding a club the bulbous end of which was studded with knobs of black rock. The kragh brought the club crashing down at Asho, who sidestepped just in time. The club swooshed past his face, missing him by an inch, and shattered the stone beneath Asho's feet.

Clutching his sword with both hands, he stabbed at the mountain kragh's face, but it released its club and raised its left palm to block the attack. Asho's sword slid through its palm, punched right through, but in doing so was deflected. The tip missed the kragh's head, the sword running through its hand all the way to the hilt.

Around which the mountain kragh closed its fingers. Asho, wide-eyed, couldn't stop the kragh from tearing his blade away. Before he could react, the kragh punched him straight in the chest with its right fist. It was like getting kicked by a mule.

Asho was lifted off his feet. He only went back two feet before colliding with other soldiers. He bounced, fell to his knees. He couldn't breathe. His chest was one endless spasm.

Screams echoed all around him. Boulders flew overhead. The mountain kragh gripped Asho's blade by the hilt, pulled it free of its hand, and lifted it overhead. It looked puny in the kragh's massive hand.

Then a sword of white flame severed the mountain kragh's arm at the elbow. Blood burned and sizzled where the wound was cauterized. Before the kragh could turn, the blade reversed its trajectory and cut down through the kragh's shoulder, deep into its chest. The kragh fell, and Asho saw Kethe, her eyes wild, her sword a brand of lightning in her hands.

She extended her hand. He took it, let her haul him to his feet, and then snatched up his fallen sword and turned. A pocket had opened around them, a space in which to breathe. Theletos – he was a couple of yards deeper in, and everything that fell upon him died. The pile of kragh dead at his feet was knee-high.

Even as Asho watched, two kragh leaped over the mound, roaring. Theletos laughed and leaped to meet them, somersaulting, his blazing blades held out horizontally. He slipped between them, cutting them in half as he did, and the kragh hit the ground behind him in four pieces.

"Damn," breathed Asho.

"You okay?" Kethe stared him up and down.

"I – yes." He wanted to pause for a moment, to collect himself, but the kragh were closing in on both sides. "Fall back!"

A boulder stood to his right. He ran to it, leaped, caught a hand-hold, scrambled, was up. He crouched and looked over the battlefield.

It was a massacre. The kragh were carving their way through the Agerastians. The boulders had shattered Agerastians' organization, and the kragh were making the most of the chaos. Fear had the humans by the throat. The ground before the Portal was a butcher's field. More kragh were coming through every second, twenty with each rank, flooding the killing field even as arrows fell fitfully amongst them.

Yet there were still almost two thousand humans pushing in all around them – pushing in and getting cut down. Asho bit his lower lip. Where to throw himself? Where could he make the greatest difference?

The boulders had stopped, he realized. That meant —

He stood up and cupped his hands about his mouth. "Trolls! Incoming!"

Four massive shapes darkened the Portal. Thirteen, maybe fourteen feet high, they came through at a gangly run, all elbows and hunched shoulders, heads thrust forward, hammers trailing behind them. Blue-skinned, hides rock-encrusted, their ears ragged, faces scrunched up in rage, they knocked the kragh aside as they charged into the massed warriors.

If Asho had heard screams of fear before, now he heard panic. Nobody here had seen anything like this, had ever had to face a monster straight out of legend. The hammers were raised, then swept down, and bodies were sent literally flying, tumbling like ragdolls. The trolls pounded into the Agerastians, cutting deep into the fourth, sixth, tenth rank of humans, sheer momentum making them unstoppable.

Men were throwing themselves back, shoving at each other, dropping their weapons. More kragh were coming in through the Portal. Oh, what Asho wouldn't give for a heavy cavalry charge right then, forty of the Black Wolves sweeping in from the flanks to crash into the foe!

But, no. They had nothing. Just massed ranks. Spearmen and swords, archers now in sufficient disarray that they weren't even fighting. All order had broken down. Asho couldn't make out regiments, ranks, anything. Just a compressed crowd of men who didn't have room to swing.

How many kragh had entered the killing field? A hundred? A hundred and fifty?

And where was Theletos? Asho saw the Virtue fighting all by himself in front of the Portal, spinning as if he hadn't been terribly wounded only the evening before. His swords left trails of flame behind them.

Kethe was fighting her way back to his side.

There were ten thousand kragh on the other side of that Portal, lined up and waiting to pour in. Asho felt a cold certainty grip him by the throat. This battle was lost. It would be a grinding, grueling slaughter, but even with Theletos holding the center, the killing ground had been lost. The kragh-held space was widening by the moment, making more room for reinforcements.

A kragh swept a scimitar at Asho's shins. He threw himself into a dive, turned his shoulder and crashed into another as it charged past him. The impact sent Asho spinning brutally to the ground, but the kragh was also knocked off its feet. Somehow, Asho held on to his blade. He climbed up, panting for breath, his back wrenched, and then ducked and sprinted after Kethe.

He didn't engage. Didn't fight back. He simply avoided fights, stabbing out as he passed kragh, and ducked and wheeled as he made his way deeper into the melee.

Kethe had nearly reached Theletos. Consecrated were trying to follow her and failing. She was going to isolate herself out there.

"Kethe!" He ducked a decapitating blow, fell into a roll, came up staggering. He hurled himself aside as a kragh charged right through where he'd been, then sprinted on. "Kethe!"

They reached Theletos just in time. He brought both blades down upon a kragh, cutting off its arms, then he stumbled and fell.

Kethe caught him in the crook of one elbow. Theletos' head rolled back. His eyes rolled up in their sockets, and an exhalation of mist puffed out of his mouth as if he were releasing his soul. His blades from his limp hands, and Asho discarded his own to awkwardly scoop them up. He hissed as their heated hilts burned the palms of his hands, but held on.

"Run, Kethe! We must get back to Iskra! The battle's lost!"

Kethe let out a cry of frustration, then crouched, hiked Theletos over her shoulder, and rose smoothly to her feet. Asho covered her retreat, lashing out and clanging the swords against an approaching kragh's blade. It lunged, and Asho stumbled back. It lunged again, and Asho sidestepped and brought both swords down on the kragh's extended arm. The blades were wickedly sharp and sheared through its forearm.

Khoussan had appeared at Kethe's side, and the large Consecrated took Theletos up onto his shoulder. They retreated together, moving through the swirling combatants, intent on getting Theletos clear.

"Should we tell Pethar to sound a retreat?" yelled Kethe.

Asho shook his head. "No. That'd lead to a massacre." He had to pitch his voice to carry. "We need to hold back the kragh as long as we can. Buy time for the Ascendant and everyone else to flee!"

Khoussan almost stumbled as he turned to stare at Asho. "You're condemning these men to die?"

"No," said Asho. He felt hard. Brutal. He met Khoussan's gaze coldly. "The Ascendant did that when he sent them down here in the first place."

A kragh charged them from the right. Asho spun toward it, pivoting on the balls of his feet underneath its axe, and slammed both blades home into its chest. They punched through leather armor, through hide, and sank with unnerving ease to the hilts into the beast's chest. Momentum carried the kragh forward, but it was dead on its feet; it crashed to the ground moments later.

Asho knelt, tore the blades free, and flicked the blood from them.

"Sorry, Kethe. Aletheia has fallen. It's time to go."

Chapter 6

A udsley emerged from the secret Fujiwara Portal into a well-appointed hallway carved from living rock. Morose tapestries sewn in burgundies, black and deep blues lined the passage, interspersed with oil lamps that burned with steady flames. The carpet underfoot had once been luxurious but was now threadbare down its center, and the air was uncomfortably chill.

Zephyr looked back at him as if to assure herself that he was there, and gestured peremptorily for him to follow. A stream of Fujiwara servants and important officials was bustling down the hallway ahead of them, and more were pushing in from behind, all intent on fleeing the compromised estate back in Aletheia. Biting down on his questions for now, Audsley set off after her, all the while gazing avidly about him.

Haugabrjótr. A hidden stonecloud, lost in legend, referenced only as a myth in his encyclopedic tomes on the matter. It immediately seemed the antithesis of Starkadr; while the Sin Casters' stonecloud had been immense, built on a scale to beggar the mind, Audsley quickly came to realize that Haugabrjótr was a warren of tightly interconnecting tunnels and chambers, an ant's nest that bordered on the claustrophobic. The tunnels were narrow enough that he was constantly twisting his shoulders so as not to knock into people going the other way, and never once did they widen into proper halls or caverns.

Instead, it was as if they were striding around inside a collection of bubbles that had been trapped within the rock, small chambers about which the tunnels coiled and twisted. He almost immediately lost his sense of direction, as the tunnels did not adhere to a level plane either; he rose, then descended, then turned, then seemed to coil back up over a chamber they'd just passed in a tight spiral.

Little Zephyr led on without doubt, however, and Audsley fixed his gaze on her. He ignored the curious glances from those who were seeing him in these tunnels for the first time, and fought down the urge to peer into the many chambers they passed. The atmosphere of the stonecloud was one of alarm and speculation; everywhere, people had gathered as best they could into tight little knots where they whispered furiously to each other, only to fall silent as Little Zephyr passed them by.

"Here," she said at last, stopping before a broad double doorway. It was imposing not only for being made of reinforced black oak banded with heavy iron, but also for being the first door he'd seen in the warren. "Ready?"

Audsley tried for a cold smile. "Given my complete lack of awareness as to what you are about to show me, dear Zephyr, I can only attest naively that yes, I am."

Little Zephyr's cheeks dimpled with amusement, and then she pushed on one of the doors. It swung inward easily, perfectly balanced, and he followed her within.

They stood on a balcony above the largest room he'd yet seen. It was without tapestries and carpets, and was dominated by an obsidian table. Iron manacles were affixed to each corner, and Audsley realized that the entirety of it was meant to restrain somebody on its surface.

Two tunnels led off from its rear wall, and several men were busy cleaning stone shards on tables arranged alongside the walls. Cabinets with glass fronts were hung above those, and all of it was lit by a dozen lanterns that hung from the ceiling from cords of different lengths.

Something about the chamber, about the clinical manner in which the men were washing their cruel-looking spikes, the massive density of the black table and its ponderous manacles — all of it sent a chill through Audsley. Yet the chill lingered not; like a cloud passing before the sun, there was but a moment of doubt and shadow, and then it was gone, having failed to latch on to his soul. In its place was left only a bright and avid curiosity.

"This is what you wanted to see," said Little Zephyr, making her way down a set of stairs that led down from the side of the balcony. "Did you not? I am most intent on keeping my promises."

"So that I shall have no excuse but to keep mine," said Audsley, following her.

The four men laid their tools down on black cloths and turned to regard them, a hint of wariness beneath their blank expressions of respect. The eldest of them, a severe man with closely cut gray hair, a high brow and piercing sky-gray eyes, stepped forward and gave a sharp little bow. His cheeks were riven by deep creases, as if he had been desiccated not too long ago, and the veins along the sides of his neck and the backs of his hands were plainly, almost painfully, visible.

"My lady," he said as he straightened, his gaze moving over to Audsley.

"Athanasius," said Little Zephyr, inclining her head. Her black hair slipped free, and she reached up to curl it behind one perfect ear. "May I introduce a new friend of mine, Magister Audsley of Nous. He has expressed a deep curiosity as to your activities here, and I was hoping you could give him a brief tour of the facilities. Perhaps even a live demonstration?"

The man's gaze was as incisive as a scalpel. Audsley raised his chin and adopted a quiet smile, refusing to let Athanasius' intensity visibly ruffle him.

"But of course, my lady." Athanasius' smile betrayed absolutely no pleasure. "As you desire. There is indeed a subject ready to be refracted. We are in luck." So saying, he turned and raised his eyebrows at one of the other men, who immediately bowed and hurried down the left-hand tunnel.

"Refracted?" asked Audsley.

The table was weighing on his mind, pressing against him as if it had a spiritual density that did not brook being ignored. It gleamed as if wet, newly washed, but that was but a property of the obsidian; when Audsley shifted his weight, even minutely, the reflected ribbons of light seemed to slither over its surface.

"That is the name to which we give our procedure," said Athanasius briskly.

He moved to a cabinet, opened its doors with sharp, economical movements, and drew forth a small case of polished cedar. This he set down on the side table and flipped open, revealing four tubes of glass, each stoppered with cork and a sealment of wax. He drew one forth with the utmost care. The bottom two-thirds was filled with a liquid of the most absolute black, without visible particles and completely opaque.

"Observe the finished product. Twelve drams has been determined to be the minimum amount needed for an effective dose. When properly sealed, its potency lasts for decades. Exposure to the light rapidly decays its efficacy, however, so the vessel must either be held within a case, or opaque in its own right."

Audsley stepped in closer, linking his hands behind his back as he leaned forward. "And what does an effective dose accomplish?"

Athanasius arched an eyebrow. "Beyond the customary usages?"

"Including," said Little Zephyr, her tone cold.

"Including, then. Well." Athanasius turned the tube about, as if examining the liquid within from all sides. "The most common application has been to retard the process of attenuation that all Virtues undergo. While it is impossible to completely reverse the process, a steady diet can delay their sublimation into the White Gate, allowing them to extend their lifespans by as much as two score years."

Audsley felt a thrill. "But how? And why? Why does the White Gate – attenuate, you described it? — the Virtues? Why does this potion delay that effect?"

Athanasius produced that predatory smile once more. "Fascinating questions, all. There are no clear-cut answers, only theories. But

I believe that the power of the White Gate is, at its most basic, that of draining the elemental spark of life from the world. Virtues, being an extension of the Gate, can extend its reach. Hence their lethality against all beings of primordial energy and those who are able to channel it."

Audsley wanted to sit down. He was getting glimpses of a whole new way of seeing the world. Hints of an understanding that promised to shatter old myths and misconceptions.

"Primordial energy?"

"Magister Audsley, you are asking questions that far exceed the scope of this demonstration. But, yes. Primordial energy. That which flows into the world through the Black Gate — or did — and which is wielded by those who walk the Path of Flames, as it was once so poetically called."

Audsley blinked. He thought of Kethe's blade, how it had wounded the errant demon outside Hrething when all other weapons had failed to pierce it. How her usage of her powers had led to her wasting away, her skin growing translucent, her vitality ebbing until she managed to undergo her Consecration.

The sound of sobs came from the left-hand tunnel. Pitiful, sniffling sobs. The broken weeping of a man who was past the point of resistance. The assistants returned, escorting a youth between them. Their prisoner was emmaciated, his rough brown hair shiny with grease, his skin almost gray. His white cotton shift hung off his shoulders loosely, and he stared forward without focusing on anything, looking right through Audsley before his gaze locked on the table.

He shivered, dug his heels in, pushed back. His weeping became a series of stutters, as if a word too awful to be spoken had suddenly clawed itself athwart his throat and stuck there.

The assistants forced him forward. He was too weak to resist, and instead resumed weeping once more and shaking his head as they helped him up onto the obsidian table and began the process of locking the manacles about his wrists and ankles.

Audsley felt a profound sense of horror and revulsion pass through him. He knew that what he was witnessing was foul beyond measure, but once more the emotions failed to find purchase. It was academic, almost; he was but a spectator here, outside this awful experience. He was not a part of this, nor was this his responsibility. He was here merely to gain knowledge, and this – this was the best and most immediate way to do so.

"Now, there are many ways to synthesize our product," said Athanasius, his tone not changing in the slightest. "The easiest means is through quarried illirium stone that we import from the mines around the Abythian Portal in Bythos. The process of purifying illirium is tedious, however, and producing twelve drams of product takes a shockingly large amount of stone and effort. It is much more effective to drain the product directly from one born with the ability to channel primordial energy."

"A Sin Caster," breathed Audsley.

Little Zephyr snorted. "You sound like an Ennoian serf. If you're going to wax eloquent, at least call him by his proper name. A Flame Walker."

"Even that is fanciful," said Athanasius. "He was born with the ability to channel primordial energy. He was arrested a decade ago by the Virtue Ainos when he manifested his ability. He was brought to Aletheia for trial and handed into our care thereafter. He has been producing for us ever since, though with time, the quality of his product has dropped sharply. Soon, he will be disposed of. No matter. He will suffice for today."

With the manacles firmly secured, the assistants set about forcing a clear tube down the young man's throat. The Sin Caster choked and gargled pitifully but was unable to resist. More tubes were threaded into his veins through gleaming needles of silver until a half-dozen such were embedded in his flesh. His skin, Audsley saw, was horrifically scarred in those areas from past treatments.

"The tubes are made of porcine intestine reinforced from within by an ingenious wire mesh. Now, there is precious little ambient primordial energy to be milked, with the Black Gate being closed," said Athanasius. "Thus, we must find a way to stimulate his talent artificially.

This is where these illirium spikes come in. It has taken centuries to refine this science, but we now know exactly where to perforate his body to best stimulate his reflexive channeling. While our artificial methods of synthesizing product from illirium directly are crude at best, one such as he can draw incredible amounts, filtering out impurities and refining the product to a state of near perfection. Watch."

The assistants took up the shards of black rock. Each was about eight inches long, perhaps an inch wide at the top and tapering to a needle point at its base. The two men worked in tandem. The first held a spike over the left-hand side of the imprisoned man's lower abdomen. The second raised a mallet, and with a confident tap drove the spike deep into the man's body.

The Sin Caster didn't even scream. He writhed slowly as if in some heinous ecstasy, and tears began to leak from the corners of his eyes.

This process was resumed. Eight spikes were hammered into his body in all. By the eighth, the man had stopped reacting.

"Now, you will observe that our source has gone completely still. When first subjected to this process, channelers will draw product reflexively and without surcease until they are completely drained. At this advanced stage of usage, however, the process is gradual. We must coax the product out by creating weak vacuums at the ends of our conduits."

The assistants brought forth large glass spheres which they set around the base of the table. They lit candles within each, then screwed on a brass lid. The flames grew quickly shorter, then extinguished themselves. The tubes, Audsley saw, terminated in brass sockets. These were affixed to valves at the tops of the spheres and rotated around till something clicked and the assistants left them alone, satisfied.

Audsley couldn't tear his eyes away from the supine form, from the invasive tubes, the crudely inserted spikes. The man was again writhing, his lips opening and closing around the tube that ran down his throat. A decade, Audsley thought. For ten years, this man had been subjected to this horror.

Audsley's breathing stopped when the first black liquid began to creep out of one of the tubes inserted into the man's left arm. Just drops. Pulled forth, it seemed, by some fell power within the glass spheres.

"That is the gist of it," said Athanasius, turning to Audsley with a clap of his hands. "We'll leave him here for a few hours, until he has totally used up the illirium spikes. The nature of his casting causes those wounds to heal themselves, fortuitously, though we won't be able to refract him for another month." He smiled at Little Zephyr. "Luckily, we have many other channelers to rotate into his place, so that's all right."

Little Zephyr looked, if anything, mildly bored. "Yes, yes. Content, Audsley?"

"I — yes." His revulsion was falling away from him. Instead, new questions were crowding his mind. Did the Virtues know the source of their tonic? Did the Ascendant? How much was produced? Who had discovered this process? What would the Virtues do now that the Fujiwara source had been cut off? "Though I have many other questions."

"Later," said Little Zephyr, giving his arm a push. "Let's leave Athanasius to his work. If you want to discuss theology and the like, it must wait. Now, let me show you to your room."

"It is always a pleasure to host you, Little Zephyr," said Athanasius, giving his sharp half-bow once more.

"Yes, yes, thank you for your time," said Little Zephyr, skipping up the steps.

Audsley followed her slowly, staring down once more at the man on the obsidian table. The man's eyes were rolling from side to side, and tears were still flowing down his ravaged cheeks. Turning away, Audsley followed Little Zephyr back out through the massive doors, and felt a shudder of relief when they closed behind him.

"Now, this way. Hurry."

Little Zephyr rushed along the corridor, and Audsley was forced to put aside his horror and questions as he fought to keep up, not quite wanting to break into a jog. Up and down and around they went, taking tunnel branches until they climbed for a while and finally turned off into a tunnel quieter than most. There were doors set into the walls here, and he was led to the third door on the right, which Little Zephyr pushed open.

She stepped aside and gestured grandly for him to enter. "Your quarters, Magister."

It was a small room, little more than a hole, with room for a narrow bed, a shelf, a desk, and a tiny window that had been bored through perhaps four feet of rock to the world outside.

Unable to control himself, he moved to the window, placed both hands on the ledge and peered through the thick glass. He saw smudged gray skies, vague storm clouds, and nothing more. Crestfallen, he turned. Little Zephyr was still standing outside.

"I hope you enjoy your room," she said ominously, eyes wide. "For you shall be staying here a long, long time. Good night, Audsley. One day, I shall return for you."

And with that, she slammed the door closed.

Audsley let out a cry of fear and rushed forward. He pounded on the door, then stepped back, raising his hand to blast it with fire only to stop when Little Zephyr threw it open again. She was bent almost double with high-pitched giggles.

"Your face! You should have seen it! Oh!" She entered the room, pushing his upraised hand down nonchalantly as she passed him to sit on his bed. "Good night, Audsley," she repeated in her usual dire tone, and then she smacked her knee and laughed once more. "Oh, that was a good one. Right? Come on. Relax, already. It was just a joke."

Audsley forced himself to smile and leaned against his new desk. "Yes. Quite hilarious."

"Anyway. This really is your room. It's not much, but you may have noticed that space is at a premium here in Haugabrjótr. But it should suffice. You're free to wander around, but you'll annoy people quickly if you keep getting lost, so you should probably wait for me to escort you in the beginning."

"All right," said Audsley. *That man is being drained at this very moment.* He shuddered again and pushed the thought away.

"Now, I've shown you the deep, dark secret of the black potions. In fact, I would say I gave it the highest priority. Which indicates, obviously, that I take my obligations to you very seriously. The Fujiwara estate is probably still being ransacked, everyone else is panicking and debating the future of the clan, and here I am, acting as your personal guide." She paused and cocked her head to one side. "Agreed? I've done my part?"

"Yes, very much so."

Audsley pulled out the chair and sat down. He ran his hand over his hair. His hand was trembling. He looked at it in confusion. He felt quite calm. Why was it shaking so?

"Very good. Which means we can now start fixating on your end of the bargain. Helping me get rid of the Minster of Perfection, as you know him, though that's probably not going to be his official title for much longer."

"Getting rid of him. Right." He inhaled deeply and gave her a smile. "What is your plan?"

"I don't have one. Not yet, at any rate." She scooted across his bed till her back was against the wall and raised one knee so she could rest her chin on it. She looked down at the bed's simple cover and began picking at it. "That's where you come in. Fresh eyes and so forth."

"Right." He watched her morosely, and then a question left his lips before he could stop himself. "What happens to the Sin Casters when they can no longer create... product?"

"Did that disturb you?" She glanced back up at him through her hair. "Be honest."

"Yes, of course." He said it calmly enough.

"Yes, it is pretty horrible, really." She pulled on a thread, causing the fabric of the cover next to it to suddenly furrow and grow tight. "But it is what it is. You might as well protest disease, or heartbreak. Facts of life, or at least, a fact of my life."

"The man?" Audsley's voice was soft. "What will happen to him?"

"Oh, he'll still have his use," said Little Zephyr. She released the thread and interlaced her fingers over her knee. "Can you guess?"

Audsley shook his head.

"It's a complicated process. It makes milking him for product look like child's play. But he'll serve our clan for eternity." Her voice changed. The playful edge fell away, and though she didn't move, didn't change her posture even a little, she suddenly seemed alien, dangerous, predatory. "Where, after all, do you think our demons come from?"

Chapter 7

Impotent, scalding fury roiled within her, like water left to boil in an unattended pot. Kethe wanted to scream and throw herself into the midst of the kragh, to lose herself in bloodletting and violence. To let the singing call of the White Gate drown out the bellows and roars and pitiful pleas for help.

Asho stood before her, tall and self-possessed, shoulders back, Theletos' twin blades held in his hands. He looked like a stranger. His face could have been carved from marble. Four flecks of blood were splattered across his jawline. Even as madness raged around them, he stood as if they were alone, uncaring for the destruction that was being wrought against their forces.

"Fine." She nodded to Khoussan. Her second retreat in as many hours. "We have to get the Ascendant out. Go."

Khoussan began to shoulder his way through the milling ranks of Agerastians. Kethe spared a glance to General Pethar up on his platform. The man was yelling his defiance at a troll that was stalking toward him, sword raised, its other hand clutching the railing. The troll raised its hammer high, and Kethe looked away. She was fleeing the battlefield. Leaving these men behind.

Gritting her teeth, ignoring Asho, she ran after Khoussan. Her passage seemed to draw men after her; why should they stand when a Virtue had fled? Twice, they'd underestimated Tharok. Twice, he'd defeated them with ease. Even as she ran, her mind raced in another direction. How could they defeat a foe that was always five steps ahead of them? He'd seized the initiative, and they'd failed to wrest it back.

And now? Madness was going to engulf the stonecloud. How many thousands were going to die as the kragh poured in unchecked? How were they going to get the Ascendant out? Was the war over? Had Tharok already won it all?

They fled out the main tunnel, leaving the din of battle behind them. A stream of soldiers ran alongside them, intermittently halting and turning to gaze back, unsure of where they were going. *Away.* Cowards. No, not cowards. Just men. Agerastians fighting for a cause that meant nothing to them, at the behest of a foreign empress.

Iskra. Her mother.

They broke out into the main spiral. Voices echoed all about them, people crying out questions, men barking commands, the sound of incipient panic. Kethe tried to ignore the people who called out to her. She ran behind Khoussan, her eyes focused on Theletos' body. He'd collapsed so suddenly. Had he simply pushed himself too far? Fought beyond his reserves? She realized on some base level that she had thought him literally unstoppable. Seeing his head roll and bounce against Khoussan's back did more to undermine her faith than anything else.

Suddenly, she stopped. What were they doing?

"Khoussan! Asho! Organize these soldiers. Go back to the mouth of the tunnel and take command. Form them into regiments and send them to the entrance to Starkadr. We're going to need them in the days to come."

Khoussan paused and looked back down the way they had come. "I don't speak Agerastian," he rumbled.

"Doesn't matter," said Asho. "They'll obey. They're looking for a leader. We'll see you at the Portal. Hurry."

Kethe nodded tightly and then began to run once more. The White Song filled her. She felt like her bones were made of the brightest light, that her flesh was being seared from her frame. Gravity could barely tether her. She ran faster and faster, her frustration and fury lending her wings. She whipped around the circles of the spiral, the balls of her feet barely touching the floor.

Henosis was dead. Mixis, Akinetos, and Synesis were lost. Theletos was down. Ainos had never returned from the blade towers. She was the last of the Virtues still in action. That fact beat upon her as if she were a drum. The last Virtue.

Makaria. Kethe. Makaria. Kethe.

Should she have listened to Asho? To her own doubts in the council chamber? Should she have argued for flight?

Makaria. Kethe. Makaria. Kethe.

No. They couldn't have abandoned the White Gate. No matter what, it had to be defended. Defended right up until this point. Until it was lost.

Its song filled her. The purity of it, the beauty, brought tears to her eyes. They were going to abandon it. Leave it for the kragh. Impossible; it had never been taken. Even as its song grew stronger, she felt it falling away. She was the last Virtue, and she had agreed to abandon the heart of Ascendancy.

She burst out onto the first level. The open area in front of the palace had been turned into a makeshift infirmary. The Vothaks were still recovering in a tent of their own, their bodies wracked with pain and debilitating nausea. If only they'd been available for the fight below! What a waste to throw them at Theletos.

Kethe ran past them all, past guards, and servants, and endless numbers of courtiers, and entered the palace. She ignored the bows, the shocked gasps, the hands over mouths. She ran right to the council door and threw it open.

The Ascendant was standing at the window. He turned to her, and she felt herself falling into his stillness, his calm. Her words choked her throat and would not come out. There were others in the room, even her mother, but she could only look at him. The tears that had brimmed in her eyes overflowed, and she fell to her knees.

She couldn't speak. Couldn't breathe.

"Very well," said the Ascendant. "We did our best. It is time to depart. We shall not concede complete defeat. With the Solar Gates taken from us, we will have to use Empress Iskra's Lunar Portals."

His voice was almost soothing. The nobles rose to their feet, some stammering, others gripping the table's edge for support.

"Kethe," said her mother. "How much time do we have?"

"Time?" She forced herself to focus. "I don't know. The battle is lost, but we're still fighting to hold them back." *We?* She'd run. "An hour, perhaps, before the massacre is complete."

"That — I can fetch my family in that time," said the Minister of the Sun. "Very well. With your permission, Your Holiness?"

"An hour? Evacuate Aletheia in — no. No, no, no," said another man.

The Ascendant ignored them. "Will you take me and mine to this Portal, Virtue?"

"Yes," said Kethe. "Of course, Your Holiness."

"Then, let us depart," said the Ascendant. "The palace staff are ready. My emergence will set the process in motion. Come."

He walked around the table and extended his hand to her. Kethe's breath stopped as she took it and allowed him to help her rise.

His smile was heartbreaking. "We are not defeated, Virtue. Not yet."

She could only nod dumbly. "We have to descend to the seventh circum, Your Holiness. We will have to pass the battle. It won't be... safe."

"There are other means of descending," said the Ascendant. "Private stairwells, platforms that can raise and lower large amounts of goods. We will use those, and I will ask that they also be opened to the public at this time."

Kethe nodded. There was so much to Aletheia that she didn't understand. Comprehend.

The Ascendant ignored the cries of protest of his nobles and pushed open the council doors, then strode out briskly into the hall beyond. Immediately, servants and chancellors leaped into action, calls and commands racing ahead of them as the palace began to move. People, it seemed, had been forewarned; servants carrying bundles, pushing wheelbarrows, and lugging crates were racing through the halls toward the western wing of the palace.

The Ascendant followed them, the palace guard closing around their small group. As they progressed, Kethe was blind to the wonders around her. She walked as if through a dream. When they emerged into an ornate chamber dominated by a heptagonal platform, she did little more than move as directed. The platform could accommodate fifty of them.

The nobles from the council chamber stepped up alongside the Ascendant.

The platform shuddered and then began to descend. Kethe looked up, keeping track of the palace room as it rose away. Her mother moved to stand beside her and took her hand. Kethe squeezed it gratefully but couldn't meet her eyes. Instead, she watched the smooth stone walls rise around them, then open to a new chamber on the second level. It was a great room, filled with activity as dozens of servants rushed around, preparing for the evacuation. Numb, Kethe stared at them, and then they were gone as the platform descended farther.

The third level. Fourth. Nobody spoke. The platform was tightly crowded. The tension was fevered. Kethe strained to hear the sounds of battle. Its absence was strange. Eerie, almost, as if she were being deceived. The fifth chamber. The sixth. Increasing signs of panic. People rushed up to the descending platform, intent on boarding it, only to be repulsed by the honor guard.

Down to the seventh, and the platform shuddered to a stop. Kethe let go of Iskra's hand and stepped down, blade drawn. A Vothak, face gray with exhaustion, led the way. They marched through a series of private chambers, more guards joining their entourage, and then out into a hallway which merged with a second that led to the main circum.

The people of Aletheia were out in force, their voices raised in fear, their fashionable outfits making it seem as if a thousand songbirds were mobbing each other in alarm. They parted before the Ascendant, however, their cries falling to a hush. Kethe saw in their eyes disbelief followed by despair. They knew what was happening, and suddenly believed: the Ascendant was quitting Aletheia. The Empire had fallen.

Kethe hardened her heart. She strode at the fore, ready to cut down anyone who sought to stop them, but nobody did. They moved quickly. Crowds were joining them: regiments of soldiers, organized bodies of scribes, imperial servants, noble houses. Soon the circum, broad as it was, was choked with traffic.

Kethe raised her sword up on high and allowed the White Song to flood her being. Her blade was engulfed in white fire, and the crowd parted before her in shock. She strode through them, meeting no eyes, and her countenance was such that nobody sought to question her, beg for her mercy or aid.

The doorway to the Portal had been torn free, leaving a gaping hole into a dusty corridor. Agerastian soldiers, wounded and roughed up, were standing guard outside it. Khoussan, Dalitha, other Consecrated – and Asho stood waiting at their head. At the sight of Kethe, they let out a small cheer, but it was a weak, faltering sound.

"Hurry," said Asho as Kethe reached him. "The battle's over. Our forces broke and ran. The kragh are no doubt spreading out through the fourth circum even now."

Kethe's throat was dry. She couldn't have spoken even if she'd wanted to. Instead, she nodded and plunged into the hallway, Asho at her side. She made a turn and then stopped before a simple archway carved into the wall.

The Vothak stepped forward, conspicuous in his purple and yellow robes. Geometric patterns in the floor, faded tapestries, marble busts of forgotten poets – the location was ornate, but she had no eye for it. Instead, she stared at the blank wall as Asho gave the lone Vothak a nod.

The man, his skin waxen, his body stooped, raised a hand and let forth a series of harsh syllables. Black ink flooded the archway. The way was opened, and Kethe didn't wait. She stepped through.

Ice flooded her marrow, her mind and spirit were contorted, twisted savagely, and she felt at once as if she were falling and being flung upward. She felt a brief, flickering moment of horror, and then she stumbled out into fog-shrouded gloom.

Starkadr. The floating stonecloud of the Sin Casters. There were others present – Agerastians, from the looks of it, the remnants of the army, or perhaps its logistical support. The huge cavern that housed the twisting spires of Portals was filled with activity. A stable had been erected to one side, a smithy beside it. Hundreds of cots stood assembled between two pillars, while perhaps a hundred servants, couriers, stable boys, army officers and porters were going about the business of maintaining camp.

Kethe moved forward, blazing sword in hand, not knowing what to say, how to communicate with them. They stared at her, eyes wide, gazes flicking from her sword to her face, and the soldiers amongst them drew their own blades. People cried out in their foreign tongue, their voices echoing dully in the low-hanging fog.

But Iskra's arrival immediately put an end to the nascent aggression. She stepped forward, hands raised, and cried out something in Agerastian. People froze, confusion replacing shock, and a number of men rushed forward to attend their empress.

More people were coming through. Honor guards. Asho and the Consecrated. The greatest nobles of Aletheia in all their unworldly finery. Finally, the Ascendant himself stepped through, and it was as if a spell had been laid upon the milling crowd.

As one, people turned to regard history in the making. The Ascendant in his simple robes of white seemed to almost glow, his frame dwarfed by the massive columns, but he held his own, was not made insignificant. He seemed more real, somehow, than the world around him, made of a truer substance than the dark floors and pillars.

"Mother," said Kethe. "Where should we go?"

"Anywhere in the Empire," said Iskra, gazing around at the pillars and their manifold Portals. "But let's put the question to His Holiness."

Together, they stepped over to where the Ascendant was standing, curiously looking around at the harsh, alien grandeur of Starkadr's Portal chamber. "Your Holiness," Iskra said. "Where to? I can host you in the Agerastian palace. Mythgraefen Castle is at your disposal.

We could instead travel to Ennoia or some other part of the Empire if you so desire."

More people were flowing through the Aletheian Portal. People of rank and power, the lowliest servants bearing goods, tightly knit ranks of Agerastian troops. They were flooding in without surcease.

"The kragh cannot follow us here?" the Ascendant asked.

Kethe looked to Asho, who shook his head slowly. "No," he said. "I don't think so. Unless they have magic users who can guess the names for the Portals... No, I think we're safe."

"And these Portals that I see around me. They all function?"

Kethe followed the Ascendant's line of sight, looking up at the doorways embedded by the hundreds into the sides of the huge pillars.

"Yes," Asho said again. "I believe so. We don't have an easy way of figuring out how they all work, but I believe the Vothaks were making progress in learning how to read the runes."

The Ascendant nodded.

It was almost too much to bear. Even now, at this very moment, the kragh were rampaging through Aletheia. Destroying. Killing. Taking the heart of the Empire as their own. Yet, somehow, the Ascendant stood there calmly, deep in thought, as if he were being asked where he wanted a vase placed for best effect.

"Then, this chamber shall suffice for now," he said, looking to Iskra. "We need no creature comforts beyond cots, food, and water. Of far greater value is information, and the ability to use these Portals to travel my Empire as needed."

"As you command, Your Holiness," said Iskra, and she turned to an Agerastian at her side to give him commands in Ennoian. The man listened intently, bobbed his head, then hurried away.

Kethe fought to keep her voice calm. "Your Holiness. What are we going to do?"

"Regroup," said the Ascendant with a tired smile. "Gather our forces. Gather intelligence. Only once we know what forces we have at our disposal and where they need to be deployed will we act."

Agerastian soldiers were still filing in through the Portal. Many were grievously wounded, some supported by their fellows. They were all directed to the cots, which they soon outnumbered. Kethe watched as a Vothak opened another Portal, and soon the overflow of soldiers began to march through this new exit.

Some Aletheian guards were coming through as well. Bowing low to His Holiness, she stepped back and moved toward a group of them. Information – that was what they needed the most.

There — five soldiers. They were wearing the same style of uniform, a fashionable array of thin robes over light chainmail armor. None of them were wounded, but they all looked dazed as they staggered away from the Portal and then came to a stop, lost and unsure of what to do next.

"Soldiers," said Kethe, stepping up to them. "Fall in."

The men took a moment to understand who was addressing them, and then scrambled to stand in a line. The very act of falling in seemed to breathe some life back into them, and they stared straight ahead, their backs rigid.

"What's going on in Aletheia?" she asked. "What was the last thing you saw of the battle?"

The man to the far left of the line made a half-bow. "Virtue, the battle against the kragh is lost. We were part of the final contingent to flee the Portal chamber."

"Details," said Kethe. "How many were able to escape?"

The man glanced at his fellows and hesitated. "Perhaps half, Virtue? The kragh did not give chase once we began to flee."

"They didn't?" Kethe frowned. That was when the gravest casualties were normally inflicted upon a foe. "What did they do instead?"

"They remained by the Portal, Virtue. I could hear commands being yelled, but of course I couldn't understand them. The last I saw, more were still coming through. More than our original army by that point, perhaps even three thousand of them."

"Excuse me, Virtue," said one of the soldiers. He was almost painfully young, his face marred by craters and inflamed red skin. His nose was unfortunate, and his mouth was little more than a gash, but his eyes were lively and blue. "I saw black-skinned kragh giving orders to the others. Reining them in, you could say."

"Black-skinned?"

"Yes," said the boy. "Black as soot, but with strange red glimmers to 'em, like — ah — coals. Different, I thought, than the big ones with really dark green skin. Their leaders, maybe."

Kethe bit her lower lip. She'd not seen any like that other than Tharok, but she smiled at the boy. "Thank you. Well-spotted. Your name?"

"Caelfas, Virtue. Ennoian, like yourself."

Agerastians were still pouring through the Portal. Why had Tharok allowed them to escape? It made no sense.

Still, over the next hour, some semblance of order began to manifest itself. Areas amidst the great pillars were demarcated for the courtiers and nobles, the Empire's administrators and other government officials. Families were moved to what was rapidly becoming a large refugee camp; orders from Iskra saw supplies and cots being brought in from Agerastos, but it was still far too little to accommodate their numbers.

The huge room was soon filled with the sounds of several thousand people talking to each other, the crying of children, the weeping of the bereaved, and angry shouts as fights broke out. Hundreds of lanterns were lit to banish the gloom, but instead they created an ethereal sight as their pools of warm light receded into the distance in every direction, surrounded by the ever-present mist. Agerastian soldiers were pressed into keeping order, but their very presence often provoked conflict.

Kethe walked amongst the people, using her status as a Virtue to calm and reassure, offering blessings whenever she was asked, though she felt hollow and fake for doing so.

Eventually, she found her way to the Ascendant's new quarters. General Pethar's pavilion had been given to the Ascendant and his innermost court. The guards bowed to her and pulled the tent's flap open. She stepped inside and saw that the pavilion had been divided into one main room with several curtained-off sections to the sides. Thick carpets had been laid over Starkadr's stone floor, and lanterns cast a rich, honeyed glow over the sparse furniture and people within.

The Ascendant was standing at the head of a long table. Her mother was seated to his left, the Minister of the Sun to his right. Down the length of the table were arranged the other notables of the resistance: an older woman in the colorful robes of the Vothaks, important ministers and military figures, Theletos slouched in a chair with his eyes closed, Noussian high priests and Sigean sages. A vigorous, handsome man in his early forties was sitting close to the head of the table, wearing thick white furs over a sky-blue tabard. Some twenty men and women all told, speaking to each other in low whispers. The atmosphere in the pavilion was one of quiet desperation.

Asho, Kethe saw, was standing behind her mother's chair. He watched her with a stony face, and she was unable to meet his eyes. Instead, she took a chair at the foot of the table and slid into it silently.

"Aletheia has fallen," said the Ascendant, and the talking ceased. "In a little over one day, the kragh warlord Tharok has breached the walls of Abythos, taken Bythos' Solar Portals, and has now conquered Aletheia. The White and Black Gates are lost to us. He now commands two of the six Solar Portals. Our forces at Abythos are gone, and Empress Iskra's Agerastian army is down to a third of its former strength." The Ascendant looked from one person to the next. "All within the span of one day."

People lowered their gazes to the table. Others stared straight ahead, unseeing. Kethe saw frowns, saw faces composed into rigid masks, saw bleak despair and fury.

"It is clear," said the Ascendant, "that we cannot afford any further losses. Our Empire stands with its back to a precipice. Whatever we decide here today must advance our cause. We must find a way to defeat this Tharok. We must find a way to wrest advantage from this position we have been thrown into."

The Minister of the Sun rose to his feet, his expression grave. He smoothed down his robes with one hand as he leaned forward. "We are without a Grace, Your Holiness. A leader of your armies. Ever since Empress Iskra saw fit to assassinate our former martial leader, we have been acting without direction on the field. May I request that you nominate a new one, so that we may organize our forces under one central figure?"

Kethe didn't miss the way most of the faces around the table hardened as they looked at her mother. Iskra appeared not to notice, however; she remained perfectly poised.

"Yes," said Theletos, his voice but a whisper. "I concur."

The Ascendant nodded. "Very well. There is no time, nor is this the place for the traditional ceremony and purification rites. Instead, I shall simply ask Lutherius of the Cerulean Guard if he will assume the mantle."

All eyes turned to the broad-shouldered man in his early forties sitting two chairs down from Iskra. His face was striking, from his hooked nose to the heavy brow under which his eyes were nearly shadowed, yet piercing like those of a hawk. His close-shaven black beard was already speckled with white at the chin, and his hair was pulled back into a tight braid. His left hand was missing, the wrist covered with a simple cup of black leather, and a cloak of white wolf fur was draped over his shoulders.

The man stood up, pushing the chair back with his knees. "I accept, Your Holiness. But I have not the patience for politicking that my predecessor did. I'll offer my apologies now to you all for the offense I am sure to give, for I won't be offering them again."

Mutters came from some of the nobles, but nobody gainsaid the man.

"The Cerulean Guard is at this moment gathered in Sige. We number five hundred and twenty-seven, and all are good men. Our abandoning the peaks and our stations leaves the outskirts of Sige and the far-flung monasteries unguarded and at the mercy of the kvathka, but there's no way around that. What other forces remain to us?"

Theletos stirred. "We sent word to Commander Mathewelin when word of the kragh invasion first reached us. He should have begun the journey home several days ago. He left Ennoia with a thousand light cavalry; they should reach the capital within the week."

Lutherius nodded. "Good. What else?"

Lady Iskra sat forward. "At the last count, my army numbers about eight hundred. Many, however, are wounded. I have nearly two dozen Vothaks at my disposal, but they are also grievously drained. Within a week, however, they should be able to join the resistance."

Kethe bestirred herself. "We fled Bythos with two or three hundred soldiers and fifteen Consecrated. Ten of the Consecrated have made their way here. Of the soldiers, I've not yet made an accurate count."

The Minister of the Palace licked his lips as he leaned forward. "The Ascendant's personal guard numbers fifty. They are all accounted for."

"Lord Melchior was also sent for," said Theletos, his chin sinking to his chest as his eyes closed. "He will no doubt be amused, given that he was banished to the hinterlands of Zoe to defend against a mythological threat that never, it seemed, fully manifested."

"How many does he command?" asked Lutherius.

"Five hundred. A mixture of archers, light cavalry, and skirmishers. If he deigns to obey the summons, he might arrive in Zoe within a week, perhaps a bit longer."

"Lord Melchior," said the Minister of the Sun with obvious distaste, "I can't believe it's come to this."

The name was familiar to Kethe. A former Black Wolf under her grandfather's command, the man had been expelled for being too sadistic even for that dark company.

Lutherius ignored him. "The question, then, is one of strategy. In a week or so, we will have at our disposal some three thousand or more mixed troops. A sizeable force." There was a forcefulness to his words that assured Kethe. Then he looked to the Ascendant. "How are we to defeat Tharok?"

"You're asking us?" spluttered the Minister of the Sun. "You're the Grace!"

Iskra was pinching her chin thoughtfully with thumb and forefinger, studying Lutherius as she did so. "It's a good question. Pitched battle will not work in our favor. The Empire is about to be engulfed across its breadth in panic and fear. We must choose our next confrontation very carefully."

"Indeed," said Lutherius. "Here are the facts we are contending with. First, Tharok has a direct channel to his own land, from which he can draw reinforcements as needed. Thus, killing a thousand kragh here or there won't make a marked difference in this war, whereas our losing a thousand men will."

Kethe nodded, and saw Asho and Theletos do the same.

"To compound that problem, our men are now suffering from low morale following shocking losses. The people of the Empire will be gripped by fear following the loss of their Ascendant and the White Gate."

More nods.

"Our greatest advantage is this... stonecloud. I forget its name. We have access to different corners of the Empire through its Portals. To our knowledge, Tharok cannot open them. Am I correct?"

The old Vothak lady nodded stiffly. "Unless his powers extend to the demonic, I believe you are correct."

"Given our morale, our numbers, and Tharok's genius in accomplishing what he has done thus far, we cannot afford to engage him in battle." Lutherius' face was grim. "Another loss will be our last one."

Nobody spoke. The Grand Controller opened his mouth, then closed it, looking confused. Theletos, Kethe saw, was smiling where he slouched, eyes still closed.

It was Asho who broke the silence. "Hit and run tactics?"

Lutherius nodded. "Yes. It's how we Ceruleans fight amidst the peaks. We never engage the kvathka directly. We track them and pick off stragglers or their weak, like wolves will with a herd of deer."

Kethe surprised herself by cutting in. "You just said, however, that defeating a thousand kragh wouldn't help us. What use, then, is killing off their weak and wounded?"

Lutherius inclined his head. "Virtue Makaria. An honor to make your acquaintance. The primary benefit will be to begin achieving victories against the kragh for the purposes of morale. The secondary benefit will be to show our people that we are still fighting for the Empire. The third benefit is to force this Tharok to spread his forces thin. If we can strike at him from any quarter, he will have to defend the entirety of the Empire from our attacks. Every front will be a target."

"To what end?" asked Asho.

"I don't know yet," said Lutherius. "But the kragh are little more than beasts, correct? Tharok can direct them like a battering ram; this, we have seen. Can he rule them once they lose momentum? Can he hold the Empire, command them from a distance, or will his horde fall apart? If we execute this strategy correctly, we should sow chaos amongst his kragh and create an opening for us to exploit."

Kethe felt like she was being led, that Lutherius wanted her to ask this question for effect. "An opening for what?"

Theletos opened his eyes at last, and in their depths gleamed a new fire, a dark and virulent hatred. "To assassinate Tharok, obviously."

Chapter 8

I t had taken both Ulein and Leuthold to lift the kragh's damn
hammer. Nok had watched with something suspiciously akin to
amusement as the two men hefted it onto their shoulders with a grunt
and then followed the group back up the verdant hill.

Marcus and his two scribes were standing beside a makeshift pallet
made of their robes, sleeves rolled up and ready to tend the wounded.
They looked up as the group emerged through the trees, ready to see
wounds and blood but completely unprepared for Nok's appearance.

"Easy," said Tiron, raising a hand as Olina stepped in front of
Marcus, a knife reversed in her fist. "Believe it or not, they want to
talk. At least, she does." He nodded at Shaya. "The kragh's going to
sit tight and not make anybody nervous. Right?"

"Yes," said Shaya, running her palms down her leggings nervously.
"Correct." She coughed a few kragh words, and Nok grunted and
stepped over to a tree, at the base of which he lowered himself to a
cross-legged seat.

Ulein and Leuthold quietly counted to three and then hefted the
hammer down onto the dirt. It landed with an audible thud.

"All right," said Tiron, not sheathing his blade. He and Ramswold faced Shaya full-on, the others completing the circle. "You've kicked off an improbable tale. Now, make us believe you."

"Yes." Shaya bit her lower lip, clearly thinking. "Nok and I both knew Tharok before he became the warlord he is today. A few months ago, he was only the warlord of the Red River tribe, a group of mountain kragh no larger than a couple of hundred individuals."

"Mountain kragh?" Isentrud pointed with her elbow at Nok, sword resting over her shoulder. "Like him?"

"Sort of," said Shaya with a half-smile. "Nok's big even for mountain kragh, but yes. They're much larger than their lowlander cousins. Anyway, we met him when he was only the warlord. But not much time before that, he was nobody at all. Just a warrior in another tribe."

"You expect us to believe he rose from obscurity to where he is today in a matter of months?" asked Ulein, anger riding his voice.

"Yes." She said this with absolute conviction. "Because he didn't do it alone. When his original tribe was massacred, he fled into the high mountains and found the remains of Ogri the Destroyer. Have you—?"

"Yes," said Tiron. "Yes, we've heard of Ogri the Destroyer."

"Well, he found his blade, World Breaker, and something else. Something of incredible power. A circlet. When he wears it, he changes. He becomes almost another person. Brilliant, calculating, absolutely ruthless. It was that circlet that helped him become first the warlord of the Red River, then take control of the minds of trolls, enlist the aid of a medusa—"

Ulein spat.

"— — and conquer first the mountain kragh, then take over the lowland tribe of the Orlokor. He was unstoppable."

"Is unstoppable," said Tiron wryly. "So, why are you trying to stop him?"

"Because this circlet is warping him. Taking control of him. The same way it did Ogri." She glanced at Nok, who was listening with sober gravity. "And both Nok and I owe our freedom and our lives to the Tharok from before. He freed us from a slave market in Gold one day when he wasn't wearing it. And now we barely recognize him. Last night, when he broke through into Bythos, he also broke his word to me. His kragh attacked my people. It was then that I realized he was out of control, no longer tethered to himself. When we confronted him afterwards, he had a moment of lucidity."

Shaya's hands were knotted into fists. "He told us to find his Red River tribe. He had sent them away with the few shamans the medusa hadn't corrupted so that they could act as insurance against his turning completely into a monster. He sent us to go find them and join forces with them. To save him from himself."

Tiron rubbed his jaw, feeling the scritch of his stubble. He glanced sidelong at Ramswold, who looked impressed despite himself, eyebrows raised, lips pursed. Nobody spoke.

"And how are you going to do that?" asked Tiron at last. "If he's truly turning into a monster — which I fervently believe, given what he did at Abythos — then he'll not welcome you and this tribe back with open arms, will he?"

"No," said Shaya quietly. "But that's why we must find the Red River. They have the last of the kragh shamans with them. If anybody knows how to handle the situation, how to figure out a solution, it's them."

"A question," said Leuthold, raising his blade to point it at her chest. "Are you for the invasion or against it?"

Shaya's eyes glittered as she raised her chin. "I'm for it. And before you spit like your friend, think of who I am and where I come from. You're an Ennoian soldier, perhaps a knight? I'm a slave. Born a slave, whipped, abused, and treated like dirt. Why? Because my parents had the misfortune of being Bythians themselves. So, yes. I'll support Tharok. I'll support his desire to tear down the Empire and free my people. Bring equality to everyone."

Ramswold went to speak, but she turned on him, spots of color high on her cheeks, and spoke right over his words. "You can't understand and you won't understand, and I don't expect you to. Fine. But the Tharok I know — the one who freed me, who treated me with respect, who allowed me to determine my future – he's the noblest person I know. I trust him. The creature he is becoming? No. So, I'll ruin his chances. I'll betray his invasion if it means freeing him from this darkness. He may not thank me, but he once freed me from slavery. It is the least I can do to do the same for him."

Her words hung in the quiet glade, vibrant and passionate. Leuthold's face remained hard and cold. Ulein had crossed his arms and hunched his shoulders, his expression ugly. Isentrud looked at a loss. Even Marcus and his scribes seemed overwhelmed.

"Kill them," said Leuthold at last. "You heard her. She supports the invasion. It's a simple matter."

"Agreed," said Ulein. "Lord Ramswold?"

The young lord shook his head, then held up his hand. "Hold, Sir Ulein. First and foremost, we are members of the proud Order of the Star. We do not execute women or prisoners who have surrendered to us with honor. But before I decide whether we should help her, I would hear Ser Tiron's thoughts on this. Magic circlets? Kragh shamans? Possession? This is far beyond my ken." He looked over to Tiron. "Your thoughts?"

Tiron was studying Nok. The kragh was sitting straight, huge clawed hands resting on his knees, at once relaxed and alert. His skin was the dark green of a forest seen at night, and his features were striking and alien. Broad, square jaw, with massive tusks emerging from behind his lower lip. Harsh cheekbones, angular ears, thick black hair falling down his back in braids, some enclosed by bronze and silver rings.

Yet it was his gaze that held Tiron's attention. There was a profundity there that captured Tiron's eye, a resolve and confidence that didn't need to assert itself. Tiron would almost call it a dignity, a level of self-possession that he'd rarely seen in another man.

"Ser Tiron?"

Tiron tore his gaze away with difficulty. "For fuck's sake," he said softly. "What else have we got going? I don't know any more about kragh shamans and circlets than you lot, but I do recognize one thing here: an opportunity. A chance to learn more, to perhaps make a difference in this war that might be already lost."

Leuthold was nodding slowly. Not in agreement; more as if Tiron had just confirmed his worst suspicions. Ulein's expression was just as sour.

"Listen up, boys. One more dead kragh's not going to make a lick of difference in this war. It'll just leave us here scratching our arses and waiting for hunger to drive us to some act of suicidal folly. So, we're not going to kill him. I'm not saying he's become our best and most trusted ally, but let's see where this goes."

"With all due respect," said Ulein, "you are not my liege lord, Tiron. Lord Ramswold is. I'll do what he commands."

Leuthold and Isentrud nodded.

Marcus stepped forward. "I know you're wedded to the blade and all that, but this is not the time for violence. What the young lady has said—"

"Marshal," said Ulein, raising a hand to cut him off without even looking at him. "We're not in the citadel. You've got no authority here. Please be quiet. Now, my lord?" He took a step forward. "You heard her, my lord. She supports the invasion. She's with a kragh that's no doubt killed our kind. Our friends, even. Now, they're asking that we let them go free? Or, worse yet, do what Tiron's suggesting and accompany them deeper into this forsaken land, to look for more kragh? No. Let's end this here, and go back to focusing on the citadel. Find a way to get back home, and help in the war."

Ramswold had his arms crossed tightly over his chest. He rocked back onto his heels, brow lowered in thought. Finally, he shook his head.

"I understand where you're coming from, Ser Ulein. I understand the impulse. But we are not cutthroats. We are knights. I must believe that we escaped Abythos for a reason, that the Ascendant has set us on this path so that we can accomplish a great quest. This, as far as I can tell, is our summons. We shall aid this young woman and her kragh. It is most... unorthodox, but if military might will not win this war, then perhaps personal courage and a faith in the Ascendant will instead."

Shaya's shoulders slumped with relief.

Ulein's lips writhed with displeasure, but then he controlled himself and bowed. "As you command, my lord. So shall it be."

Isentrud smiled. "I've never been on a real quest before."

Leuthold snorted and turned away, moved to where their meager possessions were laid out and knelt beside them.

"Looks like you've got yourself some company," said Tiron to Shaya. "Though I don't know about this being an Ascendant-ordained quest. Now, where exactly are these Red River kragh? How many days' march?"

"I — ah." Shaya glanced over at Nok and grimaced. "We don't know."

Everybody stilled. "You don't know?" asked Ulein, his voice carefully neutral.

"No," said Shaya. "We haven't spoken with a member of the tribe in months, and Tharok didn't know, either. So, instead, we're following Death's Raven. He's going to lead us to them."

"Back up," said Tiron. "Pretend we don't know who Death's Raven is, or why he's being so generous with his time."

"Death's Raven is... well, he was the Red River shaman. He was known as Golden Crow back then. But the medusa twisted him, perverted him with her touch, and now he's serving her instead of the kragh. Remember how I said the last free shamans are with the Red River? He's been sent to capture them and bring them back to her so that she can pervert them as well."

"That first group," said Ramswold. "They're going to lead you to the Red River?"

"Yes," said Shaya. "We just need to stay out of their sight, and when they find the Red River camp, well..."

"Well, what?" Tiron felt irritation flare within him. "What then?"

Shaya lifted her chin defiantly. "We'll charge past them and warn the Red River before it's too late."

Chapter 9

Tharok stood before the portal to Aletheia, hands resting on World Breaker's cross guard. He stared fixedly at the swirling white fire that filled its frame. Past him flowed kragh without end, mighty warriors who roared their salutes before diving through the fire to do battle. How many had gone through already? Two thousand? And how many soldiers did the humans have defending their precious Aletheia?

Not enough.

He felt suffused with might. He was no longer Tharok. He was a symbol, a focal point in history. People forevermore, both kragh and human, would look back and speak of this moment in hushed tones: the moment when a kragh had finally risen and destroyed the sovereignty of mankind.

Every instinct within him bade him charge forward with the other kragh, World Breaker raised high. He was their greatest warrior. He should be at the forefront of the attack, cleaving helms, lopping off limbs, shattering bones. But, no; he was now the lynchpin of this attack. He could not afford to fall. He could not trust the vagaries of fate.

So, he held back. Waited. Watched. His whole body thrummed with tension and control. Around him stood his warlords, his key chieftains, his medusa-Kissed leaders, scores of messengers, his banner kragh. All waiting. Watching not the portal, but him.

More kragh poured through into Aletheia. There was no end to their numbers. Perhaps three thousand had entered the stonecloud by now, but even so, he still had double that number waiting behind him, filling the plain, weapons held at the ready, baying and roaring in anticipation of the combat that was being waged at this very minute just beyond their reach.

A kragh stepped back through the fire into Bythos. He was massive, an old mountain warrior, one-eyed, his jaw scarred where it had been split in his youth and had healed awkwardly. Scarred and blood-drenched, he moved forward and fell to one knee, fist to the earth.

"Uniter," he growled. His voice was history summoning Tharok forth. "The humans are broken. Their army has fled. Their will to do battle has been shattered. Aletheia is yours."

Tharok inhaled till his very ribs creaked, and then he shoved World Breaker high and roared, giving vent to his dominance, a primal scream of satisfaction. His cry was picked up by the others like wildfire, and as one, the six thousand kragh who filled the plain roared their ecstasy. The sound caused the agony vultures overhead to wheel in dismay. The power of the horde's roar reverberated within Tharok's chest, and then he walked forth and passed through the portal.

As before, the world wrenched him apart, tore at the ligaments of his mind, compressed and stretched the fabric of his spirit all at once. It was a yawning, screaming passage through the void, but through it all he felt — he saw — his circlet burning with an even darker might that defied that selfsame void, that made Tharok its master even as it terrified him.

Then he was through.

Out into Aletheia.

He strode forth, World Breaker held tightly in one hand, its power flooding his frame, making him shake and shiver with the desire for release. For war.

A vast chamber lay around him, the antithesis of Bythos. The cavern was raw rock and darkness; this huge room was exquisite craftsmanship and white stone. White stone that was streaked in blood. The fighting here had been brutal. Bodies lay everywhere, heaped up in mounds. The stench of blood and feces was rank.

His kragh saw him emerge and raised a welcoming shout. Good. His chieftains had managed to keep them in this entry chamber and had not allowed them to run riot. Tharok moved forward. More came behind him. His personal guard, his advisors, his attendant shaman.

His boots squelched in the blood. The kragh parted before him, opening an avenue for him to walk along toward the distant tunnel.

His eyes rose to the ceiling. Incredible paintings adorned it, limned in glorious light. Depictions of knights and warriors, sages and generals, workers and slaves – the full panoply of human society. The ranks of the Empire, painted with such skill, it stole his breath away. Each figure would be three times Tharok's height, a testament to the culture and power of the Empire.

An empire that he had crushed.

Tharok entered the tunnel. The circlet was fairly vibrating on his brow. Eagerness? Desire? Tharok knew not, other than that it exulted. Down the hallway he walked, his thousands behind him. The tunnel, massive as it was, was deserted, but everywhere, there was art. Large vases, busts, tapestries, paintings. The floor was a complex mosaic of geometric lines of inlaid gold. What wealth. Everywhere he looked, he saw the products of money.

Tharok smiled. This, he understood. He knew that each object of beauty had been paid for with blood. Kragh blood on the fields of war. Bythian blood on the hafts of pickaxes deep in the mines. The blood of traders on their ships, of the human knights encased in their steel. All effort, all striving, all sacrifice had been channeled toward producing this wealth. This beauty reeked of blood, just as the floor of the portal chamber had, but at least that prior reek had been honestly won.

He emerged onto a vast, spiraling road. There, Tharok stopped and gazed up. Around and around the road went, coiling about a central void, climbing to a terrible height. At the sight of this feat of engineering, he felt his soul quail. What kind of beings were these humans that they could carve out the heart of a mountain and form such an elegant route to the Sky Father?

Mortals, he told himself. Men who died and shat themselves like all others. Whoever those ancestors had been, those miracle workers who had brought these wonders into being, they were long dead — and the product of their genius was now his.

Tharok led his horde up the avenue. Humans watched him come and fled. He let them go. His army had strict orders not to pillage, not to explore, not to race off into the depths of the stonecloud. Instead, they were shepherded after him by the medusa-Kissed commanders. They did not need much controlling. The scale and grandeur of that which they had conquered had conquered them in turn; the roars and cries had fallen silent. It was a quiet horde that Tharok led up, and up, and up, a horde overwhelmed by the scale of its own accomplishment.

Finally, Tharok emerged onto the roof of the world. The wind whipped about him as he strode out onto a great open square in front of a palace. He braced himself, shocked once more by the vista that opened around him. No other mountain peaks. No sources of reference, scale, anything. Nothing but sky and clouds. He stood thrust into the very realm of the Sky Father. He was amidst the gods. If there was a heaven, he was in it, and he laughed, throwing his arms wide, madness and delirium, joy and despair digging their claws deep into his mind.

The square in front of the palace had been used but recently. Bloody pallets, makeshift tents, the detritus of camp all sat there abandoned. Tharok cared not. Something was driving him on, a whip that lashed at his mind, forced him forward. He didn't know what he was search-ing for, but he needed to see something, so into the palace he stalked, and his horde came after.

Through hallways and great rooms, he went, his boots crunching precious stones that were inlaid into the ground beneath their heels. Everywhere, he saw signs of recent abandonment. Silence greeted him. There were no pleas, no supplication, no raw words of desperate fervor. The palace was empty.

At long last, he reached a doorway that dwarfed all others. It was edged in gold, cunningly wrought, and the entirety of the wall in which it was embedded had been brought to life by an impossibly gifted sculptor. Endless ranks of humans, horses, beasts and more had been partially freed from the marble by his chisel. It was a wall of frozen movement, all of it worshipping what lay beyond the doorway.

The doors themselves were of stone, sheets of white marble carved in those geometric patterns that so beguiled the eye. Bands of silver and gold joined the patterns. The doorway would have dwarfed a troll, but Tharok didn't wait for help. He stepped forward and pressed both palms against the doors and shoved.

The doors swung open, revealing a great hall. Pillars like trees rose on each side. At the far end was a set of steps that rose to glory. Tharok's throat closed. The white fire that filled the Solar Portals' interior was nothing compared to the incandescence that wreathed this final Gate: a massive, pulsing light that was caged by silver webbing, attenuated shafts of glittering metal that restrained that white fire back and kept it from flooding forth. It rose, and rose, and Tharok craned his head back to try to see its top.

The White Gate. The pinnacle of human achievement. The focus of their every thought and effort, their very lives. He knew but rudiments of their religion, but it was enough: this was the flaming heart of the Empire. If he could destroy it, the humans would never rise again.

Tharok grinned at the temerity of the thought and raised World Breaker. Its silhouette was the darkest night against the white fire. Its strength poured into him like lava. He started forward.

No one followed him.

Down the length of the hall, he marched, eyes locked on the White Gate. It was mesmerizing. Its pulsations were magnetic. They seemed to pull at his thoughts, make them flow from the confines of his skull and disappear. He thought of Kyrra and the fiery depths of her gaze. That was akin to this in some ways, but even her eyes failed to match the power of this construct. He felt as if he were walking into a veritable bonfire, that he would be immolated before he could even swing his sword.

He was only two-thirds of the way down the hall when he felt the circlet on his brow begin to burn. Its presence adumbrated his will, but now it was searing his flesh faster than World Breaker could heal. Tharok squinted his eyes against the white glory and walked on. It was like marching into a headwind. He leaned into it, hand raised to shield his eyes.

The first step. The pain in his brow was incredible. With a grunt, he reached up and plucked the circlet free. The sight of it in his hand nearly caused him to drop it. Black fire was raging around its circumference – spasms of crackling flame, shooting up in terrible arcs like negative bolts of lightning.

He couldn't see the iron of the circlet proper. His hand was buried in the flame up to his wrist. And then he realized, this was it. The circlet was nullified here. He was free of its control. It was defending itself, unable to exert its fascination over his mind.

Tharok looked up the distant Gate. All he had to do was cast the circlet into its white fire, and it would be gone forevermore. Never would he be tempted to put it back on. Never would he be urged by its foul brilliance toward acts of world-shaking devastation. This was the closest he'd ever come to being truly free to destroy it.

Tharok placed his foot on the first step, and howls sounded from both sides. Rearing back, Tharok saw humans spill forth from alcoves carved into the far walls. Dozens of them, wearing robes of the purest white, blades held in both hands. Men, he realized. Some positively ancient, barely strong enough to wield their blades. Some thirty of them all told, their eyes wide with outrage and terror, their screams echoing one phrase repeatedly: *"For the White Gate!"*

Tharok let them come. He closed his eyes and felt the pulsing of the White Gate against his front like the kiss of a livid sun. His left fist was encased in the circlet's black fire. It excoriated his flesh up to mid-forearm.

The pain was distant. He was alone. He was nothing. He was a void. He was an absence of desire.

And yet.

The humans fell upon him and were slain. Tharok opened his eyes and killed them. They fell before World Breaker. His blows cut clear though whatever he struck, be it thigh, arm, chest or abdomen, yet he felt no battle lust, no joy, no fervent exaltation. He slew methodically, and within moments he was done.

Blood gleamed brightly on the steps. Bodies lay twisted all around him. The last of the human defenders, the final votaries of the Empire.

Tharok looked up at the White Gate and began to climb. Up he went, step by step, and he felt the skin peel back from his left fist. Felt the flesh char as the circlet's flames grew more frantic.

Cast it into the fire. Let this be an end to its mad reign.

The White Gate filled his vision, and he heard voices raised in song. Not human, but kragh. The deep chant of elders, the sound he'd stayed up listening to as a child. The powerful soul chanting of shamans and warlords, of wise women and chieftains. The spirit of the kragh set to music, sorrowful and strong, noble and resolute.

Tharok took another step. The light of the Gate was so bright now that he had to close his eyes, yett it was as if he could see more clearly with them closed; the black fire in his left fist was a chasm in the world, a raging sun that sought to consume him. World Breaker in his other hand was a frozen bolt of black lightning, just as dark, just as deep.

And his own body? Tharok felt himself growing transparent, the substance of his flesh admitting the passage of the Gate's light, revealing in that process how foul it had become. The passage of his life had ruined him. He was a dark thing, a constellation of impurities and murderous acts. The light of the Gate revealed that to him.

Another step. He was growling now, head bowed under the punishment, the pain. Memories rose from the depths of his mind. The first time he had lifted a warhammer, feeling the rightness of it in his hand. The sound of young kragh screaming with laughter. His father dying in his arms. The light of the sun glittering off the Dragon's Breath. He saw Maur's eyes, saw the purple blaze as Jaemungdr's tongue caught fire in the Valley of the Dead.

Another step. His whole body was shaking with the effort. The world had fallen away, leaving only the center of this white inferno. His flesh was sloughing off his bones. No, that was his spirit being purified. Or was it his death approaching?

Memories. His very sense of self. Power. Might. The beauty of the wild. Laughter. His mother's milk. The give of flesh the first time he had stabbed another. The bright golden lights he'd seen the first time he'd spasmed inside a female. Fire in his belly. Rage. The urge to conquer. Lust. Laughter. Friends. Joy.

And through it all, the circlet burned and raged. Tharok felt himself rising, his feet no longer touching the steps, held back only by the circlet's presence. It anchored him. All he had to do was let go. Then he would rise to his ancestors, forgiven for all of his crimes, released from his responsibilities.

Let go.

No, whispered a voice from the depths of his mind. You are not yet done.

Tharok stared down into that black fire. He was beyond thought, but something pulled at him. Pulled him back.

Stubbornness? Refusal? A will to survive? To live?

To conquer?

Tharok let out a cry, a wounded, raw scream that felt as if it split him in two. He roared until he felt he would keel over, and then, overbalancing, he fell back.

He toppled and crashed onto the steps, rolling down and down till he collapsed upon the floor of the hall and sank into oblivion.

Chapter 10

Audsley stood alone, hands linked behind his back, staring at the small rectangle of light embedded within his bedroom wall. The door was closed behind him. He had been plunged into a silence so absolute it ached. He'd not moved since Little Zephyr left him. An hour ago? Perhaps two. The light from without was starting to dim. Evening was falling.

He felt cavernous. Empty. The sensation reminded him of a mouse frozen by the approach of a snake, but that didn't feel quite right; instead, it was as if his soul had been encased in ice, and now only its faint vibrations indicated that it existed at all.

He knew, on an objective level, that he should be nauseated by what he'd seen. Sickened to his core, and perhaps filled with a righteous fury. Yet he felt nothing. This was, he knew, due to his merging with his demons. It was thus an artificial equanimity, but knowing that did not make it any less enervating.

Was this, then, what it meant to be possessed? To be able to be callously academic about matters that should drive one to one's knees? If so, then there was a certain utility to it. Of course, he knew that it was ghastly to even think so, but if one set aside knee-jerk reactions and morality, his newfound ability to gaze upon horrors allowed him to remain undetected amidst his enemies. To deceive Little Zephyr. It afforded him the flexibility to pursue his investigations to their horrific end.

And then? Once he'd divined all of Haugabrjótr's sordid truths? He would return to Iskra with his hard-won information. He would reveal how the Fujiwara had polluted the Empire, how they had twisted its highest members, and allow the world to sort out the consequences.

Audsley closed his eyes. Before, he'd always been able to visualize his three demons lurking in the back of his mind. Now, they were gone.

Hello? It felt foolish to vocalize so. To speak, as it were, to himself. *Anybody home?*

Hello, came a familiar voice. It sounded almost fond. Yet no face appeared before him, no eidolon dressed in the guise of a mortal man.

There you are. Audsley clamped down on his sense of relief. *I had thought you gone.*

Not gone. Merged, perhaps, with your very essence? A terrifying thought, I am sure.

Yes. Quite so. But here you are. And the others?

A different voice, that of the Zoeian demon, said, **We are present.**

And enjoying our newfound expansion, said the Sigean monk.

Why can't I see you?

We are no longer imprisoned within your mind's eye, said the Aletheian demon, his main interlocutor these weeks past. **Now, we are free to float through your very substance like mist through the mountain passes.**

And numb my sense of morality, said Audsley, without, he thought, rancor.

I prefer to think of it as giving you a new perspective, said the Aletheian. **The ability to put aside your mortal foibles and focus on the bigger picture.**

Which is?

More terrifying and liberating than you have yet dreamed, dear Magister. You have set your foot upon a most enlightening path. We all are aware of your fondness for knowledge. This path will bring to light truths that have been forgotten for millennia.

Audsley smiled. **The Fujiwara don't seem so forgetful.**

The Fujiwara don't count, Magister. The Aletheia's tone was almost dismissive. **They are but tools. You, I am pleased to say, are a free agent.**

That is the height of irony, coming from you.

Touché, allowed the demon. Audsley could imagine its smile. **But you understand the thrust of my argument. We are bound together, the four of us. You are young and, augmented by our power, will go far. I almost quiver to think of what we will accomplish together.**

There is no need to entice me, at least, not any longer. Audsley opened his eyes and stared at the dimming square of glass. *I have accepted the yoke. We can speak plainly to each other at last.*

I take it as a point of pride to have never spoken plainly, said the Aletheian. **I am, after all, a great poet. Why waste my gifts?**

So, it's true. You were once a mortal like me.

Yes.

How did you become a demon? Have you been through the Black Gate? Am I going to become a demon myself?

Oh, my beautiful boy, such questions. Everything will be answered in good time, and when it is most appropriate.

A snarl of anger flickered through Audsley's being like a curlicue of flame. *No more games. Answer me.*

Oh, I shall, but not yet. There is a method to this madness, an order to our revelations. Think of yourself as a shy, virginal, blushing young maiden. Would it be right, would it be courteous for me to bend you over a rough wall on our first outing? Oh, no. First comes the poetry, the roses, the promises of eternal devotion. That, we have done. Then, the first, chaste kiss. That was your acceptance of us into your soul. Next come the steps of more carnal seduction. A hand placed lightly upon your breast. A tongue flicking the lobe of your ear. Breath hot and warm against your neck, till you are veritably panting, squirming, begging for more, and then – oh, and then shall we bend you over, then shall we kick your legs apart, and the three of us shall have our way with you.

Audsley stood transfixed, staring at the square of light, not seeing, his heart thudding in his chest. The demon's voice was more intimate than anything he'd ever heard. Despite himself, he realized he'd grown hard, was straining against the fabric of his own leggings. Horror stabbed him to the core.

And what's best, whispered the demon, **what's truly delicious is that by that point, you'll be loving every second of it. So, no. We'll not ruin this sweet seduction. Trust us, dear Magister. We'll fuck you when you're good and ready.**

Audsley gulped. It felt like swallowing a handful of small stones, pebbles which swelled to the size of oranges as they sat heavily in the bottom of his stomach.

Silence, he whispered. *Enough.*

He stood, trembling, but heard nothing more. He felt alone, though he knew this to be the ultimate lie. Shaking, he sat on the edge of his bed and placed his hands on his knees. *I am Audsley of Castle Kyferin, magister to Lady Iskra — Empress Iskra — and tasked with rooting out the evil that has polluted the corpus of Ascendancy.* He squeezed his eyes shut and repeated that mantra repeatedly, till the words lost meaning and became a mere concatenation of sounds.

"Oh, dear," he said, and rubbed at his knees. His fear, however, was evanescent; after a few more minutes, it left him, and once again he sat in a state of lucid concentration. This was his reality, and he had to fend for himself as best he could. Obviously, he would refuse any offers his demons made him; there was no obligation to damn himself further. What he had to do was please Little Zephyr until he learned a way back to Starkadr or Aletheia.

Little Zephyr had bade him ring a bell set outside his door when he was ready to resume his 'education'. The thought of staying a moment longer in this empty cell with only his demons was suddenly abhorrent; he rose, tightened his sash around his ridiculous Aletheian robes, and stepped outside.

He could hear the distant murmur of voices down the shadowed corridor. The bronze bell was sitting on a small wooden shelf set beside his door; he raised it, gave it a sharp tinkle, then set it back.

A moment later, a servant jogged down the hall and stopped before him, eyes lowered, hands by his sides. He was a short, lean youth in rough woolen garments; his face was flecked with old scars, and his spine was as rounded as his shoulders. He didn't speak.

"Please take me to Little Zephyr," said Audsley.

The boy nodded, turned, and hurried down the corridor. Audsley strode after him. They wound their way through the tunnels, and sooner than Audsley had expected, they stopped outside an elegant black door with a silver knocker. The boy bowed and stepped back.

Audsley patted his sides reflexively for a coin to give the servant, then felt a fool. Instead, he rapped the knocker twice. The door opened, and a middle-aged Sigean woman with aristocratic bearing regarded him. She was handsome, her figure full under her severe gray dress, but her eyes were strangely lifeless and flat.

"Magister Audsley," said the woman. "I am Lady Assaveria, Little Zephyr's attendant. Please, come in."

Audsley bobbed his head and stepped past the woman into a small living room. It was sumptuously furnished, but there was no hiding the rough rock walls, the lack of windows, the damp, mineral tang of the air.

Assaveria gestured to a chair and passed through a short tunnel into the room beyond; there, Audsley heard the gentle murmur of voices again, and then Little Zephyr appeared, dressed in nothing more than a white linen shift that barely fell to mid-thigh. Her black hair was done up in an efficient knot, and her face was without make-up of any kind. Audsley was shocked; she seemed no older than fifteen.

"We are friends, are we not, Audsley?" She sat on a chair across from him, tucking one leg underneath her and pressing her shift down with both hands. Her expression was sincere, her eyes large, her voice soft. "After all we have been through, promised to each other? You have entrusted your soul to me, and I – well, I've entrusted my every hope of a future to you. We are in each other's hands. We know enough of each other's secrets to assure our mutual destruction if we so chose. But we don't, do we? We're friends?"

"Yes," said Audsley, his mouth dry. "Friends. But of course."

"I know you're just saying that, and I don't blame you." Little Zephyr looked down at her lap. "After all, you must see me as some kind of monster. Perhaps you've already written me off as insane, or without emotion or empathy. And, to be honest, you'd be right. I am a monster. I own it." She looked up, and tears glimmered in her eyes.

"Little Zephyr, I—" began Audsley, but she smiled and shook her head, cutting him off.

"No, it's true. I'm barbarous, callous, cruel, strange and perverted. For goodness' sake, I don't even blink at Athanasius' experiments. Those wretched victims of his don't even prey on my mind. They haven't since I was, oh, twelve? I think that's the last time I had that particular nightmare. So, how else could you see me but foul?"

"It's not your fault," Audsley said hesitantly. "You didn't ask to be raised here."

"No, I didn't. But perhaps I could have done something. Escaped sooner. Tried to, I don't know, rescue some of the flame walkers. Show them small acts of kindness. Rebel in a more meaningful way. But I haven't, and perhaps that's because I am weak. Or too warped. Perhaps I am beyond redemption. Do you know, I have never been completely trusted by a single living being? Ever?" Her smile was part mock amazement, part sadness.

"Not even your parents?"

"Oh, no, definitely not by them. I have a demon within me, you see. Of course you do. As do all of my blood. And, so, we don't trust each other. We use each other. Apply leverage. Look for advantage. Bow to those with greater power while scheming how to topple them. Is it surprising, I wonder, that I have turned out this way?"

"No, I suspect not," said Audsley. He interlaced his fingers and sat back. "Why are you telling me all this, Little Zephyr?"

"Oh, drop the 'Little'," she said with a wave of her hand. "Zephyr will do. Only my family needs to continuously remind me of my station. But why? Because, dear Audsley, I don't want the horrors of Haugabrjótr to drive you from my side. You are the rope that has been lowered into my personal oubliette. I may be a monster, but I yearn for freedom. To not be a tool. And — perhaps — this self-reflection may prove the first steps in my own redemption?"

Audsley shrugged. "Perhaps. I cannot say."

"No," said Zephyr, biting the corner of her lip. "Neither can I. I feel as if I live within a hall of endless mirrors. Nothing I see is natural, true, or straight. Everything is distorted, to the point where I don't even know where to step."

Audsley knew that he should be feeling pity for her. To some degree, he did. But that same detachment held his judgement back. He watched her carefully instead, trying to read her body language. She was picking at the hem of her shift. Bouncing her knee. She appeared distracted. But was she?

"Well," he said. "You told me you had a clear plan when you made this offer."

"Yes, but it's not to walk through the maze. I've given up trying to find my way to freedom by finding the way out." Her eyes flashed. "We're going to break our way out. Shatter the mirrors, leave this place in ruins, so that they don't even dream of chasing us."

"By killing the Minister of Perfection," said Audsley. "Your grand-father."

"Yes," said Zephyr. She looked down at where her nails were wreaking ruin on the hem of her garment. "I just haven't figured out how yet."

"And that's the answer you wish me to supply."

"You have *three* demons within you," she said, her voice suddenly tight with urgency. "Three. That's unheard of. You *must* be able to help me."

"Perhaps," he said. "Why don't we start with the basic facts? What are your grandfather's powers? His weaknesses? His habits and rou-tines?"

"Those are hard to predict now," said Zephyr with a bitter laugh. She raised her shift to scratch at her pale upper thigh; Audsley averted his eyes from her bare expanse of leg. "With the Fujiwara estate lost and our clan without a presence in Aletheia, everything has been upended. Grandfather is holding an extended council with his most trusted advisors and sons as we speak, trying to determine their next course of action."

"Perhaps this time of chaos is to our advantage, then," said Audsley. "We can use it to find an opening that would not otherwise be available to us."

"Yes! Precisely. But, even so, he is rarely alone, and as I said before, he doesn't trust me."

"His weaknesses?"

Zephyr frowned. "He's largely immune to normal weapons. Stabbing him in the back won't work. He simply knows when his food or drink is poisoned — I think his demon warns him. Drowning, perhaps? But it would be incredibly hard to hold him underwater, given how powerfully he flies."

"Demon fire?"

"If it were exceptionally intense, yes." Zephyr sat forward. "As I believe yours must be if all three of your demons are behind the effort."

"I see," said Audsley. "So, what are you thinking? I petition him for an audience and then burn him on his throne?"

"No," said Zephyr. "Because I know you won't agree to something that will get you killed. We have to get him alone, when nobody knows he's with us, and kill him then."

Audsley snorted. "That sounds easy."

"Yes, tell me about it." She leaned back and bit at the corner of one of her nails, elbow resting on the chair back. "But there must be a way."

Audsley half-closed his eyes. "He's looking for a means to resume power. To regain the authority he's lost. A new weapon, a new angle, a means to strike back at those who hurt him. Correct?"

Zephyr paused her chewing and regarded him. "Yes."

"Then, that's what we have to offer him. That's how we bait our trap."

"Very well, in theory. But in practice?"

Audsley tapped his chin. "Does he know about the Sin Casters' stonecloud?"

A vertical line appeared between Zephyr's brows. "You refer to Starkadr?"

Audsley nodded.

"Yes, of course."

"But does he know how to get there?"

Zephyr sat up. "Do you?"

Audsley smiled. "I do. It's an amazing place. It would offer him unparalleled power. There is a chamber in its belly filled with hundreds of Lunar Portals. It would allow him access to the breadth of the Empire. But more alluring is the secret library of the Sin Casters – sorry, Flame Walkers – along with the lost laboratories of the artificers, complete with their abandoned experiments..."

Zephyr's eyes were so wide, she looked almost comical. "You can take him there?"

"Yes. On the sole condition that we absolutely make sure he dies and never takes advantage of it."

"Incredible," breathed Zephyr. "Starkadr. I half-thought it a myth."

She's lying, said his demon with sly amusement.

"You have been there?" she asked breathlessly. "In truth?"

Audsley nodded.

Zephyr looked away so as to disguise her interest. "And, by chance, did you see... well. I've heard that there is a command hall at the stonecloud's very apex...?"

"There is. Long and broad, with a ceiling of tessellated glass panes and cunningly wrought pools that reflect the sky in iridescent hues."

"And, at its very end? A throne, perhaps?"

"Mmmhmm," said Audsley, watching her carefully.

"And, before that throne? A pedestal?"

Audsley nodded.

"You have seen it? With your own eyes?" It was Zephyr's turn to search his face. "Can you describe it?"

"It's made of the same black stone as the rest of the stonecloud, and rises to about waist height. Topped by a hemisphere around the base of which runs a grooved indentation. Why? What do you know of its purpose?"

"Its purpose? Oh, nothing." She gave him a winning smile. "Just fanciful myths and children's tales."

"What kind of children are told tales about Starkadr?" Audsley asked, then raised a hand to pre-empt her response. "Ah, yes. Of course. Fujiwara children."

"Regardless," Zephyr said briskly. "That offer would most definitely entice my grandfather. But how do we offer it to him without his taking his entire entourage?"

"That, I don't yet know," said Audsley. "But say that we accomplish our goal. Say that we lure him to Starkadr, and then time our attack perfectly and blast him with demon fire. How can we be sure that he would die?"

"Yes," said Zephyr, sitting back once more. "We have to unleash hell itself upon him. There can be no risk of failure. Together, you and I, we can burn almost anyone to cinders. But my grandfather?" She lapsed into silence.

Audsley watched her mull over their intended murder.

Lady Assaveria entered the room, bearing a gilt tray on which rested two elegant glasses of white liquid. "Your drinks," she said with a smile, lowering the tray toward Zephyr, who took a glass absent-mindedly. Audsley did the same. Warm milk, he realized. He sipped and tasted honey. Once Assaveria had left, Audsley gestured in her wake with his glass.

"She is your...?"

"Assistant," said Zephyr, sipping her milk pensively. "It's awfully transparent, I know. Adopting into my service a woman my mother's age who serves me warm milk and sings me to sleep. But, what can I say? I enjoy it. It comforts me, though I know it's ridiculous." She shrugged one shoulder and sipped her milk once more. "Family. It's the one constant in everyone's life that's destined to fuck them up."

Audsley snorted. He thought of his own mother, a shadowy figure who had spent her years locked away in her tower suite, pining for her husband. Shrewish might be the word to use, if Audsley were feeling uncharitable. Bereaved was what he'd used in public. Her every compliment a put-down, her every complaint spoken in a piteous whine that would turn to deeply hurt silence if it was ignored or protested.

Zephyr had been watching him closely, and a soft, understanding smile curved the corners of her lips. "Shall we drink to mothers? Surrogate and otherwise?"

"Yes," said Audsley, leaning forward to tap his glass against hers. "And to the moment we shrug off the leash."

"Oh, we never shrug it off," said Zephyr. "We only exchange it for new ones. I wonder what my new prison will be when I am free to wander Ennoia or wherever I end up? An internal one, no doubt, fashioned from my own regrets, foibles, and paranoia." She paused, gazing into her milk, then downed it in one go. "No matter. What were we discussing?"

"Murder," said Audsley flatly.

"Yes. And how to ensure that my dear grandfather is properly killed. Perhaps... it's risky, but there are several individuals I could destroy if I chose by revealing a few choice secrets. I could blackmail them into helping us. Lending us their demonic flame."

"Risky," said Audsley. "The more people involved, the greater the chance for betrayal."

"Very true. But I don't see any other way. We'd have to place them in our chosen ambush spot ahead of time, of course. Then, when the moment of truth arrives, they would step forward, and four or five of us would blast Grandfather all at once. That should do it."

"Unless he's immune to demon flame altogether," said Audsley.

"Nobody is. Resistant, yes. Immune? No. Don't you worry, Audsley. The smell of burning flesh and the sound of splintering bones will be the hallmarks of our freedom. From that moment on, we shall part ways, you and I, and ah, such sweet sorrow. All I must do is consider how best to leverage my secrets against my targets to ensure both their silence and their complicity."

"Perhaps I can help," said Audsley. "Or, more accurately, my demons can. They are, if nothing else, most persuasive."

"Hmm, you *would* have dynamic demons, wouldn't you?"

"Dynamic?"

"Self-motivated. Looking out for their own interests. Cunning and duplicitous."

"That about describes them, yes. You don't?"

"Oh, no," said Zephyr. "That would be too dangerous. A lifetime spent with someone in my head trying to corrupt me completely? No, thank you. I have a sundered demon. The wreckage of a poor Flame Caster's soul. I've learned to tune out his groans and broken pleas. I simply benefit from his power."

Audsley leaned forward. "A sundered demon. Do all key Fujiwaras possess the like?"

Zephyr nodded. "They're much safer. More reliable. Not as powerful, of course, but it allows the elders of our clan to not spend their every night awake in fear of a member going rogue due to demonic blandishments."

"Of course," Audsley said with a smile, his cheeks stiff, his expression mechanical. "Who would want that?"

"But, if your demons are willing to help...?" Zephyr asked. "Have they revealed their ranks?"

Audsley thought back to a discussion he'd had with them back in Starkadr, what felt like years ago. Just before he had passed into Mythgraefen to fight alongside Asho and Kethe against the Black Shriving. "Yes. The most powerful is *nahkhor'ir*."

Zephyr let out a low whistle. "*Nahkhor'ir?* My dear Magister, I don't know if you have been greatly blessed or profoundly cursed. That is a mighty demon you house in your soul. And the other two?"

"*Urth'akak*," Audsley said reluctantly.

Zephyr waggled her head from side to side. "No slouches, either. Wow."

"Yes, well." Audsley could only manage a polite grimace. "We fortunate few, as it were. And the, ah, ranking of your own?"

"Being a direct descendant of Grandfather, I was gifted one of the more powerful demons from our stable. *Kal'shan*, a step above your two, a few below your *nahkhor'ir*."

"And your grandfather?"

"The subject of much speculation. It is said that he is invested with a *ysil-athamgr*, a potent force of great darkness that is a step above your own *nahkhor'ir*."

"These terms, these names, mean little to me," said Audsley, smoothing down the fabric of his robes over his knees.

But much to us, said the Aletheian demon. **An** ysil-athamgr **is a dire being to contend with.**

On the, ah, scale of the demon we fought at Mythgraefen? The one that led the horde from the Black Gate?

No. That was a mal'orem. **A different level altogether.**

Audsley closed his eyes and pinched the bridge of his nose. *This all means nothing to me.*

Then, think of it this way. I, being nahkhor'ir, **am the equivalent of a knight. An** ysil-athamgr **would be a landed baron.**

Zephyr's kal-shan?

The demon sniffed. **Heavy infantry, perhaps.**

I'm beginning to understand. What would a mal'orem *count as, then?*

A duke.

And the great demons bound in the largest of the cubes we saw in the bowels of Starkadr? The ones you called ur-destraas?

There was a pause, and when the demon spoke, Audsley could have sworn he heard a quaver of fear. **I do not like to even think of those beings of incandescent might. If a** mal'orem **is a duke, then an** ur-destraas... **well. That would be an emperor.**

Audsley shivered.

"Magister?"

"It's nothing," said Audsley. He didn't even bother to try to force a smile. "But, yes. We're going to need help. If we're to challenge a baron, we're going to need more than a knight and assorted footmen."

She quirked her head to one side, much like a bird. "You're babbling."

"Perhaps. But we will need the most powerful allies you can muster. Unless all of them are invested with mere *kal'shan?*"

"Mere?" Two dots of color appeared on her high cheekbones.

"My apologies. But the fact remains. Can we acquire allies of power? Otherwise, we will be as ants crawling around the paws of a wolf."

Zephyr didn't respond at once. Her gaze remained narrowed, her mouth a horizontal line. *Great,* thought Audsley. *I've insulted the size of her demon's equipage.*

"Yes, very well," she said stiffly. "The greater their demon, the harder their host will be to control. But I know of several candidates we can approach. May I count on your demon's assistance?"

Audsley hesitated. How easy it was to ask them for help, to justify their usage even as he fought to free himself of them. But how could he proceed otherwise?

He could feel his demons' smugness as he sighed and nodded. "Yes," he said heavily. "Of course."

Chapter 11

Iskra couldn't remember the last time she'd had a full night's sleep, though she knew it had been before Roddick's death. Ever since that terrible moment, she'd been unable to stop her thoughts, to quell her pain, to relax, to let go. The nights and evenings had begun to blur into each other, a mélange of lantern-lit hours and velvety darkness broken only by the brief snatches of rest she'd managed to steal from the vigilance of her mind.

The fastness of Starkadr, for good or ill, made sleeping a rare proposition. She could have retreated to Agerastos. Might even have done well in doing so, showing her face to the populace — *her people* — but, no. She couldn't remove herself from the Ascendant's inner circle. Couldn't turn her back.

Was it paranoia, fear, or cold realism that made her think that the minute she did so, they would make decisions that would cast her far from the center of power?

So, instead, Iskra had a tent erected on the cold Starkadrian floor, not quite as large as the Ascendant's, and filled it with braziers, fur rugs, a decadent divan on which she could recline if she had any inclination to sleep, a table replete with maps, and a surfeit of Agerastian nobles, guards, and Vothaks.

Orishin handled the masses. She sat back in her leather-bound chair, her finger laid along the seam of her lips, and stared in a state of near-stupefaction at the closest live flame as Orishin spoke to all who approached her desk.

She should partake. Ask that he translate. But, to be frank, she didn't care. The world was collapsing. The world as she had known it, the Empire, even. Kragh had seized the White Gate. Her daughter had become a stranger. Her son, her precious boy, was dead. Enderl Kyferin was now no doubt melded with the earth on which he had fallen and died. Castle Kyferin stood abandoned. She was wearing the regalia of an empress, but it meant nothing to her. What did she care what terms Orishin negotiated, what promises he made, how best he decided to manage the affairs of Agerastos? They could pluck her crown from her brow tomorrow, and she would only sigh with relief.

An Aletheian appeared at the entrance of her tent. The new Grace, Lutherius. She caught a glimpse of his guard remaining behind as he handed his blade to her own soldiers. Of the Hundred Serpents who had attacked Theletos, only seventeen remained fit to fight on. Yet those seventeen were as lethal as non-Virtues could be. She had them all gathered close.

The impromptu court of Agerastian notables drew aside as Lutherius approached, following her personal chamberlain to her desk. Word had spread quickly regarding his new appointment, and she saw in the eyes of her people a glittering appraisal that was part fear, part hope.

"Empress," said Lutherius, giving her a shallow bow.

Iskra sat upright. Her thoughts were restive, hard to marshal. She felt as if she had sipped too much wine, but that was only the exhaustion and grief. She considered the man. There was something of Tiron to him, she thought. The same practical brutality, perhaps. The lack of idealism or softness. She'd meant to investigate his past, his family, how he had come to lead an elite force at the very edges of the Empire against monsters most people considered to be fanciful nursery tales. It was a testament to her fatigue that she'd forgotten to do so.

"Does it bother you, Your Grace, that I had your predecessor killed?"

He stiffened. In fact, the entire court froze, murmured conversations ending abruptly. She held Lutherius' gaze.

"No," said Lutherius. "Not really."

"I must admit to being surprised."

"My predecessor was a political appointee. I knew the man. The best I can say of him is that I respected his office."

Iskra tapped her lips. "Fair enough. I must admit that, at that time, I was seeking the destruction of the Empire, a goal I no longer pursue. We are allies, it seems, Your Grace."

"Yes," said Lutherius. He hesitated, then spoke softly. "Empress, are you well?"

Iskra laughed. "A chivalrous question. The answer is no. Now, to business. What do you need?"

Clearly, he was having trouble navigating her responses. "The Ascendant has sent me to ask your opinion on a matter."

"I didn't know that the inner council was still meeting."

"It's not. I was in a private conference with His Holiness."

"Then ask."

"Would you go in the Ascendant's name to Ennoia and reassure its lords that we are not defeated?"

Iskra's gaze drifted down the length of his arm. "How did you lose your hand, Lutherius?"

He didn't so much as glance at it. "I didn't lose it. It was bitten off."

"A *kvathka*?"

"Yes. Now, will you be His Holiness' ambassador?"

"And why would they listen to the Empress of Agerastos?"

"Not all of them are aware of your blessed rise in station. You could approach them as Lady Kyferin, Ennoian lady, known and respected by all."

"The last they heard, I was murdering my brother-in-law and certain heads of state in Castle Laur."

"Well, they will no doubt be overwhelmed with joy at your propitious return to the fold. From all I've heard, you are an astute and capable woman. If you put your mind to it, I have no doubt that you will succeed."

"And, what of our cause in general? Do you harbor any doubts in that capacity?"

"Of course." He smiled broadly. "I've never been given such a shitty hand of cards. But I'll play what I'm dealt. It would help, however, if I could spend my time sparring with the kragh and not yourself. I've not the wit."

"Flattery?"

"I almost said patience instead. Will you go?"

"There's no one else?"

"Surprisingly, no. Our other preferred candidates either lie dead in Abythos or were killed by you."

Iskra didn't rush to answer. She leaned back instead, considering the man. No, not like Tiron after all. Too well-spoken. Too sure of himself. The man Tiron might have been if life had never cut his heart out, but formidable all the same.

"Very well. I'll go. Are delegates being sent to the other cities?"

"They will be."

"You came to me first." She smiled. "How flattering of you."

"You insist on thinking I aim to flatter."

"Only as part of your overarching strategy, Lutherius. Don't think I make the mistake of taking it personally."

"Well, good. I will tell His Holiness that you have assented. Will you be ready to go at dawn?"

"I'll go now." She rose to her feet. "The lords of Ennoia will be in session, debating the end of the Empire and how best they can wrest some modicum of glory from its fall. I see no reason to make them wait."

Lutherius bowed once more. "Very well. I will leave it for you to decide, but if you think it... indecorous to take Agerastian soldiers into Ennoia, I am willing to assign Ennoians from my own Cerulean Guard to protect you instead."

"Do so. Your men will no doubt help in privately corroborating my report." She raised a hand. "I tease. I will be ready in fifteen minutes. Have them wait for me at the Portal."

"Very well." Lutherius paused, and for the first time, she caught his eyes flick up and down the length of her body. "Thank you, Iskra."

"My title is Empress, Lutherius." She made her smile sweet. "Lest you forget. Good evening."

Lutherius spluttered, caught himself, and then laughed. It was a loud laugh, rich with genuine amusement, and he walked away shaking his head. A moment later, he was gone, and Iskra realized that she had watched him cross the entirety of her tent.

"Empress," said Orishin gently. He had stood to the side throughout. "Your commands?"

"Oh, you know my commands all too well," she said. "You've been giving them for me for the past two hours."

Orishin's expression paled, and she relented. "Don't mind me. I am beside myself with rapture to be serving the will of the Ascendant once more. You are my rudder, Orishin. The Empire of Agerastos would founder without your guidance. I will leave matters in your hands while I am gone. In fact, I believe it is high time I gave you an official title: Preceptor of the Court. How does that sound? I will let it be known that all imperial concerns should be directed to you."

Orishin bowed deeply. "You do this poor servant too much honor, Your Imperial Majesty."

"No, I don't. Now, don't forget that Starkadr is mine. I lay claim to it through both my discovery of it, my Agerastian occupation, and our dependence on the Vothaks for its operation. If any should seek to usurp that right, be sure to defend it."

"Yes, Your Imperial Majesty."

"Good. Send for Asho. Ask him to meet me at the Portal to Ennoia. I am going in search of my daughter." She looked over the crowd that still filled the tent. Despite their finery and make-up, their jewels and poise, she sensed a flickering fragility within them all, a sense that all they held dear was crumbling; the walls of their society were falling, their very sense of self as defined by their stations coming to an end. Iskra felt pity for them, and that pity moved her to act, if only for this one moment, as their empress.

"Translate for me, Orishin." She moved to stand before her desk. "I depart as ambassador for the Ascendant, but know that I am yet and shall always be your empress. I safeguard our values, I hold dear the sanctity of our realm, and I bend every ounce of my imperial might to influence events so that our Empire shall prosper."

She paused for Orishin and watched as the words fell like rain on a dusty field. Shoulders were pushed back. Chins rose. Eyes narrowed as people listened intently and then nodded.

"Await my return, and know that you are the heart of our polity, that you safeguard the culture of our realm, that in you shines the spirit and fire of Agerastos. Hold firm. Cling to your adamant faith. We shall prevail."

There, enough. The words had come easily, but she had felt nothing at all beyond her initial bout of pity. Yet, even as she marched toward the exit, the nobles lowered themselves to one knee, and she sensed their gratitude, even saw tears in the eyes of this man and that. Relief – not that her words had been that stirring, but relief that she had chosen to act her part. Had chosen, through her participation, to validate their own.

Her honor guard, led by Commander Patash, immediately formed a circle around her. Patash looked alert despite his haggard appearance, and bowed low as she emerged. "Where to, Your Imperial Majesty?" He'd been studying Ennoian diligently under Orishin. His accent was terrible, but she inclined her head appreciatively.

"My daughter, Kethe. Though these days, she seems to go by the name of Makaria. Let us try the area close to the Ascendant's main tent. I would say goodbye to her."

Patash gave a brisk nod and led their group through the refugee camp toward the Ascendant's high tent. Ennoians in their Aletheian household guard uniforms watched them pass. It had to be tough for their morale to not only lose to kragh, but then depend on rank heretics for their safety. Good, she thought. This enforced humility should prove salutary.

They found Kethe sitting cross-legged on the stone ground, mist floating about her middle, some fifteen men and women as disparate as if they had been randomly gathered from the far-flung corners of the Empire sitting in a group facing her. They all had their eyes closed, hands resting on their knees. No one spoke.

Iskra watched in silence, counting to sixty as she examined the gathering. Consecrated, she guessed. Too many to belong to just Kethe's cohort, so a cross-section of those who had survived the battles thus far. Prayer? Meditation? It was most strange, almost fascinating, to see her daughter sitting there so serenely. At peace, her face devoid of expression. Where was the fiery girl she had always known, impatient and intemperate? Where was the Kethe who had been riven to her core by Tiron's attack, half-sulking, half-defiant?

Gone, it seemed. Replaced by this stranger. Makaria. No, Iskra chided herself. Not a stranger. This was her daughter still.

"Kethe." She spoke the word, broke the silence as one might choose to purposefully step onto a skein of ice that lay over a puddle on the path.

Kethe opened her eyes, inhaling deeply as she did so, as if leaving a dream, and stared over the heads of her Consecrated, meeting Iskra's eyes.

"I would say goodbye," said Iskra. "Will you speak with me?"

Kethe nodded and pushed herself lithely to her feet. She held up a palm to those sitting before her, bidding them remain, and circled the group to where Iskra was standing — only to walk on a dozen paces, leading Iskra away.

"Where are you going?" Hands on her hips, Kethe turned to regard Iskra with her shoulders back. Was that a front? A pretended reserve?

"Ennoia," said Iskra. She resisted the urge to curl a lock of Kethe's hair behind her ear. "You're looking well. At peace."

"Hardly," said Kethe, arching her right eyebrow. The familiarity of that gesture struck a pang in Iskra's heart. "But I'm glad you think so. It means the others might believe the same."

"Kethe." Iskra pitched her voice soft, as if she thought she might pass it over Kethe's walls through gentleness alone. "I've missed you so much."

Kethe stiffened and half-turned away, glancing back at her Consecrated. "And I you, Mother. I'm sorry I've not been close, or able to find time, but with events—"

"May I hug you?" Iskra smiled to mask her pain. "Or do Virtues not hug in public?"

"I — yes. Of course." Kethe looked even more uncomfortable, and made no move forward.

No matter. Iskra had love enough for both of them. She stepped forward and took hold of her daughter, wrapped her arms around her cold armor, pressed her cheek against Kethe's. "Oh, I've missed you. In my bones, I've missed you." She closed her eyes and held her daughter tight.

Kethe slowly relaxed into the embrace. Neither of them spoke. Suddenly, Kethe's shoulders hitched in a violent hiccup that caused her to step away.

"I can't," said Kethe. She disengaged and would not meet Iskra's eyes. Looked down and to the side, wiping at her face with the back of her hand. "I can't. Not now. Too much depends on me. If — I can't."

"There may not be another time," Iskra said softly.

"All the more reason to stay strong," Kethe said with a sharp sniff. She exhaled through her mouth and forced a hard smile to her lips. "I shall grieve for him when I can. But not now."

"You're all I have left, my love," said Iskra. It tore at her heart to see her daughter shouldering such weight, such terrible responsibility. Only two or three years ago, Kethe had been but a girl; now, she was a warrior, a leader, a Virtue, and the fate of the Empire rested on her shoulders. Was there no end to the world's cruelty?

"Yes," said Kethe, though Iskra didn't know what she was agreeing to. "I love you, Mother." Again, Kethe looked away. "I wish you good fortune on your trip to Ennoia."

"Oh, wish the lords fortune," Iskra said wryly. "I don't intend to go easy on them."

Kethe laughed. "Yes," she repeated, then took a step back. "I have to go."

"I love you," said Iskra, reaching out for Kethe's callused hand. "Never forget that. I love you and am more proud of you than you will ever know."

Kethe gave Iskra's hand a squeeze and then pulled free, hurrying away as she wiped at her eyes once more.

Iskra watched her go. There was a knot in her throat that she couldn't swallow, a weight in the pit of her stomach, and her own eyes were so dry that they almost ached. With a sigh, she looked to Patash, who had stood a respectful distance away the entire time. "To the Portal, whichever one it is. Let us go."

They strode through the camp. Iskra looked straight ahead. She should have ordered chests of clothing to be packed, selected two or three maidens to accompany her, washed and dressed in her best finery, done all sorts of courtly things before leaving on her trip. But she couldn't summon the energy to care. Let the lords of Ennoia see her as she was. If they judged the importance of her words by the cut of her gown, then they deserved to die.

Asho was standing beside the Gate at the base of one of the horrendously twisted pillars. He had found his plate armor, it seemed, but had donned only his cuirass and pauldrons. A shirt of black chain reached his wrists and hung down to mid-thigh, buckled tight at the waist by his sword belt, while black leather leggings were all the protection he'd donned for his legs. His white hair was pulled back, and his pallid face was forbidding.

"My knight," said Iskra.

Asho bowed low. "Your Imperial Majesty."

"Oh, no," said Iskra, reaching out to touch his shoulder. "Not after all we've been through together. To you, I am but your lady, nothing more. Please."

Asho straightened and did not smile. "My lady, then."

They stood in silence, facing each other. How he had changed, she thought. As much as Kethe. Gone was the gangly youth of a year ago, lurking in Enderl's shadow as wary as a whipped dog. This man before her had been baptized in flame. He'd filled out, and now stood with a quiet certitude, had the bearing of a knight. And yet, in the depths of his eyes she saw a pulsing anger, a fierce resentment, a cruel pain. Perhaps he had not changed that much after all.

"Why are we leaving Starkadr, my lady?"

"The Ascendant has bid us speak with the lords of Ennoia and reassure them that all is not lost."

"Why you? You are the empress of Agerastos. Your place is here."

"I hold the highest rank of all the Ennoians present. The lords know my name."

"Theletos the Longed-For, or even Kethe, could accomplish as much. Lutherius, the damned Minister of the Sun. Any of them could go in your stead. So, I ask again: why you?"

Iskra felt a terrible weariness drape itself across her shoulders. "Because the Ascendant asked me to, Asho. Because it is a meaningful way to contribute to the war. Because I believe I have unique leverage with the lords of Ennoia. It is the greatest city in the Empire. The bastion of our armed resistance. Would you have it surrender?"

"No. But don't you see? They're removing you from the center of power. Even as they benefit from your soldiers, your stonecloud, your everything, they send you off like an errant messenger. Who knows what decisions and strategies will be adopted while you're gone? You can't leave the war in their hands — they have botched every opportunity they have been presented with thus far!"

His anger was scalding. Never had he spoken to her thus.

Iskra closed her eyes and steadied herself. If only she were not so exhausted. Her emotions, already stirred by Kethe, were rising in a tumult. She gestured to Patash, and he backed away, taking her guard with them, so that she stood alone with her knight.

"Perhaps you are right." She felt like an autumn leaf, trembling, barely holding on as the cruel winds of winter sought to pluck her free. "But I am doing my best." She heard her own voice thicken with emotion. "I have many excuses for my conduct. For being — overwhelmed. For not fighting, not clawing my way to the fore as I know I should. Do you think I don't recognize the madness, the foolishness of listening to those court ministers as they bleat and posture? Thank the Ascendant for Lutherius' arrival, but Asho, I can't — I can't — "

"Can't what?" His voice was cold.

She met his gaze. "I'm sorry. I said before to someone that I am a poor tool for this job. It was Audsley, I think. But I am doing my best. Do you know what I wish I could do? I wish I could flee. Find a dark corner, a cave in the mountains around Mythgraefen, and roll a stone across the entrance so that I would never have to see the world again. To tear out my hair, to rub soot against my skin and rend my clothing. To grieve. My son is dead. My daughter? She is moving farther away from me with each passing moment. My friends and advisors have left me, one by one, till only you are left. I am the empress of a nation that means nothing to me. The man I might have loved — perhaps still love? I drove him away when he spoke wisdom. I have fought, I have struggled, and I managed to bring an army to the door of the Ascendant himself and exact concessions — only for everything to be sent spinning out of my grasp by the arrival of the kragh. So, I apologize, Asho. I know you are disappointed with me, and for good reason. I know I should be doing more, but believe me. Trust me when I tell you that it is a miracle that I am still standing. That I am still able to persevere, even in this small matter."

Tears were running down her cheeks, but she managed to smile. "I don't have it in me just yet to argue with these Aletheians about tactics and war. I know nothing of the matter, so how can I assert myself? But I shall do better when I return. I promise you that."

Asho looked stricken and fell to one knee. "Forgive me, Lady Iskra. I should never have spoken to you in that way. I — I forgot what you have gone through. I've been too caught up in my own anger. We've made so many sacrifices. We've fought so hard. We came so close. But now, it looks like the Empire is using the kragh invasion to avert the danger we presented. The changes we threatened."

"I know, Asho." Iskra took his arm and pulled him gently to his feet.

Gone was the coldness, the hard expression. His own grief and pain were clear to see. "It feels like you and I are the only ones left who want to change Ascension," he said. "We've lost everyone else. Audsley. Tiron. Kethe. Ser Wyland. Maeve. Kanna. Kolgrimr. Even the fucking Agerastian emperor." He laughed bitterly. "All gone. It's just you and me."

Iskra took his hand. "We're not finished yet. Don't lose faith."

"No," he said, and then sighed. "I won't. I can't." He visibly gathered himself. "To Ennoia, then. And wherever else you may lead. I am still your knight."

"My truest knight." Iskra smiled warmly at him, pain and sorrow warring in her heart, and then nodded to Patash. "Let us go. We've a long night ahead of us yet."

As if on cue, a squad of fifteen Ennoian soldiers approached, feet tramping on the stone, five deep and three across. They were wearing the colors of Aletheian household guards, but she couldn't begin to guess which one; despite that, they appeared a competent lot. Their captain was a hirsute and swarthy man whose shoulders were rounded by heavy slabs of muscle; his head jutted forward as if he had no neck, and his legs were bandy and bent.

"Captain Uxe reporting for duty, Your Imperial Majesty," he said, his voice surprisingly rich and pleasant. He had the broad, lipless mouth of a frog, a nose that had been broken countless times, and a receding forehead; it was a most unfortunate combination, but his smile was almost a smirk, and the glimmer in his eye spoke of a sharp intelligence.

"Captain Uxe," said Iskra, inclining her head gravely. "Thank you for your service. This is my knight, Ser Asho."

"The Bythian, aye." Uxe regarded Asho for a moment. "Heard about you, I have. As dangerous as you're improbable, it's said."

Asho drew himself up. "Is there going to be a problem?"

"Problem?" Uxe barked a sharp laugh. "Not on my account. I'm so sick of licking Aletheian boots that I'd welcome a testy Bythian for a change. You a Kyferin Black Wolf, then?"

"No," said Asho, and Iskra could tell he was having trouble maintaining his frown. "They're all dead."

"Pity, that." Uxe sniffed. "I heard they were right monsters, the lot of them, begging Your Majesty's pardon – I mean, Your Imperial Highness — but we could use a few monsters of our own right now, hey? Fifty Black Wolves with your old husband to lead them into battle would be a sight for sore eyes."

Iskra couldn't help but laugh. "How on earth did you maintain your position in Aletheia?"

Uxe closed one eye and grinned. "You're referring to my charming honesty, Your Imperial Majesty? My lord August Glade came to appreciate it, believe it or not. Seems he was tired of being lied to by everyone from his wife to his manservant. That, and I'm pretty good with Frog Splitter here." He patted a strangely curved short sword at his hip. "People are willing to make allowances when you're the best at what you do."

Iskra shook her head bemusedly. "Well, if you're half as good with your sword as you are loquacious, then I will indeed believe myself to be the safest woman in the Empire. Now." She turned to Asho. "I'm ready."

Asho stepped up to the Portal and stared at the runes above the arch. "A Vothak told me how to pronounce this, but it's my first time..." He swallowed, then grated out something horrific.

Nothing happened.

He coughed, tried again. Still nothing. He took a moment to work his jaw from side to side, then tried one more time.

Darkness flooded the interior of the arch. Asho drew his blade, and, as if they had been awaiting that signal, Captain Uxe and his men did the same. At Iskra's nod, Asho took a deep breath and stepped into the swirling ink. Iskra looked back over her shoulder, trying in vain to catch a final glimpse of Kethe, and then followed.

Chapter 12

The stench of the city hit Asho like a soiled glove across the face. He blinked in the gloom and covered his face with the crook of his elbow as he was assailed by the smell of rich mud, rotting vegetables, horse manure and urine. Over it all, like a pall, lay the acrid smell of smoke, shot through with a caustic sting that made him think of spoiled vinegar.

Gagging and coughing, he staggered forward, blade held at the ready, and realized that he was within a small stone chamber. Three arched windows rose to his left, without glass, and the breeze that blew in through them was the source of that unimaginable foulness. Forcing himself to focus, he swept the rest of the room with his gaze and saw nothing but ruin: a battered and leaning armoire; shelving nailed to the wall that was collapsing upon itself; a huge, hoary desk whose surface was obscured by a dank puddle; torn and muddied sheets of paper underfoot; the remains of tapestries on the wall.

"Ah, there we go," said Uxe, emerging from the scintillating Portal. He inhaled deeply and smiled at Asho, showing all his teeth. "Smell that, ser knight? That's the city. That's the stench of civilization for you."

More guards were coming through, each showing a variety of reactions to the smell. Sharply alert, they fanned out, moving to the windows and to the door that listed in its frame, and only then did Iskra herself come through.

If the smell appalled her, she gave no sign. "We are indeed come to Ennoia," she said. "Now, to determine what part."

"I can tell you that, Your Imperial Majesty." Uxe tapped the side of his nose. "We're close to the river Magryte, we are. Most likely, we're on the south bank, fetched right up against the western wall. Within a half-mile of the Iron Gate."

Asho stared at Uxe in disbelief. "Are you man or bloodhound?"

"A bit of both, perhaps. But you smell that sharp, puckery sting in the air? Making your eyes want to water? That's the unmistakable tang of lye. Means we're near the tanneries, which are all placed by fiat on the very western end of the river where it flows out of the city. We must be right close to the three blocks known as the Tanner's Tongue."

"You're a native of the city, Uxe?" asked Iskra.

"That I am, Your Imperial Majesty. Though it's been a good five years since I last walked its streets. Much might have changed."

"Then, let us be quit of this house and make our way to the Grand Fortress. You know the way?"

"That I do. When you're ready?"

Uxe led them out into a small courtyard. It, too, was abandoned, the broad eaves of the buildings casting much of it into dense shadow, though the moon high overhead brought the worn cobbles in the center into sharp relief. They marched out into the street, and from there made their way quickly, boots squelching in what Asho hoped was mud, surrounded on both sides by three-story buildings that seemed to lean over them as if they were whispering conspiratorially.

Dogs were sleeping in great piles here and there, all of them mongrels, filthy and oblivious to the world. Asho noted a reflective flash high up under the eaves of a building and made out a small owl, its head turning to watch them pass. Clotheslines arched overhead, shirts pinned along their lengths by the sleeves so that they appeared to be frozen in attitudes of surrender.

The alley was crooked, edged in here and there by the buildings, and Asho felt a tangible sense of relief when Uxe led them out into a broad and cobbled street. There were people moving along here, cloaks pulled tightly around their frames. Some were slouching along slowly, dragged down by the toils of a long day, while others seemed to be rising for the first time, rubbing at their eyes and blinking myopically as they shuffled by. They spared Iskra's group passing glances but nothing more. Signs hung from small shops, but Asho couldn't make them out in the gloom. Here and there stood stalls within impromptu canvas tents, knots of men huddled within them holding cups of steaming liquid, muttering to each other as they munched on rolls of bread and rubbed shoulders.

The city was huge. It extended in every direction. Asho had always heard tell of Ennoia's sprawling size, but even after seeing the wonders of Starkadr and the heights of Aletheia, he found it impressive, almost intimidating. There was nothing here that spoke of godly might; it was instead a testament to humanity itself. Tens of thousands of people had to live here, cheek by jowl.

"Uxe," he whispered, stepping up beside their guide. "How big is Ennoia? How many people?"

"How many?" Uxe scratched his chin. "I've no head for numbers, ser knight. But if you asked them to file past you single file, you'd no doubt die of hunger before they were all gone by. Wait till you see a real crowd of 'em gathered together. It's said that the Empire's Square can hold twenty thousand people, and I've seen it packed to the gills. A hundred thousand people must live here. Maybe double that. Who knows?"

Asho fell back, hand on the pommel of his sword. A hundred thousand. It staggered the mind.

They entered a broad square. There, a man was standing on a statue's pedestal, haranguing a small crowd of some fifty people, his face lit from beneath by their torches. "...And in these times of despair, we must all ask of ourselves why the Ascendant has turned his back on the world, how our sins could grow so grave that he would forsake us all, leaving us in the mire and the muck to reap the harvest of our own iniquities..."

They hurried on. A few minutes later, they emerged at the base of a great bridge that ran straight across what had to be the River Magryte. Upstream, the river was as placid as it was broad, but it foamed and roared as it plunged between the narrow brick caissons that supported the length of the bridge. Unable to resist his curiosity, Asho hurried from one side of the bridge to the other; the level of the river was a good three yards higher on the upstream side, and emerged in torrential waterfalls on the other, foam scrawling luminous skeins on the churning river's surface.

Even at night, boats were plying their way across the river, lanterns on their prows. Asho saw narrow skiffs and barges being rowed across, the chanting and call of their sailors carrying across the water.

"There," said Iskra. "The Grand Fortress."

It loomed over the far bank, a squat fist of stone, its battlements illuminated by both the moon and the torches, the flags of Ennoia and the Ascendant fluttering in a wind that Asho didn't' feel. The windows were brightly lit.

"Good," said Iskra. "The lords are in session. Let's hurry."

They crossed the bridge and plunged into the north bank, and here the buildings were finer, more stately; the street was broader, the cobbles better kept. Guards were moving past in groups of six, but they made no move to intercept Asho's group. Asho expected a great space to open in front of the fortress, but the shops and homes ran right up to its base.

A crowd was gathered at the fortress' steps, hemmed in on both sides by two massive ballistae that stood nearly ten feet tall. The war machines looked almost like museum pieces, heavily waxed and preserved from an older era. A ring of guards kept the crowd from the main doors, but that didn't stop them from crying out questions, making demands, shaking their fists.

"We demand to see the Imperial Provost!"

"Is it true? Has the Black Gate been opened?"

"They can't hide in there forever!"

Uxe waded into the crowd with aplomb, shouldering people aside as he went, his guards forming a wedge after him that widened the space, allowing Iskra and Asho to walk forward unimpeded. Men yelled their annoyance and then quieted at the sight of sixteen armed soldiers; people began to part before them, and they soon reached the steps.

Asho stepped up alongside Iskra, one hand wrapped loosely around the hilt of his sword. The fortress guards watched them approach, their captain moving forward to intercept them, the front of his leather armor spattered with fruit stains and pulp.

"The fortress is closed while the council is in session," said the captain in dolorous tones. "No one, no matter how pressing their need, may enter."

"I am Lady Iskra Kyferin, and by right of tradition and law, I have a place on that council. Step aside."

Asho heard her name being spread around in a flurry of whispers.

"Lady — Lady Iskra," stammered the captain in dismay. "But — I heard — "

"I don't care what you heard, my good man," said Iskra firmly. "Step aside."

The captain sketched a quick bow and did so. Iskra moved forward briskly, and Asho followed, through the huge doorway and into a broad hall. Twin fireplaces large enough to roast oxen blazed on opposite walls; war banners, tapestries, weaponry, and stuffed animal heads adorned the spaces around them in such profusion that Asho could barely see the walls themselves.

Iskra knew the way. She swept forward, up a staircase, and out onto the second floor.

The fortress was alive with activity. Servants rushed past them, guards patrolled, administrators hurried by with arms full of scrolls, and scribes with their writing kits ran as if late for their exams.

They made their way deep into the fortress and stopped before a pair of high, closed doors. Guards in imperial livery stood there, pikes in hand, and the hallway on either side was choked with soldiers wearing the colors of different Ennoian lords. Some eighty men stood in isolated groups, watching each other coldly, only to turn their attention upon Iskra as she made her appearance.

Asho stepped before her and gave a curt bow to an old man at the doorway whom he took to be the chamberlain. "Lady Iskra Kyferin wishes to join the council, as is her right by tradition and law."

"Lady Iskra Kyferin?" The old man peered over his glasses at her. "By the White Gate, it *is* you, my lady. Or should I say empress? One hardly knows how to keep up with current events these days."

"Master Olyx," said Iskra, smiling tightly. "You look like you haven't aged a day."

The man snorted. "Tell that to my knees. And my gout. And my eyesight. Still, it is good to have you with us. They have been at it for six hours already, and by the quantities of red wine that have been sent for, I fear they have made no progress."

"Let me see what I can do about that."

"Very well." Olyx nodded to a strapping guard, who pushed open the mighty door, and then led Iskra inside. Asho saw that Uxe had already taken his men to stand to one side. The captain gave him an encouraging wink.

The council chamber was dominated by a twelve-sided table, yet only six men were seated about it, each with a knight standing behind him. A cartwheel of black iron hung from the vaulted ceiling, thick candles flickering along its perimeter and adding their soft light to the lanterns that were placed within small alcoves in the walls. Heavily waxed wainscoting gleamed along the bases of the walls, while more war banners hung from the ceiling, all of them faded, some torn, others soiled by dark stains. Fires were burning in three fireplaces, and servants hurried like mice along the edges of the walls, pitchers in hand, darting forward to refill the great pewter goblets that stood before each lord.

"Your lordships, I present Lady Iskra Kyferin." Master Olyx's announcement cut through the low conversation, and the six men immediately turned in their chairs to glare at the doorway.

"Well, this defies belief," said a powerful-looking man Asho guessed to be in his late sixties. He rose to his feet, clutching at the back of his chair for support, his smile predatory. He was completely white-haired, bearded and handsome, with a stout chest and thick shoulders despite his advanced years, but age had proven cruel; his hands were gnarled, his knuckles were swollen, and he clearly had difficulty resting his weight on his left leg. "Lady Iskra Kyferin. There's the proof you were looking for, Lord Seulfryd, that the end of the world truly is nigh."

This elicited a snort from a saturnine man who made no move to rise. With a striking widow's peak, a vulpine face and quick, lively eyes, he was resting comfortably within his massive chair, goateed chin resting on the base of his palm, his purple coat and gold buttons strangely complimenting his ashen skin. "Lady Iskra. Have you come to beg our support in your claim for Kyferin Castle? Oh, wait. That's old news. Perhaps you've come to explain why you had Lord Mertyn and the Ascendant's Grace put to the torch?"

"Neither," said Iskra, and then she strode around the table to one of the empty seats. She pushed aside the chair and stepped up to the table's edge, placing her hands on either side of the wolf's head engraved on its surface. "I come at the behest of the Ascendant himself."

"He's dead," said a prim, tightly buttoned old man sitting with a ramrod-straight spine and spectacles perched on his sharp nose. He looked, Asho thought, like a cunningly built doll, every part of him perfectly combed and polished and assembled, but altogether without any vitality or vivacity.

"No, Lord Volkmar," said Iskra. "Your information is poor. I was at his side when we fled Aletheia through a Lunar Portal to a safe harbor. He is very much alive."

"Surely you don't expect us to believe this, Iskra?" The white-bearded man lowered himself carefully back into his chair, smiling chummily at her. "That the Ascendant not only abandoned the White Gate, but sent you of all people to spread his word?"

"I don't care what you believe, Manfred," said Iskra, her tone acidic with disdain. "But know this. Lutherius of the Cerulean Guard has been named the new Grace—"

"He had better watch his back around you," said Lord Seulfryd, not bothering to lift his chin from his palm.

"And I, as the empress of Agerastos, have pledged my armed forces to help him defeat the kragh."

A fourth lord gestured languidly to one of the servants, who sprang forward as if he had been pricked to refill the lord's goblet. "Oh, this is rich," said the man. His face was seamed and weathered by hard living, his clothing martial in cut, and he was the youngest lord present, barely in his forties, Asho guessed. He flashed a white smile at the others. "A comical interlude before we return to business."

Asho felt an ugly snarl of anger ripple through him. He stepped forward, and something about his expression drew eyes and stilled their smiles. Hand on the hilt of his sword, he glared at the youngest lord, but Iskra's hand on his shoulder stilled his words before he could throw them in the lord's face.

"Lord Elbel. You've gained your father's seat at long last."

The lord set his goblet down very deliberately. "Only by proxy. He leads our men in Abythos."

"Led," said Asho.

"Abythos is fallen," said Iskra, her voice pitched to carry. "All five thousand men are lost to us."

Several of the lords raised their voices in protest. Lord Seulfryd was the only one to remain quiet, smiling a private smile that needled Asho.

Iskra raised her hands. "It is fallen, and your querulous bleating will not change that fact. Tharok has captured Bythos and Aletheia. The White Gate is his. The Ascendant has moved to a safe location, a lost stonecloud with Portals to many different points of the Empire. I came to you tonight through one such Portal. With him are Theletos and Makaria, the last of the Virtues."

"The last...?" Manfred's arthritic hands twitched on the table before him. "Surely...?"

"Akinetos, Synesis, and Mixis were lost in Abythos. Henosis died in Bythos fighting Tharok. Ainos has not been heard of since that night. Now, the Empire is reeling, but it has not fallen, and if we can unite under Lutherius, it will not fall. We are changing strategies, my lords."

She placed one hand flat on the table and leaned forward, looking like a hungry she-wolf at the lot of them. Miraculously, they stayed silent, listening. "We are gathering our forces from across the Empire. Lutherius and his Cerulean Guard have already joined us. Many more are coming, and under our Grace's command, we will be launching a series of strikes against the kragh that will cause them to stumble, lose momentum, and then tear themselves apart like the wild animals they are."

"Come dawn," the prim lord – Lord Volkmar — said, blinking rapidly, "should we expect a torrent of kragh to come flooding through our Solar Portals?"

Iskra pushed back to standing straight. "It's possible."

"Possible?" Lord Manfred's complexion was darkening. "We have only the city guard and a few regiments left! Everything was sent to Abythos. How are we to defend ourselves?"

"You can't," Iskra said coldly. "There is nothing you can do if Tharok decides to take this city."

"Preposterous!" cried Lord Elbel, slamming his fist on the table.

"What sort of message is this?" growled a fifth lord that Asho recognized as Lord Herterech. He had the look of an old wolf to him, grizzled, with iron-colored hair falling to his shoulders, his left eye a milky white. He'd fought alongside Lord Kyferin numerous times when Asho had been but a squire. "You come telling us not to despair, then tell us we are helpless?"

"I'm returning to Castle Volkmar," said Lord Volkmar, his voice growing shrill. "And I shall take my guard with me."

"And I," said Manfred, rising to his towering height once more, though with difficulty. "I have bled my lands dry and have sacrificed my three sons and my standing army for the Ascendant. But I will not die here like some fool martyr."

"Agreed," said Elbel. "If my father is truly lost — and our men — then I won't be staying in Ennoia, either. I must prepare my lands and my remaining forces for the siege that is to come."

"Cowards," said Asho. He said it quietly, but the word cut through the room like an assassin's knife through silk. Everyone froze and stared at him. "Drinking and sweating and posturing for each other here in your little room. And now that you've learned the truth of the situation, you're going to turn tail and abandon two hundred thousand citizens to their fate."

"Iskra, muzzle your dog," said Manfred.

"You are supposed to be bloody Ennoians!" roared Asho, slamming the flat of his palm on the table. Goblets jumped. "The swords of the Empire! Fighters, one and all of you! That's the entire point behind your bloody existence, to fight! Nobody else can! Nobody else knows how! Because of Ascendancy's stupid system, everyone else is helpless before the kragh, and you – you're going to abandon them all, even your own people, and flee?"

"I won't be spoken to this way by a mere Bythian," said Volkmar, rising to his feet and tugging fretfully on his coat. "Good evening, my lords."

"Yes, I'm a damned Bythian," said Asho. "And during all of my miserable existence, I've heard that my pain, my privations, all the abuse I and mine have suffered was because that was our *station*. That we labored so that you Ennoians could fight when there was fighting to be done. And now that the greatest challenge of your lives is banging down your doors, now, when the very cause of your existence is being tested, you're going to flee?"

The lords hesitated, eyeing each other. They'd all risen to their feet except for Lord Seulfryd.

"If you abandon your posts, abandon your people, if you quit the field when the Ascendant needs you most," said Asho, "I'll laugh. Because you'll be proving I was right all along. That you Ennoians aren't special. You aren't charged by your religion to be the sword that defends the Empire. You're just a bunch of cowards who couldn't stay true to their calling when they were needed the most."

Lord Manfred was trembling with fury. "If I were twenty years younger, I would cut you in half, you Bythian maggot."

Asho smiled at him. "That wouldn't make you less of a coward."

"My father and two hundred of our best men died in Abythos," said Elbel. "You dare say we have not done our part?"

"My son—"

"My brother and five hundred of our—"

"My land has bled—"

Each lord sought to be heard, yelling over each other, their faces either pale or crimson with outrage.

Asho crossed his arms and shook his head. "That doesn't matter. It doesn't matter what you've lost. Whom you've lost. That's your fucking job. To fight. To die."

"Asho," said Iskra.

"No," said Asho. "I've had it with the whole Empire. With everyone from Theletos down to these cowards. They spout religious rhetoric when it suits them, and then cut and run when they're inconvenienced. Enough. Go on, then. Run to your castles. But if you go, admit one thing: that you're no better than anybody else in this Empire, from the Bythians on up."

"Ser Swydiger," said Lord Volkmar quietly. "Cut this slave down."

"No," said Lord Manfred. "That honor will fall to my house. Ser Thadeus, bring me his head."

One by one, the lord's attendant knights drew their blades and began to move around the table toward Asho.

"Enough of this madness!" cried Iskra. "Cease at once!"

Five knights. Each no doubt the best in their lord's household. These being the lords of the realm, that was no easy position to hold. Asho stepped to the wall so that they couldn't surround him. His left hand crept into the pouch at his belt where nuggets of gate stone rested.

"What would you have us do, then?" Lord Seulfryd still hadn't lifted his chin from the palm of his hand. He was still lounging over to one side, looking dissipated and bored.

The knights paused. The other lords glanced at him in confusion. Lord Seulfryd gazed only at Asho.

"Do?" Asho's mind raced. "Defend yourselves. Defend your city."

"Yes," said Lord Seulfryd, giving an airy wave of his other hand. "But how, precisely?"

This was it: the moment he'd goaded them toward. The lords, still furious, were watching him. Listening. Waiting to hear what he had to say. But how could they defeat Tharok, protect the city, and save its hundreds of thousands? How could they fight back with only the city guard and a few hundred knights?

It was impossible. Wasn't it?

An image came to Asho's mind: the monstrous war machines that stood guard outside the fortress' main doors. "How many ballista does the city have?"

Lord Seulfryd arched an eyebrow. "I haven't a clue. Why?"

"The kragh can only come at you through the Bythian and Aletheian Solar Portals," said Asho. "When we tried to stop them coming through into Aletheia, we didn't have time to prepare. We didn't know what we would be up against. Now, we do. Gather every ballista you have and place them at the edge of the Empire Square. Point them at the Aletheian and Bythian Portals. When the kragh start coming through, massacre them."

"You didn't try this in Aletheia?" asked Lord Manfred, sitting back down and rubbing at his left thigh.

"We didn't have time," said Asho. "The kragh came right after us. We could only pack the space in front of the Portals with soldiers and hope for the best. Instead of charging us, they had their trolls hurl rocks through the white fire. Nobody expected that. The rocks plowed through the ranks. People panicked, and someone led an attack through the Gate. It was then that Tharok struck."

"But this time we know what his strategy is," said Manfred, still rubbing at his thigh, digging his thumbs in.

"But I've heard he's some kind of military genius," said Seulfryd. "He'll not use the same strategy twice."

"True," said Asho. Then he sheathed his blade altogether and walked back to the table's edge. "But there is one reality he cannot avoid: the Portals are natural choke points. He must come through them. Cities like Nous or Sige, he can simply ignore till starvation lays them low, but Ennoia? Just like Zoe, we can outlast any siege. He has to come through the Gates, and the best he can do is send twenty kragh through at a time."

"A killing ground," said Lord Herterech.

"I do like the sound of that," said Lord Volkmar.

"Exactly," said Asho. "Which brings me back around to my first question. How many ballista do we have?"

"That, we can find out," said Manfred. "By the White Gate, we can. What else can we do?"

"Archers," said Lord Volkmar.

"Trenches," said Lord Herterech with a grin. "With spikes at the bottom."

"Walls," said the youngest lord. "A palisade that guides the kragh into a trapped enclosure."

Manfred pounded his fist against the ancient wooden table. "I like it!"

Asho met Iskra's eyes. She gave him the slightest of nods and a smile.

"Very good," he said. "Then, we'd best get to work."

Chapter 13

It was good to move. To quit their small hill and stretch their legs, to *do* something, even if it was just following a broad set of prints stamped into the plains of this land. Tiron led the way, settling into the old familiarity of a long march; he'd grown soft over the final years, expecting always to ride a horse not only in but to the battle, but for the first fifteen years, soldiering had meant marching. In a way, it was good to return to the basics.

Nok had been given back his massive hammer, in large part because nobody wanted to carry it for him, and he was walking in the center of the group, where everybody could keep an eye on him. Shaya was always at his side, and they often conversed in the kragh language. Tiron tried not to let that bother him.

Ramswold was bringing up the rear of the group with Isentrud, while Leuthold and Ulein had been sent up front a half-mile to be their scouts. Marcus and his scribes were walking just in front of the kragh, at first in high spirits, but increasingly focusing on just putting one foot before the other.

The land was beautiful. Pristine, with little sign of civilizing influences, the rolling meadowland broken by patches of forest that were wild and primary growth. Tiron saw dozens of places in which a village could have thrived, set right alongside clean, rushing streams and on level ground.

Tiron called for a break around midday. They followed a small stream to where it plunged into a pool, and there sat on the rocks while Isentrud kept lookout. Tiron felt good. The kinks in his hips and knees were mellowing out, a fine sweat covered his brow, and he felt like he could march forever.

Marcus and his scribes, however, sat heavily on the rocks. Olina immediately pulled off her boots and lowered her feet into the pool, letting out a sigh of relief as she closed her eyes. Garvis pulled his left boot off and began to morosely inspect a blister on his heel, while Marcus sat in the shade of a small, wizened tree that had grown between the boulders and simply closed his eyes, red-cheeked and looking faint.

"That was just five miles," said Tiron. "We've a fair way to go yet. Are you three going to be able to keep up?"

"Five miles?" Garvis winced as he flexed his foot. "Are you sure it wasn't ten? I'm joking. I know it wasn't ten. I'm just saying it felt like ten. Or twenty."

"I used to be able to swim all day," said Olina, not opening her eyes. "My best memories are of playing in the ocean around the towers of Nous, diving down, playing White Gate, Black Gate with my friends... but that was sixteen years ago." She winced and shifted her weight, plucked a pebble out from under her ample rear and flung it away. "I've spent every day since then seated at a desk."

Nok crouched at the waterfall and cupped his hands in the falling water. It swirled and frothed in his broad palms, and then he threw it in his face and ran his wet hands over his hair and across the back of his neck. He eyed the three scholars with his inscrutable gaze, then said something to Shaya, who laughed.

"What's so amusing?" asked Olina.

Shaya sat down and undid her braid, running her fingers through her long hair. She brought it to her nose, made a face, then tossed it back over her shoulder. "He was wondering if we could shoe the three of you like they do the hooves of mountain goats."

Garvis' eyes widened. "What? Like horseshoes? Into our feet?"

"He said it in jest. Don't worry." Shaya also cupped her hands in the waterfall and then drank deep. "He has a sense of humor, you know."

"Doesn't seem like it," said Olina.

"Marcus," said Tiron, and the old man opened one eye. "Why aren't these lands settled?" He didn't truly care, but the marshal's silence was worrying him.

"Why?" Marcus pulled free a handkerchief and extended it to Garvis, who passed it to Olina, who dipped it in the water and handed it back. Marcus placed the sodden rag over his face and spoke through it. "Because of the kragh, ser knight."

"But we've been allied for more centuries than I can count, Ogri notwithstanding." Tiron glanced up at Isentrud. She was gazing steadfastly northwest in the direction of the tracks. Her expression was neutral, so he looked back to the marshal. "So, why has nothing ever been tried? This land is just begging to be farmed."

"Yes, granted, we've had long periods of peace with the kragh. But the land is deceptive. A few settlements were assayed, but all were ultimately abandoned. There are dangers here that are not immediately apparent. People complained of horrific and recurring nightmares. Visitations by demons or foul spirits. When asked, the kragh explained that their ancestors who failed to ascend to their Sky Father — perhaps their version of the Ascendant? — had been doomed to haunt the land. That we humans didn't have the fortitude to resist their hauntings."

Ramswold smiled. "Superstitions."

"Not superstitions," said Shaya quietly.

"No?" Ramswold's smile became generous, almost patient. "That's as generous a term as I can allow for such heretical beliefs."

Shaya's smile was cutting. "And do you think Ascendancy truly encompasses everything that exists?"

"Of course. Surely, even Bythians have a basic understanding of the theological underpinnings of the world?"

"I'm sorry," said Shaya sweetly. "But those big words went right over my head. Maybe you can explain them to me right after you explain how Tharok was able to control wyverns and trolls with his mind?"

Ramswold flushed. "Easy. It's demonic."

"I should have guessed," said Shaya, rising to her feet and staring at him across the pool. "Everything beyond your comprehension will be blamed on the Black Gate. Even though, last time I checked, it was closed."

Ramswold stepped to the water's edge. "Your understanding of Ascension is as crude as your manner, my lady."

Tiron stood up, but Shaya gave him no time to interject. "I'm no lady, my *lord*. No need to pretend."

"All right," said Tiron. "That's enough. What's gotten into the two of you?"

Shaya and Ramswold were glaring at each other, and Shaya only turned away when Nok reached up and placed a hand on her shoulder.

"Well," Olina said archly to no one. "I thought we were talking about ghosts, but I've no idea what that was about."

"Nothing," said Tiron. "And it's time we started moving. On your feet, everyone. Fill your water skins if you have them, and let's go."

So saying, he hopped over the pool and climbed out of the small fold and back onto the path. The rest of the group emerged slowly, the marshal and his scribes last of all. Tiron stood pacing back and forth, and, once they were assembled, led them on.

He did his best to keep his concerns at bay. They were very low on food. They had only enough to keep them walking for perhaps another two or three days. The marshal was too old for such rugged activity. Should they cut him and his scribes loose? It made sense from a coldly logical point of view. Fewer mouths to feed, and they'd make faster time. But not only did he know Ramswold would never go for it, he also doubted he could. Once, perhaps, when he was a Black Wolf, he might have found a way not to dwell on the reality of what he was doing, but now? It would be tantamount to murder.

So, they marched, following the tracks of the hundred kragh as the sun wheeled slowly toward the horizon. The land remained blessedly pleasant, but even though the trail led mostly through rolling meadows, they still moved at an agonizingly slow pace.

It was late afternoon when Tiron heard a cry of panic from Olina. Turning, he saw that Marcus had fallen and lay half-buried amidst the knee-high grass. He jogged back, hand clasped to his pommel to keep his sword from banging against his knees, and knelt beside the old man.

"We're pushing him too hard," said Olina, holding Marcus's hand and leaning over him. The old man's eyes were closed, his face was mottled red and white, and his thin hair was slick with sweat.

"Marcus?" Tiron pressed his fingers to the side of the marshal's neck. The pulse was far too quick. "Damn it."

"What can we do?" asked Isentrud.

"We won't leave him, if that's what you're thinking," said Olina.

Ramswold joined them. "Is he awake?"

"No," said Marcus feebly. "He's not."

Garvis was biting his thumbnail anxiously. "Could we perhaps fashion a stretcher?"

"And carry him from here to the Ascendant knows where?" Tiron shook his head.

"What do you think?" asked Ramswold quietly.

Tiron sucked on his teeth as he examined the countryside around them. A large copse of trees stood footed in their own shadows just ahead. The field of grass and low bushes rose to their right to a low hill; there were no buildings, no obvious place for shelter.

"You're not going to abandon us, are you?" Garvis' voice nearly broke.

"I can walk," said Marcus, opening his eyes and struggling to rise. "Just needed to take a little nap. Nothing to get alarmed over."

"Shaya," said Tiron. "Ask Nok how far he thinks we might yet have to go."

She did so in a low voice. He rumbled his response.

"It's possible the Red River returns to the mountains, he says. If that's the case, we've got at least a week of hard marching ahead of us."

"And arriving late is as bad as not arriving at all," said Tiron.

He sat back on his heels. It was clear what he had to do, clear what the right course of action was – but he couldn't bring himself to say it. He thought of his vow to uphold justice, to do what was best for the people and no longer swear to serve mere lords and generals. It had seemed so simple a vow to uphold. But where was the justice here? Did he owe it to Marcus, or to the Red River clan, and perhaps even the Empire? Old instincts bade him cut the scholars loose. His new resolve, however, precluded that option. But what else was available to him?

Olina let out a second cry and fell back, spilling onto her rear as Nok stepped forward and reached down for Marcus. Ramswold's blade slipped free immediately, and Isentrud quickly followed suit.

But Nok did no violence to the old man. Instead, he lifted him easily into the air, turning him as one might a child, and sat Marcus athwart his shoulders. The old man's eyes were wide in shock, and he waved his arms as he desperately fought for balance. Nok placed his hands over the old man's knees and locked him in place. He regarded Ramswold and Isentrud's swords blandly, and them rumbled something to Shaya.

"He says this is how the kragh transport their youngest children." Shaya's voice was flinty. "Of course, he's willing to put Marcus down if you prefer to carry him yourselves."

"Ah," said Ramswold, sheathing his blade immediately. "I — ah — see. Most generous of him." Then he turned to Nok directly and gave him a stiff bow.

"Marcus?" Olina stepped up to Nok's side. "Are you all right?"

"All right? Delighted. The prospect of not taking another step is enchanting. I could sit up here all day and night." Marcus looked down at the back of Nok's head and then carefully placed his hands on his own hips. "Why didn't someone tell me before that this was an option?"

Tiron grinned. "Don't get too comfortable, old man. We've a long way to go yet." He caught Nok's eye and nodded his thanks. Nok dipped his chin in response.

From then on, they made good time. Tiron marched them late into the evening, and they made camp in the lee of a forest, not daring to light a fire and chewing instead on cold, salty strips of cured meat in silence. Ulein and Leuthold found them shortly after, startling Olina as they emerged from the shadows, much to Ulein's amusement. Both were breathing heavily, as if they had run hard.

"Things have become very interesting," said Leuthold, lowering himself into a crouch and accepting a strip of meat. "The six black-robed figures got very excited after they made camp. We watched them from higher up in the valley and saw them sit in a circle and start praying or something. The other kragh kept their distance, looking almost spooked. Hell, I was getting spooked myself, and I was almost a thousand yards away."

"Very good. I love the narrative," said Ramswold. "But, let's cut to the chase. What happened?"

"Magic, as far as we can tell. They prayed for a while, then green fire flowed into the space between them and formed a circle about three yards high, I'd guess. Like a hoop that had been stood on its side. Set my hairs on end."

"A green circle?" asked Tiron. "Shaya, does that mean anything to Nok?"

The mountain kragh shook his head when asked, and rumbled back to her.

"He says that the shamans we're following are unnatural, perverted by the medusa. He has never seen normal shamans cast such magic."

Tiron rose to his feet and began to pace. "What were the other kragh doing? You said they were making camp?"

"Well, no, actually," said Ulein. "It was strange. They weren't doing anything at all beyond waiting. None of the usual activities you'd expect to see."

Tiron stopped. "Great. How far away was this?"

"Half a mile," said Leuthold, glancing to Ulein as if to confirm the distance. "Just about."

"How much longer did you stay after they brought this green circle into existence?"

"Not much more after that. We thought we'd seen enough, and came back to report. The shamans left the circle standing and went to argue with the biggest of the kragh escorting them."

Ramswold was watching Tiron carefully. "What are you thinking?"

"That we must move out," said Tiron. "Get to their camp as quickly as possible. Think: the distance we have to cover is vast. A week to ten days. These shamans are in a hurry. What if they've opened up a magic portal of their own to cut their travel time?"

"If they have," said Olina, "then we're out of luck. We'll not know which way they went, or where the Red River is."

"Which is why we must hurry," said Tiron. "Up! On your feet. We're going to have to move fast."

"But why?" asked Ulein. "What do you hope to do?"

"I don't know," said Tiron. He wanted to swing his blade at something, cut down a tree, but he reined in his anger. If they lost their trail now, their little party was doomed. "But we won't accomplish anything sitting here in the dark. Fast march!"

Ulein and Leuthold led them on a mad scramble under the light of the moon. They skirted the woods, then climbed up the gentle hill, which dipped and then rose to a new peak. Down they went, Tharok holding Marcus against his chest, the others nearly jogging to keep up with Tiron's brutal pace. They traveled along the base of the hill, then onto a narrow goat track that wended its way along the shallow valleys till finally Leuthold placed his fingers to his lips and led them up a final slope.

When they were near the top, Tiron gestured for the others to stay back and crawled up alongside Leuthold and Ramswold to the peak. The valley below was dark, but the circle of fire was shocking visible, a coruscating ring whose size was impossible to tell at this remove.

"See any of the kragh?" asked Tiron, scanning the deep, velvety shadows.

"No," said Leuthold after a moment.

"Nor I," said Ramswold. "Do you think they went through?"

"One way to find out," said Tiron. "Call the others. I'm heading down."

Blade in hand, Tiron jogged through the darkness toward the green circle, the high grass whispering against his legs, his pulse pounding in his ears. Every looming shadow was a kragh rising to swing at him, and he had to fight to control his breath. Sweat ran down the back of his neck, and he felt the aches and weariness of the day evaporate as every sense came into high alert.

Blood. Burned flesh. He smelled it as soon as he reached the base of the valley. Tiron slowed, casting around warily, listening for the slightest hint of an approach. Other than his comrades descending after him, he heard nothing.

He walked forward, blade held upright before him in both hands. The oval of green flame was less than a yard high, and even as he watched it, he saw it shrinking, growing smaller, gradually but inexorably. Its center was swirling nothingness, a void in the night, a hole that betrayed nothing of what was on the other side.

He tripped over the corpse on the ground. It was that of a kragh, not as massive as Nok but still huge, and it was badly charred. Tiron grimaced as he knelt at its side and felt the grass. No burns there. The kragh had been immolated where he'd stood.

Ramswold knelt beside him. "I suppose he wasn't eager to go through the green flame."

"An example, for sure," said Tiron. He rose to his feet and looked back at the others. "They're gone. Through the Portal. I'm sure of it."

"What do we do?" asked Isentrud. "Follow them?"

"That — that could lead us right into their camp," said Garvis, taking a step back. "Surely, that isn't wise?"

Marcus stumbled as Nok set him down. "The Portal is shrinking. We don't have much time."

Nok said something to Shaya, who translated, "This magic is warped. We cannot trust it."

"We don't have a choice." Tiron stepped up to the Portal. It came up only as high as his waist. The fire flickered around its circumference, streaming as if before a high wind. It cast no light, however; Tiron held his palm close to the flame and saw a reflective green glow on his hand.

"We go through," he said. "And if we come out in their camp, we take them by surprise."

"Madness," said Ulein, making the sign of the Ascendant's triangle. "It could be a portal to hell, for all we know!"

"True," said Tiron. "But I'm not going to debate it. I'm going through. My lord?"

Ramswold was staring at the portal with wide, glazed eyes, but he nodded stiffly. "Yes. I'll follow."

Tiron looked to Shaya and Nok. "You two?"

Nok placed his massive hand on Shaya's shoulder and nodded.

"Very good." Tiron grimaced as the Portal sank another inch. "Nok, you go first, while it's big enough. Hurry!"

Nok needed no translation. He unslung his warhammer and moved forward, lowering himself to hands and knees in front of the oval. He muttered something in kragh, then crawled into the swirling void and was gone.

"I'll go next," said Ramswold.

Tiron wanted to argue, but there was no time. "Fine. Go."

Ramswold crouched down, then also got on all fours, sword in front of him and pressed to the grass. He whispered, "My soul to the White Gate," took a deep breath and hurried through.

"My lord!" cried Isentrud, and she went after him, barreling past Tiron even as he went to follow. With a curse, he stepped back, and she was gone as well.

The circle was still shrinking. Tiron tried to think of something to say, a quick prayer, but nothing came to mind except Iskra's face. He gritted his teeth and crawled into the swirling blackness, painfully aware of the green fire inching its way toward him.

It felt like plunging into ice water. The shock was tremendous, and even as he fell though nothingness, he opened his mouth to gasp. The frigid air froze his tongue, congealed the air in his throat. He felt the blackness press in all around his eyes, under his eyelids, felt his heart shake and stutter, and a pain lance through his chest. His sword gleamed like a brand of white fire in his hand, however, and he focused his attention on that flame, blocking out all else, bringing it close to his face till its searing light banished the darkness from his vision completely.

Then he was through. Tumbling out into the air, he landed heavily on his side on fist-sized rocks covered in rime. Instinct took over even as he scrambled to understand where he was; he rolled up to his feet, blade held before him, its white flame gone, and backed away, looking wildly about in the darkness for signs of danger.

They were in the mountains. Their high peaks reared up, blotting out the brilliant stars all around him. Nok and Ramswold were standing to one side, weapons drawn, but nothing was attacking them. There were no campfires, no signs of life anywhere close. A mountain pass, it looked like, as Tiron's eyes slowly adjusted to the gloom.

There was a curse, and Leuthold toppled through the circle of green flame to the ground. The circle on this side, Tiron saw, was about chest-high, suspended in midair. A moment later, Ulein came through, letting out a low wail as he pitched forward and hit the ground hard with his shoulder.

"Isentrud?" Tiron moved over to where Ramswold was standing. "Where is she?"

"What?" Ramswold placed a hand on Tiron's shoulder. "What are you talking about?"

"She came through before me. Where is she?"

Shaya came next, somehow tucking her head as she fell so that she hit the ground in a rough roll and came up stumbling to her feet.

"Isentrud!" hissed Ramswold, turning in a tight circle. "Where are you?"

Shaya moved up alongside Nok as Olina squeezed through and fell awkwardly with a cry to the rocks. Ulein was waiting, however, and caught her roughly, breaking her fall.

"Isentrud!" Ramswold began to walk in a circle around the fiery Portal, pitching his voice a little louder. "Answer me, damn it!"

"The Portal's closing!" said Olina, holding on to Ulein.

Tiron whipped around and saw she was right; it was losing size with increasing speed, as if the smaller it grew, the less able it was to maintain its shape.

They all stopped and stared. From two feet, it collapsed quickly to barely a foot wide. An arm suddenly emerged from its dark center — but there wasn't room for the rest. The Portal irised closed with a sizzling *pfft* and was gone.

The arm, severed, fell to the rocks.

Olina covered her mouth with both hands and choked back a scream.

Tiron stared, unable to move. Blood oozed from the arm, black against the moonlit rocks, but quickly ceased to flow.

Leuthold crouched down. "It's Garvis'."

"Marcus," said Olina. "Garvis!"

Tiron bared his teeth and turned slowly in a circle. Dark fir trees had grown thick on either side of the pass, rising up around them on the sharp slopes of the mountains, blotting out all detail. The trail extended roughly down and away behind them, and climbed steeply up ahead. A cold, cruel wind was blowing down its length, and Tiron saw ice glint in the moonlight higher up the mountain slopes.

"Isentrud!" Ramswold's voice was nearly a roar.

"Enough," said Tiron. He strode over to Ramswold and shook the man by the shoulder. "She's gone. Everyone, with me, into the trees. Move!"

Olina bent down and picked up Garvis' arm. Ulein guided her after Tiron, the others stumbling over the rough rocks as he led them under the branches into the cool, still air beneath their clustered canopy. It was almost completely dark, and he moved as quickly as he dared, nobbled tree trunks leaping out at him every few paces.

Olina was sobbing. Ramswold was breathing harshly, and everyone but Nok seemed stupefied or in shock. Tiron led them on, movement giving him time to think, till at last the ground began to rise so steeply before them that they would have had to scramble upwards on all fours if they were to continue.

"All right, gather round," said Tiron, his voice harsh even in his own ears.

The others formed a tight circle around him and then followed his lead and lowered themselves into crouches.

"We've lost Isentrud, Garvis, and Marcus. We'll grieve for them when we can, but for now, we're at risk of being murdered if we don't keep our wits about us. There's a hundred kragh out here with six twisted shamans. So, take your grief, stow it away and forget it."

Olina was staring down at the arm she was holding in both hands, shaking violently. Tiron reached out, took it by the sleeve, and set it on the ground behind him.

"How?" asked Ramswold. "You're sure you saw her follow me?"

"Focus. They're gone." Tiron let the words sink in. "I need you here. With me. Understood?"

Nok was a boulder to Tiron's left, a looming presence that he found himself drawing comfort from. If things got ugly, he knew Nok would be ready.

Ramswold took a deep, shuddering breath, then gave a jerky nod. "Yes. I'm here."

"It worked," said Tiron. "We're in the fucking mountains, wherever they are, and we've not lost their trail. Better yet, we didn't stumble into a camp and get slaughtered. The way we were running around like headless chickens there, we'd not have stood a chance. But think. Why was there no camp?"

It was Shaya who spoke first. "If they didn't camp, it's because they had to do something first."

"Right," said Tiron. "Those six shamans could probably fix their portal to arrive wherever they wanted, so they picked this spot for a reason. Why? Where do you think they went? What's the advantage of arriving somewhere at night?"

"Ambush," said Leuthold.

"Ambush," said Tiron. "They're going to hit the Red River tonight. Shaya, ask Nok: does he recognize this place?"

Nok nodded to her question and replied in kragh. Shaya translated. "Yes. It's called the Chasm Walk. He thinks we're close to an old medusa temple."

"How close?"

"Very close."

Nok suddenly stiffened, raising his head and inhaling sharply. Tiron sniffed as well. He could smell pungent pine sap, the cold, mineral tang of the mountains and snow, the sweat and heat of the bodies pressing in around him. Nothing more.

Nok rumbled to Shaya.

"Screams," she said, her voice dropping to a whisper. "He hears screams. The attack has begun."

Chapter 14

The closest Kethe could get to privacy was a small space enclosed by the tents belonging to the Consecrated. It was barely five yards by five, its edges made perilous by guy ropes and pitons that had been hammered into the black rock, but it suited her all the same. It was a space in which to dance with her blade. A space in which she could be free.

Even as she whirled and parried, slashed and stabbed, memories assailed her. She saw Akkara, bleak-eyed and gaunt on the training ground in Aletheia, wielding her overlarge sword with clumsy desperation. Saw Akkara hurling herself through the kragh during the siege of Abythos, her face blanching even as she leaped to Kethe's aid, detonating with a flash of white light that had saved Kethe's life and left Akkara a withered doll.

Kethe grimaced and dropped into a spinning crouch, her blade whispering through an opponent's shins, then rose, her blade trailing after and opening another opponent from crotch to gullet.

She saw Henosis leaning against the balustrade with her, arms linked, a smile on her generous lips as she welcomed Kethe to the ranks of the Virtues, the setting sun burnishing her hair. Saw her eyes open wide in shock as Tharok's black blade punched through her chest and lifted her off the ground, only for the kragh to grasp her arm and tear her free.

Kethe clenched her jaw and advanced with a series of sharp chops, the blade darting forward six inches each time before being pulled back, her feet stamping the black stone, twelve cuts delivered in quick succession.

The memories came fast and furious. The demon hovering just beyond the walls of Mythgraefen, the heat from its wings caressing Kethe's cheeks. Pulling her helm off after winning the tournament against Lord Laur's knights, victorious and terrified, and meeting her mother's eyes. Asho's hand slipping into her own. Meeting Tharok's gaze across the causeway in Bythos. The White Gate encompassing her, sublimating her very soul.

She was finding it hard to breathe. Her throat was tightening. There had been so much death. So much blood. How many lives had she taken? She couldn't guess. How many times had she nearly died?

She felt Iskra's arms around her once more, that last hug, and how she had desperately wanted to pull away, to block out the emotions, the pain, the weakness that embrace had summoned.

Kethe let out a cry and spun, swinging her blade around to decapitate an invisible foe — only to have it ring loudly and send a powerful shiver up her arms as it was stopped cold.

Theletos.

He'd stepped in somehow just as she'd spun and had parried her blow. It had felt like hitting a wall. Absolutely no give, even though he was holding his blade with just one hand.

Kethe fell back, panting for breath. "You shouldn't be up."

"There are miracle cures to be had for those who need them," he said. "I have that need. Though I regret to say our supply is running low."

"The black potions?"

He nodded. "I've taken more of them in the past two days than I have in years. We've only two left." He lowered his sword. "I'm not sure what we'll do when we run out."

Kethe licked her lower lip. "Where did they come from?"

"The Fujiwara clan," said Theletos softly.

"Your clan."

He inclined his head. "It was, yes. Now, I have none."

"What are they, these potions? No one ever told me."

Theletos stepped in closer, looking around them casually to make sure nobody was close. "They are the essence of the Black Gate, Makaria."

Her head snapped up. "What?"

"So it was explained to me. A pure distillation of the sin that comes through the Black Gate in Bythos. The Fujiwara perfected a means to condense the magic from the air around the Gate and then purify it so we can drink it and be healed."

"But — that doesn't make any sense. The Black Gate is pure evil."

"Perhaps. Another way to look at it is that the Black Gate represents all worldly ties. The weakness of the flesh, the appetites that bind us to the world of the living and prevent us from ascending. Which, for most, is a detriment. We, however, are too pure; our affinity for the White Gate thins us out, saps our vitality. We evaporate and die young. By drinking a draught of this worldliness, we are grounded, we are made flesh once more, able to persist long after we would have passed away."

Kethe frowned. "So, you're saying that a little evil balances us out, lets us stick around longer so that we can do more good."

"Precisely." Theletos gave a languorous shrug. "I didn't invent the system, but it works. There is even a sense of penance to it — we must stain our souls as a form of contrition if we are to refuse the call of the White Gate so as to serve the Ascendant."

Kethe nodded slowly. "There is so much I don't know."

"Yet, you are intuiting it all beautifully." He reached up and touched her cheek. "You gather the Consecrated and give them strength. You lead where others falter. You are consumed by doubt, yet still you fight on for what is right, what is good. You are exemplary, Makaria."

Kethe pulled her head back, her cheeks burning, and looked away. "Hardly exemplary. Lucky, maybe."

"Luck is but another name for the Ascendant's blessing."

"Then, why doesn't he snap his fingers and undo this invasion?" A spark of fierce anger leaped within her. "Why is he sitting in that tent and doing nothing?"

Theletos shrugged. "An old question. I asked it myself, once. The answer I was given was thus: the true scope of the Ascendant's divinity cannot be fitted into his mortal shell. We see but the tiniest fragment of his glory, and as such, that fragment, while divine, is not complete. Its fragmentary nature renders the mortal guise of the Ascendant limited and faulty; though he is incomparably greater than any true mortal, he is similarly incomparably less than his true spiritual self."

"Yes, I remember Father Simeon saying something like that back in Castle Kyferin." She rubbed the side of her jaw. "But, then, why is he here at all?"

Theletos' smile widened. "Because he loves us. He is willing to exist in a state of fragmentation so as to be a visible symbol of the journey to perfection that we all must walk. That is his sacrifice, and it should both humble and inspire us. If a god can sustain a state of imperfection, then who are we to complain about the rigors of our own journey to purity?"

Kethe nodded reluctantly. "I'd still like him to perform some miracles and cast the kragh out of Aletheia."

Theletos stepped back into a fighting stance, blade flicking up. "That would defeat the entire purpose of his being here. There must be doubt for faith to have meaning. Nobody is lauded for believing in a stone they can hold in their hand. But a being who can open their soul to the beauty of Ascendancy and risk all on the strength of faith alone? That is the truest miracle of all."

Kethe raised her own blade. "You missed your calling. You should have been born a Noussian and gone down to proselytize amongst the heretics."

"Hardly," said Theletos, and he tapped her blade with deceptive slowness. "I enjoy swordplay far too much. Defend yourself!"

Without warning, he came at her, and Kethe fell back, nearly tripping over her own feet, then whipped her blade up and parried left, ducking and spinning around a horizontal slash, grabbed her sword with both hands and desperately parried left, right, left — feint! Left again, three quick steps back, an impossible parry behind her, stabbing her sword down over her shoulder, then she spun away again and fell back into a crouch, her heart hammering like a frenzied horse kicking at its stall door.

Theletos grinned, and she hated and admired him all at once. Worse, she felt a deep and sudden ache within her, an urge to bite his flawless neck, to push him down on the ground and defeat him, pin him, and wipe that smile from his perfect lips.

"Not bad," he said. "You'd not have been able to block half those blows a week ago. You're growing quickly, Makaria."

The playfulness of the moment suddenly felt jarring. She saw again Akkara's twisted, withered corpse. Saw Sighart being knocked off the tower top in Abythos by the troll, sent careening down to his death. No, she wasn't ready to laugh just yet. Instead, she closed her eyes, bit her lower lip and searched within herself, like a swimmer striving to dive down to the bottom of a dark grotto.

There. A faint, pure note arose within her, and she felt a soft blossoming of light well up from within her depths. Her relief was palpable — whatever Tharok had done, he'd not destroyed the Gate.

Her breathing slowed. She opened her eyes and saw that her sword was aflame.

Theletos' gaze was pensive. He gave his sword a flick, and white fire raced up its length as well. Neither of them moved, but Kethe had never felt more alert, more in tune with another's body. She gazed through him, gently focusing on his shoulders, his hips.

She relaxed. She felt suspended in light.

For the longest time, they just stood there, neither of them moving, and then Kethe parried to the left a moment before Theletos' attack appeared, sword clanging off her own, white sparks flying. She spun around, not trying to track him with her eyes, and parried an attack she couldn't have seen coming again — and again.

She wasn't reacting to him. Instead, it felt as if something was guiding her, as if there was a better place for her sword arm to be, and she need only move her body to align with that improvement, swiftly, fluidly, and her sword would block his own.

Theletos laughed and stepped back. "Yes."

Kethe's smile was tentative as awareness of her own actions infiltrated her mind.

"Now," he said. "Tell me why Asho is so angry with you."

Kethe blinked, panic and anger and confusion coursing through her calm, and suddenly a blow to her stomach lifted her to her tiptoes before she collapsed to the ground, unable to breathe.

The fire along her blade winked out. She tried to inhale and couldn't, and simply lay on her side, gaping and wheezing.

Theletos knelt beside her and rubbed her back. "There you go. Easy. Easy. You'll be better in a moment."

Suddenly, her throat unlocked and she inhaled a gasping, shuddering breath, and with it came anger, a furious resentment that caused her to push away from him and climb shakily back to her feet, snatching up her blade.

Theletos watched her from his crouch, eyebrows raised.

"That," she gasped, "was uncalled for."

"Oh? It worked, didn't it? Perhaps there's a lesson in there somewhere. Take a moment. Think about it."

Kethe willed the fire to return to her blade, but it stubbornly refused. "Come on. Up."

"Why are you so upset? You've surely taken blows while sparring before?"

"You know why. Up."

Theletos rose to his feet but didn't lift his sword. "That attack went deeper than I had expected. Asho – do you still have feelings for him?"

"None of your damn business," said Kethe. She felt bile in the back of her throat. How hard had he hit her?

"He must love Kethe, who is dead. You must be trying to understand your own emotions for him through the prism that is Makaria. And it must be confusing."

Kethe felt her cheeks begin to burn. She wanted to throw herself at him or run off between the tents. Instead, she fought for calm. Sought the White Gate.

"If you've spoken with him about this, I doubt it went well. Is that why he's so upset? Or have you avoided speaking about it altogether? Ah, I see. The cold shoulder. Pushing him away, since you don't know what to say. You'll find that to be the worst tactic in the long run."

"What do you know about it, Theletos?" She was shocked to feel tears come to her eyes. "Damn you and your toying with me!"

"What do I know?" He stepped up to her till the tip of her sword was pressed against his chest. "More than you might guess. You think me inhuman? Incapable of love, of lust? Oh, I am more than capable. I have had my heart broken, and have broken hearts in turn. Once, my bereavement nearly killed me. Rendered me unfit for battle. The closest I have ever come to losing a fight. And I see it in you, Makaria. That same weakness. A brittle spot where a careful blow will make you snap."

Kethe didn't know what to say. She felt all of twelve years old again, wide-eyed, mesmerized by the power in his eyes.

"The Empire, the Ascendant, and all its hundreds of thousands of souls depend on your strength, Makaria. Do not disappoint them. Do not fail them. Deal with this weakness. Cut it out of yourself before it causes the deaths of those who love and trust you. When you are ready, come to Lutherius' tent. We are planning our first strike."

He turned and walked away.

Kethe was left shaking, sword still held upright, staring unseeing at the spot where Theletos had stood. Cut it out? What did that mean?

Then she saw Asho's face, its bewitching mixture of handsome strength and pained vulnerability, and she thought of the gentleness hidden beneath the wounds and emotional scars. She remembered how they had stood together on the wall of Mythgraefen, hand in hand, and waited for the end of the world.

She looked down at her blade. The White Gate was real. The Ascendant was but a stone's throw away. She was a Virtue. The Empire was on the verge of being destroyed. The lives of countless innocents lay in the balance. How could she even be deliberating this issue?

Kethe wiped her arm across her eyes. Her time with Asho had belonged to a previous life. Those emotions — they had belonged to another person.

Kethe straightened her back and sheathed her blade. She was a different person now. She had obligations and duties that far exceeded her own importance. She wasn't Kethe, not any more. She couldn't afford to be. What the world needed now was Makaria.

How could she feel such serenity and pain all at once? Tears continued to run down her cheeks even as she inhaled deeply and felt something fall away from her soul. A chapter in her life was over. She heard the clamor of the thousands camped all around her and absorbed the sound, internalized their need, their pain, their confusion and fear, and thought: *This is what I must focus on. This is my calling. These people need me, and I shall not hold back.*

Kethe turned and walked toward the command tent that Lutherius had had erected beside the Ascendant's. It was half the size, and flew both the Grace's banner and that of the Cerulean Guard. Kethe smiled wryly. It seemed she wasn't the only one who was struggling to give up a previous identity.

The four guards at the entrance were clearly of Lutherius' old cohort; each of them was wearing a white wolf pelt over his back like a short cloak, the claws fastened over his chest. Their uniforms were a combination of the deepest sky blue and white, and they had blades strapped at their belts on one side and murder axes on the other. Small bucklers were slung over their shoulders, and each was holding a massive spear, taller than any of them, with a foot-long leaf blade and a broad cross guard at its base to prevent it from sinking in too deep.

The man on the left was built like a donjon tower, nearly as broad as he was tall, and he sported a long, pale gold beard that was shot through with small braids. He caught Kethe looking at his spear and grinned, showing broad, even white teeth that might have looked more at home in the mouth of a horse.

"They're beauties, all right." He took the spear with both hands and planted its butt against the ground, angling it forward at forty-five degrees. "Designed to stop a charging *kvathka*. The haft is made of ash so it's supple. Anything rigid would snap into splinters. The cross guard here—" He tapped the horizontal bars. "Stop the damn things cold. The goal is to keep 'em at bay, hold 'em back while your archers shoot for their eyes. We get all close together, five of us forming a fist — two kneeling, three standing behind — and let the damn thing run into our *kvathka* spears." He paused as if considering the situation. "Usually stops 'em cold."

Kethe studied the foot-long spear head. It was wicked. Its edges were serrated and broader than her palm. "A... *kvathka* can survive being stabbed with five of these?"

The guard laughed as if she'd told the world's best joke. He grinned over to his friend, who was smiling despite himself. "Survive? Often, you can't tell if they're even feeling 'em. Anyway. How can we help you, my lady?"

"I'm Virtue Makaria. I've come to speak with his Grace."

"Virtue...?" The Cerulean guard gaped, then snapped to attention. "My pardon, Virtue. For the, ah, conviviality. Please go on through."

Kethe hid her smile, nodded gravely, and ducked into the tent.

Several men were clustered around a central table that dominated the interior, its surface lit by five lanterns hanging from the overarching support poles. A pallet and small chest had been set to one side, but otherwise there were no furnishings.

Lutherius stood staring down at what proved to be a large map of the Empire, small models placed here and there across its length. Theletos was standing at his side, arms crossed. The others were clearly commanders and soldiers of various kinds — two looked Agerastian, another one seemed to be a member of the Cerulean Guard, while the remaining three looked to be Ennoian.

"Virtue," said Lutherius. "Welcome, and thank you for coming. We were discussing our need for intelligence on the movement of the kragh. Come dawn, the Solar Portals are going to open, and we're going to need to know where Tharok is planning to strike next. Nous? Sige? Zoe? Ennoia? All at once?"

Kethe stepped up to the table's edge, two of the men making room for her, and gazed down at the map. It showed the Empire as a series of islands, each connected by their Portals, with kragh forces placed in Bythos and Aletheia, and their own located primarily on the isolated representation of Starkadr, as well as moving toward Zoe and stationed in Sige.

"Representatives have been sent by Lunar Portal to each city to alert them to our continued resistance," continued Lutherius. "But we're going to need to establish active networks of communication. We're limited by the number of Vothaks at our disposal who can operate the Portals, but we have sufficient to maintain contact with the four cities that are yet unconquered."

Kethe nodded, arms crossed over her chest. "How can I be of assistance?"

"We need people to wait within each city so that when and if the kragh make an appearance, they can judge the situation, evaluate whether a strike is possible, and then send for an exact number of reinforcements so that we can affect a demoralizing blow. We're not looking to defeat the occupying presence, but rather shock it; hit hard and fade away. Leave them confused and angry. Then do it again, and again, and again, till their paranoia and rage make them impossible to control."

Theletos stepped in smoothly. "At that point, Tharok will be off-balance. His defenses will be down. His army of kragh will be slipping from his control. That's when we send a strike team to kill him."

Kethe nodded. "I see. And you want me to lead one of these evaluating teams?"

Lutherius nodded. "Yes."

"You'll take four Consecrated with you," said Theletos. "You'll position yourselves close to the Solar Gates and watch for signs of invasion. Remain out of sight and watch their deployment. Once you've determined the extent of their activity, report back with suggestions for a counter-attack."

Kethe nodded. "Which city do you want me to go to?"

"Nous," said Lutherius. "It's the smallest, and thus in the most danger. You need to make sure that you can escape, always. Don't get trapped. This isn't the time for heroics. Not yet, at any rate."

"And if I see Noussians being slaughtered?"

"Hold firm," said Lutherius, his voice hard. "People are going to die. We can't save them. What we can try to do is save the Empire."

Kethe inhaled deeply and nodded. "I — very well."

Theletos' gaze bored into her. "Khoussan and Dalitha will of course go with you. Pick your other two Consecrated, and then report back here. Your Vothak will be waiting to send you through. We have only a couple of hours till dawn. You need to be in position before the Gates open."

"Yes." Kethe took a step back and then gave a half-bow. "As you command, my Grace." That said, she turned and strode from the tent.

Could she watch innocents be massacred? Mind spinning, she realized that despite her assurances, she didn't know.

Chapter 15

————— ⟨◦◗◉◖◦⟩ —————

"Come," said Zephyr, pushing open Audsley's door and startling him from his bed. "We might as well get the most unpleasant of our new associates over and done with, and I shan't even pretend to have breakfast till we're done with her."

Audsley had fallen asleep fully clothed, his elegant Aletheian robes now so terribly wrinkled and dirty that he'd never recover from being seen in public in such a state of dishabille. But this wasn't Aletheia, and Zephyr clearly couldn't care less, either about his privacy or his appearance, so he stood and made his way to his wash basin.

"Whom are we calling on, then?" He splashed his face and snorted to keep the water out of his nose.

"She goes by the name of Aunt Mayze to some, Aunt Mayzie to those she's fond of, and Auntie to those she'd smother in her ample bosom." Zephyr made a face. "I have had to call her Auntie since I was little. She's Grandfather's eldest sister, a veritable dragon, but her bark is far worse than her bite. Come on. My skin is crawling at the thought of what we're about to do. Let's hurry."

Audsley toweled himself dry and followed Zephyr into the narrow hall. What could make Zephyr this uneasy? He didn't have a chance to ask. Up they went, ascending one set of steps after another till

Audsley was quite out of breath. Then, not knowing why he had been holding back, he simply willed himself to fly.

His feet left the ground.

Zephyr glanced back, let out a bright cry of laughter, and did the same. "This is considered quite inappropriate, you know," she said over her shoulder as she led him floating up the tunnels. "It's seen as a slight to all my poor cousins who can't pull it off. But no matter. Let them chew on the hems of their threadbare cloaks!"

Moving swiftly now, they soon reached an unusually broad tunnel, and there Zephyr alighted. Audsley did the same and watched with a mixture of amusement and trepidation as she took a deep breath, then marched forward into the hall, down to its very end, and there knocked on a grand if dilapidated door.

It opened a moment later, and a wizened crow of a man peered out at Zephyr, his back massively hunched so that he seemed locked into a permanent bow.

"Ah, it's the mistress. Auntie will be so pleased. Do come in, please, this way, come, yes, do come." He backed away, fawning and making falling motions with his hands, simpering and smiling and showing far too many yellow teeth.

Audsley followed Zephyr into a wall of musky perfume, a close, warm atmosphere that smelled of talc, old sweat, honey and cinnamon. The room beyond was large and boasted a window considerably bigger than Audsley's, though thick curtains had been pulled shut over it. Thick carpets lay underfoot, layered over each other so that each step was as springy as if he were walking on a field of moss, and everywhere he saw lacquered wooden furniture gleaming in the light of countless small lanterns with colored glass sides.

Firecats were perched on the backs of chairs, settees, in corners and near a dead fireplace; for a moment, Audsley's heart leaped, and he thought of a name he'd not dared speak to himself in far too long — *Aedelbert* — and then he realized that none of the firecats were moving. They were all stiff, frozen in lifelike poses, but dead and stuffed and with eyes of glass.

"Who is it, Osebius?" The voice was querulous, high-pitched and ready to take affront, but the woman who strode into the room was the opposite of what Audsley might have imagined; she was the size of a blacksmith, a solid rectangle clothed in deep patterned fuchsia and with a shock of white hair that floated about her head like smoke. Her face was just as pale, but this was paint, Audsley saw, a white coating that was thickly lathered on from the edge of her scalp down her throat so that not a hint of actual skin showed. Deep crevices were cut into her ruinous face. Her eyes were small and almost lost at the bottom of a well of wrinkles; her powerful nose and chin dominated all her other features. Her cheeks were rouged crudely in pink, and gold glittered on her ears. Yet, for all the frightful ridiculousness of her appearance, her gaze was steady and fraught and perilous.

This, Audsley thought, was not a woman to be trifled with.

"Auntie," said Zephyr, skipping forward as the old woman clapped her hands and leaned forward to receive an air kiss on each cheek. "I just had to come see you and introduce my new friend. You will absolutely love him. He insulted the Minister of the Moon so deeply that he was forced into a poetry duel, and he has three demons squirreled away within his skull! Let me introduce Magister Audsley."

Audsley bowed low, trying for a combination of gravity and elegance.

Auntie held Zephyr's hand in her own and studied Audsley with such blank coldness that his smile, despite being forced, died on his lips. Then she sniffed and gave the slightest of nods. "Insulted Beruleus, did he? Well, he can't be all bad, then. Now, it's been too long since you've visited. Tea? I heard that our estate in Aletheia has been burned and lost, and the Empire is falling to kragh. Osebius! Get the buttered toast out, and — let's see, it was black currant jam you liked, was it not?"

They all presently sat down in a small circle, Auntie lowering herself ponderously into a chair that groaned piteously beneath her bulk. Zephyr and Auntie exchanged gossipy small talk that would have convinced Audsley that they were truly the best of friends, but when the toast and tea and other delights were served and Osebius had withdrawn into the shadows, Zephyr set her cup down, placed both hands on her lap and fixed Auntie with a mock-stern gaze.

"Now, Auntie dearest, I've come to ask you for a favor."

"Oh, anything, my little dove. You know you have but to ask." Auntie's smile didn't come close to thawing the look in her eyes, that same blank, null gaze with which Audsley imagined she could gaze upon anything — no matter how hideous — and not blink.

"I'm going to be visiting Grandfather this afternoon to lead him into an ambush and kill him. I want you there to help set him ablaze." Zephyr gave the old woman her most winning smile.

Auntie ground to a halt. She didn't simply freeze, but rather slowed until she was completely immobile, teacup held in one great gloved hand, smile locked on her battle-ax face, her whole frame still.

Audsley squirmed.

"Excuse me, my dove?"

"Yes, your younger brother. I want to have him killed, and so I've come to you, Auntie dearest, for help. We've got it all worked out, Audsley and I. We just need to ensure he's bathed in enough flame that he has no chance of surviving. So, will you come?"

Auntie set her cup down. Audsley felt the hairs on the back of his neck rise. He wanted to stand, prepare for battle.

Hold still, said his demon. **Don't draw attention to yourself**.

"And why would I do such a thing?" The light twitter had gone from Auntie's voice. Now it was a dolorous sound, as desolate as a wind gusting up from the dark heart of a ruined castle.

"Because, Auntie, I know about your little indiscretion." Zephyr's tone became almost chiding. "I was *quite* shocked to learn about it. Arranging to have a self-possessed demon placed inside Janastha? Is it any wonder she turned out the way she did? So wicked of you! Oh, think of how your daughter will react when she learns the reason behind Janastha's suicide. Heartbreaking."

"You cannot prove it," said Auntie in the same leaden tone.

"Oh, but I can. I, shall I say, *seduced* Icanth into writing it all down and sealing it. There's a lot of lurid detail there about how you induced *him* to commit such a crime. I blushed to read it! But, no matter. Now, if you don't want that letter delivered to your daughter, and duplicates sent to a few other choice family members, I suggest you agree to help me in my little venture. After all, how different is it to murder your younger brother than to arrange for your granddaughter's inevitable death?"

"You mincing cunt," said Auntie with no inflection.

"Yes, I know. We'll send word, won't we, Audsley, when the time is right? You'll have to go through a portal to a select location, and when the time is right, well, you'll know what to do. Won't you?" Zephyr bounced to her feet and kissed Auntie's craggy cheek. "Now, we're on to our next house call. Audsley? Have you finished your tea?"

Audsley blinked as Auntie's head swiveled so she could regard him. Averting his eyes, he climbed to his feet and nodded. "Ah, yes. Quite finished. Thank you for the, ah, repast, which was most salubrious, and the company, the, ah — yes. Quite."

Zephyr smiled winsomely at him, then led him to the door and let them both out. Auntie didn't move. She simply watched them go.

As soon as the door had closed, Zephyr's shoulders sank, and she leaned against Audsley. "Augh. I hate visiting Auntie. That make-up! That fake voice! At least she doesn't pinch my cheeks anymore. Horrible, isn't she?"

"Ghastly," said Audsley absently. "Did she really...?"

"Oh, yes," said Zephyr, standing straight once more. "Janastha was just four when it happened. She killed herself five years later, and, let me tell you, the entire stonecloud breathed a sigh of relief. She would have proven a formidable rival with a proper demon inside her, but with a self-possessed one? She was a terror. Nasty." She shuddered. "The things she did. Ugh."

Audsley trailed after her, mutely grateful for the emotional insulation the demons provided him. He simply didn't know how to comprehend what he'd just heard, what it said about the woman he was helping. It was so beyond the pale of what he'd understood people could do to each other that it didn't make sense. But, as he watched Zephyr walk to the end of Auntie's corridor and rise off the ground, he forced himself to think: *She knew and didn't tell anybody just so that she could use it to her advantage. The suffering, the pain caused by Auntie's action — all of it was a tool.*

Yet he felt... nothing. His horror faded, and in its place came a cynical thought: *What care I for what these monsters do to each other? They no doubt deserve it.*

"Now, our next ally is a quite different matter. Eulos." Zephyr turned onto her back, hands laced behind her head, and gazed up at the roof of the tunnel as she floated alongside him. "I used to dream of marrying Eulos when I was little. Handsome, dangerous, powerful, independent, mysterious... everything a little girl could want. Too bad he proved to be a fool. Still, it's of no matter. All to our gain."

Down they went, descending from the internal heights of Haugabrjótr through the clustered tunnels to the mouth of one that was different in nature from the others: it was smoothly carved out from the rock, its walls looking as slick as melted butter, but they proved cold and hard to the touch.

Zephyr noticed Audsley's interest in the walls. "He did it himself, Eulos did, when he recused himself from polite society. Demon fire. It's a testament to his power that he could melt rock so cleanly. It goes in quite a ways, too. Come on."

They floated down the tunnel and into the dark. Audsley blinked, and the demons afforded him night vision so that Zephyr appeared before him ghostly and thin, and the tunnel was a blank grayness around him. On it went, wending to and fro, until it ended at a plain door.

"Now, Eulos is not the chatty kind, so this will probably be a quick visit."

"Zephyr, why are you bringing me on these visits? It seems I'm in no way needed."

"No way needed?" Zephyr placed her hand against her cheek in mock dismay. "Don't disparage yourself, Audsley! I need you by my side. My brave champion, my tower of strength, my sole boon companion—"

"Zephyr," Audsley said warningly.

"Fine. We're a team, you and I, and this mission implicates us both. Your showing your face here means that you can't backstab me and get away with it — Auntie, Eulos, and the Doctor of the Almanac will seek out your immediate destruction if I should die. Insurance! What can I say. Now, ready?" And she rapped her knuckles on the door.

Audsley stared at the back of her head. Never before had he met someone for whom his feelings oscillated so rapidly.

Nothing happened, so she knocked again. Finally, they heard footsteps, and the door was wrenched open.

The man who greeted them was leonine. His brow was lowered, pinched at the bridge of his nose, and his mouth was drawn into a displeased slit, but Audsley could see how a young girl would find him dashing, even handsome. Thick hair fell to his shoulders, and his body was that of a warrior. Audsley could make out ridges of muscle where his white shirt was open down to his chest, and couldn't help but notice how his leather coat was tight across his broad shoulders. His eyes were piercing despite being in shadow, and they narrowed at the sight of his guests.

"What do you want?" he rasped.

"Eulos! No witty banter? Shall we dispense with that? All right. I'm here to blackmail you. Do you want me to do it in your doorway or inside?"

Eulos slammed the door shut.

Zephyr sighed and half-turned to Audsley as she rolled her eyes. "Always with the melodrama." She raised her hand, and flames roared from her palm, roiling in tight, incandescent curls of orange and crimson to blast the door open.

Audsley cried out, throwing his arms over his face and stumbling back from the intense heat. The door shattered inwards, and Zephyr strode through its burning ruins.

"Eulos! Knock-knock!"

Audsley raised his hands, ready to unleash his own flames if necessary. Beyond the burning planks, he could see Zephyr facing their displeased host, who had both fists raised as if he intended to fight her — except that both fists were wreathed in black flame.

"I've not had a good fight in years," he growled. "And now you've provided me with the perfect excuse to kill you."

"Except that if you kill me, you'll never learn where Demarthis' body lies."

Eulos froze. "You don't know. You're lying."

"Oh, I'm not lying. I know exactly where it's hidden. I hid it there myself. Of course, she'll be looking quite different at this stage, what with all the years that have gone by, but that's what happens to the dead."

Eulos leaped forward and seized Zephyr by the throat. He lifted her to the tips of her toes, his face but an inch from hers. "You're lying."

"Not lying," said Zephyr, her voice grown tight yet still unconcerned. "I noticed how stupid you were about her and thought, *Ah, that will be useful one day.* So, yes. It was me. I'm the one who hid her corpse. And, if you help me, I'll tell you where it is."

"Never," said Eulos, releasing her. "Whatever you have planned, I want no part in it."

"Think about this," said Zephyr, massaging her neck. "If you help me, not only will you gain her body back, but you'll be able to escape in the chaos and bury her where you will. That little cottage you shared with her in Sige during that one romantic summer – remember? Maybe you can bury her there. I'm sure there's a precious spot where you both made love that would be suitable."

Eulos' shoulders hunched with anger, and black fire began to burn from his eyes.

"Zephyr?" whispered Audsley. "Easy. Easy, there."

"Look," said Zephyr. "It's simple. I'm going to kill Grandfather. With him gone, you'll be free to slip away. So, it actually will even help you to help me. Freedom! You never need see me again. Take Demarthis, bury her, make your peace, and do what you want for the rest of your life. Yes, it's distasteful to work with me, but what of it? One last job, and you're free forever."

Eulos didn't answer. Instead, he stood there breathing heavily, the black fire wreathing his brows where it licked out of his eyes.

"This is Magister Audsley, by the way. This is all his idea."

Audsley stood up straight as Eulos turned to consider him. "I — what? I mean, yes, I'm trying to help, but — this? No. Of course not. Never even heard of you before."

"Shut up, Audsley," said Zephyr. "Now, will you help? If you don't, I'll have a piece of her body delivered to you each year till she's all yours, a rotted mound that will take the rest of your life to accumulate."

Eulos pressed the bases of his palms against his eyes, breathed deeply once, twice, three times, then lowered his arms. The flames were gone, but there was a hatred burning in his eyes that was infinitely worse. "How can I trust you?"

"Here," said Zephyr. "I thought there might be some trust issues." She dug into a pouch at her hip and fished out a ring which she tossed to him.

He caught it in one hand without taking his eyes from her, then turned it around in his palm and froze.

"Yes, her ring. I'm glad you recognize it. Proof enough? Be thankful I cleaned her off it. Now, we're going to lure Grandfather into an ambush on a stonecloud called Starkadr. Yes! I know. We've actually found it." She beamed at him. "When he enters the chamber where you and two others will be waiting, we'll all set him on fire and burn him to a crisp. Simple enough, correct?"

Eulos didn't answer. Tears were brimming in his eyes.

"Good, very good," said Zephyr. "We'll send word when we're ready. Until then."

She turned and hurried away over the smoldering planks. Audsley followed her, and he almost looked back at the sound of stifled sobs that came from the dark room. Zephyr, who seemed not to have noticed the sound, lifted into the air and flew quickly away, faster and faster, till at last she slowed and set down just before entering the main warren.

"Stupid, pathetic man," said Zephyr, looking back the way they had come. "What a waste! What a terrible waste. Urgh."

"Zephyr," said Audsley. "Were you telling the truth? You have the body of his beloved?"

"What?" Zephyr looked at him blankly. "Oh, no. I don't. Only that ring. I stole it from her corpse on the second day she was pinned up." She bit the nail of her thumb. "He'll be upset when he finds out, of course. You'll have to watch for the right moment once Grandfather is dead and kill him."

"Me?" Audsley clamped his hand over his mouth, shocked at how loud his protest had been. "Me? Never."

"Of course, you," said Zephyr. "He'll be watching me the whole time. Now, that's two done. Time to speak to our third and final ally."

Audsley followed. The result was unquestionably good; killing the Minister of Perfection would be a huge boon to the Ascendant and the Empire, removing a terrible foe and source of evil from the world. But how far was he willing to go to effect this assassination? Could he kill this Eulos?

He tried to imagine a scale. He placed the Minister of Perfection on one golden saucer and imagined it dropping immediately to the table. On the opposite side, he added Little Zephyr's freedom. The minister rose. He added Eulos' death, and the minister rose again. Revealing Starkadr's existence to Zephyr and her accomplices – the scales were now balanced.

Could he pull out now? Find an exit to the surface of this stonecloud and fly away? Perhaps. But, then, what would he have accomplished? All his investigations and sacrifices, his struggle to reach this very position, would all be for naught.

It reminded him of the time he had offered up his poem to young Birch Leaf, an aspiring but doomed poet who, at the last, while awaiting death, could not pen an elegy to his own passing. So, Audsley had written a glorious poem, perhaps his best, and then paused, moments from handing it to the young poet in his cell. Could he sacrifice his greatest work of art, have it ascribed for eternity to Birch Leaf, and never receive the accolades that were rightly his?

Audsley stopped, confused. Who, by the Black Gate, was Birch Leaf? He'd never — that wasn't his memory, yet it had been so real. The vision of the dismal corridor that had led to the cell, the plangent playing of a *kot* coming through the narrow windows, his own burning sense of shame as he'd palmed the poem and chosen not to share it...

He was too frightened to question his demon. Was he losing his mind? Were they merging somehow? Was he even now only Audsley, or had he already changed? Chilled, he hurried after Zephyr, his thoughts dashed, his mind scrambling for self-control.

They walked into the heart of the stonecloud, to a series of interconnected halls that intersected each other like dropped playing sticks. From any one point, Audsley could see into three or four halls around him, and everywhere there was chaos: servants and courtiers from Aletheia rushing to and fro, carrying papers and chests, organizing desks, or even sitting numbly as they stared out at nothing, hands sunken into their hair.

"Poor things," said Zephyr over her shoulder as they walked amongst them. "They've not yet come to grips with the loss of their importance to the Fujiwara. Ah, well."

They proceeded to a corner of the third or possibly fourth hall, where several chests were piled atop each other, and perhaps a hundred scroll cases covered a broad desk and lay on the floor. An elegant man was standing behind the desk, perhaps in his early fifties, his hair the color of iron and pulled back into a tight ponytail, his robes refined to the point of severity, jewels gleaming in his cuffs. His face was long, and his brow was creased as if he was perplexed by some crucial problem.

"Doctor of the Almanac," said Zephyr, stopping before his desk and curtseying gracefully. "Is this an opportune moment to interrupt your scowling?"

"Wonderful," said the doctor, focusing on the young girl, his lips thinning. "Precisely what I need right now. A visit from you."

"Let me introduce Magister Audsley. He—"

"Yes, I am familiar with your friend. I was in the audience that witnessed his humiliation at the Minister of the Moon's estate." The doctor's eyes were sky gray and just as warm. "I will skip the civilities, Magister, as your presence in no way induces me to feel civil."

Audsley could only manage a pained smile. He had nothing to say.

"The doctor," Zephyr said to him, "was once a most important man. He advised the ministers on all matters pertaining to astrology and how the alignment of the stars predicted the outcome of this or that possible action. A *very* esoteric pursuit, and one which held much sway over the credulous, the ignorant, and the superstitious. Tell me, Doctor, how lucky you must feel to have access to the stars' truths! You must have been the only Fujiwara to have foreseen the coming of this tragedy."

The doctor's jaw clenched. He lifted a slender scroll and tapped it against his other palm. "As much as you seem to be enjoying yourself, Zephyr, I know you are not one to merely gloat. What is it? How can this most humble of doctors be of assistance to such a divine creature as yourself?"

"Sarcasm doesn't suit you, Doctor." Zephyr hopped up and sat on the edge of his desk, scattering several scrolls to the floor. Audsley winced in sympathy as the doctor watched them clatter and roll on the ground. "I have need of your services. Not your star gazing, of course; what a dreadful waste of time. Rather, I need your help in a most delicate matter."

Audsley edged closer to Zephyr, glancing around them nervously. They were sufficiently removed in their corner that nobody seemed to be eavesdropping, but he couldn't be sure.

"I would never help you willingly," said the doctor. "So, I assume you are going to leverage my peccadillo to your advantage."

"Mmm-hmm." Zephyr picked up an ivory scroll tube and examined its beautiful artistry. "Precisely. Though it was rather more than a mere peccadillo, was it not?"

The doctor didn't respond. He continued to tap his palm with the scroll, staring at her.

"You're going to help me assassinate my grandfather. I have already enlisted the aid of Aunt Maize and Eulos. The five of us will ambush him and incinerate him before he can react. All you need do is be present and put the flames of your *kal'shan* to greatest effect."

Audsley watched the doctor carefully. An outburst here would surely draw attention. Shouldn't they have drawn the man aside?

The doctor set the tube down and then crossed his arms. He blinked several times and made no answer.

"Come, say you will. We both know your position of 'Doctor' is over. And without your utility—"

"There is no need to lecture me, Zephyr. Fine, I will help. If I am certain of anything in this world, it's your self-interest. You won't enact a scheme in which you don't have the greatest confidence. His death will result in a quite alarming shake-up of our own internal hierarchy. One which might benefit me well."

"Good," said Zephyr, hopping back off the desk. "Now, when—"

"A word of caution, however." The doctor smiled as if aware of how little Zephyr liked to be interrupted. "Try to fuck me on this, and I will make sure you pay. I will be putting into place safeguards that will be enacted if I don't return from this little venture. Am I making myself clear?"

"Very," said Zephyr, her voice flat. "Be ready to act today. We will be all relocating to another stonecloud. Be sure you're easily found this afternoon. Clear?"

"Most clear. Now, go away." He half-turned away and began sorting through the contents of an open chest.

Zephyr didn't move, but Audsley saw her hands curl into fists. He reached out, took her by the shoulder, and pulled her back, then turned her and guided her away from the doctor's corner.

"How can I fuck him?" Zephyr hissed. "Safeguards. I'll have to leave a trap waiting for him, something that will only spring a week or a month after this deed is done and I am long gone. Yes." She brightened. "He thinks I mean to move up in rank, just like him. That I will be staying around. What will his safeguards matter when I'm long gone? Oh, that will be delicious. I'll arrange for letters to be delivered to key people a month — no, say three months after I'm gone."

She took Audsley's hand and smiled up at him. "That's long enough for him to settle into his new role, to grow comfortable, to feel safe, isn't it? Oh, yes. And just when he's really starting to enjoy himself, that's when I'll tell the people who matter about his little predilection. He'll be finished. Even our clan won't tolerate that kind of behavior."

Zephyr squeezed his hand. "I feel much, much better. Well, what do you think? The doctor possesses a *kal'shan*, as I do, while Auntie and Eulos both boast *nahkhor'ir* like yourself. That should be enough to make Grandfather feel quite toasty, yes?"

Is it? he asked his demons.

Three nahkhor'ir **and two** kal'shan? **That should be enough to take down even a** mal'orem, **though it would be quite the battle.**

Audsley thought of the vast, rune-inscribed cube that lay within the bowels of Starkadr. *What if... what if he possesses an* ur-destraas?

Audsley could sense the demon's smile. **No mortal could.**

But if he does?

If so, we are all going to wish for death long, long before he grants it.

"Yes," said Audsley weakly. "Quite toasty, indeed."

Chapter 16

Iskra strode toward Lutherius' tent filled with purpose. She'd never seen Asho filled with such reckless abandon and certitude, had never heard him speak with such rash passion and spite. And, more impressively still, it had worked; by the end of the lords' council, they had been listening attentively, nodding, sketching out defenses on paper and calling for their captains and guards.

She'd contributed little, but had vowed to secure the Grace's support. That much, she could do. Pausing in front of his tent, she ignored the sideways glances from the two Cerulean Guards, swept back her hair, smoothed down her dress, then stepped inside.

Lutherius was standing alone behind his war table. He was staring down at the map while a scribe read to him from a messenger's scroll.

"...Due to the lack of adequate baggage train and preparation. Notwithstanding such privations, I send my assurances — though I know how little weight they carry — that I shall endeavor to be at Zoe within the week—"

The messenger cut off as Lutherius raised his hand. "That will be all for now, Paras. Thank you."

The scribe bowed, set his scroll aside, and sat down on a simple stool.

"Your Imperial Highness," said Lutherius with a polite half-bow. "You are swiftly returned. I trust all went well?"

"The visit was both lucrative and surprising, Your Grace." Iskra decided not to smile; instead, she became aware of her lack of an entourage – should she have collected Agerastian officials en route? It was too late now. "I have much to report."

"That does sound good." Lutherius took up a pewter jug and poured wine into his goblet. "And good news is scarce these days. Wine?"

"No, thank you. Six of the great lords were gathered in council. Upon hearing my news, they stated that they would abandon the capital and retreat to their lands to prepare for siege and wait out the kragh."

"Understandable," said Lutherius. "Wise, even. That would buy us time for our own mission."

"The capital city has over two hundred thousand souls within its walls, Lutherius. What do you think would happen if the kragh took the city?"

"I am aware of the consequences of occupation." His tone took on some bite. "I am no stripling at my first command."

"Well. Asho convinced them otherwise."

"Asho. Your knight?"

"Yes. He called on their honor and devised a plan that they are enacting now. And, Lutherius, it is a good plan. I believe it stands a chance of stopping Tharok in his tracks."

"Hmm," said Lutherius, looking down at where Ennoia was marked on his map. "I would put more weight behind your words if I thought you knew aught of military matters."

Iskra raised her chin and bit down on the words that nearly slipped out.

He flicked his gaze up at her. "Continue."

"The lords of Ennoia are more than passingly acquainted with military plans, and they were enthused. Asho pointed out that we had lost Aletheia from lack of preparation. There was no time to set up a defense. As such, we were swept away. That is no longer the case. They are digging trenches before the Portal, lining up regiments of archers on the rooftops—"

"Your Imperial Highness," said Lutherius, smoothly but firmly. "Trenches? Archers? How many men do they have? A thousand?"

"No," said Iskra, again clamping down on her anger. "Half that."

"Half that. And, should Tharok throw his might against them, how many will they face?"

"Kethe reported that Tharok has some ten thousand or more kragh at his disposal."

"That, and a military acuity that has seen him demolish every obstacle in his path. And you speak to me of trenches? Archers?"

Iskra wished desperately that Asho were beside her, for him to step forward and contest with the Grace, to speak with the confidence and fire that had so charged the Ennoian lords. "They have a choke point, Lutherius. That gives them control."

"No, Iskra." Lutherius leaned forward across the table on both arms, his handsome face as hard as granite. "It gives them the illusion of control. It gives them a false sense of confidence that will see them dead. I regret that your knight has convinced the Ennoians to throw their lives away. It is a grave miscalculation. And with his being your knight, their massacre will be your responsibility."

Iskra opened her mouth to cut Lutherius down, but instead saw a vision so real, it stopped her heart: Roddick, as she laid the cloth over his wan face, and how his blood had blotted the linen.

"Iskra?"

"You are wrong, Lutherius." She had to muster the right words. Asho was depending on her sending reinforcements. "This is a unique opportunity to hold on to our one strategic advantage. If we cede the Portals in their entirety, then we will be at Tharok's mercy."

"No, we won't be at his mercy. We will be allowing him to stretch himself thin." He spoke with forced patience. "His horde coheres only through momentum. As soon as it stalls, as soon as it stops and sets to occupying, it will fragment. How will he feed ten thousand? Pillage will only go so far. I doubt he will be able to mimic the logistical supply lines that see Ennoian grain taken to Nous, Noussian fish to Sige, Zoeian crops and beef to Bythos. His ten thousand kragh will slow, and then stop, and he will no longer be able to unite them through conquest. They will have conquered. And in victory will they find their defeat: we will tear at their weaknesses like wolves at the underbelly of an elk; all his great strength will avail him nothing if he has no fixed opponent to throw it against. With our command of the Portals, we will be as shadows, tormenting, assassinating, and beguiling him till his authority collapses and the kragh turn upon each other. *That* is when we will strike, when we will launch our attack, killing Tharok and recapturing the Empire."

Lutherius stood up straight and raised a hand. "I shouldn't expect you to understand the nuances here. I know you have done well, surviving this long, but that is a testament to your ability to inspire your knights who have defended you this long. Nobody is challenging your political acumen. You've made yourself empress, by the Ascendant. But, please, leave the strategy to those who have devoted their lives to such matters."

Iskra felt a pang of humiliation and fury. Oh, if only Tiron were by her side. She ached for him, for his brutal strength, his rasping and indomitable will. But he was gone. This was her battle, and she felt like she was drowning. Lutherius' stare was patronizing, mildly exasperated, but, worst of all, long-suffering. As if she were a necessary problem he had to deal with in order to accomplish his job.

"Your forces are in truth my army," Iskra said coldly. "Your access to the Portals comes due to my Vothaks. You know nothing of me or my struggles, Lutherius, but know this: I have but to give a word, and a thousand Agerastians and all my Vothaks will march to Ennoia to support Asho."

"Yes, I'm well aware." Lutherius cast around and found his chair. He hooked it with his foot and pulled it close, then sat down with a sigh. "There's nothing to stop you from ruining everything. We are indeed at your mercy. But tell me, Iskra. Is that really how you want to go down in history? As the woman who married a heretic so as to wrest power over an army that she then threw away in a fit of pique at the most critical hour of the Empire? Hmm?" Lutherius raised an eyebrow and took up his goblet.

"If I believe it to be the right strategy, yes, I am willing to risk it."

The Grace sipped his wine, then leaned forward to set his goblet down on the table's edge. "Your daughter, Makaria, is in Nous. If you send your army to Ennoia, she may very well die."

Iskra felt an icy hand curl its fingers around her heart. "What are you talking about?"

"She agreed to lead the scouting party to determine what Tharok's next move was going to be. She is fully counting on our ability to send in soldiers if Nous proves to be his focus. If you take your army, you'll be leaving her to die."

"If I take my army, you will have to recall her."

"No," he said. "I won't recall anybody that I've placed in position. You don't understand – we're committed now. We have set upon a strategy and have deployed our most valuable pieces to enact it. You will destroy that plan and, in effect, kill those brave souls who have already left for Zoe, for Sige, for Nous. And for what? To stand behind trenches and fight Tharok's forces toe to toe? Think, woman. Think!"

He slapped a hand loudly on the table's surface, causing her to jump. "Ten thousand kragh. Plus trolls, and the Ascendant knows what else. Ten thousand? Do you think your two thousand will survive more than half an hour in a pitched battle? They'll be overrun."

"The choke point—"

"The choke point will limit him to sending in twenty kragh every three or four seconds. In one minute, he can therefore send in three hundred kragh. In ten, he can send in three thousand. And they won't stop. They'll fill in your precious ditches with their dead, they'll keep coming till your five hundred archers are out of arrows, and then they'll break against your Agerastians and swamp them. And, like that" — he snapped his fingers — "the last hope of the Empire will be snuffed out. Now, look me in the eyes. Can you risk that?"

Iskra's throat was dry. She couldn't deny his accusation: she was no military expert. She'd always depended on Ser Wyland, Tiron, and Asho in these matters.

"I've heard of this Asho knight of yours. The Bythian, am I right? Raised by Lord Enderl a decade ago on some bet. Oh, yes, I know about that affair. Who doesn't? A slave made squire. Madness! And do you know why it was such a folly? Because you can't turn a dog into a wolf. You can't turn a slave into a knight."

"You're wrong," said Iskra. "This, I know."

"Oh? Tell me he doesn't harbor hatred for the world that enslaved and mocked him. Tell me he's not twisted with fury at all those who oppressed him and his. There is a reason the Ascendant saw fit to arm the Ennoians and nobody else, Iskra – because we are born to the blade. We are raised to our duty. We consider it sacred. We can be trusted with the art of war. But a Bythian? He can only see as far as his anger, his sense of injustice. Can you truly swear that he is acting for the good of the Ascendant and not being influenced by his own spite?"

Iskra saw Asho standing before the Ennoian lords. Again, she heard his fury, how he had ridiculed them for their cowardice, and recalled his bitterness in the halls of Aletheia, how he had reproached her for doing as the Ascendant had asked and not what he thought was best.

"Yes," said Lutherius softly. "You see what I mean. I see the doubt in your eyes. For one to gamble with the fate of the Empire, with the lives of the millions who worship the Ascendant, one must have absolute and utter conviction married with a lifetime of experience from which one may derive wisdom. I have that. I know to the bottom of my soul that what I am doing is right. Can you say that, Iskra? Can you swear to me that you have that same conviction?"

Another memory assailed her: Audsley floating in the air above Laur Castle, screaming in horror as he unleashed one conflagration after another upon Laur's soldiers. The Grace and Lord Laur dead at her behest, and hundreds more dying for the sake of her revenge. Could she trust her own judgement? Could she claim with absolute certainty that what she was doing was the right course for the Empire?

Iskra bowed her head.

"I applaud your concern and your willingness to explore every option available to us. I am sending a team of four Consecrated to observe the events at Ennoia, and, depending on their report, I may indeed send our soldiers to that city. But for now, we will hold the course, hard as it may be."

Iskra stared at the map. She felt the situation slipping through her fingers, her control evanescing. She felt a wave of exhaustion wash over her, filling her with pain and anguish. She was like Tharok's horde, she thought. Momentum was all that was carrying her forward. If she stopped, then she would be dragged down by grief.

Tears watered her eyes, making the map waver and break into prisms of light.

"You are weary, Your Imperial Majesty. Shall I escort you to your tent?"

"No," whispered Iskra. "No." She swallowed and forced herself to lift her head. "I know the way well."

"Then, good evening. Or should I say good morning? Dawn is upon us. Soon, we will know what our next move should be. Do you wish for me to send for you when the reports come in?"

"Yes," she whispered.

"Very well. Will there be anything else?"

"No," she said, and turned away.

She strode from his tent, out through the flaps and past the guards, moving blindly through the camp till she was sure she was gone from view, at which point she covered her face with her hands and was wracked by a sob.

What had happened? What had she done? She felt as if she'd been slapped.

"Asho," she whispered, horrified by her own failing. "Asho, forgive me."

Chapter 17

The seven great Solar Portals dominated the center of Empire Square just north of the River Magryte. They rose, their soaring arches improbable, connecting to each other at their bases, forming a septagon on a massive scale. The cobbled square was large enough to house a castle, almost four hundred yards across and surrounded on all sides by impressive buildings that rose five stories high.

It was on the roof of one such building that Asho was standing, Uxe beside him, along with a number of the lords and their commanders. Asho gazed down at the work that was being done, that massive labor that was racing the rising sun. Looking up, he saw the sky to the east growing perilously light; dawn was perhaps only fifteen minutes away.

The roof of every building around the square had been caved in and cleared away, exposing attics that now bristled with archers. They had scrounged every man and woman who could put shaft to string and set them in long double lines so that some three or four hundred Ennoians were gazing down at the square. Professional soldiers marched up and down the ranks of the citizen archers, barking at them, keeping them in line, keeping them poised and in good mettle.

Down below, six ballistae had been hauled into the square. The two monsters in front of the fortress had proven to be beyond repair, but six smaller versions had been found and brought with much cursing and heaving through the city streets to be placed at the square's edges, their great bow faces aimed at the Aletheian and Bythian Portals. Each could fire a shaft over a yard long with enough power to punch through five men. Asho prayed it would be enough.

Around the bases of the Portals themselves, teams of men were laboring frantically, mounds of cobbles and dirt forming rough walls about a yard high that would direct charging kragh at the ballistae in as concentrated a wave as they could manage. Trenches were being dug right in front of the Portals, then again every three yards, each now over a yard or more deep.

Carpenters were busy sharpening stakes of wood which were being affixed to the far edges of the trenches and solidly embedded in their depths. Below, milling around the ballistae themselves, were the Ennoian guards and other professional soldiers who had been at hand, some four hundred men and knights who would defend the ballistae and cut down any kragh who made it through the hail of arrows and bolts.

"It's looking pretty wicked," said Uxe, puffing on a long-stemmed pipe and standing beside Asho. "A pity we don't have enough oil to flood the trenches and light them on fire when the kragh come through."

"A good idea," said Asho, biting the corner of his lip. "But we're out of the time." He looked up at the horizon again. "Ten minutes, perhaps."

"What else could we do that would bother 'em?" Uxe tapped his chin. "How about we just knock down the Portals themselves?"

Asho shook his head. "The lords ruled against it. They won't secede from the Empire."

"Ser Asho?"

Asho turned and saw a group emerging from the stairwell. Consecrated, he judged, four of them in their white robes. A plain-looking Zoeian lady with her black hair tightly braided and pulled back into a topknot, a Bythian youth with the sides of his head shaved and a nasty scar puckering his lips, a Sigean man in his forties with a wounded arm in a sling, and a second Bythian. It was she who had addressed him.

She looked to be in her early twenties. Her alabaster hair was parted down the center and pulled back into a long ponytail. Her features were sharp, her expression haughty. She was wearing form-fitting black leather armor and had two murder seaxes strapped to her hips.

The Ennoian lords stepped in close, and they all formed a ring. Clearly, the young Bythian woman was in charge.

"Consecrated," said Asho.

"Your request for reinforcements has been denied." She spoke briskly, as if she expected an angry response and did not care.

"Denied?" growled Lord Herterech. "Why?"

"His Grace has outlined a clear and simple plan." She looked over to the lord, ponytail swinging. "We are to reserve our forces for calculated strikes, not for general defenses against what could potentially be the entirety of Tharok's forces."

"Take a look down there," said Asho, pointing below. "Tell me that doesn't stand a chance of stopping him."

"I don't have to look. I walked through it." If she felt any kinship with him, she didn't show it. "I laud your efforts. They will slow Tharok if he comes through, but nothing more. We won't pour our meager resources into a doomed battle."

"Well," said Lord Seulfryd, popping the collar of his furred cloak, "I'm glad they saw fit to send a charismatic talker to smooth over our feelings."

"Her Imperial Majesty Kyferin thought otherwise," Asho said stiffly. "She isn't sending her army?"

"His Grace convinced her not to," said the Bythian. "She is holding her forces in reserve."

Lord Herterech turned and spat.

Asho felt like he'd been dealt a blow right to his core. "I see. So, you've come to bear the good news, I take it, but not to help fight?"

"No," said the Consecrated. "We're here to observe and report back."

A hot, dangerous anger began to smolder within him. He took a step forward. "Well, then, get the hell off my observation deck and observe from somewhere else."

Everyone stilled.

The Bythian arched her brow. "Excuse me?"

"I think you heard me. You won't help? You want to watch us fight for our lives? Fine. But not here. Go find yourself a bolthole somewhere else."

"Ser Asho..." said Lord Seulfryd.

The Consecrated took a step forward. "Have you lost your mind? Do you know whom you're speaking with?"

"Maybe," said Asho. He stared down into her upturned face. "But I couldn't care less. Now, go."

The other three Consecrated shifted their positions subtly. The woman looked up at him. "I am Shameka, of the Virtue Theletos' own cohort, and I have gazed upon the glory of the White Gate and been blessed by the Ascendant himself. No one speaks to me that way."

"I couldn't care less who you are. This is my last warning. Go." Asho placed his hand inside his pouch of gatestone.

Nobody moved. Her eyes were narrowed and fierce with anger.

"Dawn's about two minutes off, I reckon," said Uxe from the side. "Oh, my, is that the Portal I see flickering?"

Shameka shook her head. "I could cut you down before you even moved. But I wasn't sent here to kill fools." She looked to her three companions. "Come. We'll find another spot." That said, she led them away and down the steps.

"By the Ascendant's bunions, you're crazier than a drunk six-year-old," said Lord Herterech.

Asho let out a deep breath and turned back to the square. "They've botched this every step of the way. I'll be damned if I keep listening to them."

"Hmm, well, we do still need them as allies," said Lord Seulfryd, by his side. "Let's keep that in mind, shall we?"

The eastern horizon was a pale, robin's egg blue. The archers massed on the eastern buildings were dark silhouettes.

"We don't need them," Asho said quietly. "If this fails, we'll be dead. If it works, well, then, they'll be the ones who come running to us."

Uxe knocked his pipe out on a spar of wood that had once risen to support the demolished roof and stowed the pipe away. "A bit grim, but fair enough. Do you need me any longer? If not, I'll be going down to lead my men."

"Go," said Asho. "And good luck."

Uxe grunted and headed downstairs.

"Any moment now," said Lord Herterech. He was watching the Portals carefully. "Truth be told, I'm glad we resolved to stand and fight. Best way to go. I'd hate to waste away in some damn siege with no hope of relief."

"Speak for yourself," said Lord Seulfryd, hugging himself against the cold. "I'm perfectly fine with spending my last few months hip-deep in wine, listening to my bard instead of having a kragh lop off my head an hour from now."

"There," said Asho.

White fire flickered and filled the expanse of each Portal except that of Agerastos. Cries sounded out from around the square, commanders preparing their archers, sergeants readying their soldiers and forming them into tight groups. Asho heard the deep, winching groan of the ballistae being drawn back and loaded.

He leaned forward, staring intently. They were positioned directly across from the archway to Aletheia. Unfortunately, the Portal to Bythos was three arches over, almost to the far side; he couldn't see its face, but he knew he'd hear yells the moment a kragh emerged.

Silence filled the square. Isolated coughs rang out, but nobody spoke. Nobody so much as moved. Almost a thousand people watched and waited, bowstrings drawn back. The last of the workers fled the trenches and streamed back to safety, tools over their shoulders, trenches unfinished but still a deterrent.

The waiting became intolerable. Asho gripped the wooden siding of the attic wall so hard that the wooden beam creaked.

A flock of pigeons flew overhead, fluttering around in confusion as they found all their usual perches disrupted or taken.

"A few more minutes, and we'll give out the order to stand down," said Asho. "Conserve our strength."

"And bowstrings," said Lord Herterech.

"There!"

A hundred voices cried out as a kragh emerged from the white flame. He stumbled, shield held at the ready, adjusting to his new reality, but he never had a chance. On reflex, about a hundred archers released their arrows, which hissed down from the roofs to punch into the creature before he could even register the threat. Most of the arrows missed, thunking into the exposed dirt, disappearing into the trenches or into the Portal itself, but some thirty of them punched into the kragh, driving his shield hard against his body and embedding themselves in his shins and head.

The kragh collapsed to the ground, twisting and twitching and then going still.

Ragged cheers floated out across the rooftops, accompanied by the angry barks of the commanders. The archers had not waited for the order to release.

Asho bit his lower lip and waited. Another kragh poked his head through, not emerging completely, and again arrows rained down on him, three of which *thocked* home, one in the eye, the second punching deep into his cheek, the third skittering off his forehead. He fell back and was gone.

"None of them have been able to report back what they've seen," said Asho. "That's good."

"Not exactly a determined charge, though," said Lord Seulfryd. "A bit hesitant."

Nothing else happened for a good five minutes. A few groups started singing victory chants, only to be shushed by their sergeants. Asho remained completely focused. Time stretched out and ceased to have meaning. There was just the blank, flickering fire of the Portal. Nothing else existed.

A boulder came flying out through the Portal. It arched over the trenches and slammed into the open cobbled expanse, bounced twice, rolled five yards, and then came a stop.

Asho grinned. "That's not going to work this time, you bastards."

More boulders came through, but not nearly at the rate they had done back in Aletheia. Five, six, seven of them, and then nothing. A couple of archers released their arrows in shock, shooting down at the rocks only to be jeered at by their fellows.

"Here they come," said Asho. "Ready below!"

And he was right. Twenty kragh came storming out through the Portal at a full charge, shields raised high. Commanders yelled at their archers to hold, not to fire, and for the most part they did — perhaps only fifteen arrows all told flew down.

The kragh slammed into the first trench that was only a yard from the base of the Portal and went down, two of them having the presence of mind to leap at the sight of the gap beneath their feet only to crash into the spiked stakes embedded on the far side. Their screams were immediately replaced by the roars of the second rank that came charging through. Shields held high, they ran forward, took two steps, then fell upon their fellows in the ditch.

"Not deep enough," said Asho, fighting back his frustration. The first two waves had already filled in the first ditch.

A third wave came through, hard on the heels of the second, and these clambered over the bucking and rearing first and second ranks, squirmed through the sharpened stakes, roaring and bellowing even as they stared around wild-eyed — and it was then that the commanders gave their signal.

Two hundred shafts darkened the air and fell upon the trenches. Kragh screamed, spasmed, fell over. A fourth wave came through. Another flight of arrows hissed down upon them, laying them low. By the time the fifth wave arrived, the bodies of the dead kragh had filled in the first two trenches and had knocked askew the stakes. The fifth wave sprinted forward, leaping and tripping over their dead friends, staggering out past the second trench and reaching the third before the arrows sliced down amongst them and knocked them low.

Five of the kragh persisted. Even with arrows buried deep in their shoulders and chests, they powered forward and leaped over the third and final trench.

"Release!" came a cry from the base of Asho's building, and twanging *thwop* echoed loudly as a huge bolt crashed into the chest of the first kragh, knocking him flying back off his feet, his chest obliterated.

The bolt sailed through and into a kragh that was climbing out of the second trench, then into a member of the seventh wave that was emerging from the Portal.

Two more bolts sped across the open expanse, and more arrows rained down upon the kragh who had broken through. In moments, they were dead, but members of the seventh and eighth wave were coming right after them, some fifteen in all racing over the cobbles.

"Too fast," said Asho. "They're already overwhelming our defenses!"

Knights and soldiers moved forward to engage the kragh who were running at the ballistae, and in short order cut them down. But more kragh were coming through. The archers were loosing their arrows continuously now, picking targets at random, so that kragh everywhere were falling. The piles of dead near the Portal itself were growing, forcing other kragh to run around them, shove bodies aside, leap over the dead.

The tenth — or was it the eleventh? – wave came through, making it some two hundred or more kragh who had already attacked. Asho gazed across the square at where their forces were waiting to engage any kragh that came through the Bythian gate. None had, leaving the men to watch the fight on the far side helplessly. He cursed and snatched up a green flag from the floor beside him, raised it high and waved it back and forth.

Immediately, archers from the flanks of the Bythian position, some fifty men on each side, ran into their buildings and disappeared.

Every twenty seconds, the massive ballistae sounded off, sending huge bolts powering through the kragh ranks. Their dead were proving to be more of an obstruction than anything else at this point, piled almost a yard high. But the enemy came on, however, howling, and now without shields, simply brandishing their axes and hammers and swarming forward without regard for their own safety.

The men below finally met the kragh in hand-to-hand combat, forming a skirmishing line that extended across the front of the ballistae. Asho stared down and saw Uxe and his Ennoians right in the thick of it. The ballistae were mounted on platforms raised four yards high, and continued to shoot right over the heads of their defenders.

The summoned archers streamed out of the doorways of their buildings and formed rough lines far out to the sides of the attacking kragh. Their commanders yelled, and they began to fire into the kraghs' flanks, dropping them as they emerged from the Portal.

"Will we hold?" asked Lord Seulfryd, his voice but a whisper.

"Not for much longer," said Lord Herterech.

He was right. The waves of kragh kept coming, and they showed no fear, no hesitation, no panic at the mounds of their dead or the death that was raining down upon them. Instead, it seemed to goad them into greater heights of fury, causing them to bolt forward, ignoring the arrows that hit them until they fell, each of them peppered with five or even ten shafts.

"I'm going to have to get down there," said Asho. Leaning forward, he saw the line of their men beginning to bow to the pressure of the kragh, who now stood three deep. The ballistae were still firing, but the men working the machines were beginning to panic, their aim growing haphazard, their rate of fire dropping.

Asho placed one foot on the edge of the roof and dug out a chunk of gatestone. He drew his blade and took a deep breath. It was a five-story drop to the square below, but with magic coursing through his veins, he'd be able to handle it.

"Look," said Lord Herterech, grabbing his arm. "They've stopped!"

Asho looked up from the melee below and saw that the wolfish lord was correct. The kragh were no longer emerging from the Gate. The archers on the flanks closed in, firing now into the rear of the kragh who were running to join the battle, taking them down and then lifting their aim to send shafts whistling into the back of the kragh combat line.

"Why?" Lord Seulfryd was on Asho's other side. "I thought you said they had thousands?"

"Ten thousand or more," said Asho.

"And trolls and other impossibilities," continued Seulfryd. "I count — perhaps four hundred kragh below. Herterech?"

"Yes, just about."

They watched as the archers' concentrated fire from behind whittled the kragh numbers. The human fighters, sensing the shift in the fortune of the battle, let out a roar praising the Ascendant and pressed forward. Asho saw Uxe fighting almost in a crouch, his short blades held in reverse grips as he spun around, darted forward, and spun again. Wherever he went, wounds opened across kragh legs, hamstrings were severed, and the great warriors fell.

"We've survived," said Seulfryd.

"For now, at any rate," said Asho. "This must have been an exploratory force. Testing our resistance. I saw a dozen or so kragh retreat back through the Gate to report."

"Which means they're hitting another city," said Herterech grimly.

"Nous, or Sige, or Zoe," said Asho. "Yes."

"By the White Gate, we nearly fell to their exploratory force," said Seulfryd. "What happens when they come against us with all their might?"

"We'll do better," said Asho. "We might have the day and tonight to regroup."

The sounds of battle, the wretched screams and yells and roars, were still filtering up from below, but the kragh were fighting in tight pockets now, their numbers rapidly dropping.

"First, we clear the dead," said Asho. "Cart them out. Strip them of their weapons and dump the bodies."

Herterech nodded. "I'll speak with Cunec, the captain of the city guard. He'll know how to organize the guilds to get that done."

"Then, we need to work on those ditches," said Asho. "I want them as deep as we can make them, and stretching all the way to the ballistae."

Seulfryd leaned forward, his eyes narrowing. "I make that about fifteen trenches, then. A yard wide, three yards between."

"I want the side closest to us to be lined with stakes," said Asho. "So thick and planted so deep that the kragh won't be able to push past them."

Herterech nodded. "I'll get soldiers to work on that."

"More ballistae, too. I'm going to send for a man who can help us in that department. A blacksmith who's stationed in Mythgraefen Hold. If anybody can fix those monsters set up in front of the fortress, it's him."

Herterech studied the battlefield. "We'll need more arrows. I'll have the guildsmen collect what they find when they clear out the bodies, but even so, from the way the rate of fire lessened toward the end, there, I'll warrant a good number of our men were running short."

"And oil," said Asho. "Uxe mentioned filling the trenches and lighting them up with fire arrows. I don't know how much we can gather, but even if it's just the one trench, I'll take it."

"What about crossbows placed by the ballistae?" asked Seulfryd. "To take down kragh who charge the line? Their range won't reach the Gate, but they should be effective at dropping attackers from close range."

"Good thought," said Herterech, clapping Seulfryd on the shoulder. "We'll make an Ennoian lord out of you yet."

"That's the most disheartening thing I've ever heard," said Seulfryd, which provoked a harsh laugh from Herterech.

Asho studied the buildings that hemmed in the square. "We should consider blocking the roads that lead into the square. Board up the windows and doors of the buildings as well. That way, if the kragh overrun the ballistae and foot soldiers, they'll still be penned up for a while as they figure out where to go, and they'll be at the mercy of our rooftop archers."

"The boys won't like that," said Herterech. "Knowing they're trapped in there with the kragh."

"Too bad," said Asho. "There's nowhere to run. If we lose this square, we lose Ennoia. It might even be better to drive that point home."

They stood in silence, their staffs standing attentively behind them, and watched as their men below cheered as the last kragh fell. The cheer was picked up by the archers on the ground and then carried by those on the rooftops. The men raised their weapons to the sky and yelled their defiance, pounding each other on the back and screaming their relief and elation.

"We did well," said Herterech. "Looks like we have perhaps twenty wounded, a handful dead. They lost five hundred."

Asho nodded, but he felt sober, cold, calculating. They all knew that with a few more minutes of pressure, their entire force would have been wiped out. "Let's get Captain Cunec working on our task list. The next attack could come at any moment."

The two lords nodded and strode away, followed by their staffs and knights, leaving Asho alone at his post. He saw Uxe look up at him and lift his blade — Frogsplitter? – and laugh. Asho couldn't help but grin back.

Could they hold off a full attack? He wanted to say yes. He desperately wanted to believe that they could. But he knew how large Tharok's horde was. And worse, they weren't taking into account one crucial factor, a factor that they couldn't prepare for, and which had been strangely absent in today's raid:

Tharok's military genius.

Chapter 18

Tharok awoke with a groan, rolled onto his side and placed the base of his palm to his forehead. A sense of urgency gripped him, an imperative to hold on to his dreams, the fragments of which were already slipping from his mind.

Luminous beings, messages of great import, a song that would forever change the world... but no. Even as he focused on capturing them, they were gone, and it was with a sense of irrevocable loss that he sat up, shoulders hunched, eyes closed, regretting his return to the world.

Something was different. He opened his eyes, blinked rapidly. He was in a small chamber without windows, barely large enough for the bed, the sole adornment a golden band of geometric patterns that ran along the top of the wall where it met the ceiling. A candle had burned down to its last inch on a small side table. The floor was bare, made of stone. The bed on which he was lying was ample, but its simple sheets of linen were mussed and had been kicked to the footboard.

Tharok raised his hand to his brow. The circlet was gone. He leaped to his feet and turned wildly, searching the room. Under the bed? He flipped it onto its side with a crash. Nothing. World Breaker was gone as well. He wanted to shatter furniture, but there was nothing to destroy, nowhere it could be hiding.

The door opened, revealing Jojan, former warlord of the Black Clouds, now the leader of a full thousand kragh under his command. His medusa-Kissed black skin seemed to absorb the golden candle-light, and his eyes were slitted, his face inscrutable.

"Where is it?" growled Tharok, advancing a step. "Where is my circlet?"

"On Uthok's head," said Jojan. "World Breaker is in his hand."

Tharok absorbed the words like blows, his head snapping back. "He's claiming the role of Uniter?"

Jojan closed the door quietly, not hurrying to answer, then crossed his arms over his chest and nodded. He had earned a reputation for cunning and slyness and had led the Black Clouds, if not to great-ness, then to heightened relevance amongst the peaks. That cunning showed in his eyes now. "Yes. He is saying you are dead. That Ogri struck you down for approaching the humans' white fire Portal. That he is now to lead the kragh to victory."

"The Sky Father curse his spirit," said Tharok.

He pulled the bed back down and sat, cradling his head in his hands. He felt the circlet's absence like a physical void, as if he'd awakened to find both hands cut off, or all of his teeth and tusks removed. He needed to think, to plan, but there was nothing there in his mind, no genius to reach for. Only himself. His own mind. Only Tharok.

He looked up at Jojan. "Tell me what happened."

"You collapsed," said Jojan. "You looked dead. Uthok moved first. He took your circlet and placed it on his head, then he fell over as well."

"I don't doubt it," grinned Tharok savagely. "It is a heavy burden to bear."

"But he rose soon enough. He looked... disoriented, but he ignored our shouts and threats and took up World Breaker, and that seemed to calm him. Several kragh attacked him, seeking to take the circlet, and in that confusion, Ithar and I stole you away. We brought you down here and hid you, and have lied ever since as to your whereabouts."

"How long?"

"Not long. Twelve hours. It is now late morning."

Tharok gritted his teeth. "Damn. And the horde? Has Uthok given orders?"

"Yes," said Jojan. "He has sent five hundred kragh to explore resistance in the lands beyond the four remaining Gates. He is gathering the rest of the horde in the Portal room here in Aletheia to witness his rise to Uniter."

Tharok rubbed his thumb along his chin. "And the kragh? How have they taken my fall?"

"They took it well. Uthok has given them permission to loot and kill through all of Aletheia. Its halls run with blood and are filled with smoke."

"Curse him!" growled Tharok, leaping to his feet. He began to pace from one side of the small room to the other. He'd not wanted the kragh to loot the stonecloud, but he couldn't remember why not. It had been important, though. "Any word from Kyrra?"

Jojan shook his head. "Not that I have heard. Uthok suspects me, and will have me killed soon. But not yet. He needs the framework you created to manage the horde, and I lead a thousand kragh. To kill me would be too much change, too soon. So, he is keeping me out of his council and biding his time. In a week, maybe less, he'll start replacing your warlords with his own."

Tharok nodded. He kept expecting his thoughts to take flight, to make intuitive leaps that would connect different points of information and cause a plan to fall into his lap, a way to turn this turn of events to his advantage. But it didn't happen. Nothing brilliant came to mind.

Jojan was watching him, waiting to see how his gamble paid off. Tharok had to keep his confidence.

Uthok had the circlet and World Breaker. He would be wrestling to stay afloat, to not be drowned by the influx of power. Would he be able to resist the circlet's commands? The fact that he'd not gone to the Black Gate immediately was a good sign, but then, he'd not yet dared to face Kyrra. That was probably why he was holding the gathering here in Aletheia. He'd only face the medusa and her shamans when he had ten thousand kragh at his back.

"What is your plan, Uniter?" Jojan's voice was soft, almost probing.

He doesn't know that my genius came from the circlet. He thinks it only a symbol. A front. I must convince him otherwise.

"When is the gathering to take place?"

"This evening. Already, the kragh are building bonfires and roasting cattle and pigs in the Portal chamber. More and more are leaving their sport to gather. I reckon Uthok will speak when the festivities are at their height."

"Yes," said Tharok.

He could challenge Uthok to a duel before the assembled kragh; Uthok would have no choice but to accept, but with the circlet and World Breaker, he would have little difficulty in cutting Tharok down. Go to Kyrra? She would laugh at him, consume him, or help him in such a way that even if he regained his circlet, he would be forever in her debt.

No, he thought as he continued to pace. The kragh respected strength. They would not follow him unless he defeated Uthok, and he couldn't defeat Uthok in a fight. His allies were few, and liable to leave him if he showed weakness.

Jojan was still watching him, eyes gleaming in the candlelight. What Tharok wouldn't have done for Nok, or Maur, or any of the Red River to be here! True allies. Tribe. Clan. But they were gone. He had to face this alone.

He stopped, hands on his hips, and stared into the candle flame. Had his position as Uniter truly been so precarious? Was there nothing he could do? How had he fought before the circlet came into his life? How had he won his battles?

The memory came easily: the last fight he had won before finding Ogri's corpse in the Valley of Death. A dozen Orlokor kragh had been hunting him down with their dogs. He had fled into the mountains for days, only to turn and take them down as they charged him, one by one, with his mountain bow.

That had been clean. That had been simple. And when they were upon him, he had cast his bow aside and leaped into their midst like a boar amongst pups and destroyed them.

A sense of calm settled over him. "Very well. I know what we must do. "

Chapter 19

Kethe emerged through the Portal into Nous and clamped her hand over her mouth to prevent herself from crying out in surprise.

Water.

She was plunged, submerged, engulfed in wet darkness. She fought to keep the air in her lungs and swam forward with frantic strokes, feeling the weight of her boots and sword, her coat and belt dragging her down.

Gradually, her eyes adjusted. The darkness was a thick, velvety, cobalt blue, and though at first it had seemed to extend in every direction, she saw that it grew lighter above. Darker below. To the sides — impossible to tell. A tapestry of shadows that could have been walls with doorways within them, or just her imagination.

Their Portal shimmered with a darkness more absolute than that of the water, and Kuliver came through. His tall, lanky frame immediately stiffened, but Kethe was ready. She clamped her hand over his mouth, feeling the short, sharp bristles of his mustache and goatee, and clenched his arm tight.

His eyes were wide with shock, but he was as sharp as she'd guessed — she pointed upward and gave him a shove. He needed no second urging, and kicked and swam away.

Khoussan came next. He bellowed in surprise, the sound muted by the water, and a cascade of bubbles erupted from his mouth and rose through the darkness. Kethe grabbed his arm and shoved him upward, pointing after Kuliver, and then turned back to the Portal.

Could she slip back through? She waited for the Portal to grow dark, but just as she dove forward, she collided with Braex. He clutched her to his broad chest in alarm, but had the wits to bite down on his air — instead, he whipped his head from side to side, crushing her to his chest.

Kethe pointed, shoved, and he was gone, swimming with broad, clumsy strokes. Dalitha came through right on his heels, and Kethe again pressed her hand to her Consecrated's mouth. The young woman reacted more speedily than any of the others — she immediately wriggled free and with the suppleness of an eel shot upward.

Kethe's chest was growing tight. How far were they from the surface? Would she be able to make it up? Where was the damn Vothak?

Finally, he came through, an older man whose fine silver hair immediately formed a billowing cloud around his startled face, his cry of shock burbling up with his bubbles. Kethe felt her heart sink — his heavy Vothak robes would be the death of him.

She couldn't wait any longer. Grasping him by the hem of his cloak, she began to swim up. The old man fought to follow, but he floundered helplessly in his thick robes and seemed if anything to fight against her. Kethe's heartbeats were pounding in her ears. She strained to lift him, thought about trying to get him to undress, and kicked off her own boots instead. Dancing motes of black were appearing in her vision.

They reached the ceiling of a room, but were still underwater. Oh, by the White Gate and the Black — where to? Smooth as marble, slimy to the touch, the ceiling was a great expanse — there, movement! Dalitha, waving. Kethe tugged on the Vothak, but he was starting to thrash madly. Kethe spun around and punched him straight in the face. The blow was muted by the water, but she still felt his head crack back. She slipped an arm around his chest and began to swim, clawing with her free hand as if to find purchase in the water ahead of her.

Dalitha was there, waiting, and she reached out and took the Vothak by the arm. Together, they swam into a stairwell. It was from there that the faint light was coming. Down and inside they went; then, together, they hauled on the Vothak, kicking their legs. Kethe's air was fighting to erupt through her throat. It was like pulling on an anchor. Around and around went the stairwell, one turn, two.

The water grew lighter. They swam out into a second chamber, this one a luminous aquamarine, and there was Khoussan, passed out and sinking toward them.

Kethe let go of the Vothak and sped toward the Zoeian. She grasped him under the arms and fought to lift him. He was massive, heavy beyond belief. She tugged him up inches with each kick of her legs, only to sink back down.

Her head was aching, pounding, and she could barely think. Then there was a rushing roar, a crashing boom, and Kuliver appeared beside her, wreathed in bubbles. He pushed her up and took hold of Khoussan.

Kethe couldn't think to argue. She bolted up, thrusting desperately. Up, and up; she couldn't hold her breath, opened her mouth to scream, and just then broke the surface, out into the glorious air, to inhale with a sucking gasp that filled her mouth with salty water. She spluttered, spat, inhaled again, fought to keep her head up. Her hair had run into her face, into her eyes, and she raked it back.

Where? What — there! Braex was hauling himself up onto what looked like a balcony, water streaming from his clothing. A moment later, Kuliver and Khoussan broke the surface beside her.

"Dalitha!" Kethe was still sucking in great torrents of air, her head swimming, but she had to dive down — had to help…

Dalitha appeared a few yards to her right. "He's still down there!"

Kethe sucked in a bruising lungful of air and dove. Down she swam, fighting for each yard, into the gloom. The room descended perhaps ten yards, and she could make out a multitude of tightly packed balconies all the way down the walls. Where was the Vothak?

There! He'd sunk to lie across a mass of rotted furniture — pews? Kethe fought to reach him, kicking and thrusting her way down. The water was clear enough that she could make out a stage of some kind at the far end of the room, brilliantly colored crabs scuttling away under ruined chairs, something like a great eel withdrawing into a window.

She clutched the hem of the Vothak's robe and heaved. He came up slowly. Dalitha appeared at her side. Together, they fought to lift the Vothak, his face obscured by his silver hair, his robes billowing out around him. Each yard was a struggle. Kethe was about to let go when Kuliver dove down beside them again, and he seized the old man under the arms. The three of them powered up though the water and reached the air once more.

Gasping, nearly retching, swallowing salt water and spluttering, Kethe focused on keeping her face above water, and she inhaled huge quantities of air. The ceiling was only three yards above them, and was gorgeously painted with some expansive scene, framed with gilt molding and depicting faded Virtues, golden rays of sunlight, and the stonecloud of Aletheia in the center. Skylights were cut into its surface, too high above them to be reached.

Kethe tore her eyes away and swam to where the others were climbing onto a balcony. Braex grabbed her by the upper arms and hauled her up easily, lifting her over the marble railing and down next to Khoussan, who was shaking and spitting bile and sea water onto the slick floor.

"The Vothak," said Kethe, fighting to her feet. But Braex was already helping the others lever the old man up and over. He laid the man down next to Khoussan, forcing Kethe to hop up onto the broad balustrade, hiking her legs out of the way.

Kuliver swung himself over the railing and landed next to the Vothak, crouched down and got to work. He'd been a sailor in his previous life, before he became a Consecrated, and wasted no time in pumping the Vothak's chest.

Kethe watched, her mind still numb. Kuliver placed one tattooed hand over the other and shoved hard on the Vothak's pigeon chest, three, four, five times, then cocked the man's head back and breathed powerfully into his mouth.

Nothing.

Again. Three, four, five times. "Breathe!" he demanded.

Nothing.

Kuliver kept at it for another minute, Kethe and the others watching in horror, until finally the wiry man sat back on his heels and shook his head. "He's gone beyond my ability to call his heretical arse back."

"Wait," said Dalitha. "What does that mean? For us? Are we stranded here?"

"No," Braex said heavily. He'd unshouldered his thick coat and draped it over the balustrade, and was working on pulling off his boots. "There's always the Solar Portals."

Khoussan spat. "That doesn't help us much if there are some ten thousand kragh coming through."

Kethe rubbed at her face in an attempt to banish her shock. "If the Vothak is dead, we'll adapt. Deal with it. Now, where the hell are we?"

"Looks like some old playhouse," said Braex. "Balconies, that stage below."

"Whatever it is, we're deep down in Nous' belly," said Kuliver with a tone of wonder. "The city's sinking, aye? Each year, a few more feet of white stone slide down into the Eternal Sea. Some say there's miles of dark, flooded halls and chambers below. I've always wanted to come explore. Dive down for the treasures that are rumored to glitter and gleam in the depths, waiting for a canny soul to bring them back to light." Kuliver's smile grew pensive as he looked down at the Vothak. "Never thought my first salvage here would be a dead priest."

Dalitha had edged around their group to explore the back of the balcony. "Look, this opens up into a small room. And there's a door."

Kethe helped Khoussan to his feet. She realized the other three were waiting for her to go first, so she moved after Dalitha. There was indeed a small chamber set within the wall, with warped and moldy furniture decaying to each side. A place where spectators of the show below could have retired for private conversation?

No matter. The door set into the back wall was waterlogged and swollen. Dalitha tugged on the iron handle, and it came off in her hand.

Kethe placed her palm against the door and gave it a push, to no result.

"Here," said Khoussan. He waited for them to step aside, and then simply charged it. He exploded through the boards of the door, which didn't snap so much as fall apart into long shards of soft wood, and stumbled out into a dark hallway.

Kethe drew her blade. She inhaled deeply, focused on the White Song, and white fire licked up her sword, casting a sharp white illumination up and down the length of the curved hallway.

"We're close to the surface," she said softly, leading the way. "The skylights prove that. It should be easy to find our way out."

There were numerous other doors leading to private balconies, and then the curving hall descended into a set of flooded stairs. Dalitha jogged in the other direction, but when she returned, she reported a dead end.

"All right," said Kethe. "Kuliver, you're our best swimmer. See what you can find below."

Braex tapped the wiry man on the shoulder. "These steps will most likely lead to a large reception room. There'll probably be a set of main doors leading to the outside from there."

"How'd you know that?" asked Kuliver, shucking his boots.

Braex's smile was grim. "My girls back in Zoe used to frequent the imperial playhouse. That's how it was set up. This place reminds me of it."

His girls, Kethe knew, were the nearly three dozen whores that he'd operated for high-class clientele before being called by the White Gate. His ascension to Consecrated had caused no end of consternation amongst the elite of Sige and Aletheia who had been his customers before.

"Good to know," said Kuliver with a grin. "If I'm late coming back, it's 'cause I ran into one of Braex's ladies coming up the stairs." He flashed them all the sign of the triangle and then dove lithely into the water.

"I don't fancy another swim," said Dalitha, hugging herself tightly.

Kethe watched the water and counted. She'd reached sixty when she saw a shadow shimmer beneath the surface, and then Kuliver's head emerged and he gasped for air.

"Success!" He walked up the steps till he was halfway out. "Just as Master Braex guessed. A grand ol' room below, with a pair of double doors standing open. I stuck my head out and saw the sun winking down at me through the waves overhead."

"Good," said Kethe. "Kuliver, you'll come last to help anyone in difficulty. Khoussan, Braex, you're first. If you have any trouble, Dalitha, Kuliver and I will be there to help."

Kuliver emerged from the water. "Best you all strip down to your skivvies and wrap your clothing around your weapons. You'll swim better that way. Watch."

He stripped down to his braies, wrapped his clothing tightly around his sword, then cinched his boots to the bundle with his belt. "Pull this along behind you. It'll feel like a rock, but you'll move quicker, believe me."

Kuliver was all lean muscle and freckled shoulders and chest, his angular face seeming unable to maintain any expression but a wicked smile for long. Crude tattoos were inked over his arms, depicting everything from boats to improbably endowed women to six names in a list down his left arm. Over his heart was a swallow, while other assorted icons and glyphs were inked around his back and torso.

The men set to stripping. Kethe and Dalitha undressed to their leggings and shirts, and then, once everyone had their bundles ready, watched as Khoussan dove into the water, followed immediately by Braex. A second later, Kethe and Dalitha dove in. Kethe skimmed down just over the surface of the steps, kicking strongly to descend into the gloom, and this time she kept her mind and heart on the White Gate, visualizing its burning white glory, and found strength flowing into her limbs.

Down they went, a good ten yards, Khoussan's and Braex's boots pulled along just ahead of them. They swam out into a broad, dark chamber wherein objects floated in the murk. Kethe saw rotted pieces of furniture, fronds of weeds, and a school of fish flitting away in flashing glimmers over a chandelier of cut glass that glittered like a fallen mass of stars.

Kethe swam powerfully, feeling now as if she could stay submerged forever. Khoussan and Braex were picking up speed, swimming with strong strokes, but Braex moved with ever-greater clumsiness. Ahead were the double doors, and in a moment they were out, the four of them kicking toward the surface that shone like hammered silver above them.

They emerged amongst a set of waves, and were raised and dipped into troughs as they gasped and grinned at each other. Kethe turned, and for the first time saw the towers of Nous emerging from the waters, gleaming white stone thrusting upward for what looked like a mile into the sky, topped by great onion domes of bronze. The towers were engulfed in a complex mass of balconies and bridges like spun sugar, with embedded plazas and open courtyards cascading down and into the water.

Several large ships were at dock at the water's edge, the docks themselves having the look of mobile, impromptu affairs of wood fastened to the main towers by ropes and buoyed on huge gray bladders, so that they rose and fell with the waves. Gulls were wheeling overhead, a mass of them circling and weaving complex patterns, and the sunlight was rich and warm; already, its rays were coloring the water a bright blue even as it caused the salt-crusted towers to glow white.

Kuliver breached the surface a good ten yards off to Kethe's side, spat a long stream of water, and waved at them. "Come on, then! No sense in lollygagging!" He began an overarm swim toward the closest set of docks, no more than twenty yards away, and the rest of them followed.

They climbed up onto the pier, one after the other, and sat there gasping. A few Noussians had been working aboard the sole boat at dock stood frozen, staring wide-eyed down at them.

"Morning," called Kethe, rising to her feet, water streaming down her legs to soak the wooden boards.

"Good morning," said one of the men, stepping up to the boat's railing, wonder in his eyes. His skin was a rich reddish brown, and his hair was thick and smooth, pulled back into a folded topknot. His clothing was broad-sleeved and white, with a bright blue waistcoat over it. "You came... from below?"

"Yes," said Kethe. "We've been sent by the Ascendant." She was busy buckling on her sword as she said this. "I am Virtue Makaria, and these are my Consecrated. What is the quickest way to the Solar Portals?"

"I am Roanu, captain of this ship." He hopped down onto the pier. "It would be my honor to take you to the square. You are a Virtue?"

"Yes," said Kethe, looking at the others. Braex pulled on his last boot. Khoussan adjusted his chain shirt. Dalitha fixed her hair into a ponytail and gave a nod. "Please, lead on. We have to hurry."

Roanu looked like he wanted to ask a dozen questions, but instead simply nodded and jogged down the pier. They fell in line behind him, following him up a set of narrow stairs carved into the face of the tower. It followed the tower's massive curvature, and soon they were high above the water, the glory of the sunrise sweeping around and out of sight.

Kethe looked out over the Eternal Ocean. It was said to run in every direction without end, to have swallowed countless brave Noussian youths who had set out to find land, to chart a course to Ennoia or Zoe. Perhaps a mile out, she could see a mass of small fishing boats, far too many to count.

Kuliver was just behind her and must have caught her studying them. "They'd have headed out a few hours before dawn," he called up. "They'll be back in soon enough with the day's catch. Unless they decide today's a good day to stay out."

Up and around they went, passing doorways, running up past windows whose shutters were painted a deep blue. Birds had roosted everywhere, their nests scooted into improbable nooks and crannies. The tower itself was not one uniform surface, but was built like a tightly bound bundle of thick reeds with staircases winding between them, the passages interweaving amidst their verticalities barely broad enough for one person to pass through. There were nine massive towers topped in bronze, and each, she realized, was composed of a dozen smaller, tightly clustered fragments.

"This way," said Roanu, finally leaving the stairs for a bridge perhaps a yard wide that arched out over the water far below. The Noussian ran without fear, darting across the span to the next major tower.

Kethe followed, light on her feet, and gave a quiet prayer of thanks to the Ascendant that there was no wind. The far tower was encircled by a broad, shallow ramp, and people were standing about on its length, talking nervously to each other, clad one and all in the same white and blue style, though here and there Kethe saw dashing caps of crimson or sashes of gold.

On they ran, then the Solar Portals hoved into view. They were placed in the center of the nine great towers on a massive pedestal of their own, connected to each tower by a huge bridge wide enough to drive two oxen carts across. The Portals rose twenty yards high into the air in a heptagon with a narrow band of clear space around their bases from which to traverse to one's chosen bridge.

Roanu came to a stop, hands on his knees, panting for breath. He pointed. "There. Those you see gathered on the pedestal have come to die, the poor fools. They said last night that they would face the kragh and not let them take the city."

Kethe felt but lightly winded. The fire within her soul was giving her wings. She stepped up beside the Noussian and gazed at the crowd that had clustered around the Aletheian Gate. Some two hundred men and women stood ready with everything from harpoons to short blades to fishing knives.

"Damn," said Khoussan. "They're going to be massacred."

Kethe turned and looked up. Every window, every balcony, every minor bridge was crowded with Noussians, their faces grave, their eyes wide as they watched.

"Why were you on the boat below?" asked Braex, his voice light, almost careless.

Roanu hesitated. "I was getting ready to cast off. To take to the water if the kragh truly came."

"You're a smart man," said Braex, clapping Roanu on the shoulder. Roanu visibly relaxed with relief. "But you're also a coward," said Braex. "Pity."

A thousand gasps were torn from throats around them, and Kethe saw the white fire fill the Portals. The crowd at the bases of the arches stumbled back, and a woman turned to harangue them. Her black hair was pulled smooth over her scalp and then erupted into a black, frizzy cloud behind her head. Kethe couldn't make out her words, but when the Noussian lifted her sword with a cry, it was echoed by the others and they stood firm.

Dalitha was at Kethe's elbow. "What do we do, Makaria?" The slender woman was biting the corner of her lip, worrying it and shaking her head. "What do we do?"

"Nothing," said Braex, folding his arms. "We were sent here to observe. That was made clear, was it not? So, we observe."

"And then what?" asked Khoussan, turning to stare at him. "Then, what do we do once we're done observing?"

Braex scowled but said nothing.

Kethe felt something akin to a light-headed joy pass through her. She could hear the White Song in the crash of the waves below, in the scream of the gulls, in the hushed murmur of the crowds watching above them. It was everywhere, she realized. It infused the world if you but had the ear for it.

"Come," she said, and began to walk across the bridge.

"We were sent to observe!" Braex yelled in protest.

Kuliver spat over the side of the bridge. "Then stay back here and observe, whoremaster. I'm with the Virtue."

Khoussan and Dalitha were right behind her. Kethe felt like, at any moment, she might slip the bonds of gravity and float up into the sky. Instead, she raised her sword and laughed as white fire engulfed it with an audible *whoomph*.

Her laugh was met by a second round of gasps and cries, and Kethe kept her blade aloft as she marched onward. The people at the crowd's rear turned to regard her, and then they yelled and elbowed each other till they had all turned and were staring at her in wide-eyed wonder, grinning and amazed.

"The Ascendant has heard our plea!" cried out the Noussian woman, who then pushed her way through the crowd to fall to her knees at the bridge's base. Her face was strong-boned and would have been plain if not for her striking, vivacious eyes. She seemed almost fevered as she gazed across the bridge at Kethe's approach. "We are saved!"

"No," called Kethe, feeling a great tenderness pity for her. "You are not. The Ascendant has sent us, but we are not enough."

Confusion flickered across the woman's face. "Your pardon?"

Kethe reached her and extended her hand. The woman took it, her own as callused as Kethe's, and rose.

"You are brave beyond belief," said Kethe, pitching her voice to carry. "But bravery will not win the day." Suddenly, a plan came to her fully formed. "You must do as I command."

"As you will, Virtue!"

"Take your people to the tower behind us. You must clear it of people. It is soon to become a battleground. You must move fast. We have perhaps only seconds. Go!"

Her final word was a cry, infused with the sharp crack of command, and the woman nodded and ran. Her people followed her, two hundred men and women who gazed with wonder and relief at Kethe and her burning blade as they streamed past her small knot of Consecrated and ran back over the bridge, shouting for people to get away from windows and balconies, to move to other towers.

The space in front of the Solar Portals cleared. The white fire continued to writhe and dance between the arches as Khoussan and Dalitha stepped up to Kethe's left, Kuliver and Braex to her right.

"So," said Khoussan carefully. "What's the plan, Virtue?"

"Follow my lead," said Kethe.

The first of the kragh emerged, shields raised high, hammers and axes lifted to strike down upon their enemy. They hesitated, blinking as they oriented themselves, then relaxed when they saw only five men and women standing before them. Kethe heard them laugh, twenty kragh in a line, and they moved forward, relaxing as they did so.

"Five against twenty," said Kuliver. "I think we can take them."

Another twenty kragh stepped through behind the first wave, and then a third.

"Shit," said Kuliver.

Instinctively, Kethe reached out with her blade and touched it to those of the Consecrated. White fire ran up Khoussan and Dalitha's swords, then flew up Kuliver's twin curved blades and engulfed Braex's hammer.

"Steady," said Kethe as the kragh advanced upon them. The white fire had wiped the grins from their brutish faces, and they approached with renewed caution. "We bloody them, then we flee for the tower. Stay with me if you can. When the time comes to split up, you'll know it."

"You're mad," said Braex.

"I love me a madwoman," said Kuliver, shifting into a deeper fighting stance.

The kragh at the front slowed. They were glancing around, trying to find a trap. Trying to understand why the five humans weren't running. The bridge forced them to narrow down to a dozen across, the others filling in behind them.

"Kethe?" asked Dalitha, her voice fraught with fear.

"I'm here," she replied. "Embrace the White Gate, Dalitha. Hear its song. Let it sing through you."

"I don't hear it!" Dalitha said.

"It's there."

"I don't hear it!"

The kragh roared and burst into a charge.

"Hear it in my voice! For the White Gate!" cried Kethe, thrilling at the charge, holding her blade aloft. "For the White Gate, for the Ascendant, for Nous!"

Chapter 20

A ction was always the best recourse.

Tiron rose from his crouch, and his fatigue and confusion fell away from him. In these moments, implicit with violence, he felt young again, immortal. His knees be damned.

The others stood. Everyone looked to him for direction.

"Lead," he said to Nok, drawing his ancient family blade. It gleamed in the gloom beneath the canopy like a spar of white ice.

Nok didn't need a translation. He unshouldered his massive hammer and began to lope through the trees, weaving his way around the trunks. Occasionally, he brushed one with his shoulder and set it to shaking.

Tiron came fast on his heels, the others running behind. Olina's breathing was ragged, half-hysterical, but that was all right; he didn't expect it to be otherwise. The others were intent. Slowly, they were turning from the naive knights he had met on the border of Ramswold's land into wolves: focused, trusting in his leadership, committed to executing his orders.

The slope began to rise precipitously, and soon they were reduced to striding powerfully uphill. Tiron wanted to maintain his run, but he knew they needed to conserve their strength. Bitter experience had taught him what happened when you ran into battle winded.

They broke free of the trees. The sound of roars came to their ears, then a crackling snap like a thousand twigs breaking at once, and the hair on the nape of Tiron's neck stood on end.

Magic.

The mountains glittered around them. There was no path, just a rocky scree that rose to a ridge up ahead of them. The sounds of battle were coming from the far side. Up they went, boots scrabbling and slipping on the loose stones, and then Nok cleared the rise and they were among enemy kragh.

Well, among three of them, left behind to guard the baggage train and the mountain goats. Lowlanders, Tiron thought, judging from their stature.

They turned and saw Nok. The closest one was wearing a torn and bloodied knight's tabard over his leathers. He looked up just as the mountain kragh swept his hammer up high into the air, and then with a grunt brought it slamming down as if he were pounding a spike into the dirt.

The hammer smashed the lowlander's head right into his chest, caved in his ribs, shattered his sternum, and buried itself all the way down into his pelvic cradle, then sheared through the bone to exit in a welter of gore and slam into the rock.

The other two kragh froze, eyes wide. Tiron didn't give them a chance to react. He was around Nok in a flash, his blade flickering out to slip across the first one's throat, a neat, simple cut that was mostly wrist, and the kragh gargled and dropped the reins of the mountain goats, hands going uselessly to his neck.

A dagger blossomed in the third kragh's eye, and then Ramswold was there, sliding his blade through the kragh's stomach, angling it up into his lungs. Despite his terrible wounds, the kragh pulled the dagger from his own head and went to stab Ramswold, who was stunned by the kragh's continued life.

Nok stepped in and punched the kragh in the head. Bones crunched, and the lowlander was knocked clear off Ramswold's blade to go down without a sound.

The others staggered over the rise. There were some twelve mountain goats, each as large as a knight's charger, most of them still carrying bags and crates, six of them with crude saddles. They were shying and jostling each other, apparently offended by the blood spilt at their hooves.

Tiron moved to the far side of the ridge. A shallow slope descended to a bowl in which a massive ruined building stood. Tiron would never have thought the kragh were capable of building such an edifice. It was a great circular building, gutted and hollowed out, easily some five or six stories tall, inlaid with alcoves and arches and great high windows that allowed him to glimpse the interior. Portions of it looked strangely melted in the light of the moon, with smooth, organic curves like melting ice.

Kragh were fighting kragh outside the building's main entrance. The hundred lowlander kragh who had come through the main Portal were hacking at an equal number of mountain kragh, but, despite the disparity in stature, the fight was uneven; black-robed shamans stood at the back of the attacking line, hurling balls of green flame at the defenders that carved huge, bloody holes through five or six of the fighters at a time.

"Black shit," said Tiron. He searched for a way to make a difference, a place they could attack so as to change the tide of battle. But it was on bloody scrum, a devouring mass of blades and hammers, tusks and black magic that would embrace them and destroy them without pause.

"There," said Ramswold, touching Tiron's arm and pointing to the far left of the battle. A group of kragh were fleeing the battle, climbing a trail that led up into the mountains. Perhaps a dozen individuals in all, they were rushing as fast as they could, helping several of their slower members — older kragh, it looked like — climb the rocky slopes.

"Nok," said Tiron, pointing them out in turn. "Who are they?"

He spoke swiftly to Shaya, who translated with one word. "Our shamans."

The enemy had seen the departing group. One black-robed shaman floating on a geyser of black smoke that seemed to be erupting continuously from the ground pointed a clawed hand and screamed an order. Twenty kragh peeled away from the fight to charge after the fleeing contingent.

"Tiron?" Ramswold's voice was taut with tension.

It was a good sixty yards down the slope to the battle, and another couple of hundred yards past it to the base of the mountain slope that the contingent was climbing. The kragh giving chase were halfway there already. They'd never reach them in time on foot.

Tiron sheathed his blade. "Time to mount some mountain goats," he said, sounding almost manically cheerful. "Nok, how the hell do you ride these things?"

Shaya translated. "They have a herd mentality. Will follow the leader. Nok will ride at the front. You just hold on."

"Sounds great."

Tiron stepped up to the closest goat. It swung its head around to regard him with liquid black eyes that were framed with surprisingly long and delicate lashes. Twin horns rose and curled back from its brow, each the length of Tiron's arm. Its coat was shaggy and white, thick enough that he could lose his hand within its delicious pile. It had a deeper chest than a horse, with massive shoulders that tapered down to comparatively narrow hindquarters. The legs weren't as long as a horse's — Tiron guessed that it could march forever, but could only sustain brief charges.

"All right, my friend," said Tiron, taking the reins. "My name's Tiron. We're going to go have some fun. Mind if I get on up?"

The goat shied away as Tiron grabbed a fistful of hair at the nape of its neck and hauled himself up onto the broad saddle. Thank the Ascendant, the kragh used stirrups. The goat was broader across the shoulders than a horse, making Tiron feel as if he were sitting athwart a furry boulder, but its movements were surprisingly light and graceful.

Tiron turned around. The others were climbing up as well, Nok having chosen the largest. "Olina, grab the pack beasts!" called out Tiron. "You're responsible for bringing as many of them as you can with us. Are we ready?"

They gave out nervous cries in response. Tiron rose in the stirrups and raised his sword. "I asked, are you ready to ride down into hell's chasm on the backs of some fucking goats?"

Laughter erupted: despairing, panicked, elated. It was the best he was going to get. He nodded to Nok, and then held on with grim strength as the goat nearly jolted out from under him and charged after Nok down the hill.

This was all wrong. The goat didn't move like a horse at all. Tiron kept trying to adjust in ways that jarred with what was happening beneath him. Down they charged, the ride surprisingly smooth despite the mass of jumbled rocks they were running over, a terrain that would have crippled a horse within seconds. Nok pulled his goat to the left, shearing around the back and flank of the attackers, whose rearmost members turned to regard them in surprise and dismay.

Tiron held his blade back along the goat's flank, at the ready. The night was split here and there by crackling, nightmarish flashes of green light. The din of kragh warfare was terrible, the roars only matched by their howls. The battle flashed by to their right, and then they were past the main part of it, racing through a mass of rounded tents, leaping over small campfires, female and young kragh yelling in fear and anger and scrambling to get out of their way.

The twenty kragh who had been giving chase heard them coming and turned at the last moment to face them. Nok led his goat right through their midst, swinging his hammer down and back up and lifting one of the lowlanders right off his feet, knocking him flying into the darkness.

Tiron was right behind him, and, without thinking, he swayed out of the arc of a hammer that came at him, letting his sword move forward almost of its own accord to take the kragh's arm off above the elbow. His goat lowered its head as it smashed into another kragh. Tiron heard bones snap as the kragh was butted aside. The goat stumbled, and Tiron thought he was going down — and then his goat recovered. He managed to swipe at another kragh's head as he passed him, his curses and cries tearing at the night, and then he was through.

Nok was pounding on ahead, his goat laboring under his mass. Tiron gripped the reins and looked behind. They'd carved a bloody swath through the center of the twenty kragh, leaving them reeling. Olina came last, benefitting from the chaos, leading five mountain goats in a tight bunch behind her own.

They reached the base of the mountain, turned their goats onto the narrow path that scrawled its way up the slope, and climbed after the shamans. They lost speed, but not as much as Tiron would have expected; the goats powered up the slope with incredible fortitude.

Nok called out something in his basso profundo voice, and the shamans ahead stopped and turned to regard them. There were twelve of them, Tiron saw: two women, three warriors, and the rest looked to be the shamans themselves.

"Hurry," said Tiron as they stopped before the kragh. "Olina, bring up the goats!"

Ramswold, Leuthold and Ulein, who were guarding the rear, half-turned to face the ten kragh who were edging up after them.

Olina slid down from her saddle and led the goats up, squeezing through their ranks, the goats nimbly picking their way, and reached the front, where Nok took the leads and spoke to a kragh woman who seemed to be in charge.

The refugees quickly mounted up, cutting only a few of the sacks and crates free. Tiron reached down and hauled Olina up behind him, giving her goat to the kragh. In a matter of moments, they were up, the refugees clearly used to riding the beasts.

"Watch out!" cried Ramswold. "Fireball!"

Tiron snapped his gaze down to the valley below. One of the black-robed shamans had approached, and Tiron saw a mass of green flame leave his hand and arc up toward them, leaving a lurid tail of sickly light behind it. It came too fast for them to avoid — and it was as large as one of their mountain goats, arching up high and falling upon them with wicked, mesmerizing speed.

Nok was faster. He dropped down from his goat, grasped his hammer with both hands, spun around once, and then, with a ragged roar, hurled his weapon into the sky. Tiron watched as the hammer shot up into the night and slammed into the center of the fireball just as it fell toward them — and caused it to explode.

A thousand smaller fragments of green flame cascaded out from the central mass to fall upon them and the mountainside, sizzling and searing whatever they touched. Tiron hissed as one landed on his arm and quickly burned through the leather and caused his chain to grow so hot that it burned his flesh.

"By the Ascendant," said Ulein in awe.

The afterimage of the fireball hung in Tiron's vision even after it was gone. Rubbing his hand across his eyes, Tiron looked at where Nok was standing, hands on his knees. He'd never, in all his years, seen the like.

"Move!" cried Ramswold from the back. "They're coming up!"

Nok mounted, then pulled Shaya up behind him. The kragh up ahead clucked to their goats, and in moments their entire line was climbing, leaving the huge building and the raging battle below. Tiron saw the defending kragh begin to surrender, raising their hands and dropping their weapons. Just before their trail curled around an outcropping and cut off the sight of the battle altogether, he saw the attackers rounding up the defenders and forcing them down to their knees.

They rode in silence for almost two hours, higher and deeper into the mountains. The cold was vicious, and when Olina wrapped her arms around Tiron, he felt nothing but gratitude. The goats moved with an eerie silence along the trail, rarely dislodging rocks, their white coats gleaming in the moonlight. He could hear the kragh up ahead conversing amongst themselves, but felt no urge to ask what they were discussing; it was enough to simply gaze out over the mountains and give thanks for having survived one more battle.

The view was stunning. The ice and snow just above them glittered with a ghostly lambency. The peaks themselves were jagged and raw, thrusting their way up against the multitude of stars as if freshly gouged from the womb of the earth itself. They were above the tree line now, the path barely a foot wide, and the drop to their left was precipitous. Tiron would never have dared this trail on a horse. His goat, however, seemed unperturbed.

He was almost asleep when they finally stopped. Rousing himself, he saw that they'd arrived at a small plateau, barely large enough to hold their dozen goats. Kragh were dismounting, some more stiffly than others, and their harsh, dissonant language was muted as if in respect for the grandeur of the vista that spread out before them.

Tiron groaned as he levered himself out of the saddle. His legs had stiffened terribly. He helped Olina down, then moved forward to where Shaya was standing beside Nok, facing the Red River kragh.

Their leader was a female. In the moonlight, her hair looked the color of dried blood, the strands coarse and thick, with most of it tucked back and beneath a huge bear fur that enshrouded her shoulders and chest. Twin tusks emerged from her broad mouth, but they were nubs compared to those of the males. Her brow was broad and heavy, and her cheekbones were harsh. Her bare arms were comparable to Elon the smith's, heavily muscled and with veins visible across her forearms, and she stood tall — an inch taller than himself, at any rate.

It was her eyes, however, that held his attention; her stare would have given Iskra pause. She was examining him closely in turn, her expression closed and hard.

"Ser Tiron," said Shaya. "This Maur, leader of the Wise Women of the Red River tribe."

Tiron gave her a nod. "Maur."

Maur exchanged words briefly with Nok, who rumbled his responses. As they spoke, another kragh stepped up alongside her. He was an older male, his skin a dark olive green, his frame without the muscled bulk of the younger males, but rather lean and rangy as if he was accustomed to hard living. His left arm was missing, but something in the way this kragh held himself, with calm confidence and a flat gaze, told Tiron that he might be as lethal as any warrior Tiron had ever fought.

"This is Barok, the Red River's swordmaster."

The shamans themselves approached. Tiron saw with surprise that they were all blind; each of them had empty eye sockets, though that didn't seem to trouble them; they gathered around as if the moon lit their path as clearly as the sun.

Tiron was introduced to each of them in turn. Under Wolf, a spindly old male so small he could have been a child, his knee joints wider than his thighs, topped by such a massive pelt of white wolf fur that he seemed to almost disappear beneath it, with the wolf's head resting over his own. Owl Home, with a carved wooden mask of a white owl over his face, a profusion of sticks tangled into his hair like some wild, improbable mane. Mud Knife, with a brown cloth covering his lower face, held up by a ring that pierced the bridge of his nose; his head was covered with a brown cap whose sides fell down nearly to his waist. Bear Dancer, the largest of the group, a hulking old male with five deep scars running down across his face, clad only in a loincloth despite the cold, his hide worked with sigils of white paint. And Frozen Heart, an albino kragh with pallid, dusty skin, bowed down under the weight of a great pack that seemed to be filled a multitude of bleached bones.

Their leader was their eldest member, an ancient kragh called Forest Lord, who was wearing a dear's skull over his own, its antlers spreading out impressively on either side, the bone gilded in silver and bronze. He leaned his weight on a large branch from which hung a number of bones, bells without clappers, small crystals, feathers and other such objects, and was clad in thick mountain goat furs that were bound about his wizened body by black leather straps.

Forest Lord stepped up to Tiron and peered up at him, then extended a wrinkled old claw of a hand and touched it to Tiron's cheek. His skin was strangely hot, as if he'd been warming his hand over a fire. The old kragh traced the line of Tiron's jaw, then stepped back, looking to his shamans, and muttered something. They all nodded their agreement.

"He says that you were sent to us by the spirits," said Shaya. "That they brought you in our hour of need to ensure the completion of their sacred mission."

"The spirits," said Tiron dryly. "All right. Sure. I'm glad we arrived in time to help. Now, about your mission. Are you going to tell them about Tharok?"

The two Red River warriors who had accompanied them were at the back of the crowded ledge, where the cliff face extended out into a broad overhang. They crouched down and crawled into the shadows beneath it. Sparks flickered, and a small fire came into being several yards deeper into the cliff face than Tiron would have thought possible.

Forest Lord spoke, then turned and shuffled toward the overhang, the others turning to follow.

"He said he doesn't want to talk out here in the cold," said Shaya. "So, come. We're safe enough here for a few hours. I'm going to tell them everything."

They spent the next twenty minutes tying up the goats, checking the supplies they had stolen, and making another three small fires in the surprisingly deep cave that extended like an ax wound into the mountain. The ground was gritty but dry, and once Tiron was seated cross-legged on a fur in front of a small fire where stolen food bubbled in a little pot over the flames, he had to admit the old kragh was right: this was a much better way to talk.

Ulein sat with Olina, one arm thrown awkwardly around her shoulders as she wept softly. Leuthold stared into his fire, alternately clenching and relaxing his jaw, and startling every time a kragh moved abruptly. Ramswold sat beside Tiron, stiff with tension, clearly over-whelmed, repulsed, and fascinated by their company.

Shaya and Nok told their tale in kragh. Tiron allowed his mind to unfocus and simply ate and warmed his frozen feet. The kragh lan-guage sounded a lot like rocks falling down a cliff face: small cracks, sliding rasps, harsh guttural sounds. Maur asked questions, her voice stern. Forest Lord seemed sunken in reverie, staring into the depths of the fire.

Finally, Shaya and Nok finished their tale, and the silence caused Tiron to lift his chin from the palm of his hand. Ramswold's eyes were closed; apparently, the young lord was asleep where he sat. Tiron elbowed him awake and turned to Shaya. "What's going on?"

"Forest Lord wants me to translate something for you."

Tiron rubbed his face and sat up straighter. "Go ahead. I'm listening."

Forest Lord spoke, pausing only for Shaya to translate every so often. "The shamans of the kragh are tasked with one great and sacred duty, and that is to remember. To preserve the past, so that our previous errors do not repeat themselves. Many think our power lies with our connection to the spirits, but our true power is simpler and more profound: we guard the greatest secret that ever there was."

Tiron shifted a little, easing the stiffness of his rear. "The greatest secret ever," he said, trying to keep his tone neutral.

"Once, we were bound as slaves to the medusa. You saw their great temple below, where the Red River was camped. For countless years, we sacrificed ourselves for their pleasure. We begged to be turned to stone, killed each other, worshipped them. We were little more than animals, and they treated us as such. But, finally, a hero arose who sought to change the old ways. She was the first shaman, perhaps the greatest of us that ever there was. She went into the spirit world and there discovered the means to overthrow the medusas."

Tiron's mild impatience disappeared. He leaned forward. "A secret to defeat them?"

Forest Lord nodded gravely and croaked on, Shaya listening patiently. Tiron kept glancing between the two of them, barely concealing his eagerness to learn.

"The spirits led her on a great quest, far from our lands, and eventually she came to a place where the earth shook, where the rivers were like fire, where the mountains groaned and the sky was filled with black smoke. There, she found the khargans, and after a terrible sacrifice to the spirits, they helped her persuade them to come to our aid. She rode the greatest of their number back to our homeland and destroyed the medusas and their faithful with cleansing fire. The only medusas to survive were the ones who fled deep into the earth. She led our kind out of the darkness, and so began the dawn of our civilization."

Tiron nodded slowly. "All right. So, what happened to these khargans? Can we ask for their help again?"

Shaya didn't translate his question, but instead continued to interpret the shaman. "At the end of her life, the great shaman gathered all the other spirit talkers and told them that the khargan were too dangerous to leave free. Too powerful. Already, she saw the kragh beginning to worship them as new gods. So, they bound the khargan in a great spell, hiding them away from the world, but leaving open a path to reach them. They have slumbered ever since, waiting for the kragh to need their aid once more.

"That time has come. We journey to find the khargan. We seek to awaken them and bring them back, so that they may destroy Kyrra and her foul cult, and, if need be, destroy Tharok as well. Only then will the kragh be free to return to their true ways, to give up this mad quest of domination and war. And it is for this reason that the medusa-Kissed shamans now hunt us. They seek to prevent us from accomplishing our sacred goal."

Tiron couldn't help but grin. "Well, I and mine are happy to help you in any way we can. How far are we from the khargan?"

Forest Lord cut in and spoke carefully to Shaya. She covered her mouth, her face growing pale.

"What?" asked Tiron, looking from her to the shaman and back. "What happened?"

"I misspoke," said Shaya in a whisper. "The kragh weren't rescued by the khargan. They were saved by *dragons*."

Chapter 21

T he kragh came at them like a wall of tusks and weapons and
muscle, shoulder to shoulder, roaring and screaming, their boots
thudding on the smooth expanse of the bridge. Kethe felt all her
fear evanesce, felt a holy madness descend upon her. Her blade was
weeping fire. She was an extension of the glory of the White Gate,
and she was going to bring that glory to the kragh.

They were halfway to her when she burst forward in a charge of
her own, the dismayed cries of the Consecrated trailing after her. One,
two, three long strides, and she leaped, soaring up, right at the lead
kragh. She didn't so much kick as step on his face, then turned sideways to slide past his descending ax, her turn leading her into a rapid
spin, right over the heads of the other kragh, her blade extended out
laterally so that it blurred all around her as she fell into their midst.

Down she plummeted, like a knife stabbing into their ranks, to
fall into a crouch, carving through thighs and knees and shins. Blood
surrounded her in thick, gouting torrents as the kragh around her
toppled like felled trees, screaming and clutching at their wounds.
She didn't stop, didn't hesitate. She leaped once more, high into the
air, bursting up just as the kragh piled into where she'd been crouched,
into an arcing flip that took her five yards from where she'd been but

a moment ago. Down she came again, and there was no thought of sword forms, ripostes, high or low attacks — there was only fire, and she was the flame.

She danced through their ranks, high on her tiptoes, twirling and ducking, rising and falling, arms out and then pulled back in toward her chest, laughing as she went, leaving a spray of thick blood behind her. Arms, hands, heads, and the upper diagonal quadrants of chests all fell apart around her. Her white fire cauterized each wound, filling the air with the sound of sizzling meat.

She could hear her Consecrated doing battle only a few yards away. The kraghs' charge had been slammed to a halt, and now their enemy was heaving in shock, trying to figure out where she was, yells of confusion and dismay filling the air.

And still Kethe danced, her blade an adder's tongue, slipping in and out of bodies. She bent over backwards, an axe slicing the air where she'd been, then leaped straight up, knees to her chest as a kragh dove through where she'd been standing, only to land, one foot on a kragh's huge shoulder, then leap once more, somersaulting, blade slicing down and leaving carnage in her wake before she fell back beyond the battle line, the empty bridge behind her, her four Consecrated fighting for all they were worth to hold back the tide.

She had no idea how many she had killed, but it wasn't enough. It would never be enough. She could hear the fresh roar of new kragh emerging from the Gate. The mass beyond the Consecrated already numbered in the hundreds.

Kethe lifted her blade, which was immaculate and devoid of blood. "Consecrated! To me! Retreat!"

They stumbled back, hacking and slashing with vigor born of desperation, hurrying away from the kragh, who hesitated, seeing her somehow before them once more. Kethe lunged at them, swiping her blade in a vicious arc through the air, causing the kragh at the front edge to leap back, then laughed, turned on her heel, and ran.

Her Consecrated were right behind her.

She felt as fleet of foot as a deer. The sea shimmered far below them, the sun having fully cleared the horizon down and to her right. The huge cluster of slender towers that formed one of the nine massive agglomerations rose before her, dusty white and luminous in the morning light. She saw only a few faces in the windows, a few people on the balconies. She prayed that the majority had cleared out, but it was too late now if they hadn't.

The kragh pounded after them. Kethe reached the far edge of the bridge with no time to think, to plan. The ramp curved down and to the left, up and to the right. Ahead, a narrow pathway slipped into a shadowed crack. Into this she speared, racing but ten yards before she reached a narrow set of steps. She leaped up them and turned. Her Consecrated were climbing up behind her. Kuliver's arm was red with his blood. Dalitha had a gash across her temple. Behind them came the kragh.

The steps ended in a doorway, but two yards above and to the left was a balcony. Kethe leaped, caught the railing with one hand, and swept up onto it in one smooth movement. Braex stared up at her, not understanding, then shook his head as if clearing his thoughts and leaped after her. She reached down, caught his hand, and heaved him up. Kuliver needed no assistance despite his wounded arm, but Khoussan barely made it. Dalitha was the last, and she turned as if she intended to stem the tide of kragh all by herself.

"Dalitha!" Kethe's voice caused the young woman to look up. "Don't even think about it!"

Dalitha swallowed, turned, ran up the last five steps and leaped. Kethe caught hold of her outflung hand and heaved her up. They were packed in tight, the kragh right below them.

Braex threw his shoulder against the doors and burst into a dark and cool room. Kethe darted past him, across the room and into a narrow hall, then up some more steps, through another series of rooms, and came to a narrow window. All she needed was the sight of a sloping tiled roof outside to convince her to leap, her body closing into a tight ball, and she soared out through the open square and back into the sunlight.

The white tiles were solidly built and spattered with bright orange lichen. She caught her balance and ran across them. The kragh were yelling below, just out of sight. She sprinted to the edge of the roof and then leaped, reaching out to catch hold of a clothesline festooned with huge white shirts. Her free hand closed around the cord, which dropped quickly at first, then slowed, sagging down into a triangular shape, and when it was stretched to its maximum, she released it, momentum and the cord's resistance causing her to flip in midair to fall into a crouch in an empty alleyway between the towers.

The white walls here were glacial blue in the shadows, with brilliant profusions of purple flowers spilling down from planters at every window. Kragh were running past the far end of the alley. One saw her, stopped, and pointed. Immediately, they came in after her, and with a laugh Kethe turned and ran in the other direction just as Kuliver landed nimbly behind her. She looked up and saw Khoussan staring down in disbelief from the tiled roof high above.

"That way!" she yelled, pointed in another direction, and he nodded and disappeared.

With Kuliver at her heels, she ran out onto a broader ramp that curled around the outside of the great tower. Around this she sprinted, going faster and faster, so that when four kragh came jogging down toward her and into sight she didn't stop, but crashed into them, her left shoulder skimming the tower's wall, her sword slicing and deflecting. One kragh fell; a second overbalanced and disappeared into the void. The third fell to his knees ducking her swipe, and she leaped at the fourth to bury her knee in his face. She rode his head down to the ground, nearly fell, and then was back up, Kuliver's hand at her elbow.

She rounded the tower's curvature, and the Portals came into view some forty yards below. Her heart sank at the sight. Some four hundred kragh, maybe more, had already come through, and they were boiling up the ramps and steps toward her, swarming like ants up the sides of the tower.

A yell went up at the sight of her, and she ran. There was nowhere to go but up. She was a fleet fox of divine fire, a zephyr of endless wind. Up she went, around and around. The kragh were indefatigable, however, and followed tenaciously just behind her.

"I'll lead them off!" Kuliver cried, and shouldered a door open to disappear into the darkness beyond.

Kethe ran up and around and then cut right and went out onto a bridge that arched out perilously to another tower. She turned, walking backward across the yard-wide span, easily some two hundred yards above the ocean. Kragh ran up to the base of the narrow bridge, heaving for breath, and then began to edge across toward her.

He charged her, screaming his war cry, but she didn't meet him head-on; instead, she fell backwards just as he reached her, reaching past his hammer to grab his belt and pull him down onto her upflung leg, which she buried into his crotch. Momentum carried him up and over to slam face-down on the stone and slide off into oblivion.

Kethe rolled back over her shoulder and came up, sword raised overhead just in time to block the downward swing of an axe, the head of which her blade lopped off as it sheared through the wooden haft. The axe head nearly flew into her face, but she turned aside just in time and rose fully to her feet to slash a quick succession of cuts into the kragh's chest, arms and thighs. He screamed and collapsed.

A third kragh died, then a fourth and fifth. There were just too many.

Gasping for breath now, sweat pouring down her face, Kethe feinted at the next kragh's face, then turned and ran across the bridge to a new stairwell, soared up the forty steps, then leaped out onto a second bridge. She crossed that, and halfway over leaped down, falling twenty feet to crash and roll onto another tiled roof. She barely caught herself on its edge before tumbling into the void, then was up and through a window.

Screams surrounded her: kragh yelling commands, their voices echoing from all sides. Kethe bolted up through the tower, fighting her way through crowded stairwells, slipping past kragh before they knew she was there, cutting them down as she ran. She burst into a large room and saw some twenty of them yelling at each other, weapons drawn. Their argument ended at the sight of her, and as they charged, she leaped impetuously out a window only to realize there was nothing below to land on.

Heart in her throat, she whipped her hand back and caught the window's edge before she cleared it altogether, then fell and grabbed the sill, and her body slammed into the tower's face. A sword came down at her hand, which she swapped with the other just in time. She caught her falling sword with her now-free hand, then bunched her legs underneath her and, using her arm that gripped the windowsill as a fulcrum, leaped straight up. She flew up perhaps four yards, just high enough to grab the next window. With only one hand, she hauled herself up, the effort drawing a scream from her depths as doing so tore at her shoulder, then she was crouched on the sill.

The sound of fighting came from far below. Though she couldn't see them, she knew her Consecrated were still on the run. Kragh yells sounded from deeper within the tower.

A band of raised stone ran around the tower here, a foot of navigable surface along its top. Kethe sheathed her blade and made her way out onto it. She shuffled quickly, hugging the tower face. A whistle sounded near her ear, and then a huge clothyard arrow *thwacked* into the rock. Kethe gritted her teeth and hurried. Another arrow struck, and she risked a glance down. Some twenty kragh were shooting at her from a rooftop some sixty yards below, heaving back with massive longbows.

Arrows bouncing off around and below her, Kethe reached the next window and ducked inside, only to find another staircase. She felt delirious, every instinct honed to fever pitch. Her world had narrowed to a labyrinth of steps and ledges, rooftops and bridges. She tore through the room and up the stairwell, up and up and up. Footsteps sounded behind her, dozens if not more. Should she turn and dive into the crowd, killing as many as she could before she fell? No. That was madness. Run!

Up and up. Round and round. An open hallway beckoned her, and she darted down its length and outside onto another ramp. She was so high up now that the tower had tapered to only twenty yards wide. Around and around this she ran. The sunlight was mellow gold, the walkway dusty with disuse.

In the back of her mind beat a constant refrain: *You're running out of up. You're running out of up.*

The ramp reached an iron ladder that was bolted to the wall. She leaped up, clutched the tenth rung, and began to climb. Above her bulged out the bronze onion dome. She was near the top when kragh appeared on the ramp below her.

She reached the final rung and climbed out onto the dome. The footing was treacherous behind belief, but shallow steps had been beaten into the metal surface, each a foot high and a yard in. Her lungs were on fire, her muscles liquid with fatigue. She didn't run, but simply trudged up the side of the dome, sword held at her side.

She reached the very peak. Below her, the world spread out in every direction. The sky was illimitable and righteous and blue, and she felt as if she could reach up and touch its very substance. The ocean didn't even seem to move from this height, but rather looked to be a single plane of beaten azure scratched here and there by lines of foam.

The bronze dome glimmered and gleamed in the light of the sun, great patches of variegated lichen spreading like continents across old maps over its surface.

Sweat dripped from her nose. From her chin.

There was nowhere left to run. No exits. No escapes.

The first kragh climbed warily into view, a massive arm swinging over the roof's edge to clutch the last rung, and then he was up and crouched on the first step. He saw her standing there, raised a hand as if to say *Just one moment*, and sat.

More came up after him, all of them panting like dogs, until some fifteen of them were gathered on the lowest steps.

Kethe took a deep breath and forced herself to stand straight. The peak of the dome was a flat circle perhaps a yard wide with a spike ten yards high spearing up to the heavens. She leaned back against it and watched as the kragh gathered themselves.

They were in no rush. They had her cornered at last.

More kept coming up. The fifteen became thirty, then angry yells from below indicated that others couldn't come up while the first lot were crowding the edge of the roof. Nervously, licking their wide maws, the kragh began to approach Kethe. A few tried to leave the steps, but the second to do so slipped, his foot going out from under him. He crashed down onto his chest, scrabbled at the curved bronze, and slid down and out of sight with a scream.

The other kragh shuffled closer together on the steps.

Kethe lowered herself into her battle stance. Her only mercy was that they could only come at her two at a time. But more kept coming up over the edge, and these had great bows in their hands. A wild desperation at the sight of them arose within her, but there was nowhere to go.

The kragh with the bows yelled, and those who were edging toward her with weapons looked back and then lowered themselves into crouches, giving the bowmen a clear line of sight.

Their leader drew a black feathered arrow and set it to his string. He pulled back, sighting at her down the shaft's length. Back and back he pulled, the huge bow creaking. She doubted she could even begin to draw that bow, but he did so till the fletching was alongside his ear. Kethe inhaled and held her breath.

He released, and she stepped to the slide and slashed down with her sword. The huge arrow clattered in two pieces near her feet.

The kragh all gaped at her, and then one of them began to pound the rooftop with his fist. The others stared at him, and then a second and a third began to do the same. Soon, all the kragh were pounding the bronze dome, producing a deep, echoing knell from its center.

Kethe raised her blade once more, and the lead bowman snarled something. The other kragh with bows all pulled arrows from their quivers. There were ten of them.

There was no way she could cut those arrows down, and just one would knock her backwards off her perch, onto the curvature of the roof.

The bows creaked as the kragh drew their arrows back to their ears.

Chapter 22

They gathered before the Portal that would return them to Aletheia. Auntie was dressed in a voluminous black gown complete with a veil that rendered her face a pale but indistinct presence, like a full moon glimpsed through the clouds. Eulos was wearing black leather armor, which was artfully designed but creaked with his every move. Only the Doctor of Almanac was dressed as Audsley had seen him, seeming to have put no effort or greater thought into the impending assassination.

Zephyr was clothed in elegant, form-fitting robes that were slit up between the legs. Her black outer robe was a maze of subtle silver patterns, wide-sleeved and ending just past the elbows; below that, extending to her wrists with a hole for her thumb to slip through, was a completely black layer of silk.

"Thank you for coming," she said to the small group, her voice grave. She gave no sign that she had forced their hands in the foulest ways possible. "Master Audsley is to lead us to the stonecloud of Starkadr, and there we shall destroy the Minister of Perfection when he follows us in. Are we all ready?"

Audsley wanted to say no. He didn't know where to look, how to hold himself, what to think. His mind was like a mouse caught within a circle of firecats, darting this way and that in a helpless panic. He *knew* there was no escaping this, but that didn't make him dread what was to come any less. Every time he reflected on his role in these proceedings, his thoughts would skitter away once more, his mind not willing to consider the perfidious action he was about to execute. Only the calming influence of the demon's possession allowed him to stand there in silence at all.

"Very well," said Zephyr. Gone were all traces of coquettishness, childishness, and provocation. She moved to the Portal and spoke a harsh string of syllables. The Portal flushed with that oh-so-familiar ink, and she stepped aside and gestured for them to go through.

Auntie went first, lifting the hem of her skirt as she stepped into the rippling darkness, followed by Eulos and then the doctor. Then, taking Audsley's hand in her own, Zephyr gave him a squeeze and a searching look, and, together, they stepped through to Aletheia.

There was that swimming sense of disorientation, that sensation of a million miles being traversed by diving *inwards*, and then they emerged together into the smoldering wreckage of the Fujiwara estate. It was mid-morning. Smoke was rising in smudged columns into the sky, and everything smelled of charcoal. What had once been an ancient and distinguished home of severe beauty had been reduced to cinders and ash. Here and there, structural beams were still pointing up at the sky, but the devastation was near-total.

Nobody spoke. Audsley could only imagine how hard it must be for them to see their former seat of power so reduced. The four Fujiwaras looked about with grim expressions, and finally Auntie lifted her veil and spat.

"Eloquently put," said Zephyr. "No sense in delaying. Audsley?"

He willed himself to rise just enough so that he could skim over the complex. In a way, they should be grateful that the devastation was so complete; it meant there was no reason for people to remain, to guard, or even seek to possess. They reached the edge of Aletheia without any problem, and flew out into the sky.

The others followed without comment. They descended, picking up ever greater speed, their robes and hair streaming up as they fell feet-first. Down they went, past the complex layers of balconies, exposed roads, colonnades, courtyards and bridges. Audsley studied the bulk of creamy stone coldly. It was here that he'd lost everything in order to gain one still elusive victory. He sought out the crowds of beautifully dressed courtiers, the palanquins, but they were all gone.

Curious. None of the usual activity was in evidence. Instead, he saw a band of broad-shouldered monsters moving sluggishly down one ramp, hammers and axes over their shoulders, laughing and shoving at each other.

Audsley slowed. "What are they?"

The others stopped and hovered alongside him.

"Kragh," said Eulos, his sullen mien cracked open by shock.

"In Aletheia?" asked Auntie, her voice rich with horror. "Impossible."

They watched the kragh turn into a hallway and disappear into the stonecloud. Audsley backed away and looked at the stonecloud with new eyes. For the first time, he noticed smoke drifting out through the windows, rising in thin trickles here and there. He could hear the distant sound of shouts erupting from somewhere far below, and then screams, and then silence.

He looked at Zephyr, his heart pounding, his throat closing. "Aletheia has fallen."

Zephyr's face was a blank nullity. She blinked, much like a lizard might, and then shrugged. "Not our problem. Let us continue."

"Not our...?" Audsley almost choked. Even the demon's numbing effect on his soul couldn't contain his outrage. "Aletheia! The seat of the Empire! The White Gate – oh, mercy, have they taken...?"

The doctor's voice was disdainful to the point of harshness. "They cast us out. Who knows? If we Fujiwara had been allowed to remain, perhaps this wouldn't have happened. As it is, Little Zephyr is correct. This is not our problem. Let the Empire deal with it."

Audsley ran his hands over his hair. His mind reeled. What did this mean? Was there any point to what he was attempting to do? Had the mission for which he'd sold his soul been rendered void? And what had happened to Iskra and her Agerastian forces? "I —

but, I can't understand — Abythos, the siege — how could they have fallen so quickly?"

"Audsley," said Zephyr, floating around so that she faced him and blocked his view of the stonecloud. Her face was but inches from his. "I know this affects you deeply, that it pains you, but we must focus. You must focus. We have a goal in mind that precludes all other concerns — not least because it is your own small way of helping the Empire. And now the Empire clearly needs as much help as it can get. If you do this, if you kill my grandfather, you will have removed a dangerous player from the field. No matter how great the difficulties that the Ascendant faces, the death of the Minister of Perfection can only help him. Yes? Come. Do your part. Do not lose your zeal now."

Audsley allowed Zephyr to pull him down, but this was all too much. How could any man retain his sanity under such extreme blows? The vicissitudes of life had never been so cruel.

Down they flew, Zephyr holding him by the arm. She kept asking him in soft tones if they were close, if this was the right level.

Finally, they reached the seventh. Was it so long ago that he'd been conveyed by palanquin along this circum, hurrying to meet the Red Rowan widow? It seemed like part of another life. He flew around the stonecloud till he reached the familiar section which led to Starkadr's Portal — only to pause again in shock.

Nearly a hundred kragh were milling around in the circum just outside it, weapons drawn, talking amongst themselves.

"What are they doing here?" Eulos asked, eyeing them warily. "Standing guard?"

"Guard? Whatever for? Useless creatures." Auntie sniffed.

"They must know of the Portal," said Audsley. "I mean, it's the only reason to fill up this part of the circum. But why? Someone must have used it, fled through it, or perhaps arrived through it to fight them."

Zephyr studied the circum, then shook her head. "Even if we incinerated these kragh, more would come. Grandfather would never consent to being escorted through a battle. He would demand that his cousins and nephews be sent ahead to clear the way, or declare that Starkadr wasn't worth the effort." She tapped her lips. "Audsley? How else can we get to your stonecloud?"

"How else?' He wanted to cry. There was no other way. This was the sole Portal to Starkadr that he knew about. The other was in Mythgraefen Hold. Of course, if they could fly to Ennoia, he could pass through the Raven's Gate at Kyferin Castle to Mythgraefen— but of course that wouldn't work. How could they get the Minister of Perfection to consent to such a journey?

The four Fujiwaras were watching him. He had to come up with an answer. How could they pass so many kragh, and then, harder yet, ensure that no more came to guard the entrance?

There is another way, said the Aletheian demon in his mind.

There is?

Of course. Think, dear Magister. What is a Portal?

A means to travel impossible distances.

And how is that travel effected?

By the demon invested in... Audsley trailed off and then clamped his hand over his mouth. *Can you...?*

But of course. I am, after all, a demon of some consequence. All you need do is ask, and I will take you wherever you wish to go.

Why didn't you help me in this way before?

There was no response, but Audsley could hazard a guess. Doing so now would further the demon's purposes. Somehow, facilitating this mission would lead it closer to its own personal goals. Did he need any more reason to balk at proceeding?

"Audsley?"

"I, um – Zephyr, this may sound like a strange question, but can you — or any of you, really — can you teleport?"

The doctor raised an eyebrow.

"Without the use of a Portal?" Zephyr shook her head. "Of course not. Can you?"

"I believe I might, though I've never done it before." He swallowed with difficulty. *How does it work?*

Have them touch your skin. I will do the rest. Poor things, with their castrated demons. I wonder, do they know how pathetic and pitiful they are? How they limit themselves needlessly?

"Here," said Audsley, rolling up his sleeve and extending his arm. "Everyone touch me. And I... I shall do the rest."

They did so, Auntie peeling off a black glove so that she could lay one finger across his forearm.

Where to, dear Magister?

Audsley thought of the great Portal room in Starkadr, and then quickly changed his mind. *The secret library. If you will.*

But of course.

The world fell away, was consumed by night, and this time the sensation was less a feeling of falling than of the world itself spinning around him while he remained still. Everything seemed to blur, and then, somehow, they were within Starkadr's secret library.

The five of them were floating in the center of the large circular room. It was exactly as he'd seen it last. The walls were covered in precious tomes, endless shelves wrapping all the way around them, while below, rings of balconies descended in a telescopic manner to a circular table. The six corpses were still holding their positions of eternal rest, with the books Audsley had disturbed piled on the floor beside them to one side.

"Amazing," breathed Eulos, floating away from their group.

"Yes," said Audsley, feeling a foolish sense of pride in the place, as if it were his own creation. "It's quite a splendid repository of knowledge."

"No," said Eulos. "You. You brought us here. I didn't think it possible."

"These books," said the doctor, and then he drifted to the wall and held out his hand in a reverential manner that was all too familiar to Audsley. In fact, he found himself warming up to the man for that reason alone. "What language is this? Ancient Aletheian?"

"Where are we, precisely?" asked Auntie in a clipped voice. She sounded furious — but perhaps that was how she handled fear.

"The secret heart of Starkadr's library," Audsley said, trying for nonchalance. "The Flame Walkers' stonecloud. I discovered it not too long ago."

"Oh, Audsley," breathed Zephyr, drifting down through the rings to the very bottom and alighting beside the table. "You wonderful, brilliant man."

"Yes, well." He felt a soft glow of pride. "I will admit, I was quite proud of the leap of intuition that led me to discover its secret. I was with a knight and three guards, you see, and one of them, a rather foolish man called Temyl—"

"Look at these tomes," said the doctor. "I can barely decide where to begin. This – this will change everything for us."

"Us?" asked Audsley.

"Yes," said the doctor, not even bothering to look at him. "For the Fujiwara clan. How much lost knowledge resides here? Oh, to think of the uses we shall put it to! This is wealth beyond imagining!"

"Ah," said Audsley.

Zephyr picked up the uppermost book from the pile Audsley had collected what felt like many years ago. "*Being a treatise on the formation and enslavement of demons*," she read slowly.

"Shall we, ah, focus on the mission at hand? Your words, I believe, Zephyr."

"Yes," said Zephyr, and she put the book down with great reluctance. "There will be years upon years to absorb this discovery. For now, however, let us focus."

I thought she wished to while away the rest of her life as a fisherwoman, said his demon in amusement.

"You can choose where to appear?" asked Eulos.

Yes, said his demon. **As long as you have visited the location before.**

"I believe so," said Audsley.

"Then, we should do the following," Eulos said decisively. "The doctor, Aunt Mayzie and I will be positioned up here on the topmost level, pressed back against the books so as to be out of sight. You, Zephyr, and the Minister of Perfection will appear on the bottommost level. As soon as you do, both of you are to fly straight up. That will be our signal. We will all fill the bottom of this well with fire. The walls will concentrate our power, focusing it all on him."

"But the books!" exclaimed Audsley and the doctor together. The doctor shot Audsley an irritated glance immediately thereafter.

"We can bring them up," said Eulos. "Remove everything of value."

"Then, do so," said Zephyr. "Audsley and I must find my grandfather and convince him to come. I will take a few samples to whet his appetite." She plucked the top three books from Audsley's old pile. "We will give you at least an hour to prepare and remove the books. From then on, be ready for our arrival."

The three Fujiwaras nodded, their expressions grim.

"Come, Audsley." Zephyr extended her hand, opening and closing it as she bid him join her. "Let us return to Haugabrjótr. The trap is set. We have our bait. Now, let us lead our mouse inside."

"The Minister of Perfection," Auntie said softly, "is no mouse."

Zephyr didn't bother to respond. She took Audsley's hand as he reached her and beamed a truly beautiful smile at him, her eyes sparkling with joy and mischief. "Ready?"

For a second, a terrible, foolish second, Audsley wondered what it would be like to have her smile at him like that for no other reason than that she enjoyed his company. This was immediately followed by a sick sense of shame, and he nodded jerkily. "Yes. Hold tight."

Back to Haugabrjótr, please, he whispered, and the world fell away once more.

A moment later, they were back in his cramped quarters, the light falling gray and diffuse through his tiny window.

Zephyr released his hand and looked about with delight. "With this new ability of yours, I don't think I'll ever be able to leave your side," she said. "It's breathtaking! And all because your demon is self-possessed? So many questions, so many possibilities... Yet, of course, the primary danger remains: the loss of control, the sublimation of self into their desires... But you're managing to remain very much yourself, Audsley." She peered at him as if he were a particularly interesting species of insect. "How do you do it?"

He gulped and pushed his glasses up his nose. "I'm not quite sure I *am* 'doing it', as you say. I haven't felt quite myself in some time."

"Well, we can explore this at our leisure later on. Starkadr! What other mysteries might it hold, I wonder?"

Something about her last words struck Audsley as false; they had been said too blithely. Still, he didn't know what to make of them, so he remained silent.

"No matter; all in due time. First, we must attend to my grandfather. I requested a private audience, earlier, to which he agreed with extreme reluctance. But with these books, and the story we shall spin—! He is all but dead already."

"All but dead," Audsley agreed morosely. "How are we going to prevent his bringing half his court?"

"Simple! We claim that you can only take two people via your new means of travel, and that it greatly exhausts you. What can he say in response to that?"

"I don't know," said Audsley, and he honestly didn't. "But let's not underestimate him, shall we? I mean, he *is* the Minister of Perfection, and has ruled your clan for—how many years?"

"Some eighty or so," said Zephyr with a frown. "Fair enough. Your admonition is well-received. Now, I must go and prepare myself for our audience. I will send for you shortly. Be prepared!" And with that, she rose to her tiptoes, kissed him on the cheek, and was gone.

Audsley closed the door behind her and rested his forehead upon the smooth wood. What was he doing? Aletheia had fallen. Where was Iskra? Perhaps he could take advantage of this moment alone to report to her — yes!

Demon, he commanded. *Take me to Mythgraefen Hold.*

No, said the demon.

Audsley didn't know how to respond. He spluttered out loud, then clamped his jaw shut. *But why not? I know that you can.*

Of course I can, but why should I? It would be a salutary influence to expose you to Iskra. Have you forgotten that I'm trying to corrupt you, my dear Magister?

Audsley felt a crushing sense of frustration and impotence rise within him. "You blasted, wicked, cunning fiend," he said in a low, vicious voice.

Yes, all quite accurate.

Audsley clutched at his head and staggered across the room to sit on the edge of the bed. His heart was beating powerfully, erratically. *I command you to take me there!* He tried to summon those shards of white light with which he had imprisoned the demon before, but it had no effect; he imagined all manner of swords and cages, but there was nothing to put within them.

A vision sprang into his mind: his hands wrapped around the neck of a young woman. She was gasping and choking as he squeezed the life from her.

Audsley cried out and jumped to his feet, reeling and crashing against the wall. The vision was gone, but while it had lasted, those awful seconds, it had been so real that he'd *felt* his hands around her neck!

Do not offend me, Audsley. The demon's voice had grown soft. **I am being most gentle with you, but I can crack the whip at any time I choose.**

Another vision sprang before his eyes, replacing the room in which he was standing — he was holding a curved knife, and was doing something ghastly to an old man, who was whimpering softly and offering no resistance.

"Stop!" screamed Audsley, shoving the bases of his palms against his eyes. He fell onto his desk and then onto the floor. "Stop!"

No, said the demon. **It is time you learned which of us has dominion, and the consequences of rebellion.**

More visions manifested before his eyes, and in each one he actually experienced the ghastly actions he was committing: felt the slick, hot blood, heard the cries echoing in his ears, felt another's excitement and lust as his own. One after another, they flowed before him, and for what felt like an eternity, he rolled on the floor, burying his head in his hands, crying out in futile revulsion.

When, finally, the visions had faded, he lay still. He was staring underneath his bed, his body aching, his mind numb, his thoughts flattened with horror. He lay prostrate as if he had been speared through the mind, pinned to the ground by a lance made of nightmares.

You are mine, Audsley, whispered the demon from his depths. **You are mine. And in time, those visions you saw will pale in comparison to the acts you yourself will commit as we become as one. There is no escaping me. No escaping your destiny. And remember: none of this would have happened without your willingness to proceed. This is all your responsibility. Your doing. Your fault.**

Audsley shook his head slowly from side to side as tears welled up in his eyes. His body was wracked by sobs that he fought to stifle, shoving his fist into his mouth and biting down, but nothing could assuage his grief. Worst of all, he knew the demon was right. He was the one who had asked for its help, who had accepted its offer when he lay dying in Starkadr, who had leaned on and benefited from its knowledge and magic. The demon had been the tool, but it had been Audsley who had wielded it all along.

The sobs abated. Audsley lay still, staring glassy-eyed out into the middle distance. The visions he had seen were etched into the fabric of his mind, and different fragments kept returning, flickering through his memory. And worse, he felt a corresponding arousal at the memory of some of them.

It's the demon's influence, he told himself. *It's not me enjoying those sights. It's not.* But the words felt hollow and did nothing to ameliorate how foul and depraved he felt.

Finally, he heard a knock at the door. Stiffly, his muscles aching, he climbed to his feet just as Zephyr let herself in. She stopped, taken aback by his expression, and then rushed to his side, took his hand and pulled him down onto the edge of the bed.

"Audsley! What's wrong? You look near death!"

"Nothing, Zephyr." His voice was wooden. He felt as if he were a thousand miles away. "I had a spell of panic. That's all. It's over."

She searched his face. "Are you sure?"

"Yes." He took her hand from his cheek and folded it closed within his own palm. "I'm ready. Let's get this over with."

Her brows lowered in consternation. "You sound — you seem—"

"Different?" He smiled, though his cheeks ached. He felt like a mannequin aping a human expression. "Perhaps. But maybe it's simply that I'm resigned to my role. I'm ready for what's to come. So, shall we?"

She rose to her feet. "Yes, all right. If you're sure."

Audsley stood. He felt untouchable. Insulated from what was to come by the horrors he already harbored within his own soul. "Oh, yes," he said, smiling still. "I'm quite, quite sure."

Chapter 23

Tharok gazed up at the swirling madness of the Bythian aurora. It was mesmerizing, vast banks of cottony soft colors melding into each other, swelling into crimsons and then cooling into soft blues, expanses of emerald green blossoming only to give way to deep fuchsia. An impossible sky, and the only thing of beauty in this harsh underworld.

He tore his eyes away and turned to regard the Solar Portals. Kragh were streaming through the entrance to Aletheia, cramming into the packed hall beyond to listen to Uthok's declaration of power. Few spared him so much as a glance; Tharok was wearing a heavy forest-green cloak over his brawny shoulders with its hood pulled down low over his face. To the kragh who passed him, he was but a solitary mountain kragh awaiting his clan mates, albeit a particularly massive specimen.

The solution to his dilemma had proven incredibly simple. Would he have thought of it with the circlet about his brow? Probably not. He'd have come up with some elaborate plot that would have leveraged different political groups into conflict, creating chaos he'd have exploited at the key moment.

Sometimes the simplest solutions were best.

He'd slipped through the Aletheian hall easily, one kragh amongst thousands, embedded in a group of Jojan's largest kragh who had been ordered into Bythos. He'd peeled away once, through, and had simply stood to one side ever since.

Simple.

The speech would now be underway. Uthok had ordered that the human platform of lashed beams be repaired, creating a stage high above the heads of the crowd. The scent of cooking beef and pork had been thick in the air, and the kragh had been feasting and carousing, hundreds of barrels of white oak wine having been discovered in some room or other and rolled down to be broached and consumed.

An interesting approach. Whet their appetites and make them think that, under the new Uniter, they would be given more leeway to feast and loot. It would lessen their efficiency, but perhaps Uthok didn't care; perhaps he thought he had enough strength with Aletheia already defeated to mop up the rest of the Empire without a perfect military machine.

Tharok shrugged his cloak closer, suddenly irritated. He felt strangely alone, and his thoughts seemed to echo within his mind, as if a close friend had left him all alone in the dark. He'd grown used to the circlet's guidance, had grown to depend on the confidence it gave him, the surety.

This was the longest he'd gone without it since Wrok had bound him up so many months ago, and he itched for its return, for its mastery, its power. Without it, his mind tended to wander toward issues and complexities he had no answer for. Waiting around only made it worse.

The world was roaring past him. Events that he had set in motion were gaining their own fell momentum. Everything was hurtling toward climax. Without his circlet to guide him, Tharok couldn't help but feel lost – as if, by stepping outside the flow of events, he had lost his visceral connection to them.

Madness. Foolishness. He stilled and closed his eyes, exhaled softly and centered his thoughts. He would regain control. This was but a minor upset.

Into that focus, that silence, came a single note of music that seemed to emerge from the very core of his spirit. A single note of quavering purity, a tenuous call of beauty, alluring and fey. He could do nothing more than marvel. What was it? Where had it come from? Had it always been there?

No, a voice whispered from the depths of his mind, an ancient voice, primal and indelibly kragh. *This sound is new.*

Then, where had it come from?

Tharok hunched forward and squeezed his eyes even more tightly shut. He tried to magnify the sound, but it eluded him, like trying to catch a minnow with one's hands. Thoughts intruded as he fought for focus. Plans. Urgencies. He should be pondering a hundred different responsibilities…

The sound of the musical note rose higher within him, as if seeking his attention now, daring him to focus solely on its beauty.

Tharok fell into a crouch, elbows on his knees. It was a candle flame of astonishing beauty, rising from his dark core, and a crystalline tone was emanating from its depths. The stiller he became, the brighter it burned, and the more piercing its call became.

What he wouldn't do for a shaman to speak with, a kragh steeped in the ancient ways, who could tell him what this meant.

The note quavered and then became a song. He licked his lower lip and focused harder upon it, allowing the sound to well up all around him, envisioning the candle flame growing into a massive spear of light in whose luminous heart he was sitting.

Instinct urged him to lift his hand. He stared at his seamed palm and crooked fingers, and, guided by instinct, he envisioned the candle flame hovering there. He bent his will, channeled that song and light, and felt his palm begin to itch. He narrowed his eyes, sweat beading his brow. The song was a torrent now, enveloping him, sweeping away his thoughts, his very sense of self. All he could do was focus with obstinate stubbornness on his palm. Stare, and will, force, summon, push, and…

Nothing.

The song fell away. Tharok closed his fist slowly. He tried to reach for that sensation, but it slipped away all the quicker and then was gone.

For a long while, he simply stared up at the aurora. Frustration at being denied bubbled up within him, but then, with a sigh, he let it go.

Whatever that had been, it was finished for now, so he rose to his feet. It was time. He put all thoughts of that elusive song from his mind and picked up his bow. It was as tall as he was, a monstrosity of horn and ash, heartwood and yew. He tied the thick bowstring about one end, then placed it on the ground, reached up to take the other end with both hands, and pulled.

The muscles of his back, shoulders, and arms strained against the wood. Down it came, inch by inch, fighting him all the way. The tension was enormous, the power inherent in its deep wooden length incredible. When he finally had it bent enough, he tied off and released his hold with a sigh.

The string held. Heart pounding, he took up his arrow. It was over a yard long, as thick as his thumb, topped by a wide diamond blade. He riffled the black goose feathers, then set the arrow's notch against the string. That done, he raised the bow, inhaled deeply, and pulled the arrow back toward his ear.

The muscles of his back writhed as he hauled. The bow bent reluctantly. It took all the strength of his massive frame to hold it, to pull the string back. For a moment, he didn't think he'd be able to draw it all the way; his fingers were burning, his muscles aching, and the bow was fighting him. But, with a feral grunt, he yanked the arrow all the way back to his ear.

Tharok had no time to waste. He stepped through the Portal to Aletheia.

The whirling darkness inverted everything, plunging him into untold depths, but throughout it all he held on tight to the arrow and the bow. When he emerged into the hall, he was immediately buffeted by a wall of sound; the kragh were cheering, pounding the ground with their fists, waving hunks of meat, jostling each other.

Uthok was standing above them all, World Breaker held aloft, his face triumphant, the circlet gleaming upon his head. He was basking in the adoration, drinking it in. He turned and saw Tharok, saw his bow, and his eyes flared wide.

Tharok exhaled and released at the same time. The arrow leaped from the bow so quickly, he couldn't track its flight. One moment, it was held by the string; the next, it punched into Uthok, through his chain and leather and furs to bury itself a full foot deep into his chest.

The roars cut off. The kragh around Tharok wheeled on him, stunned. Tharok threw back his hood and began to walk toward the platform.

Uthok was still standing, gripping the railing, his mouth opening and closing in protest as he explored the huge shaft that protruded from his chest.

"Kill him," he croaked. "Kill the... the usurper."

Nobody moved. The kragh parted before Tharok, who climbed the steps of the platform. Uthok pushed away from the railing, World Breaker no doubt giving him the strength to remain standing.

"Greetings, Uthok," said Tharok. "Nice try."

Uthok let out a gargling howl and lunged at Tharok, sweeping World Breaker wildly at Tharok's head. Tharok simply stepped out wide and caught Uthok's wrist with one hand. He smashed a fist into the one-eyed kragh's face with the other.

The thousands of kragh seemed to sigh.

Uthok wheezed. Something was wrong with his chest; blood was flooding down his front and out his mouth. The arrow had gone through a lung, thought Tharok. The old kragh was drowning. Even so, World Breaker let him fight on. Uthok tore his hand free, staggered back, gripped the sword with both hands, and threw himself forward once more with a scream.

Tharok opened his arms wide as if to embrace death, and only at the last did he dart forward, inside the clumsy swing, bringing his fist down onto Uthok's forearm, crunching bone. He drew his arm back and then pummeled the older kragh across the jaw, taking advantage of the moment to rip the circlet off his brow.

Uthok reeled, his eyes rolling up in his head. His universe, Tharok knew, had just shrunk to the size of his own skull. The sensation was nauseating, overwhelming, and because Uthok had no experience with it, he was overwhelmed.

Tharok pulled World Breaker from the older kragh's hands and felt that familiar fire rush through him, the thrum and rush of strength and impossible vitality. The loss of the sword caused Uthok to fall forward. Tharok caught the dying kragh by the throat.

The thousands watching were spellbound. The crackle and spit of the dozens of bonfires sounded through the ancient hall, but nobody spoke, nobody cheered. They simply watched, waiting.

Should he don the circlet? Tharok hesitated, a split second in which to decide, and then recalled that quavering note, that beautiful white flame.

No. Not yet.

Uthok hung from Tharok's upraised arm. He weighed nothing. Tharok placed World Breaker's edge against his neck.

"I do not blame him for trying," roared Tharok, turning to regard his horde. "We are all ambitious. We all dream of glory. But I am Tharok. I am the Uniter. In me, the spirit of Ogri has come again! Uthok thought to take my place, thought he could lead this horde, and for that, he dies!"

Tharok drew World Breaker across Uthok's neck, cutting off his head in a welter of gore, and then cast the corpse aside.

"I am your warlord," he growled, stepping up to the railing and staring out over the ocean of faces. "You are my horde. It is I who have led you to success! Together, we conquered Abythos, destroyed that great citadel — together! We took Bythos, we took Aletheia — together! We are ten thousand strong, we are legends in the making, and I am your Uniter!"

Nobody spoke, nobody responded.

Tharok was heaving for breath. He should don the circlet. It would tell him exactly what to say. He shouldn't risk it — but no! He tightened his grip around its smooth edge but did not raise it.

"Do you not understand? We have done more than any other kragh in all of history — even Ogri never came this far! As great as he was, we are greater! No kragh has ever walked these halls. The humans are broken. All that remains to be done is to sweep up the shards of their Empire. Then we will be the masters of all, each of us a warlord, each of us greater than any and all who came before!"

There were isolated roars of approval.

"But we are not there yet, my great and ferocious kragh. We cannot celebrate yet! There are still humans to be torn apart, knights to be slain, castles to be toppled. Blue skies yearning for smoke, rivers aching to bleed blood-red, fields longing for the touch of flame. Do your ears not ring with the absence of screams? Do your axes not thirst to be buried in flesh? The time to feast will come, but not yet, not now, not while our enemy is building their defenses in defiance of our mastery!"

More roars echoed around him, along with the drumming of fists being pounded against the ground. The crowd was growing restive, shifting its weight as energy built up within each kragh.

"The humans think they have seen the worst that we can do. They think that now they can regroup, can fight back. Fools! We will show them what it means to fight the greatest kragh army that ever walked beneath the Sky Father's gaze! We will show them the price of having manipulated us like beasts for so many years! We are the true rulers of this earth! We will crush them where they hide, exterminate them where they run, and only when the last human sword has been snapped and the final castle destroyed, when we hear nothing but their pleas for mercy, then will we throw back our heads and laugh, knowing that we have achieved our great destiny, that we will then and forevermore be immortals!"

This time the roar that came back to him was deafening. Tharok looked out over the assembled kragh , baring his tusks and raising his arms as if daring them all to charge him, and his heart pounded mightily with a sense of personal victory: this was his doing, those had been his words, and this was *his* horde.

Finally, he raised his hands for silence. "Finish this feast, but do not drink over much. We fight come dawn. My warlords, attend me. We have much to discuss. Now, come!"

Descending from the platform, he considered the circlet. Perhaps this was the blessing hidden within Uthok's betrayal: a chance for him to break free of its tyranny. To be a kragh once more, to lead his kragh as their true warlord. To be Tharok again.

He bound the circlet to his belt and let it hang there. He was so close to victory. He and his kragh could complete this final step alone.

Many hours later, after dismissing his warlords, he returned to the great Portals. His approach was presaged by kragh kneeling and pressing their massive fists to the ground. The vast morass of warriors noticed his arrival and turned to regard him, their eyes dark like those of ravens, their expressions closed, their heads bowed. Tharok looked neither right nor left. The effect would have been magnified by the presence of his four trolls, but they were lost to him without the circlet, and reports had been brought to him that they'd descended to the bowels of the stonecloud. Ah, well. He didn't need them to command respect; his own weighty presence demanded it from the thousands who parted for him.

The Portal to Bythos flamed before him. Tharok stopped a yard from its swirling surface and turned to regard his horde. His gaze raked over them all, his regard unflinching, and everywhere he looked, kragh pounded their fists solemnly against the ground. They were his. For a moment they had strayed, but he was back. They accepted him. Bowed to him. They knew that he was the Uniter, that he would see them to glory. He gave no speech, didn't so much as nod. When he was done examining his kragh, he turned and stepped through the fire.

The bulk of his horde was camped out across the badlands of Bythos, some six thousand of them, their campfires flickering as if all the Sky Father's stars had fallen to the depths of the earth.

Medusa-Kissed chieftains and warlords were gathered in a loose crowd before the Portals. Waiting. Watching. Patient. At his emergence, they rose from their squats and roared their fealty.

The roar was like fire across dry leaves. It was picked up by those behind and spread out across the badlands. From where Tharok was standing, impassive, he could see the kragh rising to their feet like a ripple being blown across the grass of a mountain meadow. The roar was sustained. Tharok lifted his chin but a fraction, and the kragh in the very far reaches of the badlands finally rose to their feet. The sound was cacophonous and challenged the shifting aurora.

Finally, Tharok lifted World Breaker. The roar peaked and then broke as he lowered his weapon and began to march toward the Blade Towers.

A black-clad shaman stepped forward to intercept him. "Uniter, Kyrrasthasa bade that I speak with you when next you came to Bythos. She awaits you in the Abythian Labyrinth. She had been working diligently toward furthering your cause and looks forward to showing you her good works."

"Good works," rumbled Tharok. "Your name, shaman?"

The kragh was bloated like a corpse, his hide stretched thin over his puffy flesh, his eye sockets dry and showing withered flesh within their cups. He bowed. "I am now Hollow Heart, Uniter. Reborn to a greater purpose."

"Lead me to the medusa, Hollow Heart," said Tharok. "Now."

The shaman's upper lip peeled back from his teeth, and then he bowed once more. "Come."

Then he walked quickly away, moving toward a large outcrop of rough rocks just beyond the Portal roads.

Tharok raised a hand, and some twenty kragh fell into step with him, ranging from his couriers to a dozen of Jojan's best warriors, and together they followed the shaman, who led them around the outcropping and out of the horde's sight.

Once hidden, the shaman drew a black dagger from his belt and traced a circle in the air, muttering foul words all the while. Where the tip of his blade passed, it left a trail of hissing green flame, and when the circle was complete, its interior fell away into absolute darkness.

"Our power grows, Uniter," said Hollow Heart with greasy smugness. "As our mistress' blessing corrodes the constraints that held us down, we learn greater miracles."

"Miracles that you hide from the others," said Tharok, not bothering to keep the revulsion from his voice. "This is a blasphemy, what you do. You assault the spirit world."

"There is no need to provoke the horde," said the shaman. "And in time, they will come to accept our methods. And you cannot deny the utility of this magic: it will lead us directly to Kyrra, saving us hours of walking. Come."

Tharok gazed at the green burning and felt his skin crawl. He did not need a shaman to tell him this was evil, a perversion of the spirits in some way he couldn't begin to understand. The other kragh at his side were restive, clearly upset. Yet time was indeed precious.

"Very well," said Tharok. "You first."

"Of course," Hollow Heart said with a sneer, and passed through.

Tharok showed no hesitation. Not in front of the others. He ducked his head and followed, into a swirling madness of darkness that threatened to attack his mind, his very sanity. He wanted to scream, to lash out, to don the circlet so as to benefit from its protection, but then he was through to the other side and stumbling upon the ground.

The great Abythian archway that signaled the ramp descending into the depths rose behind a second shield of rocks. Tharok hawked and spat, and then glowered at the grinning shaman. "That was unpleasant."

"But useful, was it not? Now, come, Uniter."

The shaman led Tharok and his followers out from behind the rocks. Kragh were unloading the human wagons and carts, handing their war provisions to waiting warriors, who shouldered the foodstuffs and began marching back to their camps. What had once been a massive stockpile was already nearly gone; even the carts had been broken down and dragged away for firewood.

The kragh all turned at Tharok's appearance and dropped to one knee. Tharok ignored them and descended the ramp, but instead of being led down to the Portal itself, Hollow Heart led him off into a side passage, picking up one of the green buglights as he did so.

They hadn't gone far when they came across their first corpse. The light spread out to encompass the body as they walked along the corridor, showing its frozen figure. It was still standing, balanced on its two feet, fabric, hair and flesh all transformed to stone.

Tharok stopped before it and gazed into the agonized features. "A Bythian," he grunted.

"Yes," said Hollow Heart, who hesitated and then led on.

They passed more petrified bodies. Down they went, ever deeper into the labyrinth, and Tharok stopped counting the dead after he reached fifty. They were spaced out evenly, every thirty yards or so. Tharok wanted to ask why, but he knew the shaman would deflect his question. Yet, with each body they passed, his anger grew. The shaman, apparently sensing his wrath, walked all the quicker.

They all emerged at last into a natural cavern deep below the surface. Two shamans were holding great torches aloft, their orange and yellow flames dancing and casting frantic shadows across the folds of natural rock. Ten kragh warriors were watching over a crowd of Bythians, who stood as if they were numb, eyes glazed, tears drying on their faces. These kragh, Tharok noticed, bore shields on which Kyrra's serpentine hair had been painted around a single yellow eye.

Kyrra was caressing the face of a young Bythian woman, her rattle raised from her coils, her body bent over the helpless human. The woman was shivering, shaking, transfixed by Kyrra's gaze. She was unconstrained but clearly unable to move; she shook as she gazed up, and then, before Tharok could interject, she was bleached of all color, freezing in place as she turned to stone, a horrendous *crack* echoing through the cavern.

"I swore to protect the Bythians," said Tharok, drawing World Breaker. "You made me an oath breaker."

Kyrra turned slowly to regard him and his followers, her snakes forming a living corona about her striking visage. Smiling, she slithered around the newly created statue, her great serpentine body hissing over the rock, her scales smoldering in the gloom.

"Do not be wroth, Tharok. The wonder I work here will be the greatest gift that you have ever received."

"Release them," said Tharok, pointing his blade at the Bythians. "Now."

The kragh hesitated, glanced to Kyrra, and Tharok narrowed his eyes. How many kragh has she subverted beyond his control?

"You are not wearing your circlet," she said at last, her voice almost lazy with curiosity.

"What of it?"

"Would you be willing to don it for this conversation? What I am about to say will make more sense."

"No, Kyrra," he said. "Now, explain why you have broken my oath."

"Very well. I will keep my words... simple, then, for your benefit. Do you know wherein you stand? What this ancient complex they call the Abythian Labyrinth is, in truth?"

"Speak," said Tharok.

"This is a place of great joy." She moved to the cavern wall and ran her palm down its side. "It is ancient. How many millennia old, I cannot guess, but once it was filled with life, a warren, a hive of activity. Once, it was all like this, unworked by the hands of man. If you close your eyes, you can almost hear the clicking of ten thousand pointed legs moving rapidly over naked stone. You can almost feel the brush of their carapaces."

Tharok waited. Was she trying to test his patience? He'd not play her game.

"Did the humans drive them out? Find it abandoned? I do not know. But they haven't hesitated to mine it for shaman stone ever since. They have sunk so many mines through the labyrinth in their eagerness to dig up that precious ore that the original configurations are quite lost." She paused, a smile touching her lips. "Do you think it a coincidence that the Abythian Portal is located here?"

"You promised an explanation," said Tharok. "Not a reverie."

"Yes, I did." She reared back, rising and looking down at him with something akin to amusement and lethal interest. "This was once a hive of *kchack'ick'ill*. Cavekillers. Ferocious predators that subsist primarily on shaman stone. But, oh, their lethality when they turn their blades against flesh and blood..." The snakes of her hair hissed with pleasure.

"So?" Tharok fought not to be impressed. "What is that to me?"

"I summon them back, Uniter. I stake out offerings that they will smell through the rock and come swarming back to enjoy. How many are left, I do not know, but they will come in time. And if you thought trolls to be excellent combatants, oh, wait until you behold a *kchack'ick'ill* taking to the field of battle. Wait till you see what even one can do against the humans."

"The kragh alone will win the rest of this war," said Tharok. "I no longer need the assistance of trolls, wyverns, or whatever else you may summon. The humans are broken. Tomorrow, I finish them. My word to the Bythians means more to me than these monsters of yours." Tharok paused. "You aren't summoning them for my benefit alone, are you, Kyrra?"

The medusa undulated with mesmerizing languor from side to side, her bronze lips curling into a smile of sly amusement. "Have I grown so transparent, Uniter?"

"What are you trying to do, Kyrra? Control them yourself?"

"Not at all. I hadn't anticipated that your war against the Empire would proceed so quickly. Your capabilities have taken me by surprise."

"Answer my question."

"Mind your tone, Tharok," said Kyrra softly, and with disarming speed, she slid forward, swooping past him on his left, then curling back around so that, for a few heartbeats, her great coils undulated around him on all sides.

Tharok heard the alarmed cries of his warriors, but none of them tried to intervene. He could perhaps have leaped to safety, but opted instead to remain still. Waiting, watching. She couldn't kill him yet. She still needed him to command his army, to deliver the victory she would then steal from him.

"You do not appreciate my gift." She pulled away, easing back. "Such is your right. I shall cease my evocation. I shall release the Bythians who yet remain."

"You will make restitution to their families," said Tharok. "I shall have the survivors mark the names of the fallen. You will not besmirch my honor so lightly."

Kyrra's eyes widened, and he felt a wash of heat across his face and the fronts of his forearms. He tensed, prepared to raise World Breaker to block his line of sight if she dared seek to petrify him.

"Very well, Uniter. But the bait has been set. The denizens of the depths are on their way. Should you change your mind..."

She was hiding something, and she knew he knew that. But what? Was this her means to topple him from his throne after he had conquered the humans? Most likely. But, unless he personally cleansed the labyrinth of all her statues, he couldn't be sure that she would remove the 'bait'. Was now the time to kill her? On the eve of his final attack? That might precipitate a rebellion of her faithful. Or should he conquer the humans and then turn immediately upon her?

"Thank you, Kyrra. I will be busy these next few days consolidating my grip over the human lands. When I return, we will talk further on this matter."

"As you command."

Did she know he would strike at her tomorrow evening? Would she be able to mount sufficient defense against him in that short a time?

He smiled at her, baring his tusks. She returned the expression, her eyes betraying nothing but cool amusement.

"Until then," he said, and nodded to Hollow Heart to lead him to the surface.

"My heart longs for our next encounter," whispered Kyrra, her voice reaching him like a deadly caress.

Chapter 24

The square was being cleared of the dead. The sound of horses whinnying as men heaved the kragh onto carts echoed up to Asho, who was standing with his arms crossed, staring down with implacable focus. He was watching the gate to Aletheia. Half an hour had passed since the attack's rebuff, and a second could come at any moment, a fact the men below knew all too well. They were working with frantic intensity, casting glances at the sentries, whose sole duty was to cry out a retreat at the first sight of an emerging kragh.

Archers covered the rooftops, the word of their victory having flushed more volunteers out of hiding. They were busy tending to their bows, rubbing beeswax on their strings, checking their arrows, or simply laughing and enjoying the morning sunshine as food was passed amongst them by young boys who had volunteered to help.

Below, two more ballistae were being wheeled into place, having finally finished their journey from the far Iron Gate where they'd been mounted for over a century. Restless guards were standing in long lines, watching the Portals, kicking out their legs, shifting their weight, some with weapons drawn, the wiser of the men simply resting their hands on sheathed blade hilts instead.

The air above the square was thick with crows, wheeling and cawing in their rough voices, seeking neglected bodies with great boldness. Each kragh that was heaved onto a cart dislodged a good dozen of the black birds, who flapped up crying their indignation before settling down on the next corpse.

Progress was being made. Hundreds of men were prying cobblestones free and chucking them to other men who were busy molding them with into low walls, while others swung pickaxes at the exposed dirt as they sought to dig trenches as quickly as possible. The atmosphere was one of dread and elation, of fevered activity, and uncertainty that any of it would do any good.

The Consecrated had wanted to speak to him. Shameka had sent a summons, making Asho laugh. He expected her to bother him again, and was trying to decide whether to let her up onto the roof. Tables had been dragged up here and covered with plans that were being studied intently by the lords and their retainers, the captain of the guards and other officials. They were sketching out battle lines and disputing the positioning of different blocks of men. This was the heart of the resistance, and now Shameka wanted to be allowed in.

Asho looked down and saw Uxe and his men leading a group of city guards through a drill, showing them how to stand next to each other, each man's shield protecting the fellow to his left, how to stab and not swing, how to operate as a wall. The canny Ennoian had them broken up into groups of three and drilling against his own men. Their progress was slow, but it was better than idleness or letting them face the kragh completely unprepared.

Suddenly, Asho tensed. It felt like an invisible hand had seized him by the throat, clamping iron fingers around his neck and squeezing hard. His heart stuttered, missed a beat, surged powerfully, then stuttered again. He couldn't breathe. His vision swam. Letting out a cough, he fell forward, catching himself against a beam.

"Ser Asho?" said a voice from behind him, and it was followed by another question.

Asho tuned them out. His very soul felt as if it were being wrung like a wet cloth. The sounds from below seemed so very distant, impossibly faint. A rushing roar was filling his mind, a roar like that which he'd heard when he'd approached the Black Gate in the Skarpheðinn Range. But there was no Black Gate here. What was going on?

He forced himself to straighten. Something was pulling him, a force as primal as the tide. It was drawing him forward.

A need. A summons. But what? To where? A hand was laid on his shoulder, and he shrugged it off. What was it? What was happening to him?

A voice sang in the depths of his mind: *Asho!*

Kethe's voice. A cry of need, of desperation. His skin crawled, every hair standing on end. She needed him. He didn't know how he knew that, but he didn't doubt it. Her life was at stake. She was about to die, and he wasn't there. Wasn't by her side. He was going to fail her.

"No!" he cried, roughly shrugging off hands again. Only instinct guided him. He shoved his hand into his pouch and pulled out every rock of gatestone therein. Six chunks. One after the other, he shoved them into his mouth, biting down hard, cracking and crunching them, lifting his water skin to wash them down, water splashing over his cheeks and down his front.

He felt their power blossom within him. Gently at first, but with the second and third stones, the fire within his core began to grow, to burn black-hot, and still he bit and chewed and swallowed.

Four chunks. Five. It was as if he'd dipped himself into molten iron. His every sense came alive. Energy coursed through him, jittery and needing release. He ground down on the last chunk, the largest, then swallowed, the sharp edges gouging red lines of pain down his throat.

His magic – it was there. It was pulsing through his very being, burning him up from within. His body was a thin shell that could barely contain his power. He hunched his shoulders, fighting to control himself, to maintain a grip on his burgeoning might, but it was too much, too intoxicating, too deliriously intense.

Asho!

With a cry, he leaped up to the broken wall and balanced perfectly on the horizontal beam. Where was she? How could he get to her? He roared his frustration, and every man, woman and child froze at the sound of his bellow, at the fury and power behind the cry. Nearly a thousand faces turned to regard him in shock, but he didn't care. Instead, he dug his knuckles into his eyes and focused on Kethe. He summoned her freckled face, how the color of her hazel eyes changed in the sunlight, her wry smile.

He felt her presence. Could sense a cord connecting them, a line of white fire that only he could see. He snapped open his eyes and saw that it led straight to the Noussian Portal.

Without hesitation, he threw himself off the side of the building, and screams were torn from a dozen throats. He drew his blade as he plummeted, and just before he would have smashed headfirst into the cobbles, his sword erupted in black fire and his fall leveled out. He skimmed over the packed dirt, came up fast, and shot over the heads of the soldiers, his clothing rippling, his hair streaming back from his face.

Men threw themselves to the ground, diving aside as he passed over them, but then the Noussian Portal was there before him, its fiery interior dominating his field of vision, and he speared into its glorious heart.

The darkness of the interstitial void boiled around him, as if his very presence were setting it afire. There was a flicker-flash and then he was through, flying straight out into a glorious azure sky.

The ocean surged against the bases of the huge white towers around him. Kragh were scattered about the Portals, but Asho ignored them. He focused on the cord of white flame, felt it pull him upwards.

Asho flew up, arms thrown back, skimming up the side of the tower, a profusion of balconies, ramps, paths, small courtyards and other details blurring past.He pushed himself faster through the humid air, fighting to reach the bronze dome at the top. Faster... His eyes were watering. He narrowed them, gritted his teeth, and fought for more speed.

He was moving so fast now he couldn't make out any details, the tower just a white blur, and then he shot up over the dome, high into the sky, and there — Kethe!

She was standing alone at the peak of the dome, white fire blade in hand, and a group of kragh was pulling back on their bows, a dozen archers preparing to riddle her body with arrows.

"No!" His shout was instantly followed by a furious, snarling wash of black flame. Thrusting out both hands, Asho unleashed his desperation and fear through his palms, and the fire belched down, roiling and engulfing the kragh, some twenty or thirty of them, blasting them right off the roof even as it blackened and killed them, incinerating them in mid-air, so that charred, withered husks fell to the ground below along with dollops of melted bronze.

Gasping, his heart slamming frantically within the confines of his chest, Asho lowered himself to the rooftop. Kethe was staring at him, clearly both relieved and astonished.

The roaring of the ocean filled his ears. He could feel the power of the gatestones fleeing him.

"You came," she whispered.

"We don't have much time. We have to go." He extended a hand to her. She took it, and in that moment, in that touch, he felt wildfire race between them and back, coursing through their bodies, a union that amplified their powers beyond anything he could imagine. The dark clouds of pain that were already swirling around his mind lessened, the poisons that were building within his body faded away, and Kethe gasped, a visceral sound of pleasure and surprise and delight.

Asho grinned at her, all complications washed aside by their bond, and leaped up into the air. His power extended to her, so that she was able to fly alongside him. They arched up and then fell over the side of the tower and soared downward, down toward the Solar Portals.

"Wait!" called Kethe over the rushing of the wind. "My Consecrated!"

Asho scanned the tower's face. There, halfway down, two men were fighting back to back on a rooftop. He angled their descent toward them. The kragh looked up, saw their approach, and gaped; the two men followed their gaze and let out cheers of elation.

Asho swept over them, catching a spindly man's hand just as Kethe grabbed Khoussan's forearm. Straining, Asho lifted, bore them off the roof, and then allowed himself to simply fall. Down they went again, the gangly man in his grip whooping with fevered delight, Khoussan roaring in dismay. They plummeted for several seconds, then Asho angled up, pulling with everything he had, fighting the suck of gravity that wanted to tear him down past the bridges and into the cold embrace of the ocean below.

The massive Gate to Ennoia was protected by some thirty kragh, but they could only stare helplessly as Asho and Kethe flew past, dragging Khoussan and the other man over their heads, and sliced back into the Portal's white fire.

They emerged a split-second later over the Portal square. A thousand throats cried out in alarm and wonder, and a few arrows hissed down around them.

Asho was starting to flag; he could feel his very essence being torn apart by his effort. Even with Kethe's cleansing effect on his magic, he was running out of power. He released his passenger a yard over the ground, and the man tumbled neatly head over heels. Kethe did the same with Khoussan.

The air had become as thick as honey. Asho gritted his teeth, fought for altitude, and failed. His body was coming apart at the joints. Fire was searing the backs of his eyes. His tongue was swelling, bloated and desiccated. He couldn't breathe, couldn't think. All he could focus on was Kethe's hand, gripping his as tightly as he held hers.

The square's buildings were rearing up before him. He wanted to climb, to fly up into the sky with her, to disappear into the blue, but he couldn't hold on. Couldn't go any farther. With a cry, he let go. The world swirled and went dark, and oblivion claimed him before he hit the cobbles.

Chapter 25

Audsley followed Zephyr into the Minister of Perfection's camarilla chamber. It was the opposite of ostentatious, with a complete absence of decorations, ornamentation, or signs of vanity. Of personality, even. A single, stiff-backed chair sat at the head of the circular room, without cushion or curves. A row of smaller chairs had been placed around the room's circumference behind a waist-high divider of paneled dark wood; a second and third levels were recessed deeper and above the first, so that in all, some thirty individuals could attend deliberations or proceedings.

The camarilla was clearing of personages; elderly men and severe-faced women in dark robes were filing out, muttering to each other. A few gave Zephyr suspicious or disdainful looks, but most of them ignored her. She stopped before the central chair in which the Minister was sitting, clad in a severe black robe with a simple if startling sash of crimson around his waist. His carriage was erect, his skin yellowed with age, his beard a slender wisp of gray that descended in a stately spike to his sternum. His face was long, almost cadaverous, and his eyes were sunken with what Audsley might have called fatigue if he dared think of the Minister as human enough to suffer from such a condition.

He raised a skeletal digit and beckoned Zephyr closer. "You have but minutes, Granddaughter. Consider yourself fortunate. Now, you have made outrageous claims. Substantiate them."

The room had emptied out, leaving only one other individual standing behind and to the side of the Minister, clad in the ubiquitous black robes, a hood obscuring their face. Their posture was one of deference. A servant?

Zephyr's response was to step forward and extend the first of her three books. The minister glanced from its cover to Zephyr, his brow arched as if he was preparing to be annoyed, and took the slender tome.

His eyes narrowed as he read the title, and then a thin, vertical line appeared between his brows as he opened the cover and flicked through the first few pages.

"Where did you get this?"

Zephyr held forth the second book. The minister took it quickly, read the spine with his eyebrows now raised, and then scowled as he flicked through the pages with greater rapidity. He snatched the third book from Zephyr's hand, read the title, then set it atop the other two.

"Explain," he said, but Audsley knew the matter was won.

"My magister — you *do* remember him, don't you, Grandfather? He is a most marvelous and knowledgeable man. He is the one who gifted me these tomes."

"You? Audsley, was it not?" Never before had Audsley heard his name spoken as if it were an accusation. "Where did you acquire these books?"

"Starkadr, my lord," said Audsley with a little bow. *Chew on that.*

"Starkadr. The abode of the Flame Walkers." The minister did nothing to hide his skepticism. "It's been lost for centuries. You claim to have been there?"

"No mere claim, my lord." Audsley's voice was calm and sure. "I *have* been there. I have traversed its heptagonal corridors, seen its vast chamber of Portals, a hundred embedded in each pillar. I've flown past the Artificers' ancient laboratories. It was there that I acquired my three demons."

The minister said nothing, and Audsley felt the man's scrutiny so intently that had he tried to face him at any other point in his life, he would have crumbled into apologies. Instead, he met the old man's gaze with a frank one of his own.

"Remarkable," said the minister at last. "I believe you."

"There's more, dear Grandfather," said Zephyr. "We can take you there now, if you like."

"Oh?" The minister rose to his feet, moving the three books under one arm. "There is a Portal close by?"

"No," said Audsley, allowing his negative to stand alone, brazen and just shy of confrontation. After a moment, he relented. "My demon can transport us there directly."

"Teleportation," said the minister quietly. "You possess that power."

Audsley allowed himself a quiet smile and nodded.

"I have seen the Flame Walkers' secret library myself, Grandfather," Zephyr said excitedly. "Hundreds upon hundreds of books just like these, all intact, rows upon rows of lost wonders. Wonders that I offer humbly to you to redeem myself, to humbly ask that you give me another chance to prove myself of value."

The minister smiled coldly. "Then, let me summon my court. We shall all visit this ancient wonder together."

"Alas," said Audsley, feeling dangerously confident. "Such travel tires me greatly. I can only take a few people before I need to rest. My apologies, my lord. An entire court is far beyond my powers."

"Is it, now," said the minister. He didn't seem at all surprised. "How unfortunate. Then, perhaps you can take my servant, here, first, to confirm that all is as you say it is. Return with her, and if she says the way is clear, why, then, I will go myself."

His servant stepped forward. She was tall, even statuesque, and what little Audsley could see of her face was pale-skinned. A mature woman, perhaps in her mid-forties, though it was hard to tell.

"As you command, my lord," said Audsley. He stepped past Zephyr and extended his hand. "Here."

The woman reached out and touched her fingertips to the back of his hand. Though her touch was light, her skin felt rough, almost callused.

His demon needed no prompting. The world dipped into darkness, they flew, and then Audsley and the servant were at the base of the secret library, standing beside the long table at which the six cadavers were seated. The shelves around them were empty, but the next level up boasted their full complement.

Audsley glanced up surreptitiously. Good; nobody was in sight.

The servant gasped, pulling back her hand, and looked about; well might she be shocked, Audsley thought complacently. He caught a glimpse of golden hair beneath her cowl, but nothing more.

"Here you have it," Audsley said. "The secret library of the Sin Casters. Are you ready to return?"

The woman nodded mutely and reached out for his hand. Audsley gave it, and a moment later they were back in the minister's camarilla.

"Well?" asked the minister, still on his feet.

"It is as they say," said the servant, her voice husky and deferential.

"Then take me there," said the minister. "I would see this lost treasure for myself."

"Very well, my lord," Audsley said, and extended both hands. Zephyr, the minister, and the servant all reached out to touch him once more.

Audsley took a deep breath. Even with his demon's influence, his pulse was beginning to race. His mouth was dry. What they were about to do beggared the mind.

Now, he whispered, and the world fell away into darkness. Audsley blinked, and the four of them were in position, placed neatly beside that ancient table.

Audsley wasted no time. He immediately surged upward, bolting toward the faraway ceiling, Zephyr flying up by his side.

"Now!" cried Zephyr, her voice rich with elation and terror, and Auntie, Eulos, and the doctor stepped into view.

The minister had made no move. He was staring up at them, frowning in consternation. Audsley placed both hands before him, much as Zephyr was doing, and channeled his demons' might through his palms. The shock knocked him several feet higher up into the air as livid, furious fire spewed from his palms with a horrific roar.

Zephyr and the others did the same. Such fury and flame poured down into the pit of the secret library that the very air became scorching hot. A conflagration blossomed and roiled within the final layer, obscuring all view, but Audsley could see a faint shadow of the central table collapsing into cinders, saw shelving fall away from the walls, saw everything immolate in a matter of seconds.

With a gasp, Audsley closed his hands, cutting off the flames. The others did the same in rapid succession, and like that, the roar was gone.

The afterimages of the fires were seared into his vision, making it hard to see what lay below. Natural fires crackled over charred coals, and smoke rose thickly from the ruins of the furniture.

But that wasn't what Audsley focused on.

"No," Zephyr whispered, then said again in a scream, "No!"

A sphere of white fire mazed with black was only now fading away. Within its center stood the minister and his servant. He had both skinny arms raised, while she had raised only one; with the other hand, she was holding a large glass bottle filled with black liquid, from which she was drinking. Her hood had fallen back, revealing a stern, handsome visage, her golden hair thick and curled about the nape of her neck. Her black robes had burned away to reveal a glittering coat of chain that reached down to her knees.

She finished the bottle — enough to have filled five vials, Audsley guessed — and tossed it aside. It shattered against the wall.

The minister lowered his arms and dusted off his singed sleeves. "Thank you, Ainos," he said, almost as an aside.

Audsley felt his joints go weak. If he'd been standing, he would have fallen. *Ainos. Ainos the Praised, the Sigean Virtue.*

"I will have you know, brother, that I was coerced into this," said Auntie with wounded hauteur. "I agreed to murder you with extreme reluctance."

"Yes, yes," said the minister. "Of course, Maize." He craned his head back, studying the rest of the party to his assassination. "Eulos. And the Doctor of the Almanac. Why, you have collected a most eclectic group to effect my murder, Little Zephyr. I am impressed."

"No," whispered Zephyr, pressing a fist to her mouth. "No. This can't be. You can't — how?"

The minister extended his hand to Ainos, who took it as if she were about to be led onto the floor of a ballroom. Instead, they both flew up till they were level with Audsley and Zephyr. "How? Oh, Granddaughter. The curse of youth is to believe that your every thought is original. You think you are the first to attempt such a coup? Oh, no. I have lived through many such attempts, though none, I will admit, with such a fine and wondrous backdrop."

Eulos was snarling and backing up against the wall, black flames wreathing his fists once more. The doctor was standing ramrod straight, his face pinched, his brow covered with a sheen of sweat.

He's not even upset, thought Audsley. *By the Ascendant, how powerful is he?*

"Thank you, Magister, for bringing me here." The minister turned to regard him. "Now that I have visited this location, I can return whenever I so desire." He leaned forward in an artificially conspiratorial manner. "I, too, you see, have a self-possessed demon entwined within my soul."

Audsley felt all his fears fall away from him. He'd tried his best. He'd risked everything. He'd made every sacrifice he could — and had come up short. Now, it was over. No more worrying. No more self-loathing. No more fearing his ultimate corruption. In a way, he realized, he was glad; in defeat, he had finally found a form of freedom.

"Well?" cried Zephyr, floating back, her body rigid with tension. "Don't just mock me! Kill me if you're going to, but I won't be toyed with!"

"Kill you? Oh, my dear Little Zephyr. What, by the Black Gate, makes you think you'll escape your life of servitude so easily? Oh, no. You are mine, and now more so than ever." The minister's smile was a cruel and cutting thing. "This is only the beginning. I have many, many ends for which I shall use you."

"No," said Zephyr. "You can't. I won't." Tears filled her eyes, and strands of her pitch-black hair caught in the corner of her mouth as she shook her head violently. "I won't serve you! I've had enough!"

"You disappoint me, Zephyr. I had thought you quick-witted enough to realize that this was not your choice to make."

"No!" She screamed and flung up both hands. "Never!"

Before she could unleash the flames that wreathed her fists, the minister raised his hand and loosed a bolt of black flame the size of a fist. It slammed into her chest and sent her flying backward to crash into the shelving and fall amidst a flurry of books to lie insensate on the floor.

"Tiresome," said the minister. "But she will grow. She will learn. What of you three?" The minister turned to regard the others. "I don't fault you for the attempt. It is part and parcel of your situation for you to try such a gambit. But you've failed. The consequences, as you know, will be dire."

Auntie placed both gloved hands on the railing. "I am your flesh and blood." Her voice was heavy and lifeless, as if she already knew her plea was futile. "Leave me be. I will retire to my quarters and nevermore emerge."

"I, on the other hand, am yours to command in everything," said the doctor, bowing deeply. "Though everything I am and everything I have was already yours. I have nothing to give but my apologies, which I am sure are without value."

"Yes, yes," said the minister, waving the doctor off. "Maize, you will do exactly as I bid, when I bid, until you are dead. Let us not sink into indignities. Your power is now wholly mine. Understood?"

Auntie seemed to settle into herself, her shoulders sagging a fraction, her chin lowering. "Yes."

"And Eulos. My dear, poor cousin. You're still upset, I see. Let us make this quick. I can't be bothered with your mock heroics. Shall I kill you now, or do you wish to live?"

Eulos stood there shaking, his whole frame shivering like a boat being battered by a storm. "Kill me." His voice was a harsh grate. "Let me die. Please."

"Very well. On your knees. Beg for death, and I shall grant it."

Eulos staggered forward. He swayed, then fell heavily to his knees. Tears were running down his handsome cheeks. "Please," he whispered. "I can't do this anymore. This life." He bowed forward and rested his forehead on the dusty carpet. "Please, I beg of you. Release me."

The minister seemed to think about it, tapping his chin, and then gave a decisive shake of his head. "No. Of course not. *Vza'thyk'allak.* I command you to rise."

Eulos rose jerkily to his feet, shaking his head all the while. "No," he whispered. "Please."

"I command you by your true name, *Vza'thyk'allak*, to prevent your host from harming himself in any way or seeking to contravene my orders or harm me in any fashion. Nod if you understand."

Audsley watched, horrified, as Eulos clenched his jaw and squeezed his eyes shut. Tears ran down his cheeks as he fought, but, slowly, as if he was being forced by an inexorable pressure, his chin lowered and then rose.

"Good," said the minister. "Now, Magister Audsley."

Should he be feeling terror? He wasn't. He felt, if anything, as if he were watching the proceedings from outside his own body. He was no Fujiwara. There was no bond of family to protect him here.

"Do as you will, Minister. My soul belongs to the Ascendant, and nothing that you can do to my body will harm it or impede its progress in any way."

"The Ascendant? Oh, Magister, after gazing upon the wonders of Starkadr, after wielding the powers of demons, after learning so many truths, don't tell me you still hold to those pathetic lies?"

Audsley raised his chin but said nothing.

"Come, Magister. Haven't you pieced it together yet? The true history of the Empire? What actually happened so many centuries ago, when the First Ascendant rose to power?"

Audsley wanted to shut out the man's voice. It was but another form of temptation. Another attempt to seduce him toward the paths of darkness.

"Your Ascendant's Empire," said the minister, "is held together by Portals powered by demons. His stonecloud itself is held aloft by demonic power. Have you not questioned how such a holy civilization could be based on such evil?"

Audsley swallowed. He didn't know what to say.

"And the Black Gate and White Gate. You do know they predate Ascendancy, don't you? That there were men and women who could attune themselves to each of them before the first Ascendant pre-scribed religious roles to them?"

Audsley thought of the corpses below, in the huge chamber of Portals – the men and women who had fought against the Ascendant in both white and black robes. "Flame Walkers and the White Adepts," said Audsley, his voice a whisper.

"Yes, precisely. Joined, as I am joined with Ainos, in a bond that empowers us both beyond understanding."

Ainos was still holding the minister's hand, her face grave and thoughtful.

"It always pains me to meet such ignorance in men who profess such learning. Magister, a brief lesson in history, after which I shall judge you by the quality of your refutations. What came before the Ascendant Empire?"

"The Age of Wonders," Audsley said woodenly. "When the Portals were built and Aletheia was raised into the sky. Followed by a time of chaos and bloodshed, when man lived in a state of anarchy and bestial brutality. The Chaos Years."

"Very true," said the minister. "But the shadow cast by our history is much longer than that. Once, perhaps a thousand years ago or more — the dates are inexact — the Flame Walkers, whom you call Sin Casters, fought each other for dominion. They warred across the skies, burned each other's cities, and wreaked great ruin upon the land. This state of magical barbarism lasted until the rise of Enos and Zakaya, the first Flame Walker and White Adept to establish a Conduit. They quelled the others and ordered that never again would a Flame Walker wield temporal power. It was then that Starkadr was built – a refuge, an asylum, a stronghold for their kind, and power was given over to normal men and women."

Despite himself, Audsley listed raptly. *Enos and Zakaya.* The origins of Starkadr. *Fascinating.*

"A Republic was formed, with each city its own city-state. A parliament of equals, and under Starkadr's eye, peace reigned for centuries. Now, see if you can guess: why did the Ascendant, so many years later, designate Agerastos as the home of heretics?"

Audsley blinked. "Because that is their station in the cycle of Ascension. Worthy Bythian slaves are reborn at the lowest rung of belief, which is heresy."

"Yes, but why Agerastos? Why not Zoe, or Nous?"

Audsley let out a half-panicked laugh. "You speak as if he had a choice! It was Agerastos because it was so ordained! Or are you claiming that they were punished for some historical transgression? "

"I am," said the minister with a self-contented smile. "Agerastos was the first city-state to shatter the peace of the Republic. They invaded and conquered Nous, setting the others against it. When its mad king launched an attack on Zoe, the others banded their armies and crushed it — but the Republic was already dead. Aletheia, Ennoia, and Zoe formed a Triumvirate, but they had acquired a taste for blood, for power, and they found it to their liking. Not eight years later, Aletheia and Ennoia found a pretext to conquer Zoe, and a Duumvirate was formed. Can you guess where this is leading?"

"The Chaos Years," whispered Audsley.

"Precisely. The quickening could not be stopped. Aletheia and Ennoia went to war, Zoe and Agerastos threw off their shackles, and soon every city was waging war through the Portals against the others. It is said that in the fifteen years that followed, over half the population that had once formed the Republic was slain. The Portals ran red with blood."

Audsley swallowed. Open, continuous warfare conducted through the Portals? It was only too easy to imagine the bloodshed.

"It was then, when our civilization was at its nadir, that your Ascendant rose to power. He was a failed Bythian magistrate before he was a messiah. Of course, that isn't mentioned in your holy texts. He was, I believe, nearly forty when he began to claim religious visions. He was ignored and laughed at. Furious, impecunious, he retreated from the Blade Towers into the Badlands and there wandered, alone, for a year."

"The Year of Solitude," said Audsley. He fought to rouse his piety, his sense of resistance. "Voluntarily chosen so that he could better channel the divine truths that came to him."

"Yes. That's what he said afterwards. But, then, oh so fortuitously, he discovered the great Portal to Abythos."

"Yes," said Audsley. "Though you mock it. And it was through that Gate that he found the kragh, whom he led back into Bythos and so began his taming of empire."

"Yes. Quite." The minister tapped his lips. "Tell me, Audsley, don't you think it suspicious that he found a major, permanent Solar Portal in the depths of the Abythian Labyrinth? The only such Portal that stands apart from the main seven Gates?"

"The Ascendant's piety opened the way."

"Oh, don't tell me you believe that. Piety? Opened a demonic Portal?"

Audsley struggled to reconcile that. There were so many implications to the Portals being fueled by imprisoned demons that he'd shied away from thinking about it.

"No," said the minister. "He conquered a demon and forced it to open that Portal. How he knew of Abythos and its kragh, I do not know, but perhaps he didn't. Perhaps he simply wished to leave the land of his humiliation. But when he did find the kragh, surely then he recognized the opportunity they presented. So, he returned, leading them by the thousands, and conquered every city until he had formed his Empire."

"No," said Audsley.

"Is it a coincidence, then, that Bythos, where he was most humiliated, became the dwelling place of slaves? Or that Agerastos, which began the War for the Republic, became the home of heretics? But he was not yet supreme. Who still hovered in the skies, impotent, yet all-powerful? The Flame Walkers. Your first Ascendant was a jealous god. He could not tolerate their presence. They gave lie to his theology.

So, he had them declared the greatest of sinners, named their magic evil, and began a foolish, impossible war against them."

Audsley could only listen, spellbound.

"But he failed, and died without coming close to defeating them. His replacement, the Second Ascendant, was perhaps more cunning. Thirteen years after his rise to power, he was able to convince one of the White Adepts to split away from the others, and she brought with her in time almost a hundred of her fellows. Together, they formed the Order of Purity, and on that very night, the Flame Walkers broke their neutrality and assassinated the Ascendant."

"This I know," Audsley whispered. "It led to the Third Ascendant's miracle of closing the Black Gate and depriving the Sin Casters of their magic, followed by the storming of Starkadr."

"Yes, very good." The minister nodded. "You have the tail end of it. But now, tell me, Audsley: When you step back and gaze upon the entirety of our history, can you not help but see how artificial Ascension is? How it reflects the arbitrary whims of a vengeful man, who with the kragh at his back was able to conquer a land torn by civil war, and who then created a system by which he could ensure his dominance forevermore? A system that made him a god?"

"It's not like that," said Audsley. "He was blessed, visited by a greater truth—"

"And the Portals, Audsley? How do you account for them in your philosophy? The fact that Nous is sinking, bereft as it is of the sustaining powers of the Black Gate? Or that your Virtues — the descendants of the Order of Purity — are dependent upon this elixir derived from Flame Walkers and gatestone to live full lives? Do you not see the imbalance that your Ascendant created when he blocked the Black Gate, when he broke apart the Conduits, when he deformed history with his lies and cast entire peoples into slavery and eternal punishment out of spite?"

Audsley reached for his defenses, everything that he had learned and had been told was true ever since he was a child, but the words, the arguments, slipped through his fingers. His mind was whirling, the minister's words cutting into him like slashes from a blade. Then he thought of Kethe and Asho, fighting together, and how Kethe had cleansed Asho of his sin-casting taint.

"You are the father of lies," he said, his voice shaking with emotion.

"Here is the truth," said the minister. "The Black Gate and the White Gate are opposites. One pours raw creation into the world, the other drains it. Different people are attuned to each of them, but that attunement is fatal in time; Flame Walkers who only channel the powers of the Black Gate are driven mad and sickened, while White Adepts are bleached and sucked dry until they are deprived of their vitality and die. Only by establishing a Conduit, by connecting with each other, can they mimic the same balance that exists naturally in the world, and in so doing not only live, but prosper.

"The Ascendant ruined that balance. He blocked the entrance of creative power into the world. Why did the Age of Wonders come to an end? Because the Flame Walkers were deprived of their abilities to fashion new Aletheias, to raise new Nouses from the sea. Where have the beasts and monsters of legend disappeared to? Without sustenance from the Black Gate, they have all died or fallen into deep slumbers. Your Ascendant, in his bid for power, has ruined the balance of this world. The only way to correct it, to save us from eventual extinction, is to correct the grave wrong he did to us all."

"You mean to open the Black Gate," Audsley whispered, horrified.

"Yes," said the minister. "That is our eventual goal. To allow the natural forces of creation to flow back into the world. To allow the Flame Walkers to arise once more, to take the Virtues as their partners and heal the world. To cleanse the lie of Ascension from the land, and return us to the Age of Wonders."

"No," said Audsley, clutching at his head. He wanted to curse the man and call him a liar, but to do so without greater arguments was useless. He studied the man's web of lies, trying to find the weakness in his logic, to unravel it and defend his faith. But, to his horror, he couldn't.

"I do not fault you for feeling anguish," said the minister. "You have been inculcated with a primitive and barbaric morality from birth. One that has benefitted you to this point. Now that you are being faced with the facts, how can you react with anything but horror? Breathe, Audsley. Deep breaths."

Audsley found that he was doing the exact opposite. He was panting in short, shallow gasps. His head felt like it was going to blow open, and he clutched it with both hands, curling up and turning away from the minister as he squeezed his eyes shut.

"For too long has Ascendancy gloried the few at the expense of the many. For too long has the Empire closed its eyes to the horrors of slavery, oppression, and inequality."

"How do you know all of this?" asked Audsley.

"Why, my grandfather told me," said the minister, sounding surprised. "He lived through most of it and can personally assure me of its veracity."

"Your grandfather?" Audsley wanted to laugh. He felt manic. "*You're* the grandfather."

"My grandfather," the minister said softly, his eyes smoldering. "Erenthil, the greatest Artificer who ever lived. One day, perhaps soon, you will meet him yourself."

Erenthil. The name rang in Audsley's mind like the tolling of a great gong. He knew that name, had read it somewhere. It came back to him suddenly — he'd read the name in this very room, in the letter one of the cadavers below had been penning moments before her death. The Artificer who had labored in Starkadr's final hour to work with demons and create artifacts with which to repel the Order of Purity.

"He — he's alive?"

"Yes," said the minister gravely. "And he directs our actions. He always has. It was he who divined the means to create the black potions, he who first led us to Haugabrjótr. His will, ancient and timeless, directs our campaign to free this world and redress the wrongs done to us by your Ascendants. One of which," said the minister, turning to look at Ainos, "is here with us, is he not? In Starkadr."

"Yes," said Ainos. "I can feel his presence below."

"Now we know where he went," said the minister. "And how. The pieces are falling into place most delightfully. How opportune."

Audsley fought to take control of himself. "Opportune?"

"Yes," said the minister. "My clan has lost centuries of work in getting close to him and taking control of the Empire." He snapped his fingers, making a dry, cracking noise. "Gone, like that. So, we turn to an alternative plan. We will help the kragh destroy the Empire. Maize, Doctor, Eulos – accompany Ainos. She will get you close to the Ascendant so that you may kill him."

"No!" cried Audsley. He raised both hands to unleash demon flame, but froze when Ainos turned to him, her hands glowing white in turn.

"Do not disappoint me," said the minister. "You have a great role to play in the coming events. And think about this: there is nothing you can do to stop us. Resistance now is not only futile but beyond foolish. Do not fear the truth, Audsley. Embrace it."

The minister set Ainos down on the uppermost level. The three Fujiwaras moved to her side, and together they left, disappearing into the rest of the library.

Audsley felt tears running down his cheeks. Was Ascension a lie? If not, how could he explain away the inconvenient facts he had discovered himself, and deny the plausible explanation the minister had given him? Why did the Empire depend on demons? Why did the Virtues die so young? Why had Bythos and Agerastos been chosen for punishment? How could the Flame Walkers be so evil if it was they who had created Aletheia?

"Audsley," whispered the minister, floating toward him. "It is no easy thing to learn that you have been lied to for your entire life. But this is your moment of greatness. The door to your cell has been opened. All you need do is step outside and liberate yourself. You are clearly an intelligent, learned man. Think: if all of the evidence points to a different truth, how can you cling so obtusely to falsehood? The mark of a great man is his willingness to adopt new truths and grow, no matter how painful those truths may be. Grow, Audsley. Adapt. Overcome. And help me bring this truth to the rest of the world, to those who are unjustly imprisoned and oppressed. Help me, Audsley. Do the one thing that can help us win this war."

"One thing?" croaked Audsley. "What's that?"

The minister's eyes glittered. "Kill the kragh warlord and bring me the circlet that he wears."

Chapter 26

Their destination was a lake called the Dragon's Tear. They left before dawn, while a soft darkness still lay over the hard mountain slopes. The cold bit through Tiron's new furs as he emerged from the cave and caused his chain to feel so chilled that it bit his skin when he brushed against it. His mountain goat shied away from him as he sought to mount it, till Shaya stepped forward with a wry smile to hold its bridle.

His muscles ached. The cold was doing him no favors. Biting down his annoyance, Tiron boosted himself up and then swung a leg over the saddle. Only a lifetime of experience spent mounting chargers allowed him to do so without falling right off, and once he was settled, he found that the goat radiated a gentle heat that was inexpressibly delicious.

Shaya climbed up behind him, her body fitting neatly against his own. *More warmth*, he thought as he felt her press against him, her arms linking around his waist. The others were getting ready; shamans were grumbling and scrambling up with differing levels of dignity, while Maur and her swordmaster were at the lead, waiting.

"That Maur is formidable," said Tiron.

"She is," said Shaya as she swallowed a yawn. "She's the only kragh I've ever seen go toe-to-toe with Tharok and get him to back down."

Seeing that they were all mounted, Maur turned her goat's head and clucked at it, and the entire line lurched into motion.

"You knew them?" Tiron asked. "Back before Tharok's invasion?"

"Some," said Shaya, her voice quiet over his shoulder. "Tharok saved me from a slaver's market in the lowlander city of Gold and gave me my freedom. I had nowhere else to go, so I followed him. We left for the mountains the very next day, and those weeks traveling with the kragh..." She shook her head. "It's hard to explain to a man. But for a brief time, I got to enjoy all the privileges that you take for granted."

"They made you a knight?"

"No," said Shaya with biting acidity. "They did not make me a knight. They did something better. They treated me like an equal. You can't know how that felt for me. It was... life-altering."

They rode in silence for a while. Tiron couldn't stop himself from imagining that it was Iskra behind him, her arms around his waist, her cheek against his shoulder. His thoughts mellowed as he thought of their private moments together, particularly the one night they'd spent in Mythgraefen, when he'd simply held her for hours upon hours, watching her sleep, luxuriating in her lying naked by his side.

Tiron closed his eyes. Where was she? Again, he wondered if he should have swallowed his pride and gone with her to attack Laur Castle, should have remained true to her in her grief. He'd be with her now, wherever she was, helping her, defending her — not out here on this alien mountainside with a bunch of spirit-crazed kragh.

Dawn was just beginning to limn the eastern peaks, tracing their craggy outlines in gold, when the hiss of arrows cut through the air.

Tiron's reaction was immediate. It was born from a lifetime of battle and precluded all thought; he swept Shaya off the saddle behind him and tumbled to the ground, crashing onto the cold rocks as arrows rained overhead.

"Ramswold!" Tiron drew his blade and rose to his feet, clutching at the saddle and keeping the goat close.

The enemy were sprinting up the trail behind Tiron's group under the cover of their archers. Tiron couldn't make out how many — twenty? Thirty? Leuthold's goat at the very rear was riderless. Ramswold was urging his goat to turn around, Ulein at his side. The shamans were crying out in fear and consternation, while Maur was barking out orders in kragh.

"Ramswold, retreat!"

Death had come for them on the pass. They would be overrun in moments if they didn't flee.

A goat came charging down the trail from behind Tiron, and he heard Maur cry out in protest. He made out the name: "Barok!"

The old swordmaster swept past them. Hunched over his mountain goat's neck, he held his wicked blade at the ready, down and to the side. Ramswold was about to engage the kragh when Barok flew past him and smashed like a thunderbolt into the leading edge of the enemy.

Tiron watched in awe as the mountain kragh leaped sideways off his saddle to collide bodily with five of the charging kragh, bringing them down in a crash and tumble of limbs, causing those running behind them to trip and fall as well.

Ramswold hesitated, blade drawn; Ulein was fighting to control his own goat.

"Ramswold!" Tiron snapped back to life. "Retreat!"

Nok called out a sharp command and took hold of Maur's arm, giving her a shake. The Wise Woman had been about to charge after Barok.

Barok had rolled up into a crouch from which he lashed out with his blade, each sweep severing tendons and hamstrings and opening arteries. Even at this remove, Tiron could appreciate the sheer artistry of the old kragh's attacks: not a movement wasted, every attack flowing smoothly into the next.

But he was doomed. Already, Tiron could see wounds glistening wetly across his body and the flow of blood over his hide. Only his speed and discipline were keeping the kragh at bay, but there were far too many.

Ramswold rode up and took Shaya under one arm. Without slowing, he hauled her across his saddle and kicked his heels into the goat's flanks so as to burst on past.

The other two mountain kragh from their group came charging down the pass, blades drawn as they raced to Barok's assistance. Tiron marveled at their bravery as arrows *thwipped* through the air, several them hitting the two kragh but doing nothing to stop them. They threw themselves into the fray, singing what sounded like dirges, and were engulfed by the enemy.

Cursing, Tiron leaped up onto his goat and urged it after the others. It broke into a frantic gallop, and soon the sounds of battle grew faint. Tiron gasped as he held on, half-raised out of the saddle as he would be on a charging horse, holding on for dear life. Tiron had seen men die selflessly in battle, had seen the highest acts of heroism before – and had also lived long enough to know how rare such acts were. Barok's bravery had sobered him. He'd never thought a kragh could act nobly.

They raced onward and upward till the goats could run no more. Then Tiron dismounted alongside Ramswold and Ulein. "What happened to Leuthold?"

"I don't know," said Ramswold, his voice bleak. "He was the rear guard. They must have killed him just before they launched the attack."

"I didn't hear anything," said Ulein, his voice harsh with shock. "I was right there, a few paces ahead of him. How was it that I didn't hear a thing?"

Tiron rubbed at his face. They were dying too quickly. "You did well. You acted quickly, made the right choice. Don't be hard on yourself."

"But, Leuthold..." said Ulein, searching for the right words. "He was smart. Tough. He'd been a soldier for twice as long as I have."

"Death comes to us all, ser knight," said Tiron. "Being smart and strong, tough and fast might give you an edge, but in time, it will never be enough. Nothing is. We're all going to die, and this was his time. Now, come. I have questions."

They'd reached a small clearing of rocky pools covered in skeins of ice. The goats had their heads down and were drinking with powerful gulps. Tiron made his way to where Maur was standing with the others. She looked up at him, grief in her eyes.

"Shaya, translate."

Olina stared at him. "She's grieving, Tiron. Give her a moment."

"No," he said.

"It's all right," said Shaya. "Maur's tougher than any of us here."

"It's not all right," Olina muttered. "None of this is."

"Ask Maur how much farther it is to the Dragon's Tear."

Shaya did so, then translated the response. "She says we are half a day's ride away."

"Good. Now, ask—"

The shamans let out a wail. Tiron dropped his hand to the hilt of his blade and turned slowly, scrutinizing the pre-dawn shadows. He saw nothing. "Ulein," he barked. "Is anything coming?"

The young knight was standing alongside the path. "Nothing that I can see."

The shamans turned slowly, gazing up into the sky as if they were searching for something in the heavens, their arms raised, their wailing half-turned into a chant. Even to Tiron, it sounded haggard and desperate.

"What's going on?" he asked Shaya.

"I don't know. Wait." She asked Maur something in kragh, and Tiron was taken aback by the fear on the kragh woman's face. "She says a spirit is coming," whispered Shaya. "A bad spirit."

"Great. Fucking great." Tiron felt his patience beginning to wear thin. "Mount up! Shaya, Ramswold, you're together. Olina, Ulein, let's move!"

The air above them began to shimmer like the surface of a pool. Light curled and curved strangely through invisible dimples, and the hairs on the back of Tiron's neck prickled. He wanted to stand there and gape, but he gave Shaya a shove and whistled sharply to get Ulein's attention. "Hurry!"

The six shamans were facing the disturbance, Forest Lord at their lead. He raised his hands and moved them back and forth in an intricate pattern. Where his nails scored the air, they left a faint tracery of gold light like incandescent spider's thread. The others supported his chant, repeating segments, moaning a low accompaniment, and their raised hands seemed to draw Forest Lord's golden summoning and amplify it, causing the web of shimmering, delicate light to expand and blossom into the air above them.

Tiron grabbed a fistful of his goat's mane and hauled himself up onto the saddle, but the goat sidestepped and shook its head in irritation, its huge horns swinging dangerously through the air.

"Stand still, damn you!" But the goat's eyes were rolling as it shuffled backward, fighting his grip on its bridle. "Curse your mutton head! Stand still!"

Out of the corner of his eye, Tiron saw the air slit open to reveal a greater darkness that seemed to spill out like smoke into the sky. Something that looked like a crab's leg emerged and descended to touch the ground, fully six yards high and sheathed in amber bone, green fire smoldering in its joints.

Ramswold was mounted, Shaya in his arms. He let out a cry and dug his heels in. His goat needed no urging. It bolted up the path and was gone. Maur and Nok fled shortly afterward, followed by Ulein and Olina.

Tiron's goat skittered back, rearing its head away and nearly tearing Tiron's arm out of its socket. "Come here!" he snarled at it.

Forest Lord's voice rose into a fierce pitch as another leg came through some six yards away. The golden cloud of tangled light was now high above them, gleaming as if it had been freshly forged, a complex pattern like an impossible web. The antlered kragh raised his hands high, his chant coming to a climax, but then it was horrifically cut short when a third leg stabbed down out of a tear in the sky and speared straight through his chest, slamming him to the ground.

The other five shamans fell back, but quickly resumed their chanting, trying to pick up where they had left off. Forest Lord lay gurgling on the ground, twitching, dying.

Tiron made a grab for his saddle horn and was nearly knocked off his feet as his goat danced aside once more.

The five remaining shamans let out a great cry, and the webbing of golden light flew at the patch of sky that was being torn apart. The rents in the air glowed brightly and began to close; one of the spirit's legs was shorn clear off as its Portal shut, sending six yards' worth of chitin and fire crashing to the ground.

Tiron stared, his goat forgotten. The tears were sealing up — the second leg was severed and fell to the ground. But Forest Lord's chanting wasn't working completely. He could see the disappointment on the shamans' faces as the light finally faded, leaving a few gashes open in the gloom through which smoke was still pouring out.

A new leg speared down into Mud Knife, tearing through his leather apron and pinning him gruesomely to the rock. Again, the shamans lifted their hands, raising their voices in desperation, and once more the golden threads began to manifest.

Tiron cursed and lunged for his goat's saddle, surprising the animal and managing to scramble up before it could get away. Sitting up, he grabbed the reins and yanked them savagely, bringing the goat under control.

The four shamans were failing. The tears in the sky were growing wider once more, and Tiron could see the spirit pressing closer now, its huge body causing the air to distend like some tortured bubble. He got a glimpse of foamy mouth parts and bulbous eyes, and that was enough for him.

He kicked his goat into a run and raced past the shamans, leaning down and out to snag his arm around the one wearing the white owl mask. The kragh shrieked at him and writhed in his grip, but Tiron gritted his teeth and held on, nearly falling out of the saddle as they raced over the pools and then up the path after the others.

The kragh shaman was light, and after a few moments, he ceased struggling. The screams of the other three fell behind them, and soon all Tiron could hear was the rhythmic clopping of the goat's cloven hooves as they surged ever higher.

Dawn had finally broken when he rounded a corner on the trail and came upon the others waiting on their goats. At the sight of him, Ramswold punched the air. "There he is!"

"Here," said Tiron, setting the shaman down on the ground, his arm almost numb. "I saved one."

Maur slid off her goat and ran up to the shaman, speaking harshly to him. They spoke for a minute, and then the shaman simply shook his head.

"He says the medusa-cursed shamans are too powerful," said Shaya. "Her influence has shattered the balance between sanity and might. They are no longer constrained by – I didn't understand how he explained it. They're burning like bonfires, he said. They're consuming everything in their path, but they can't last. They'll burn out."

"Not soon enough," said Ramswold. "Why can't our shamans fight them in a similar manner?"

"I don't know," Shaya said softly. "That's not their role. That's like asking why a miner doesn't collapse his mine. They're here to tend the spirits, listen to them, placate them. Not order them into battle."

"That's too bad," said Tiron. "Can Owl Home still get us to the dragons?"

Shaya asked his question softly. The shaman lowered his head, clearly hesitating, then nodded.

"Great," said Ulein, his voice nearly cracking. "That's just great."

Maur said something sharp to Ulein. Tiron didn't understand the words, but the tone was clear: *Get it together.* The young knight paled and sat up straighter.

Maur then spoke to them all, looking around their small group. Only Nok still seemed impassive. Everyone else was haggard with shock and exhaustion.

"Maur says we're almost there. We just need to get to the lake. One last run. She thanks us for our help, our sacrifices, and says we need to give our all now, or the deaths of our friends will have been in vain."

Tiron nodded somberly. "Well said. Tell her to lead on. We're not finished yet. We just need to keep ahead of the kragh behind us."

Maur gave him a nod and mounted her goat. The poor beasts were clearly unaccustomed to being driven so hard. They fought the commands to keep moving, keeping their heads down and digging in their forelegs until Owl Home raised a hand and whispered something. Immediately, the goats relaxed and became pliable.

The sun rose over the peaks as they resumed their climb, bathing the mountain crags to the west in glorious hues of gold and white. They were high enough now that snow lay thinly strewn over the dark rock, and the only trees in evidence were short, stunted black pines.

Up they went, the trail wandering around cliff faces and climbing steeply between small, rocky meadows. Nok passed back some smoked goat meat, which proved harder to chew than rocks; after five minutes of gnawing on it, Tiron got his first hint of flavor, and his mouth filled with spit.

They abandoned their goats for the final stretch, and Owl Home led the way. The slope grew steep, and the icy rocks were too large and broken up underfoot to allow for easy passage. Tiron hauled his way up by gripping at slender tree trunks. His boots slid off patches of snow and crunched frozen puddles. Up they went in single file, always glancing behind them. The air became thin and hard to breathe, and Tiron's chest grew tight with the effort. His body was cold but slicked in sweat.

Finally, they scrambled over one last rise and staggered out into a shallow valley in which a great lake lay. Its beauty was cold and perilous; its black waters reflected nothing, not the sky or the sun or the mountains. A wall of shattered ice seemed to flow down from the higher slopes to the lake's far end, and spars and spikes of blue ice erupted from its front edge like a crown. Tiron couldn't tear his eyes away from the lake's black impossibility, as flat and perfect as a sheet of glass.

A circle of green fire hung in the air to one side. Some two yards high, it was disgorging a constant stream of kragh who stepped through nervously and huddled together.

Tiron's heart sank. "Of course," he said, and spat thick phlegm onto the rocks. "Of course."

There were some fifty kragh already massed in front of the circle of flame, and even from this distance, Tiron could see their fear. How they pressed against each other like cattle that had been led into an abattoir and were now quailing at the scent of blood that hung heavy in the air.

Four shamans clad in black stood at their fore. Clearly, it was their presence that kept the other kragh from fleeing. Tiron couldn't see under their hoods, but their hands were soot-black, an unnatural color, as if they had smeared themselves completely with ashes.

"Damn," said Ulein, staggering up beside Tiron, exhaling plumes of condensation and sweating heavily. He winced from some pain or other, and Tiron saw incredulity in his expression; some anger and, what was worse, fear. Whatever narrative Ulein had been telling himself, whatever enchanted tale he had been the hero of, it had suddenly and brutally come to an end on the rocky shore of the Tear.

"Ask the shaman what we must do," Ramswold said to Shaya. His long, pale face appeared almost waxen, with those twin spots of red color high on his cheeks, yet he was breathing more easily than Ulein, and there was a calmness to him that Tiron didn't trust. Shock? Fatalism?

The Bythian did so. Maur looked to the shaman, who was hanging from his staff as if it was all that was holding him up. Owl Home muttered something, then waved a hand in front of him as if he were trying to part a particularly heavy set of curtains.

"The shaman says the spirits are angry. That the presence of the corrupted is rousing them."

The shaman spoke further, more urgently.

"He says the Tear is guarded by the fallen kragh who could not ascend to the Valley of the Dead. They dance for eternity along the edge of the Tear, broken and gibbering and hating the living. The air, he says, throbs with their anger. They are offended by the arrival of the corrupted."

Ulein made the sign of the triangle.

"He didn't answer Ramswold's question," growled Tiron. At least for the moment, no more kragh were coming through the green Portal. They were now assembled in a great block behind the shamans.

Maur spoke roughly, her impatience clear. The shaman bobbed his head as if he had been chastened and dropped his arms. His response was brief.

Phil Tucker

"He says we must dive into the Tear itself," said Shaya. "The way to the dragons lies through the lake."

"The enemy will catch us before we reach the water's edge," said Tiron.

"I say we go back, then," Ulein said in a quavering voice. "Where's the sense in trying to fight sixty kragh?"

Olina was the last to come up over the ridge. She staggered forward a few steps. The life of a scholar had not prepared her for the harshness of a forced mountain march, but, although she stood there swaying, she didn't seek to sit or shrink back from the kragh. Instead, she turned to look at Ulein, scorn on her rounded features.

"Run away?" Her voice was hoarse. "After what Marcus and Garvis sacrificed? Barok and Leuthold? The other shamans and kragh?"

Ulein flushed. "I'm talking common sense. There's sixty of them."

"I'll not run," said Olina. "Give me your sword." She laughed, the sound jagged with intensity and despair. "I'll lead the damn charge."

Nok walked over to where Tiron was standing. The huge kragh's face was a graven image, dignified and hard. He spoke quietly, and Shaya paled and then translated.

"He says that the hour of his death has finally come. He will kill as many of the enemy as he can, and then will ascend to the Valley of the Dead. He wants to know if you will fight beside him?"

Tiron looked down at the sixty kragh. Nok had spoken the truth; the moment of his death had indeed come at last.

Tiron inhaled deeply and thought of his dreams of seeing Iskra once more. Of a life spent at her side, in some quiet and out of the way place, their lives rich in love and humble in all other needs. He thought of all the tomorrows he would never see, the years that were about to be cut short by death. He closed his eyes, held a moment of peace within his heart, found his calm, and then turned to Nok.

"Yes."

"Oh, come on, Tiron!" Ulein tugged at his own hair in desperation. "Why? We can slip away, try again later, or — or—"

Tiron drew his blade and slowly shoved its tip into the gravel at his feet. Then he reached up and undid the knot of his cloak. The thick fur whispered down to pool around his feet.

"Listen, Ulein. All of you." He reached behind his head, grabbed at his heavy wool tunic and pulled it off. The cold was invigorating through the thin shirt he was wearing underneath. "We fought hard. We did our best. But from the moment you decide to walk the path of an Ennoian knight, you accept that one day a blade will cut you down. Each of those blades is down there, held in some kragh's fist. We've little time left to us now, perhaps only minutes. All we can control now is how we choose to meet that blade."

Ulein sank into a crouch and buried his head in his hands.

Tiron continued, "Do we die well? Or do we die badly? That's all that's left for us to decide."

"I can't," said Ulein. Tears were running down his cheeks. "I can't go down there."

"Ulein," Tiron began, but Ramwold cut him off.

"Tiron is wrong," Ramswold said quietly. Ulein blinked and looked over at him. "We're not going to die down there."

Tiron felt an ugly anger ripple through him. "Ramswold –"

"No, I know it." Ramswold's smile was gentle. "Look where we're standing, Ulein. Look how far we've come. Did we not dream back in the Red Keep of being blessed with a moment such as this? Did we not ask for a chance at true heroism, to be challenged with a task worthy of the greatest champions? Well, here we are." He pointed with his blade. "And there is our challenge."

"Let the man die with dignity," said Tiron. "Don't fill his head with your nonsense."

"It's not nonsense, Tiron. We are the Order of the Star. On our shoulders rests the fate of the Empire. We're on a quest for *dragons*, and you think a group of kragh is going to stop us?" Ramswold's eyes glimmered with something that seemed dangerously akin to joy. "We are protected by fate. We are guided by greatness. I don't know how we're going to do it, but we will overcome this challenge. We will be victorious."

Ulein rubbed at his face. "You really believe that, my lord?"

"I do," said Ramswold. "This is our greatest hour, Ser Ulein. Come – we march into history."

"History," said Ulein, his voice soft with wonder, and slowly, he rose to his feet.

"Enough of this stupidity," snarled Tiron. "Face this moment like men, not like fools. Where is your damned dignity?"

"We're not fools," said Ramswold, still smiling. "We're the chosen."

This moment was supposed to be sacred and grave, filled with a sober dignity as they accepted their imminent death. Tiron wanted to smash the smile from Ramswold's face; he far preferred Ulein's sniveling over the starry-eyed wonder that filled him now.

"Fine," he groaned. "Lie to yourselves if that makes meeting death easier for you. Cowardice comes in all forms."

"It takes a special kind of bravery to put faith in that which you cannot see," said Ramswold. "But I don't expect you to understand, Ser Tiron. All I ask is that you not begrudge us our conviction."

"Fine," Tiron said, and stepped up beside Nok.

The kragh's impassivity made him feel ashamed of his own anger; Tiron took a deep, steadying breath, and then nodded. Maur came to stand on Nok's far side. Ramswold and Ulein lined up to Tiron's right. Olina, Shaya, and Owl Home stood right behind them.

The shaman was moaning and clutching at his head. He took a step back, looking as if he might flee. Maur grabbed him cruelly by the arm and yanked him back into place, shoved her face down toward his own and snarled at him.

"He says — he says the spirits have grown too hungry. That we will be devoured before we even reach the enemy," whispered Shaya.

"Then, let us charge! For the Order of the Star!" Ramswold yelled, Ulein joining him at the last, their voices thin in the mountain air.

Maur raised her blade and let out her own piercing cry, and was joined by Nok's basso roar.

The shamans below were chanting, weaving their hands through the air, and they drifted back through the ranks of their warriors, who parted for them uneasily. Somewhere between fifty and sixty of them, Tiron thought. Far, far too many.

Tiron raised his blade. Now – now was the time to die. Now was his hour, come at long last. "For the honor and beauty of Lady Iskra Kyferin! For the Black Wolves!"

Chapter 27

K ethe bore Asho through the Portal back to Starkadr, stumbling
with exhaustion but unwilling to let anyone else carry his weight.
Khoussan and Kuliver followed grimly, their expressions silencing
all questions. The Vothak intoned the harsh words, the Portal to the
stonecloud opened, and Kethe stepped through into darkness.

She made a beeline toward her tent, ignoring the questions that
were put to her by ministers and attendants, the curious looks, the
whispered comments. She needed to be alone. Needed to close the
tent flaps and get away from prying eyes. Her emotions, her thoughts,
everything about her was scrambled, and she could barely breathe till
she was alone with Asho.

Finally, they reached her tent. Khoussan and Kuliver positioned
themselves just outside to stand guard, and Kethe staggered inside
to lay Asho down on her low cot before her arms gave out. She fell
to her knees and rested her forehead on his chest; he was breathing
very shallowly, and there was a heart-wrenching wheeze in every
inhalation. She screwed her eyes shut and focused on his presence,
his body, on being close to him.

That moment when he had swooped down from the cerulean
skies would be forever engraved in her memory – how quickly her

terror had shifted to elation, how her heart had swelled at the sight of him coming to her rescue. But how had he known where to find her? How had he *flown* like that? She'd called out to the Ascendant, and Asho had answered. Did that make Asho the Ascendant's tool? Or was the Ascendant not involved, and this miraculous rescue was something personal, something private, something sublime between the two of them?

Kethe sat on her heels and examined him. His face was sunken, his pallor was waxen, and his eyes were rimmed with purple. She couldn't begin to imagine how much he would pay for what he'd done, despite her every attempt to drain him of the magic's taint. It had felt different from when they'd fought together in Mythgraefen; this time his magic had been... the best word she could come up with was *dirty*. Polluted, somehow. That had to be the gatestone he'd used. No wonder it took such a toll on the Vothaks.

Kethe took his hand and squeezed it gently. Was there a way for her to help him even now? She didn't know, but she had to try. Settling herself, she closed her eyes. She focused on her breathing and waited for it to grow steady. Waited for her pulse to slow. It took longer than she had expected; the feel of his hand in hers stirred her every time she focused on it, and all she had to do was remember him diving down toward her, the look on his face of both fear and devotion, and her pulse would pick up all over again.

Finally, she felt herself calm, and into that stillness came the White Song. It was distant but there, a beautiful tone like a choir raising its voice in hallowed praise. Kethe didn't push for more, but simply waited, allowing the song to grow louder of its own accord. A part of her mind remained separate this time, however, and asked: *What are you? Are you the voice of Ascension? Or something else? If so, what?*

The song gave her no answer. It rose higher and higher, and when Kethe felt herself bathed in its glory, she directed her focus to Asho's hand. She *reached* for him on a deeper level and sensed him beside her, his aura flickering and dancing like a lamp flame in a storm's powerful wind, unsettled and throwing off caustic sparks of black fire.

But there was more. She felt — sensed — *saw* in her mind's eye a channel between, a cord of white fire that turned black halfway. It went from his heart to hers.

Kethe's eyes snapped open. The cord was gone, and the song of the White Gate began to fade. She closed her eyes, and it gradually welled up once more.

Please, she said to the source of the song. *Please, heal him.*

The song was music and fire all at once, and it flowed into the channel between them, pouring slowly into the dark half that was Asho's and then out over his aura.

Where it flowed, the hissing, angry flames grew quiescent, lost their harsh flarings and became velvety smooth and quiet. Kethe focused on pouring more of the song into him, allowing it to wash away the gatestone's impurities. She didn't know how long she sat there, holding his hand, but when the song finally faded, she felt him stir, felt him squeeze her hand softly, and opened her eyes.

Asho was awake. Much of the fatigue and pallor was gone from his face, though he still looked ill. They held each other's gaze without speaking. Kethe's throat closed up, and her heart was pounding so loudly, she was afraid he'd hear it.

Slowly, wincing, he sat up. He reached out and curled a lock of her hair behind her ear, then cupped her cheek. She pressed her hand over his, and then he leaned forward and kissed her, a deep, passionate kiss that caused the White Song to explode into full volume, drowning her in its ineffable glory even as she lost herself in his touch, her lips parting as she held him close, and kissed him with an ardor that caused both of them to tumble back onto his bed.

He laughed and held her close, then turned onto his side so he was propped up on one elbow, his white hair falling down around his face. "Kethe," he whispered, tracing the lines of her lips and then her cheek. "I love you."

She went utterly still. It felt like someone had punched her right in the chest.

"I knew it when I heard your cry," he said. "Nothing else mattered. Not Tharok, not the Empire, not my cause, nothing. I had to find you.

I had to help you. I would have done anything for you, anything at all. I knew it then, and I know it now. I love you – even if you walk away. Even if you insist on being Makaria, if you never talk to me again. I love you, and I always will."

Tears pooled in her eyes and overflowed. She didn't know what to say; she could only gasp and smile as something within her cracked and opened and she felt a tenderness, a wild joy, an overwhelming happiness that made her cup her hands over her mouth and then reach up to grab him and pull him down for a second kiss.

Their legs intertwined as they held each other tightly, kissing as if this might be their last chance to ever do so. It was only when Asho pulled away, his eyes now unfocused, and put his forehead down on the pillow, wincing and blinking, that she remembered how ill he still was.

"It's all right," he said, laughing huskily. "Just — just a moment of dizziness. I'm fine."

"You're not fine," she said, then pushed him over onto his back and sat up to stare down at him in concern. "Tell me what you're feeling."

He pressed his hand to his brow and closed his eyes. "Well, let's see. Love. Lots of that. And a very improper desire to see how much of your armor I can convince you to take off... and..."

She slapped his shoulder, and he laughed. "Honestly," he said. "I'm fine. I just feel... worn out. Like I could sleep for a week. I thought — I could have sworn — that I'd be in much rougher shape."

"I think I healed you," she said. "While you slept. I saw a cord of white fire stretching between us."

"Yes," Asho said, pushing himself up onto one elbow with excitement only to groan and fall back. "I saw it too! It's what I followed to reach you. It led me through the Portals."

"What is it, Asho? Our... love?" Saying that word made her feel strange, almost squeamish.

"Maybe," he said somberly. "Or something to do with our magic. How we've connected as a team. We've always had that connection, but it's as if that's finally coalesced into something tangible. More... defined. I don't know."

Kethe frowned. "I wish there was someone we could ask. But I've learned nothing in my lessons as a Virtue or Consecrated about anything like this. Ascendancy doesn't speak about this bond at all."

"Audsley might have known something," said Asho. "Remember that book he found about the Path of Flames?"

"We haven't heard from him since Aletheia fell," said Kethe. "Some of the ministers reported him challenging the Minister of the Moon — a Fujiwara — and losing a poetry competition badly. He flew away, and nobody's heard from him since."

"Well, we know he can take care of himself," said Asho. "It would be good to have him back, though. I miss him."

"And Ser Tiron," Kethe said quietly. "I never thought I'd say it, but I miss him too. Or maybe I miss what his being around did for Mother, though I've not spent much time with her. It's been too hard. But she seemed more sure of herself with him at her side."

"We've all been struggling," Asho said as he took her hand. "I've been struggling. I'm sorry for what I said. I was..." He searched for the right words. "I was hurt. Angry. I'm sorry."

"No," she said. She smiled down at him, though she remembered the pain all too well. "I'm the one who should apologize. I retreated into being a Virtue. I see it now – it was a refuge, and a way to hide. To allow that role to dictate what I had to do, so that I need not make any choices myself. I'm the one who's sorry."

"Enough with the apologies, then," he said, pulling her back down.

Kethe wanted to lose herself in his embrace, but, with a rueful smile, she forced herself to pull away. "Asho, you need to rest. I need to report back to Theletos and Lutherius. Nous is lost unless we can find another Lunar Portal that will take us there. How did it go in Ennoia?"

"Good," he said. "But we got lucky. If they'd sent any more kragh, we would have been overrun. But it worked, Kethe. It worked." His eyes lit up. "You have to see it. We're creating the perfect death trap. Trenches, walls that funnel the kragh, ballistae... — Elon himself has come from Mythgraefen to help, and we've got hundreds upon hundreds of archers. If we could gather more soldiers, and more arrows, I think we could hold the kragh off forever."

"I'll see what I can do," she said. "I'll convince Lutherius to send as many archers as I can. But, please: you're looking worse. Lie down. And no, I *won't* lie down next to you." She grinned as she swatted his hands away. "Rest. We're going to need you soon."

"We?" he asked with a smile.

She blushed and looked away. "Fine. Me. I'm going to need you soon."

"Better," he said, and again he sat up, his chest against her shoulder. "Kethe," he whispered, turning her chin so that she met his eyes. "I love you."

Her heart lurched in her chest, and she felt her face flame with emotion. She couldn't speak, could only nod and then kiss him tenderly, hoping she was conveying everything with that one touch of their lips. Then she rose to her feet and smoothed down her sodden clothing.

Asho lay back, hands laced behind his head, watching her with an almost feline inscrutability.

"Rest," she ordered. "I'll come back as soon as I can." She bent down and kissed him hard, then wheeled and escaped his arms to step back outside.

Her cheeks were still burning, and she pressed her palms against them in an effort to compose herself. Only then did she notice Khoussan and Kuliver pretending to look straight ahead, their expressions studiously neutral.

"What?" she demanded.

"What was what, my gracious Virtue?" asked Kuliver, his voice light, affecting surprise. "Oh, nothing. Nothing, I assure thee. It's not like we were standing just three paces from where all the action was taking place."

"Action?" she asked, arching a brow. *Don't blush*, she commanded herself. *Do. Not. Blush.*

"Aye. The action, the activity, the heart of the storm, as it were." He dropped all pretenses and grinned. "Blessings upon you both, Makaria. The Ascendant knows there's little enough cause for merriment these days. A tumble with a willing — and black fire-spewing — lad is a cause for celebration."

"Kuliver, we didn't 'tumble', and as for the 'heart of the storm' –"

His grin only grew wider, and she gave up and turned to her last remaining cohort member for help. "Khoussan?"

He shook his head, smiling sadly. "Enjoy, Makaria. Enjoy."

"Fine. Well, thank you for your... I don't even know what to call it."

"Blessings," said Kuliver.

"Blessings." She realized then that Asho had no doubt heard everything that had just been said, and she felt herself blush furiously all over again. "All right, enough of this. Come on." She strode hurriedly away, much to Kuliver's amusement.

"I had a girl once," said Kuliver, hurrying to catch up as they strode between the tents. "The shipwrights used to use her as a model for their nautical figureheads. Full head of hair, and everything she wore was tight in all the right places. Now, this you'll find hard to believe, but she had a best friend who wasn't all that particular –"

Up ahead, she saw Ainos leading three strangers toward the Ascendant's tent. She held up her hand, cutting Kuliver off, and jogged to catch up. "Ainos! You're back!"

The Virtue was about to duck into the tent, but he paused and then smiled coldly. "Makaria. Indeed. I've just now returned."

"We were all wondering what happened to you," Kethe said, smiling hesitantly. "We feared you had been killed by the kragh."

"No, though it was close. I was trapped in a Blade Tower and unable to escape. A terrible waste of time. These good people here helped me. I'm thanking them for their service by introducing them to the Ascendant."

Kethe turned to regard Ainos' saviors. A massive old woman with a frightful face and a black tent for a dress stared impassively at her, while a handsome man with the air of a warrior and bleak, guttered eyes stood by her side. The last of the three was a severe academic type who smiled with bitter amusement at her as if he was aware of some joke at her expense.

"Well, thank you," Kethe said uncertainly. "You've done the Empire a great service." She turned back to Ainos. "How did they help, exactly? They were in Bythos?"

Ainos clapped Kethe on the shoulder. "I don't like repeating myself. Come inside. You can hear my tale when I give it to the Ascendant."

Kethe nodded and waited as Ainos and the three strangers filed into the large tent.

"Something's off here, Virtue," said Kuliver, stepping in close. "I don't like the look of those coves."

"Yes, it's strange," said Kethe. "But I suppose they don't have to be good people to have helped Ainos — just interested in self-preservation. I'm sure it's a curious story. Come on."

The Ascendant was rising from a simple meal, Theletos and Lutherius at his side. Several ministers were also in attendance, standing in the wings of the tent, and everything was lit by the soft glow of candlelight.

"Ainos!" Theletos wiped his mouth and stood. "You have decided to join our war at last."

"Theletos," said Ainos, bowing her head. "Your Holiness." She bowed deeply, then looked at Lutherius quizzically.

"Ainos," said the Ascendant, smiling warmly. "You have returned. This gladdens me more than you could know. We need your wisdom and strength. This is Lutherius, the former captain of the Cerulean Guard, whom I have named my new Grace."

Kethe moved to stand to one side, Khoussan and Kuliver behind her. None of the three strangers with Ainos seemed particularly impressed to be in the Ascendant's presence; the old woman had yet to show a flicker of emotion at all.

"Your Grace," said Ainos, nodding again. "Let me introduce three individuals who made my escape from Bythos possible, and without whom I would surely have perished." She looked back at them. "Please, step forward."

The three strangers did as she commanded, forming a line alongside Ainos. "It's a strange story," said the Virtue, "and one that almost defies belief. The important part, however, is that we have made it through the dangers arrayed before us and are here at last." She turned to her companions. "Now."

The three strangers lifted their hands, and black flame erupted from their palms. It engulfed the table, knocking it back, a torrent so furious that the back of the tent immediately caught fire, the whole of it lifting up as the superheated air caused it to balloon.

Kethe saw Lutherius reduced to a charred skeleton, his arms raised to protect his face. The Ascendant and Theletos both managed to throw up shields of white light, and about them the black fire billowed, both men staggering back from the brunt of the blow.

It happened so quickly and was so unexpected that Kethe had no time to react. Ainos, however, leaped forward, blade drawn, and stabbed it deep into the white sphere that encircled Theletos, who twisted so that it pierced his side and not his heart.

Kethe screamed. When she drew her blade, its blaze was terrible, its length immediately aflame. The massive old woman turned, her face still expressionless, and unleashed black fire upon her.

Kethe gritted her teeth and shoved her burning sword into the heart of the flames. It was like being kicked by a horse or being toppled onto by an entire barn. She was driven back a good four feet, her boots sliding on Starkadr's slick stone floor, the fire fulminating like a thundercloud just in front of her sword, held back by flashing jabs of white lighting that speared out to form a protective wall.

"Ainos!" she heard the Ascendant cry out. "Traitor!"

Khoussan and Kuliver stepped up alongside her, blades raised, and as they joined her, the white lightning sizzling out continuously from her sword lit both of theirs, and the three of them began to struggle forward against the torrent of black fire.

Then, suddenly, the fire and the resistance it provided was gone, and they stumbled forward unchecked. Kethe saw the old woman fly up into the air, blasting the tent into burning fragments, and tattered and flaming swaths of cloth fell about her. The other two did the same, lifting effortlessly into the air, and then, together, they unleashed another torrent that was focused exclusively on the Ascendant.

Ainos had backed away from Theletos, who had a single sword in hand and a wicked smile on his handsome face. His side was drenched in blood, however, and he pressed a hand against the wound.

"A good try, Ainos. But it wasn't enough. You can't defeat me. You can't come close. Prepare for the Black Gate."

Kethe stared in horror at the Ascendant, who was withstanding the combined blasts of the three Sin Casters. He was being forced down to one knee, however, the continuous torrent taking its toll. Not quite knowing what she was doing, she ran to his side and raised her blade, pointing it at the triad. Her fire flowed out to meld into the Ascendant's own protective sphere, and she saw him gasp in relief.

Ainos was smiling at Theletos. "Oh, I'm prepared. But, before I go, one thing." She pulled out a vial of black liquid, thumbed the cork off and extended it to him. "You're looking weak. Want a quick refill?"

Theletos' expression stiffened, and he began to advance on her.

Ainos drank the contents in one pull, then tossed the vial aside. "You do know where these come from, don't you, Theletos? The truth?"

"The Black Gate," he said.

Shouts were coming from all around them now, people converging on the chaos but then pulling back at the sight of what was going on.

Bit by bit, Ainos was giving ground. "In a way. The Fujiwara drain it from Sin Casters. It's brutal. They force them to channel until they die from it. That vial I just drank? A man suffered for nearly two days to produce it."

Theletos stopped. "You lie."

"I swear it, Theletos. On my heart and soul. Look into my eyes. You know I'm telling the truth."

Kethe gritted her teeth as she was slowly pushed down to one knee. The flames raged about around her and the Ascendant without surcease, encasing both of them. She could barely breathe; she was forced by the heat to close her eyes, turn away her face.

"No," she heard Theletos say. "I don't believe you."

"What did you think your family did with the Sin Casters they took away? Hmm? Oh, you knew. Deep down, you knew it was all connected. Golden boy. Chosen one. Your own family. Your own flesh and blood."

"Kill her, Theletos!" Kethe's cry was more scream than anything else. "Now!"

She heard the ring of blades and forced herself to squint at Theletos, who was giving ground as Ainos charged him. Somehow, her blade was also aflame, white fire dripping from its point just like Theletos'.

But he was losing. The new wound in his side was grievous, and his previous injuries and exhaustion hadn't been cured. He had run dry of the black potions. But, worse, he looked shocked beyond the ability to fight, and his parries were clumsy and slow.

"You drank their souls!" cried Ainos, her blade ringing down endlessly on his defenses. "Your power is stolen from theirs! Their sin is etched into your very being! All this time!"

"No!" cried Theletos, and for a moment he beat her back, moving with his old speed, but then he froze.

Ainos' blade emerged from his back, its white fire searing and bubbling his blood and flesh. Something akin to ecstasy filled Ainos' face, something so visceral that it caused her to gasp and smile as she shoved the blade deeper through his body.

Theletos dropped his blade. Blood ran from his mouth, and then Ainos stepped back, withdrew her sword, and hewed his head clear from his shoulders.

"No!" screamed Kethe.

Outrage and horror filled her, sickened her. With a burst of fury, she fought to her feet, the Ascendant rising before her, and then she felt an overwhelming flood of energy pour out of him. The white globe that protected them expanded outward at a terrific rate, and the black flames were cut off as the triad was sent wheeling away through the air.

Panting, the Ascendant pointed a finger at Ainos. "You are beyond atonement."

"There's nothing to atone for," she said, swirling her blade about her. "Ascension is a farce. You're simply a very talented young man, and you'll soon be a dead one."

There was a great yell, and a phalanx of soldiers charged at Ainos from behind. Black fire swept over them, and they fell, screaming horrifically.

The triad drifted forward and hovered over Ainos as Khoussan and Kuliver stepped up alongside Kethe.

"I pity you," the Ascendant said softly.

Ainos' face screwed up in fury. "Kill them!"

The bulky old woman loosed a gout of flame that hit Kuliver across the chest like the lash of a whip, knocking him sprawling with a cry. Khoussan charged, only to take in the gut the dagger that Ainos flung at him with almost casual aim. The Ascendant threw aloft his hands, and white fire surged up toward the hovering Sin Casters, only to be met by their own blast.

Kethe sprinted toward Ainos. She felt delirious with horror and fury. She wanted nothing more than to cut down this traitor, this woman who had coaxed her into believing in Ascendancy, who had seemed so sure and calm and trustworthy. With a cry, she brought her blade crashing down on Ainos, who blocked and sidestepped and lashed out with a wicked riposte.

They circled, and Kethe allowed herself to move beyond thought, letting the song of the White Gate rise within her. Her blade was a living brand, but then, so was Ainos'; they moved faster and faster, circling and leaping, ducking and spinning as they each sought some weakness, some chink in the other's defenses, a means to bring each other down.

A blast of flame hit Kethe between the shoulder blades. The pain was incredible, and for a moment she blacked out, only to come to as she hit the ground on all fours. Then Ainos kicked her across the chin, and she collapsed.

Her blade skittered free of her hand and spun away across the polished black stone floor. She couldn't think, couldn't do anything more than crawl toward her blade, biting down on her pain and nausea.

A boot stomped onto her back, smearing her burnt flesh, and pinned her to the ground. Kethe let out a scream as her cheek hit the floor. From where she lay, she could only stare at the ghastly image of Lutherius' burned skull. She fought to rise, to push the boot aside, but it was immovable.

The edge of a sword caressed her cheek. "Goodbye, little Kethe."

Kethe pushed one last time, and suddenly the boot was gone. Gasping, she rolled onto her side and saw why.

Asho was rising into view as if he were being lifted by a storm. The tents in their immediate environs were being battered as if by powerful gales. Black flame cascaded from his lower body, obscuring his legs, lifting him on a column of utter, roiling night. His eyes were black pits, his hands were smoldering gauntlets of flame, and power rolled off him in palpable waves.

"Who the hell is that?" demanded Ainos.

Joy flickered through Kethe's agony, and then she resumed crawling toward her blade. She glanced back and up just in time to see the triad turn on Asho, but he dove through their flame, apparently inured to it, and grabbed the ascetic-looking scholar by the throat.

Kethe froze. She saw Asho place his palm on the man's forehead, and then the stranger screamed, as if something were being torn out by the roots from his very soul. His eyes rolled up in his head, and when Asho released him, he fell to the ground, several bones snapping audibly on impact.

Asho grinned. It was a feral expression, and the two surviving members of the triad faltered. Kethe reached for him, *connected*, and nearly passed out from the sheer amount of magic he was channeling. No, not channeling — that he'd absorbed. She'd never felt him so powerful. He was pulsating with it, nearly burning to cinders. What had he done?

Asho raised a palm and unleashed a blast of fire that sent the formidable old woman hurtling backwards through the air, her flesh and clothing alight, her wail ending just before she hit the ground and rolled away, charred and scorched and clearly dead.

The remaining stranger faced Asho without fear. The leonine man opened his arms wide as if for an embrace and smiled, a genuine expression of relief. "Come at me, brother," he said. "End my misery."

Asho floated forward. He was exuding so much heat that his form shimmered as if Kethe was seeing it through distorting waves. When he reached the third man, he extended his arm and placed one finger against the stranger's brow. The leonine man's eyes rolled up, and with a cry, he fell from the sky as if his strings had been severed.

Kethe couldn't bear it. She was trying to channel as much of Asho's taint as she could, to cleanse his body of pollution, but it was too much. Far, far too much. Terror gripped her by the throat. He was going to burn himself to a crisp.

Asho floated down, alighting in front of Ainos. For no reason Kethe could imagine, he threw his head back and laughed, the sound spiraling almost maniacally up into the high reaches of the cavern, and Kethe remembered how affected he'd been by Mythgraefen's Black Gate, how the surfeit of power had overwhelmed him and rendered him nearly mad.

Abruptly, his laughter cut off, and he began to advance on Ainos, flames burning upwards from his eyes sockets, his white hair wavering behind him as if he were underwater. He was holding no weapon. He needed none.

Ainos fell into a defensive crouch, blazing sword at the ready, and then threw herself at him. She sliced down in a great overhead swing, but Asho simply swayed aside. Ainos reversed her blow with inhuman speed and lashed out with a series of short stabs and slashes from all angles, moving faster and faster until Kethe had trouble keeping track of her movements.

None of them connected.

Asho ducked and swayed, bobbed and danced with her. Her blade passed within a hair's breadth of his face each time, but she couldn't hit him. The Virtue let out a cry of rage and threw herself bodily at him, only to be caught by the throat, lifted right up off her feet, and then smashed down to the ground, head-first.

Asho screamed and poured fire into Ainos, immolating her head where he gripped it. He didn't stop; Kethe sensed that he *couldn't* stop. He had too much power pent up within him, and he needed to release it. A column of swirling black fire extended up from where he was pinning Ainos' corpse, and still he screamed, staring blindly at the ground, which was rumbling beneath his assault. Cracks extended in every direction, and still the fire came through, expanding outward and superheating the air until Kethe couldn't bear to look at him anymore.

It was too much. Kethe could sense it through her connection to him: he'd taken on far too much power on top of who knew how much gatestone. His screams were melding with the roar of the flames, and she could feel the very fabric of his body begin to unknit, his spirit bleeding through, the fire consuming the boundaries that protected him from its rage. Any moment now, it would come pouring through all at once, like a reservoir about to blast out its dam.

Kethe fought to her feet. She had to help him, had to do *something*, but the heat was too intense. She could feel the hairs on her arms burning away, her skin blistering. She took one step toward him and then cried and fell back.

A man walked past her with a bubble of white fire shielding him. Chin lifted, the Ascendant strode into the heart of the raging maelstrom.

Chapter 28

The sound of explosions jolted Iskra from her uneasy slumber. The silhouettes of her guards were stark against her tent walls, the shadows flickering and dancing and stretching fantastically long at oblique angles, only to snap back into vertical positions. She clutched her heavy blanket to her chest, feeling as if she were a child of six again, caught in a nightmare from which she couldn't awake.

All around her, there were screams, mixed in with the sound of men rushing past, the thud of their boots, their hoarse exclamations. It would be so easy to stay quiet, she thought, to let the others handle what was no doubt a terrible crisis – Lutherius, Theletos, the Minister of the Sun and Moon and every Star. And yet, she saw in her mind's eye Tiron's stern visage, his heavy-lidded gaze.

She took a deep breath and stood.

There was no time for donning appropriate dress. Instead, she threw a thick gown over her shoulders, tied the belt off with clumsy fingers, then pushed her way outside.

Her Agerastian guards bowed hastily. Patash was there, his blade drawn, his expression filled with wonder. Iskra followed the direction of his gaze and saw an impossibility in the air above where the

Ascendant's tent had been: three strangers pouring streams of virulent black flame into the ground below.

"Patash! Send men to summon the Vothaks, if they're not already on their way!"

Patash gave his head a swift shake, as if he was ridding himself of his indecision, and barked out her commands. Four guards took off at a dead sprint.

"Send word to General Savash. I want archers on those three. Hurry!"

Another four men raced off, disappearing quickly amongst the forest of tents.

"Now, come," said Iskra. "We move!"

She could feel the waves of heat rolling through the air even at this remove. The three broke off their attack and hovered in a line, then split up, two of them unloading more flame on a single target, a third rushing around in a curve and then firing a single bolt below.

To his credit, Patash didn't try to dissuade her. Instead, he snapped at his men, the remnants of the once greatly feared Hundred Snakes, and they immediately cocooned her within a circle of armor and blades. They moved quickly toward the battleground. All around, Iskra could hear confusion and terror; men cried out questions and cursed, horses neighed in fear, and groups of clearly uncertain people gathered with their weapons drawn, peering around, seeking better vantage points.

Iskra's passage seemed to give these soldiers confidence; many fell in line behind her, swelling her guard so that, within moments, she was trailed by perhaps a hundred Ennoians and Agerastians. She moved quickly, heart in her throat, and when she was perhaps only fifty yards away, she saw Asho rise into the air like a demon possessed.

Iskra froze, extending her arms out to either side to arrest the passage of the others. With her pulse pounding in her ears, she saw Asho destroy the attacking triad, though she didn't understand why the enemy collapsed at his touch. Then he dropped down and was gone from her field of vision.

Urgency seized her, and she ran. Discarding all propriety, she hiked up her gown and sprinted barefoot across the cold stone till she rounded the last tent and the ruined battlefield came into view.

At that very moment, Asho unleashed a column of raw flame into the sky, and in horror Iskra fell back — but with that panic all around her, surrounded by those cries of fear, she held up her fist, and Patash barked out a snarling command. Her men held fast, the Hundred Snakes steeling themselves against the impossible that lay ahead of them, and the others took heart.

Silence fell through the ranks when the Ascendant stepped into Asho's whirling hurricane of fire. The heat was so intense that Iskra could only watch through the cracks between her fingers. The Ascendant's form shimmered and nearly disappeared in the tumultuous inferno, and then he was at Asho's side. Iskra saw him reach out and place a hand on Asho's shoulder. Almost immediately, the vortex of flame diminished and spiraled down into the Ascendant.

A moment later, the last of the flames curled away into the air and disappeared, leaving Asho in the center of a crater. He lifted his head, groaned, and toppled over onto his side. The Ascendant stood over him, his young face marked by grief, and then he bent down and lifted the Bythian knight into his arms.

Iskra heard the awe-struck whispers of the men behind her and the sound of many of them falling to their knees. Only then did she see Kethe struggling to rise to her feet, the back of her tunic burnt away, the links of her chain shirt gleaming as if they had been brilliantly polished and had melted into each other.

Iskra let out a cry and ran forward, reaching her daughter just as she stumbled, and ducked under Kethe's arm to catch her before she fell.

The Ascendant was struggling to bear Asho's weight, and then others were at his side, helping him. Other men helped two of the Consecrated rise to their feet. Iskra let out a hiss of shock at the sight of Theletos' head lying on its cheek, staring sightlessly out at oblivion. All around her, small fires were smoldering on the collapsed remains of the tent, smoke rising into the air along with the sound of wails and furious shouts.

Iskra waited for somebody to take control, for some deep, masculine voice to begin bellowing orders, but nobody did. Looking around, Iskra saw Aletheian court notables and highly ranked ministers with ashen faces. She saw various military men, Agerastian and Ennoian, but no generals, no leaders.

Nobody was speaking up, but somebody had to. Standing straighter, she looked to Patash. "Have the closest tent evacuated and lead the Ascendant there. Take Kethe, Asho, and those two Consecrated with him. Find healers!"

He bowed and called out orders. Kethe, nearly insensate, was gingerly taken up and borne away.

Iskra looked about her. "You!" She spoke to a Cerulean Guard standing at the front of perhaps twenty or so other men in identical uniform. "Take the bodies to that tent there. Begin with Theletos. Go!"

The big blond man nodded jerkily and moved forward, his fellows hurrying to assist.

"Iskra," said one of the ministers — she couldn't remember which one — as he hurried up to her. "What, by the Black Gate, is going on here?"

"Not now," she said, striding past him.

Agerastians were pouring in. Orishin hurried up, followed by the archers Iskra had summoned, with General Savash in the lead. A dark-skinned, hawk-nosed man with a sullen air and brooding mien, he was as famous for his temper as for his propensity for unorthodox military tactics.

The general walked up to her, tearing his gaze from the burning ruins, and bowed low.

"General," she said. "Have your men clear the grounds. I want this area quarantined. Then I want every soldier commanded to return to his regiments. This chaos is dangerous. Finally, double the number of guards at the Portal columns."

Orishin translated, and the general nodded and turned, moved back to his men and relayed her commands. Then Iskra stood surveying the scene. Men were moving with purpose now, voices were raised in command and not in panic, and, slowly, a sense of control was coalescing where before there had been raw panic. She felt a rush of relief as she strode toward the Ascendant's new tent.

Several Aletheian nobles were trying to get inside and were shouting abuse at Patash, who was standing implacably, sword drawn, in front of twenty of the Hundred Snakes. The ministers and councilors and whoever else was there all caught sight of her approach.

The Minister of the Sun stepped forward, nearly vibrating with indignation. "Order your men to step aside, Iskra! Now!"

"I will if the Ascendant commands it," said Iskra, walking right past him. "And not before."

Shouts followed her as she and Orishin passed through the crowd of soldiers and into the tent. It was luxuriously appointed with four cots covered in thick furs, and it was on these that Asho, Kethe, and the two Consecrated were lying.

The Ascendant stood looking down at them, hands on his hips, a frown marring his youthful face. He looked up as Iskra entered. "How could I allow this to happen?" His voice was heartbreakingly bleak. "Ainos attacked us. Ainos! I knew that not all of my Virtues could be trusted, but to have her laugh in my face, to see her cut down Theletos..."

"Your Holiness," said Iskra, moving to kneel alongside her daughter.

Two men in Agerastian colors were carefully untying the leather cords that bound Kethe's chain shirt down her side. Asho lay still, barely breathing, his skull prominent under his pale skin. Other healers were working on the wounds of the Consecrated.

Iskra felt a helpless grief well up within her. Would the world ever spare these two? Would they ever be free of the pain and misery that seemed to be their lot in this life?

"Can you heal them?" she asked, turning back to the Ascendant.

"No," he said. "We were dependent on the Fujiwaras' black elixir for that. And after Ainos' revelation, I would hesitate to heal them with it even if we had an endless supply at hand."

"Your Holiness," said Iskra, fighting for calm in which to order her thoughts. "What, by the White Gate, just happened?"

"An ambush." He sat heavily on a simple stool, and Iskra was reminded just how young he was. "Ainos and three Sin Casters. They killed Lutherius. They would have killed all of us were it not for Ser Asho's intervention." He gazed pensively over at Asho. "For his magic."

"Your Imperial Majesty. Your Holiness," said Orishin cautiously. "Word is no doubt spreading like wildfire that Theletos is dead. Some may have seen Ainos approach. They saw Kethe being carried to the tents. If we do not reassure them soon that we have the situation under control, we may have rioting, or desertion, or — I don't know. But we cannot wait long before making a statement."

"True," said the Ascendant, but he sat there with his shoulders slumped, gazing down at Asho, and did not speak further.

Iskra watched him with a rising sense of dread in her gut. To see the Ascendant himself so despondent filled her with a primitive terror.

What would Tiron do if he were here? She immediately knew the answer to that question: he would act.

"Orishin," she said quietly. "Send for Toki and his Hrethings. Their presence will bolster the Ennoians. Second, have the next highest-ranking Cerulean Guard attend us, along with the Minister of the Sun and the highest-ranked Ennoians. Last, spread the word to all that the Ascendant will soon be leading all of the faithful in a ritual of mass mourning for the fallen, and that they are to cleanse themselves as permitted by their duties. Go."

Orishin bowed low and slipped outside.

Iskra hesitated. "Excuse my presumption, Your Holiness."

"Not presumption," he said, a tired smile playing on his face. "Wisdom. I must admit to being a little... overwhelmed at present. Never in my life have I confronted such darkness. Thank you, Iskra, for your help."

Iskra curtseyed, remembering too late that as an empress, she was his equal.

The Ascendant rose to his feet, pushed back his shoulders, and raised his chin. "I am in need of a new Grace. Will you serve me, Iskra?"

Iskra stared blankly at him. "Excuse me?"

"Come dawn, Tharok will attack once more. How many will die? I trusted a man who convinced me that we should hold back, that we should wait and strike from the shadows and let countless people suffer in the interim. Was that right? I don't know. But look what happened in Nous. Have you heard of the massacre in Zoe? Thousands killed by rampaging kragh. No word has returned from Sige."

"But I am not trained in military matters," said Iskra.

"No, but neither am I. And look what our military men have achieved. Nothing." The Ascendant stared bleakly at the floor, then grimaced. "Perhaps I am being unfair. But I find myself ruing not having trusted your advice from the start. I swore that I would, and instead I was swayed. I'm sorry, Iskra. Please, accept my apology."

"No," said Iskra. "Don't apologize. Or, if you must, accept my own apologies in turn. I've also been overwhelmed, felt completely out of my depth, and have been told to shut up by men who claimed to know more than I ever possibly could. I failed you by not standing up for what I believed to be true."

He smiled crookedly. "Perhaps we have both failed. But now we have a chance to set matters to right. Or at least try. Will you be my Grace?"

"Yes," said Iskra. "If you ask it of me, I accept."

"Thank the White Gate," said the Ascendant, sitting back down. "To be honest, I don't know where to go from here. Do we follow Lutherius' plan? Do we attack?"

A new voice interrupted them. "No, Your Holiness." Kethe struggled to sit up, aided by the two healers, who set about peeling away her ruined chain shirt. "We defend. We do what Asho suggested. We hold the Portals at Ennoia, or we die trying."

"I thought you were against that plan," the Ascendant said mildly. "I thought you agreed with Theletos about avoiding direct confrontation."

"Theletos was wrong," said Kethe. "I see that now."

Iskra nodded. "Asho held back the kragh with only a thousand or so men. If we sent everyone we have to hold those Portals, if we force Tharok to come through that bottleneck, we can stop him cold."

326

Kethe nodded. "If Asho thought he could hold the line, then I believe him."

The Ascendant gazed down at the fallen Bythian. "It is passingly strange that the fate of the Empire should rest on the beliefs and talents of a Bythian knight." There was no bitterness or rancor in his voice, merely wonder. "Very well. If you will it, my Grace, then it will be done. I myself will go to Ennoia and seek in some way to inspire our people toward a final act of defiance."

Iskra considered that for a moment. "A brief visit, Your Holiness. I would advise you to return to Starkadr before the Portals close. Should our lines be overrun tomorrow, I wouldn't want you to be in peril."

The Ascendant bowed his head in acknowledgement. "As you advise."

Kethe hissed as her mail was finally peeled from her body, revealing her quilted undergarment. An interwoven pattern mimicking the shirt's links was burned across its back. One of the Agerastian healers tapped the quilted shirt and said something appreciative.

"He says that this saved you, more so than your chain," said Orishin.

Kethe winced as she pulled the quilted shirt over her head. The Ascendant turned his back to give her a modicum of privacy, but Iskra moved to sit at her side, taking the jar of thick, waxy ointment from the healer with a murmur. Kethe's back was inflamed and blistered, but, fortunately, the damage did not seem permanent or the flesh too badly burned.

For the next five minutes, she focused on applying the ointment, doing so with as light a touch as she could, pausing every time Kethe hissed through her teeth in pain. After she was done, the healers wrapped clean gauze around Kethe's chest and back, looping it up over her shoulders in diagonals and then finally cutting and tucking the end away under the rest.

The healer spoke again, shaking his head, and Orishin once more translated. "He says you should rest for several weeks, not exert yourself in any way, and reapply the ointment twice daily."

Kethe nodded and moved to Asho's bedside. She reached for his hand and held it tight, gazing down at his gaunt face.

"He would have died but for my intervention," the Ascendant said quietly. "As it is, I do not think he will revive in time for tomorrow's battle."

"He hadn't even finished healing," whispered Kethe. "Oh, Asho. What have you done to yourself?"

"What he had to," said Iskra. "No matter what happens next, we shall all owe him a great debt of gratitude."

"Yes," said Kethe. She raised his hand to her lips, then pressed it to her cheek. She closed her eyes tightly, as if she was engraving the sensation tightly into her memory, then laid his hand back down with a sigh. "Yes."

The tenderness of her touch lit a warm glow within Iskra's heart. She wanted to hug her daughter tight, but instead confined herself to merely placing a hand on Kethe's shoulder and giving her a gentle squeeze. Kethe laid her own hand over Iskra's and smiled at her, tears in her eyes.

"Here," said the Ascendant, kneeling beside Asho's bed. "Let us see what we can do for him."

He took Asho's other hand in both of his and closed his eyes. Kethe did the same, and they remained kneeling for perhaps five minutes, neither of them speaking, simply meditating.

Looking closer, Iskra saw some color return to Asho's pale face, saw the lines of tension and fatigue fade away. Slowly, his breathing deepened.

The Ascendant released his hand and smiled at Kethe, who smiled broadly back, her eyes glimmering with wonder.

"That was..." She trailed off. "That was amazing."

The Ascendant bowed his head in thanks. "I've never tried that, but it seems to have eased him somewhat."

"Yes," said Kethe, curling a lock of Asho's white hair away from his brow. "I think it did."

Moving away from Asho's bed, Iskra readied herself. She was about to order all of their forces to march into Ennoia to oversee what could prove to be the final defense of the Ascendant's Empire.

Orishin stepped up to her side and gave her a tight smile of support. The Ascendant nodded, indicating that he was ready. Kethe cast a deep blue cloak over her shoulders and did the same.

Taking a deep breath, Iskra stepped out of the tent and into her new role as the Grace of the Empire.

Chapter 29

A udsley appeared in his old room in Kyferin Castle. He'd been unable to watch the Minister of Perfection lay claim to Starkadr's secret library; the sight of his pulling down the most secret tomes of the ancient Sin Casters had been too much to bear. Without consciously desiring it, he'd appeared here in his room, alone, bereft, unable to think, to progress, to plan his next step.

He stood shivering in the cold. The windows to his old quarters stood open, allowing a bitter draught to swirl the pages of books that lay tossed on the floor and scattered across tables. Scroll tubes had been crushed underfoot. Pigeon shit was smeared across almost every surface.

Had he thought returning here would help? Would ground him? As tears burned his eyes, he knew it had been a mistake, the worst of mistakes. He managed to take three steps forward before he fell heavily to his knees.

His shoulders hitched. With his hands curved into claws, he reached up, trying to take hold of his glasses, to remove them, but he was crying too hard. He couldn't do more than mash his hands against his face and hunch over, sobs wracking him, pummeling him, each one like a great hand reaching into his depths and raking up the very essence of his being, ripping up his sense of self, his sense of place, his sense of purpose, his everything.

He'd never felt so lonely. So terrified. His whole life had been a lie, devoted to a creed that was little more than a towering testament to a single man's ego and desire for power.

It made him sick to think of all those long years he'd spent inside dusty libraries, poring over esoterica. The countless hours he'd spent debating fellow students in earnest. How all his life he'd reveled in his sense of place, in his *surety* of who he was. What a fool! What a sickening, naïve, idiotic, blathering idiot he'd been all his life!

What did it mean to be a Noussian, to think himself blessed, advanced along the chain of purity?

Nothing.

All of it had been torn down, ripped asunder, and replaced with — what?

Fighting for breath, he finally tore his spectacles away and forced himself back to his feet. He tottered to his window and placed his hands on the worn stone as he gazed out over the familiar Ennoian landscape. What was this world, then, now that the lie of Ascendancy had been torn away?

What did one cling to, once the morality of Ascension was gone? He'd not dared to ask the minister. Hadn't had the bravery to hear his response. What compelled a man to goodness if there was no reward or punishment awaiting him, just death? An egalitarian evanescence through the white flame. Then — nothing?

Audsley hunched his shoulders and shook his head, his face scrunched up in horror, his soul protesting. No, that couldn't be. *Oh, please, please, don't let that be the truth. The bleak reality.* Was that why the ages before Ascension had been so marred by warfare?

He buried his face in his hands. He wasn't strong enough for this. He couldn't absorb it. He needed Ascension. He needed the Ascendant – needed his divine guidance, the sense of being watched, approved, and loved.

"Oh," he gasped, pulling down on his face with his fingertips before he dropped his hands to the sill. "Oh, please. Oh, please, no."

The sky mocked him, vast and empty. There was nothing up there. The world operated along the basest of principles: might made right. Those who could wield the power of the Black Gate could dictate the form of the world. Could raise up cities into the air, up from the very depths of the ocean.

What an ugly world. What a raw, terrible world, where grace and hate were equally countenanced. Where the greatest acts of charity were equal to the depredations of war. Audsley saw a great river, a torrent of life, rushing ever forward into the future, carrying with it the heroes and villains, the common people and the great, the wise and foolish, the rich and poor, the perverted and saintly, all of them striving for wealth, for bread, for sex, for love and friendship. For power. Rising, falling, succeeding, then… dying, only to have history erase the marks of even the most accomplished.

Mortality was the only truth. In his mind, Audsley heard the bawling of babes rising up to drown out the pleas of the dying – none of them special. Every sin forgiven, every act of grace forgotten. Everyone united in their ignorance. Every man or woman as correct and as wrong as every other, all of them fighting for truths that were as valid as any other.

Chaos.

Audsley gritted his teeth. He didn't want to live in this world. He didn't want to see its dawns, witness its random beauties. He couldn't bear to face his old friends, to gaze into the eyes of strangers and know, deep in his heart, that they were all doomed to die, that their lives were pointless, that none of it mattered.

Audsley slid down the wall. With numb fingers, he drew his knife. The blade was short and sharp – usually, he used it to pare apples. One cut, one slice down his wrist, and he too could sink into that terrible oblivion.

A true end. And why not? Why delay death if there was nothing awaiting him on the other side?

Yes, whispered his demon, as soft and intimate as a lover. **I understand your fear. The worst part in discovering that life is a charade is**

realizing that you have been dancing alongside all the other fools. I once sat where you sit, a knife in my hand, ready to end my life.

Audsley stared down at his blade. "Why didn't you?"

The silence that followed could have been a ploy. Part of the manipulation. But, somehow, Audsley felt as if the demon was truly searching for a way to answer his question.

Spite, perhaps. Yes, spite stayed my hand. I had within me a desire to impose myself upon it all. The world. Its peoples. Upon this life that had stolen my values and left me defenseless. What is the opposite of oblivion? Eternity. I decided not to die with a whimper but to persist with a snarl.

They sat in silence. Audsley could hear the distant cooing of doves, the rustle of pages as the wind blew through the room. He shivered, marveling that he could still feel something as prosaic as cold.

"You decided to become a demon? But how?"

I persevered. My will was stronger than my flesh. Long after my body should have failed me, when I should have been consumed by the taint of my magic, I used the dark arts of Flame Walking to persist. I did not have the humility to die, so my power made me immortal. But I was caught by the Flame Walkers and bound. I lost centuries in Starkadr. I slumbered, powering the stonecloud's flight. It was only when desperation led the Artificers to embed me into that blade that I awoke, that I realized how much time had passed. That, despite everything, despite the very perversity of my will, I had in some form died after all. You, Audsley, have been my resurrection.

Audsley turned the blade over, watching how the afternoon light lit fine seams along its length. "Can I find a similar eternity?"

No, the demon said heavily. **You are not a Flame Walker. You simply borrow my powers. When you die, you will pass into shadow and be undone. Eternity can never be yours.**

Tears brimmed in Audsley's eyes again, and he inhaled in a series of gasps.

But there is always spite, Audsley. There is always the will to power. When all of your graven eidolons have fallen, all that is left

is the truth, no matter how impoverished it may be. You can choose **to worship the truth, to set it free. To bring it back into this world. The inner truth to no one being special is that we are all truly equal in our unimportance. There is no reason that the Bythians should be enslaved, that the Agerastians should be punished for a war they conducted millennia ago. That Aletheians should be revered, and Noussians forced to promulgate a false religion. They all can be freed. You can free them, Audsley.**

"But to what end?" His cry echoed in his bare chamber. "Why? Why would I bring this misery to others?"

To set them free. To let them choose their own paths. To put their fates into their own hands, and in so doing, give them dignity. Self-determination. You can bring an end to this vast mockery that the first Ascendant inflicted upon the world, and allow humanity to once more pursue its own reasons for persisting, however hard doing so may be.

Audsley hung his head. The demon's words were redolent with pathos. It seemed to believe what it said. Free the people of the Empire, whether they wished for freedom or not? Bring them dignity. Bring them... equality?

His very soul rebelled, reaching for the strictures of Ascendancy, the benefits of hierarchy, the blessings of ascension — but there was nothing there to hold on to. Just lies.

Freedom. Equality. Self-determination.

He thought of Asho, and of his people, all of them slaves. And why? Because Bythians had mocked the first Ascendant? He thought of the Agerastians, of Lord Enderl Kyferin's punitive raids that had lashed their island for years, of the brutalities that had been inflicted upon them for their temerity in rebelling.

Freedom.

He gritted his teeth.

Equality.

His whole body was a coiled ball of tension, writhing, resisting.

Self-determination...

With a gasp, he opened his eyes and leaned his head back against the stone wall. He was empty. A reed. A broken vessel. The only truth he could bring to the people of the Empire would shatter them. He wouldn't bring it because it was better, but simply because it *was* the truth, anguishing as that might be.

"All right," he whispered. He fumbled his knife back into its sheath. "All right. I'll do what the Minister of Perfection bids."

That is… good. He commanded you to locate your Flame Walker friend. Where is he?

Audsley rubbed his face with the crook of his elbow, wiping the tears away, then placed his spectacles back on his nose. "I don't know. The last I heard, he was in Bythos, but with that taken by the kragh, I'd imagine he's been driven out. I'd imagine that the easiest way to find him is simply to ask those camped in Starkadr. Iskra and Kethe will probably know."

Are you ready to return?

Audsley stared at the floor. The carpet was threadbare, its colors faded, torn through and showing the boards beneath. Had this chamber truly once been the center of his existence? It was nothing but a ruin.

"Yes." He inhaled sharply and climbed to his feet. "Yes, let us proceed."

Almost instantly, his tower room and all of Kyferin Castle disappeared. In its place materialized the hexagonal tunnel that led into Starkadr's great Portal chamber. A diffuse ambient light allowed him to see about twenty yards ahead of him before everything faded into gloom. He could adopt the demon's night vision, but there was no need; he walked forward until the tunnel ended, opening into the Portal chamber, and there he gazed out over its expanse.

Thousands were camped amidst the columns. Smoke from hundreds of small campfires had risen to darken the fog that obscured the ceiling, while the stench of humanity assailed his nostrils in all of its war-camp glory. The army was stirring, however; he saw men forming up into columns, sergeants barking their commands, men breaking down tents, gathering supplies, raising standards and moving forward at a slow shuffle to disappear into one of the Portals.

It would no doubt take hours to feed every soldier through to their destination, but Audsley sensed something akin to relief in the air; laughter floated up to him, and he saw men moving with energy. He knew all too well that waiting could be a form of punishment; the Agerastian and Ennoian army was pleased to be moving at last.

In the center of the room sprawled a blackened site of destruction. Audsley peered closer and made out a ring of soldiers keeping all the others out. Whatever existed within had been cratered and charred.

He felt a lump in his throat. The Ascendant. Had he died? Where was Ainos?

He'd find out soon enough.

Audsley stepped over the tunnel's edge and floated unassumingly down to the floor. Nobody noticed him. Then he hurried forward, head bowed, making his way into the camp, heading roughly toward the center. He listened to the camp chatter as he went; most of it was in Agerastian, but enough Ennoians were about that he picked up the most salient point of news: Iskra had been made the Ascendant's Grace.

The attack had failed, then; the soldiers would be shocked and grieving if the Ascendant had died. Audsley didn't know how he felt about that. Relief, perhaps, that murder had been averted, mingled with frustration. Ascendancy would be harder to disprove with the Ascendant alive and kicking.

After asking some discrete questions, he was directed toward the large tent that Iskra had commissioned for the Ascendant. It was but a stone's throw from the site of destruction, close enough that Audsley could smell the smoke of the ruins.

Agerastian guards were standing out front. Smoothing down his robes, breathing deeply, Audsley stepped up and bowed. "Is Her Imperial Majesty Iskra Kyferin within?"

"It's no use," said an Aletheian standing off to one side. He was wearing sumptuous robes that were direly in need of being changed, and he looked sullen and angry. "We're not to be given admittance."

"Oh?" Audsley stepped over to the man, bowing respectfully. "Why would the luminaries of the Aletheian court be denied entry?"

The man sniffed and looked to his fellows. "Better to ask why the *osonti* petal, soft and delicate, is blown by the winter gale—"

"I'm sorry," said Audsley, lurching back. "I've lost my taste for poetry." He ignored the man's outraged grimace and stepped back up to the guard. "Please announce Magister Audsley to those within."

The guard stared at him as if he had been trying to hawk fresh rat skins.

"Hello? Do you speak Ennoian? Oh, dear."

The guard didn't move a muscle.

Audsley considered blasting him with fire. He was about to try again when the tent door parted and Orishin emerged, looking delighted. "Magister Audsley! It *is* you! Come, come! Where have you been? You have missed much activity, many surprises. Come in!"

The guard stepped aside, looking studiously indifferent, and Audsley entered the tent. His heart leaped at the sight of Asho sleeping on one of the cots. Nearby, several Agerastian scribes were busy at work at makeshift desks, hastily copying out messages.

"What has happened to Asho?" asked Audsley, hurrying to the Bythian's side.

"He is gravely ill," Orishin said somberly. "He expended himself terribly saving the Ascendant's life. Were it not for the Ascendant's own intervention thereafter, I've been told, Ser Asho might have died from the corruption of his own magics."

"Oh," said Audsley, pursing his lips. "Bless the Ascendant — both providentially as well as quite literally. But, tell me: What have I missed?"

Orishin proved remarkably adept at concisely conveying the events of the past few days. Audsley forced himself to make surprised sounds and shake his head gravely at the right moments, and when the scribe was done, he nodded thoughtfully. "A miraculous turn of events. Iskra, Kethe, and the Ascendant have already gone to Ennoia? Very well. Orishin, could you do me a great favor? I have a message for Asho's ears alone. Can we please clear the tent?"

"But Ser Asho is not to be disturbed." Orishin hesitated. "Of course. If you believe it necessary, I trust your judgment." He spoke a sharp command to the half-dozen scribes, who paused, blinked, then looked down at their parchments in dismay. They sprinkled sand over their lettering, then rose and departed.

"I'll just be a moment," said Audsley. "Thank you."

Orishin squeezed his arm, then exited the tent.

"Asho," said Audsley, sitting on the cot's edge. "Asho, can you hear me?" He took the Bythian by the arm and gave him a firm shake.

Asho groaned, squeezing his eyes shut, and turned his head away.

"Asho?" Was he too far gone? If only he were a Virtue and could be soothed by a black elixir. "Asho!"

Impatient, Audsley picked up a cup of water that was sitting in readiness by the cot and tipped its contents over the young knight's face.

Asho spluttered, coughed, and began to sit up before sinking back with a groan. "What? Oh — Audsley? Audsley!"

"Yes," said Audsley, pushing him back down. "Shh. You must conserve your strength."

"Where is Kethe? The Ascendant? What happened? I remember..." Asho laid his forearm over his eyes as he screwed them shut in pain. "Ah, my head."

"All is well. You saved the Ascendant! Well done. Kethe is well, Iskra is the new Grace, and it seems that the entire army is marching to Ennoia."

Asho's arm fell away, and he stared up at Audsley in surprise. "His Grace? Marching to Ennoia?" He opened and closed his mouth several times and then laughed hoarsely. "I can't believe it."

"Yes, and everyone seems very pleased with you, my dear Asho." Audsley found that he was having difficulty remembering how he had once spoken; it felt stiff and artificial, like trying to wear a mask. But Asho didn't seem to notice. "I fear your trials aren't over yet."

"I know they're not," said Asho, struggling to sit up once more. "I have to get to Ennoia. Even if I'm sick, I can help organize the defenses."

"No, no, that's all in good hands." Audsley pushed the young man back down again, though this time with some difficulty — Asho had put on more muscle than he'd expected. "No, I've come to you for a very special, ah, mission. I've come to ask you to help me with something that could change the tide of this war."

"Oh?" Asho seemed to see him for the first time. "Audsley, what's happened to you?"

"Me? Ha ha. A lot, to be honest. It has been a trying time, though isn't that true for us all?" The way Asho was frowning at him made Audsley's pulse pick up. "Surely I don't look that ghastly?"

"You look... Your eyes. I don't know. But, where have you been? The last I heard, you were investigating the upper echelons of the Aletheian court."

"I was. And doing so has led me to a new set of allies, if you can believe that. A shadow organization that has been working to improve the lot of people everywhere, including the Bythians."

"Not a very effective organization, then," Asho said dryly.

"They've had their challenges. But they have found a way to accomplish a most marvelous goal: to assassinate Tharok."

"Assassinate — how?"

Audsley couldn't meet Asho's eyes. "I have been – well, I have developed, under their guidance, certain abilities, including — ah — well, the ability to teleport. Directly. Which is why I need your help. I need you to teleport with me directly to Tharok, and then kill him."

"Teleport? As in—?"

"Mmm-hmm. I have become my own mobile Lunar Portal to any location I have already been. Which is a bit of a catch, as I haven't been to a number of places where Tharok might be, but *you* have. With your help, we could teleport into Bythos, seek him out, and then teleport directly beside him and incinerate him in hellfire."

Asho swung his legs over the edge of the bed. His face paled dramatically from the effort. "I'll — of course I'll help. But I'm not at my best."

"I know, I know. I can help with that. Or, well, my friends can. They have refined a method to boost your powers beyond that which you might normally be able to handle. It is a quite gruesome method, but it will give you the power, regardless of your current state, to accomplish this final goal."

"Gruesome, you say?"

"Yes," sighed Audsley. "It is as effective as it is repulsive. You will be empowered for far longer than mere gatestone would allow. Long enough, I hope, that we will be able to locate and execute this kragh, and, with him, the danger he poses to us all."

Asho looked down at his hands. They were trembling, so he made fists of them and nodded. "Of course I'll help. Should we send word to Iskra?"

"You can, if you like, but, either way, we'd best depart immediately."

Asho nodded, rose with difficulty, and hobbled to the tent flap, where he exchanged words with Orishin. Then he returned, his face drawn with effort, and picked up his blade.

"I'm ready. Which Portal do we go through?"

"I told you, my old friend. No Portals. This is a new age. Now, you need simply take my hand, and we will be transported immediately."

Asho did so. "Where are we going?"

"A long-forgotten stonecloud. It has a curious name: Haugabrjótr."

Chapter 30

————— ◦ ═══◦❖◦❖◦═══ ◦ —————

Forty mountain kragh were beating on their war drums – a blood-stirring cadence, deep and resonant. The rhythm was simple, but oh, how it echoed deep within one's chest, how it made a kragh itch for war! Hundreds accompanied the war drums, beating their weapons against stolen shields, pounding rocks together, or simply letting out deep, visceral grunts.

The forty drums were positioned around the Solar Portals. Tharok was standing on a platform he'd commanded be erected in front of the Portal to Ennoia. Behind him, his warriors were lined up in orderly columns twenty wide, stretching far into the gloomy recesses of Bythos' main cavern. The air was turgid with bloodlust.

Every eye was turned to the Portals. They rose silent and empty toward the flickering aurora. When their interiors finally filled with fire, a terrible roar filled the cavern. The drums were pounded faster, a wild beat that signaled that the time had come.

Tharok raised a fist, and, slowly, silence fell upon the horde, extending outward like a ripple across a pool. The drums stilled. Tharok pointed at a single kragh who was standing in front of the Ennoian Gate, a huge tower shield of iron held before him, a single horizontal slit cut into its face. His shoulders were heaving with anticipation, and, at Tharok's gesture, he stepped forward into the Portal and was gone.

Nobody spoke. A moment later, the kragh stumbled backward through the Portal, a hail of arrows following to bounce off the rocks around him. He huddled beneath his huge tower shield, then cast it aside and climbed to his feet.

Tharok stepped down from his platform as the kragh approached. He was an older male, a wiry lowlander with a sharp wit and a quick eye. He dropped to one knee in front of Tharok and bowed his head.

"Report," growled Tharok.

"They await us," said the kragh. "The ground has been torn up into endless furrows that stretch to the far buildings. Huge machines of war, like the crossbows of giants, are set on platforms, just as yesterday's scouts reported. But an army is standing in front of these machines. I would guess—" The kragh paused, narrowing his eyes in thought. "Two of our tribes. And the roofs – they are covered with archers. Many, many archers."

"Good," said Tharok. "They are focused on the Portals to Aletheia and Bythos?"

The kragh narrowed his eyes again. "Yes. But there were so many humans there that the whole square is armored."

Tharok nodded and looked to his medusa-Kissed warlords. He made eye contact with each one, waited for them to nod, then gave the signal for his drummers to begin the marching cadence.

Slowly, his army lurched into motion. Cries of anticipation and roars of bloodlust filled the air as the kragh hauled up their portable bridges and marched into the Portals that led to Sige, to Nous, and to Zoe. Tharok watched them disappear into those far lands and found himself marveling at the magic that could transport so many so far. Two thousand kragh were marching into each city. The warlords would assemble their forces in new columns, then await Tharok's signal.

Uthok's scouting missions hadn't been a catastrophic waste of time; though they'd lost a day, they'd gained toeholds in Nous and Sige. The Zoeian forces would fall back from the incursion of the kragh.

Jojan was waiting in Aletheia, two tribes under his command. When the time came, Tharok would give the signal, and all of the columns would march upon Ennoia as one. Ten thousand kragh flowing through the Portals. Five great fingers closing into a fist that would crush the humans no matter how well they had prepared.

There would be a great loss of life, but Tharok hungered now for a final victory. Subtler ploys, long-term stratagems – none of that appealed. He would not depend on his medusa's shamans, his trolls, or any of the circlet's tricks. This final battle would be won by the kragh alone. He would conquer through brute force.

One hundred kragh could charge through the five Portals at once. Two thousand kragh could be on the battlefield by the time the drummers beat sixty, ten thousand by the time they beat three hundred.

A black-robed shaman climbed up to his side. "Kyrrasthasa sends word. She is ready to assist you when needed."

Tharok waved the shaman away, not even bothering to respond.

He watched his kragh file into the remnants of the human Empire. Nothing could stop them; the next hour would see the Empire's final collapse.

This was the end of the human-dominated era. From this day forward, the kragh would rule supreme.

Chapter 31

Tiron raced down the gravel slope toward the kragh, leaping over the occasional rock so as not to lose momentum, his blade held low behind him. The elation of the charge gave his vision incredible focus, so every detail of the opposing force was terribly vivid: the bared tusks, the rippling of muscles beneath their hides, the raising of their hammers and axes as he pounded toward them.

"Now!" he roared over his shoulder. He sensed more than saw Shaya, the shaman, and Olina break away, peeling off to spring down to the Tear's edge.

The kragh had been bracing themselves to receive the charge. At the sight of the group racing toward the water's edge, they broke ranks and ran forward, a tide that sought to cut Shaya off and crash into Tiron simultaneously.

The air between them began to ripple, distorting colors and shapes. Tiron's war cry died on his lips. The kragh, who had only managed to take a half dozen steps, fell back.

Luminous white curves appeared in the air, faint outlines that quickly grew more solid. They were everywhere. Tiron slowed and then stopped altogether. The white outlines grew denser, coalescing into the silhouettes of kragh – kragh with burning white eyes like stars that had been plucked from the heavens and ensconced within their unhallowed skulls. Their hair fell in white locks. Their multiplicity was enhanced by how hard it was to distinguish one from the crowd around it.

Tiron raised his arms as if he were wading through a chest-high river. Kragh ghosts were appearing everywhere. They were the thickest near the Tear's edge, but there were hundreds – no, thousands — and more were appearing every moment.

Owl Home wailed piteously and began to chant in a desperate tone.

The black-cowled shamans began to do the same, their words furious and commanding.

A hulking ghost, bigger even than Nok, suddenly shoved its hand into the chest of the lead kragh warrior. The kragh stiffened as he let out a shriek unlike any that Tiron had ever heard. Blood began to flow into the ghost's nearly invisible arm, and where it passed, the ghost's form became solid, turning it into a silvered kragh while its victim seemed to shrivel like a fruit left in the sun.

"Tiron?" Ramswold's voice trembled as he fought for calm.

The kragh were edging back, bunching in together, ignoring the shrill orders that the shamans were hurling at them.

"Back," said Tiron. "Slowly. Move back."

Another kragh shrilled as a ghost plunged its hand into his chest, ignoring all of his armor. The first ghost released its now-desiccated prey and threw back its head to let out a hoarse, ghastly roar, more akin to a rusted blade being scraped over an anvil than anything a living being might cry.

"Back!" roared Tiron, but there was nowhere to retreat to. Everywhere he looked, the guardians of the Tear were manifesting and closing in on them. Ulein was sobbing a prayer to the Ascendant. Maur was growling, whipping her head from side to side as if she could keep the infinitude of ghosts in sight.

A third kragh screamed, then a fourth. After that, there was no distinguishing their cries.

Shaya and Olina were huddled behind Owl Home, who was leading the way to the shore, a shimmering sphere of gold hovering between his upraised hands. As Tiron watched, Olina suddenly spasmed and screamed. Blood flowed out of her body, taking the form of a kragh's arm with tendrils like the finest of shoots flooding over its hunched shoulder and forming its chest.

Ulein was the next to cry out. Tiron grabbed him by the hem of his chain shirt and hauled him toward the lake, but it was no use; the young knight was lifted clear off the ground, his body shaking and twitching as more ghosts plunged their hands into him and his blood streamed forth to become four different limbs.

"No!" he cried, slashing his blade futilely through the ghosts. "No! Ramswold! Ramswold, help me!"

"To the Tear!" Tiron lowered his head and ran toward the shaman. Olina had fallen to the rocks, twisted and shrunken, a horrific caricature of her former self.

The screams were continuous.

Green flames suddenly hammered against the lakeshore, spattering gobbets of emerald everywhere, shredding the ghosts. The three shamans were advancing on the Tear as well, lobbing their spirit fire as quickly as they could.

Tiron saw the hint of an arm reaching for him, a glint of white in the pale dawn light, and instinct led him to slice through its elbow. To his shock, the arm exploded into silver mist and was gone. Tiron barreled on, nearly tripping in surprise. His family blade was gleaming strangely.

"Follow me!" he cried, and set to hewing a path to the lake for the others.

Owl Home reached the Tear's edge. He cried out a terrified supplication and then seized Shaya by the nape of the neck and threw her bodily into the black water. Something caught her inches above the serene lake's surface; she began to float up, blood pouring out of her back as she arched and screamed in agony.

"No!" cried Ramswold. He burst past Tiron and raced past Owl Home, discarding his blade as he ran, then dove in a great leap over the water to crash into Shaya and wrapped his arms around her body. Together, they slammed into the water and were gone.

Tiron reached the lake's shore, Maur a single step behind him. He risked a glance behind him. Where was Nok? Ah, there. The huge kragh was striding toward the black-robed shamans. The spirits seemed to part before him, bowing as he walked. The three shamans saw him coming. One threw a fistful of green flame at the mountain kragh, but spirits rose in front of him, their wispy bodies shredding in the fire's passage but consuming it in turn, shielding him from harm.

The shamans cursed and threw more fire, but the spirits manifested ahead of each attack. Nok marched on, implacable, and when he reached the trio, he swung his hammer down and slammed the closest shaman's head into his chest.

The shaman's body did not fall. Instead, the spirits clamored around it, and his blood geysered up only to be consumed, filling dozens of spirit kragh with its vigor.

The second shaman's curses were ended by a sweep of Nok's hammer, a perfect lateral blow that pulverized the shaman's head.

The third shaman, a wiry, elderly figure, let loose a laugh. Placing both hands together, he unleashed a bolt of fire so potent that its brilliance blinded Tiron. Staggering back to the water's edge, he saw Nok being cut in half. The spirits did not drink his blood as he fell; instead, they rushed in to mob around the remaining shaman, whose laughter spiraled maniacally into the air.

He barely had time to notice that the sphere between Owl Home's hands was nearly spent, reduced to a flickering knot of golden filaments, before Maur seized his arm and hauled him into the lake.

Gripping his family blade tight, Tiron waded into the waters of the Tear. The lake was numbingly cold, a cold that pierced his muscles and set his very bones to throbbing. Gasping, cursing, with Maur and Owl Home right behind him, he waded forward till he was thigh-deep, then let out a bellow of anger he dove in.

The cold was like a slap that went right through him, knocking his spirit clear of his flesh. It felt like stepping through one of the Lunar Portals: that entrance into nothingness, the complete dearth of light, a plunge into the void. Tiron opened his mouth to scream, knowing that the water would flood into him and chill him from the inside out, but he couldn't hold back his cry.

He broke the surface despite having dived down. He emerged into the frigid air with a roar and found a bed of rounded pebbles beneath his feet. With the help of a few sweeps of his arms, he managed to stand.

Ramswold and Shaya were climbing out of the lake ahead of him, hunched with cold, the young lord's arm around her shoulders. Maur and Owl Home broached the surface behind Tiron with gasps of their own.

Tiron stood still, sword in hand, eyes on the shore. Where countless kragh had stood, there was now a legion of hollow-eyed figures whose number stretched back into the tree line. They encircled the lake completely, moving restlessly, pacing like firecats as they watched the new arrivals emerge from the lake.

A knot of them was engaged in violence on the shore. One of them thrust its arms forward, then slowly faded from view as first its wrists, then its arms, then its torso disappeared.

These were the spirits, he realized: endless ranks of them gathered here around the Tear.

Which meant...

His mind seemed to stop. He couldn't force the words though.

Which meant that he and the others had crossed over into the realm of the dead.

Maur squeezed his shoulder reassuringly, then gave him a rough shove. Tiron walked stiffly up to where Shaya and Ramswold were standing ankle-deep in the water, facing the countless spirits that were waiting for them, flexing their hands, their greed and hunger plain on their faces.

Both Shaya and Ramswold looked different. Ramswold was standing taller; his shoulders were filled out, and his face was handsome, almost imperial. Coruscating light seemed to dance around his head in a fey and barely visible crown. Shaya, in turn, looked more beautiful, more mature. Her expression was shadowed, and there was something dangerous in the gleam of her eyes.

"Where's Nok?" she asked, looking past Tiron.

Tiron could only shake his head, and when Shaya's eyes went glassy with shock, he pursed his lips and looked away.

Owl Home took a step and fell to his knees with a splash. He raised his hands and began to plead. "Spirits of the dead and fallen, ancient guardians of the black waters, we come with pure mind and with peace in our hearts, seeking succor and relief, for matters in the land of the living are grim. Oh, spirits, our people are suffering. They have been wrenched from their natural path into unholy acts..."

The shaman had also changed. His owl mask was a mask no longer; real feathers ruffled around his face, his voice came from his beak, and his great eyes were gleaming intently.

Tiron wanted to ask what was going on, but he shut his mouth. He'd not be asking for explanations in the spirit world.

The water behind them erupted in a great splash as a new figure emerged. Tiron turned, hoping desperately to see Ulein, perhaps, or Nok, somehow, but he saw instead the last black-robed shaman. He was a spindly, nightmarish mess of a kragh, his arms and legs like those of a spider, his face a distorted caricature, and from his scalp shadowy snakes were writhing.

Maur spat a name. "Death's Raven."

"He used to be Golden Crow," said Shaya. "The shaman of the Red River."

The shaman rose from the waters and became a massive black bird, its beak nearly a foot long, its claws massive and cruel, its plumage as dark as the lake's deep waters and gleaming with oil. With a heart-wrenching *caw*, it beat its wings and flew out over the heads of the spirits.

"Why can't Owl Home do that?" asked Tiron.

"Golden Crow was a very powerful shaman," Shaya said softly. "Owl Home is young."

Tiron watched as the kragh on the shore reached up for Death's Raven, their arms spearing up into the sky and elongating impossibly to try to snatch at the bird flying some ten yards above their heads.

Death's Raven wheeled and avoided their claws, rising ever higher, and soon was gone from sight.

Tiron shifted his grip on his sword, and only then did he realize that it was glowing with a white luminescence. He lifted it in wonder – and, to his surprise, the spirits at the water's edge drew back. Tiron moved forward, blade held before him like a firebrand. The spirits pulled back farther, and Owl Home's words faltered.

He stepped right up to the shore, and there he stopped. A ripple of fear passed through the spirits, but then they seemed to harden. Their expressions grew dour and forbidding, and they pressed forward once more.

"Looks like they want a fight," said Tiron.

Owl Home rose to his feet and stared at the blade, his golden owl eyes flickering as he blinked faster than Tiron could follow. "Where did you get that sword?"

"It was given to an ancestor of mine out of the Ascendant's own armory in Aletheia."

The shaman passed his hand over the glowing blade and whispered to himself, then turned and pointed at Ramswold. "Give him the blade."

Tiron arched a brow, but did so. As Ramswold closed his fingers around the hilt, a soft sigh seemed to escape the assembled spirits, and Ramswold seemed to grow in stature, the crown of light taking on a golden sheen.

"What's going on?" asked the young lord.

"Reverse your grip on the blade," said Owl Home. "As if you were about to stab it into the ground."

Ramswold did so.

"Now, step onto the shore. Have no fear. The caliber of your spirit will see us through."

"I am not afraid," Ramswold said, and placed his foot on the shore.

The spirits backed away from him and his burning blade, and in doing so opened a path.

"What, by the Black Gate, is going on?" asked Tiron.

Owl Home followed. Maur came next. She, too, had changed; there was a faded glory to her, like the sun glimpsed through the clouds, shorn of its beams. She exuded a sense of resolve and indomitable will that was somehow palpable in this world; Tiron felt the force of her personality impress itself upon him and shivered.

Shaya went next, her expression still hollowed by grief, leaving Tiron to bring up the rear. He stared at the young lord and felt a desperate anger, an almost panicked desire to deny what he was seeing. *This isn't a damned fable,* he thought helplessly. *This doesn't happen in the real world.* Yet, he couldn't help but follow Ramswold through the ranks of the spirit kragh.

"Geography is not a constant here," said Owl Home. "Fix your mind on our destination, Ramswold, and take us there."

"But, I don't know where to go," said the young lord.

"In your heart, you do. Feel our need. It is a force all its own here in the spirit world. Feel my guidance. Take us where we must go."

Ramswold nodded uneasily and continued walking, but as he did, the world around them began to fade and grow vague; it was as if a mist were rising from the ground to obscure the details of the landscape, erase the kragh, the mountain peaks and the lake. The deeper they walked into the fog, the thicker it became, until it seemed as if they were walking through the heart of a cloud.

Tiron jumped when Owl Home leaped up into the air with a cry of joy. His body contracted violently as white plumage erupted everywhere, and he became an actual owl. He swooped above the others, flying in tight circles, and then out ahead of Ramswold, who turned to follow the shaman's path.

"This fucking spirit world," said Tiron to Shaya, who frowned at him.

They hadn't marched long before they emerged into a cave. *Bythos?* wondered Tiron, but it wasn't. This was a different cavern, though it was similar in scope. It was lit by great pyres of flame whose tongues leaped up dozens of yards into the air but failed to illuminate the darkness overhead. Vast shadows flickered on the burgundy-hued walls, in the folds of which gleamed chunks of crystal and precious stones.

The air was close and smelled strongly of something fey and strange; it was leathery and alien, and something primal in Tiron reacted to the smell with fear.

Owl Home flew down and landed on Maur's shoulder. Together, the group stole ahead, emerging from the shadows into the undulating crimson light, and there Tiron saw his first dragon.

The sight of it closed his throat and caused his heart to stutter. It gave the impression of burnished might, its countless scales gleaming softly in the pyre light as if each of them caught a glimmering of the flame and held it within its heart. The beast was blood-red along its spine, fading to umber and mud gold beneath. Its spine was serrated by horns the length of Tiron's arm, while its sinuous neck was all languorous strength, terminating in a head the size of a drayman's cart.

Its eyes were closed. Its maw was large enough to cut a man in two, with a savagely beaked tip curving over the lower jaw. Heavy scaled ridges surmounted its eyes, the scales around which were so fine that they took on the appearance of skin.

Its wings were furled over its back. Its tail curved off into the shadows. It was easily large enough for five men to ride, large enough to clutch a plow horse in its front talons and bear it aloft.

"By the Seven Virtues and the White Gate," Ramswold whispered, lowering the blade. "That can't be real."

Tiron saw another dragon asleep on the far side of the cavern, partially hidden by a descending elbow of rock. Its hide was more crimson and incardinine, its form more slender than the other dragon's. A third was humped up in the distance, more muscled than the first two, horns rising cruelly down its length, its scales ebon and gleaming like wet obsidian.

"The saviors of the kragh," whispered Owl Home, though he was still in his avian form. "The dragons. They have slumbered here since time immemorial. They are our greatest and most dangerous last recourse. No one has disturbed them since Ogri ventured here to summon Jaemungdr forth."

Tiron was overcome. He'd never expected to see such awful magnificence in his life, and he didn't know what he'd done to deserve this vision. He realized he was smiling helplessly, feeling for the first time in years — perhaps decades — as awed and delighted as a boy.

"They're amazing. How do we wake them?"

"They have a guardian," whispered Owl Home. "She should present herself soon."

"Who?" asked Shaya.

"The first and greatest shaman. The kragh who found the dragons and brought them to us. She who gave up her name in payment, who consigned her spirit, deserving as it was, to an eternity of watching over them for the sake of us all."

Maur took a step forward, one hand raised as if she expected to touch an invisible wall. She took a second step, and then a third, and stopped when a figure manifested in front of her. Gray mist swirled and coalesced into an old kragh, her body stooped and rounded by age, her hair hanging in iron-colored dreadlocks. Despite her great age, her eyes burned with starfire, and her scrutiny cut like a knife.

Maur fell to her knees and pressed her brow to the dirt. Owl Home fluttered down to the ground, opened his wings and bowed. Shaya did the same, then Ramswold knelt and bowed as if he were facing the Ascendant himself.

Only Tiron was left standing.

Slowly, his smile died on his face. Something was wrong. This was like a minstrel's tale – no, a tale told to bright-eyed children at night by their indulgent grandfathers. He didn't deserve to be here. Instinct bade him look down at his hands, and he saw that they were glistening crimson as if they were stained with blood.

"Ancient seer," said Owl Home, slowly morphing back up into his kragh form. "We come to you in a time of great need. Our kind is falling sway once more to the medusa. We make blood sacrifices in her honor. The old chants are being sung once more, and our greatest shamans have been perverted to her will."

The ancient spirit gazed upon him but did not reply.

"We have need of the ancient guardians," continued the shaman. "For—"

Green fire slashed into Owl Home, limning him in emerald. He screamed and rose to the balls of his feet, then collapsed in a pile. Tiron let out a hoarse oath, but the flame was not yet done. Death's Raven emerged from the shadows, both hands raised, and the flame flickered out to coruscate around Ramswold, who screamed and raised Tiron's blade in self-defense.

"Rot and filth, death and defilement," rasped Death's Raven. "End times are coming, end times are here. Rejoice in your fetid depths, cut and ruin. No succor. No light! Dance, dance and fall, weep and laugh. Our mistress is everlasting, our mistress is time itself, cruel and venomous, uplifting and deserving of every drop of blood that is spilt!"

Maur ran at the shaman, but the shadows leaped up and engulfed her, bring her crashing down to the rocks.

"Cease," said the ancient shaman, drifting forward, one hand raised. Her voice was a moan out of time, and Tiron felt his skin crawl.

"Never, rot and ruin!" Death's Raven was foaming at the lips, and smoke was rising from his coal-black skin. The flames were closing around Ramswold like a coruscating fist. "My might is made double by my mistress' favor! My need will not be denied. The shackles that limit are cast aside. Everything is permitted! Though I rupture, I will jolt you from your complacent vigil. Feel the pain of life!"

The green fire ripped toward the ancient shaman, playing off her body and searing her where it touched. The old woman hissed and pushed back, golden light flooding out of her like a rising sun, but Death's Raven simply laughed. The very fabric of his being was coming apart, was being fed into his lightning. More and more of it spilled out, enveloping the seer, drowning her light.

Tiron pulled his knife from his boot and ran forward, his thoughts incoherent. Death's Raven glanced at him, then raised his hand; Tiron stopped as if he'd run into a wall.

"You?" asked the shaman in disdain. "You attack me? But you should be my creature, polluted as you are. Your will should dance to my commands. Turn, human, and slay your friends."

To Tiron's horror, he turned to look at Ramswold, who had been driven down to one knee. Tiron's blazing sword barely holding back the green fire.

With jerky steps, Tiron strode toward him, knife raised high. Anguished, furious, Tiron struggled to stop, to throw himself aside, but his limbs refused to do his bidding. His skin burned as if he had been bathed in acid, summoning memories from the depths of his mind. Memories of slaughter when he was riding with the Black Wolves, of attacking Kethe with the intent to slay her, of standing by as others raped and killed, of the brutal manner with which he'd dispatched countless foes over the years, his cold moral calculus — all of it arose within him and seemed to give purchase to Death's Raven's control.

Ramswold, however, was able to rise to his feet. The white light of Tiron's sword was glowing brighter, and the green flames seemed unable to touch him. The young lord was gritting his teeth in effort, pushing back against the attack for all he was worth.

The ancient seer lifted up into the air, fading away as she did so.

Death's Raven let out a howl of triumph which curdled into a scream of hate as Ramswold lifted his blade. It flashed brightly, momentarily blinding Tiron, who stumbled, dagger still raised, and came to a stop.

A low rumble caused the ground to shake.

The dragon's eyes had opened, and its head was rising into the air. It was a vision of predatory majesty as it shook out its great wings and resettled them on its broad back, talons splintering the rock.

Death's Raven cut off his attack and fell to his knees. Tiron gasped as the will impelling him onward disappeared.

"Your era of enslavement is at an end, glorious one!" cried Death's Raven. "I bring you the freedom you deserve, the chance to assume your rightful place at the peak of existence! No longer need you sleep away the eons, awaiting your next summons. Now you can—"

The dragon opened its maw, and a slender skein of white fire burst forth with tremendous power, a jet that blossomed into a ball of rolling flame that engulfed Death's Raven. The light was stark and shockingly intense, and the heat was stunning.

Tiron staggered back, freed from the shaman's magic but mesmerized in turn by the lethality of the attack.

Death's Raven didn't even scream.

The jet of flame was cut off by the closing of the dragon's jaws. Nothing was left but a broad expanse of melted stone and blackened dust.

Ramswold was facing Tiron. The flame had passed only a few yards above his shoulder. Ever so slowly, he turned and lowered himself to his knees.

HIS REEK OFFENDED ME, said the dragon, shaking out its wings once more.

"I — I apologize," said Ramswold. "Th-thank you for killing him."

Maur rose painfully to her feet. Even she was overwhelmed, Tiron noticed. She staggered forward a few steps and then sank to her knees alongside Owl Home. She touched his body here and there, but he was literally fading away, the stone starting to show through his body.

The ancient shaman appeared once more, the damage inflicted upon her gone. "The will to power blinds," she said. "The pursuit of dominion unbalances and ultimately destroys."

Maur bowed her head. "Yes. I have seen this with my own eyes. Power becomes its own justification. One of my tribe has risen to terrible power, but in doing so, he has brought great evil upon us."

"And upon himself," said the ancient shaman.

"Yes," sighed Maur. "And upon himself. He is a prisoner of ambition, of an intelligence that is not his own. He awakened the medusa and seeks to use her toward his own ends. He has broken our society and reshaped it to his greatest benefit. Even now, the kragh are destroying the human Empire. But to do so, we first had to destroy ourselves."

The old kragh's eyes gleamed. "You are worthy, daughter. It pleases me to see such nobility amongst my descendants."

Tiron winced and forced himself to sit up. Those dark memories were starting to fade, but the blood soaked into his hands was as vivid as before. It would be best, he thought, if he stayed quiet.

"Human," said the old shaman. "Why are you here?"

"To stop Tharok," said Ramswold. "To save my people."

"Your soul is true," said the shaman, gazing deep into his eyes. "You do not wish for power?"

"No," whispered Ramswold. "I do not."

"Nor do I sense hatred. After all that you humans have suffered, you do not wish for revenge?"

Ramswold shook his head slowly. "No, not revenge. Just peace."

The dragon lowered its head so that it was directly in front of Ramswold. **GLORY BURNS UPON YOUR BROW. I SHALL BEAR YOU INTO BATTLE.**

Ramswold rose shakily to his feet and bowed, the corona of light around his head growing even more resplendent. "It would be my life's greatest honor. I am Lord Lenhard Ramswold of the Order of the Star, master of the Red Keep and sworn knight of the Ascendant. May I ask your name?"

SKANDENGRAUR, rumbled the dragon with obvious pride.

Tiron wanted to smile, to clutch his head. They should all have died in their mad charge on the shores of the Tear; instead, Ramswold was about to become the first person in history to ride a dragon.

Gazing at the young lord, Tiron felt a wretched sense of self-loathing arise within him. If this was what Ramswold had been born for, if Ramswold was living his truth, then what did that say about Tiron himself?

Tiron looked down at his blood-smeared hands once more. The symbolism was all too apparent. The sins of his past could not be washed away by a simple vow to uphold justice.

Tiron sank down onto his haunches, feeling as if his insides were being hollowed out. How easily he'd fallen to Death's Raven's control. Numb with horror, he watched as the founder of the Order of the Star reached out and laid his hand upon the dragon's snout.

"Those who are true of heart will find their prayers answered," said the old shaman. "At least, they will in this place and time. You, dear daughter, will be given the chance to ease your woes and heal the anguish that you have witnessed."

"Me?" said Maur.

The crimson dragon behind the first stirred, its wings shifting. Slowly, its head ascended, and its golden eyes narrowed. Its horns curled back in such profusion from its skull that they almost formed a mane.

"By the Sky Father," whispered Maur.

Ramswold looked as if he thought he was walking around in a dream. The dragon lowered one wing to the cavern floor, and he climbed up its length to where the dragon's neck met its shoulders. There, he sat, his expression dazed, and settled his hands around the closest horn.

The dragon rose onto all four legs. Ramswold's face grew pale as it did so.

WHERE AWAITS OUR FOE? asked Skandengraur.

"Bythos," Ramswold whispered, knuckles whitening as he tightened his grip.

The dragon shook out its wings once more, then simply disappeared.

"What — where did — oh," said Tiron.

The second dragon approached, stepping with a leonine grace around the shoulder of rock. It seemed to personify the concept of fire, from the crimson ridges of its horns to the yellow and white streak that ran down the center of its neck and smoothed out over its stomach.

Maur was shaking. She took a step back. "I am not worthy."

OUR OPINIONS DIFFER, said the crimson dragon. **I AM FLAMSKA.**

It extended its wing down to the ground, and the Wise Woman carefully climbed up till she was astride its neck.

"I am Maur," she said, her voice swelling with confidence as she gripped the next horn up the length of its neck with both hands. "Let us fly, Flamska. Let us liberate my people!"

As before, the pair of them disappeared.

Shaya stepped over to where Tiron was standing, her expression awed. She bowed low to the ancient seer, hesitated, then spoke. "What's to happen to us?"

"If you have been spared from the dragon's fire, it is because you have been found worthy," said the old kragh.

From the depths of the great cave, a smaller shape appeared, as luminous as a Noussian pearl espied at the bottom of a murky pond. It was half the size of the other dragons, its scales so fine that its hide appeared smooth and of a white so pure that its shadowed declivities appeared almost blue. Its eyes were of the deepest azure.

Shaya, Tiron noticed, had stopped breathing. "Go on," he said, and gave her a small push. She stumbled forward a few feet, suddenly graceless, and then stood frozen as the dragon lowered its white snout to sniff at her hair.

"Is it — is it a Bythian dragon?" she murmured.

"No," said the ancient seer. "It is its own self."

PAIN, DEFIANCE, LOSS, BRAVERY, said the dragon. **SUCH STRENGTH OF WILL, SUCH HEART. I AM RAUDA. WILL YOU FLY?**

"Yes," breathed Shaya. "Oh, by the White Gate, yes."

She climbed carefully up its lowered wing and settled on its neck with her back straight and her hands clasped around the next horn up its neck.

Shaya's eyes gleamed with wonder — then she was gone.

"Well, you're stuck with me for company," Tiron said with a mirthless smile, sliding down the cavern's wall to sit. "To be honest, I'd welcome the chance to rest. Let the young ones accomplish the glorious victory."

The ancient seer gazed at him without comment.

"It's going to be a long wait if you're not up for sharing stories," said Tiron. "Unless you want me to go first? I'll warn you, though." He raised a bloody hand and examined it. "Mine are pretty dark."

Something was moving in the depths of the cavern. Something large, a great shadow given life. Glints and gleams reflected off its proud brow and its deep chest. Its great wings were like the sails of a three-masted galleon.

"Fuck me," said Tiron as the black dragon emerged into the light of the torches.

It would have dwarfed even Skandengraur, and was hoary with age, deep scars crisscrossing its hide. Its scales were like black shields, and its horns were weathered, one of them snapped halfway.

There was in its baleful regard a sense of deep time, of a life beyond Tiron's ability to comprehend, of an immensity of experience that dwarfed the mountains and challenged the stars themselves.

YOU SMELL OF BLOOD, said the dragon, its voice reverberating through Tiron's chest. **BLOOD AND DEATH AND IRON**.

Tiron climbed slowly to his feet, half-expecting a cleansing blast of flame at any moment, but there was something in the dragon's dark eyes that called to him. A hunger, he thought. "Yes, I imagine I do," he said warily. "No coincidence, that."

YET, THERE IS MORE.

Tiron tried to hold the dragon's gaze but failed. He looked down and away.

YOU CLAWED YOUR WAY BACK FROM THE ABYSS. YOU SOUGHT TO REFORGE YOUR SPIRIT ON THE ANVIL OF YOUR WILL.

"Aye, perhaps," said Tiron, finding it hard to breathe. "But I failed. I'm still a bastard. Cynical, ruinous, foul-minded and hard."

AS AM I, said the dragon, and Tiron could have sworn he heard humor in its voice. **I AM KNOWN AS DRAUMRONIN. WILL YOU FLY?**

"You bet your damn eyes I will," Tiron said hoarsely, his heart thudding painfully within his chest.

THEN COME, said the dragon, and, with a great rustling, it extended its wing to the ground. Balancing, Tiron walked up the long exterior edge of the wing, then reached down to grip the outer ridge of muscle. The scales were warm to the touch, and he felt a jolt of elation at the thought of what he was doing. He clambered up over the huge shoulder and then onto the dragon's neck. He was a good ten yards off the ground, and the dragon's head curled around to regard him as he settled down behind a great horned spine.

IT HAS BEEN TOO LONG, rumbled Draumronin. **THE WORLD HAS FORGOTTEN MY NAME.**

"To war," said Tiron.

TO WAR.

The dragon raised its wings, inhaled mightily, and then the cavern was consumed by darkness and disappeared.

Chapter 32

K ethe stood beside one of the ancient castle ballista, gazing at the Solar Portals. Silence lay like a shroud upon the great square. Three thousand men and women stood and watched. Agerastians. Ennoians. The Cerulean Guard. The creaking of bows filtered down from the rooftops some six stories above. Men coughed, shifted their weight. The tension in the air felt like a palpable force; it weighed on her shoulders, pressed her down, made it hard to breathe.

Elon was standing atop the ballista's platform to her left, one hand on its great curved arm. The few Consecrated who yet lived were scattered throughout the front lines. The Cerulean Guard was an island of blue and white to her right; she could see a large block of Hrethings under Toki's leadership halfway around the square. Men young and old were gripping swords rusted or sharp, holding pikes and spears. Everyone knew that this was the last battle for the soul of the Empire.

The Ascendant himself had told them so.

The streets and avenues leading away from the square were all barricaded, a mass of carts, wagons, sandbags, stones and trees laid in formidable piles six to seven yards high. Kethe and every other soldier on the ground was standing in a killing field. Here, they would slaughter as many of the kragh as they could — and if they failed to hold the tide, here, they would die.

That knowledge was writ large on the faces about her. Some men looked dazed. Others were near panting, shoulders heaving, opening and closing their fingers around the hilts of their blades. The professionals were calm. The day of reckoning had arrived at last, and over the course of the long night, they had made their peace.

If anything, Kethe felt relief. Here, there would be an end. In her heart of hearts, she didn't think they could win. She'd seen firsthand what Tharok could do. But she would fight with everything she had to ensure that there was such a slaughter here that Tharok's victory would be gutted. That he would become the ruler of a host laid waste.

More, this would prove an end to her growing torment. She no longer knew what to believe. Theletos was dead, which she still couldn't believe. Ainos had proven to be a traitor. That cut even deeper. She was the last Virtue – an impossibility. Akinetos, Synesis, and Mixis had been killed at Abythos, Henosis torn apart by Tharok before the Abythian Gate. Theletos had been beheaded, Ainos reduced to charred bones. She was the last, the final repository of an ancient tradition, the final manifestation of Ascendancy's greatest defense.

And she didn't even know what she believed.

She'd almost sought out the Ascendant to confess her doubts, but the young man had seemed so steeped in his own troubles that she'd held back. Was he a mystical figure or a precocious youth? To the thousands gathered here this dawn, he was someone to die for, and for that reason and that reason alone, she would keep her doubts to herself.

A kragh emerged through the Bythian Portal, hidden behind a tall tower shield. A roar erupted from a thousand throats, a primal scream of hatred and defiance. Arrows by the hundreds were loosed. Elon himself had to yell at his crew not to fire the ballistae.

The kragh backpedaled and disappeared, arrows *thwipping* into the white fire of the Portal and disappearing with him.

The ranks of soldiers around her strained, men rising to their tiptoes to gain a better view, calling out questions, letting out derisive curses and half-hearted cheers. Someone close to her called out, "Well, that wasn't so bad!" Men around him laughed nervously.

Kethe watched the Portal. That kragh had been a scout, and now he'd be relaying his information to Tharok. The futility of having the trolls lob rocks would have been readily apparent to him. What else might the kragh warlord be planning? What subtle stratagem that would render all this preparation futile? Would he not attack? Leave them to die in the heat? Attack just before dusk?

The passions that had been roused to a boil by the appearance of the lone kragh were slowly reduced to a simmer once more. Hundreds, if not thousands, were darting glances at her. She was the sole Virtue on the field. As such, she stood firm and silent, the tip of her blade resting on the ground, her hands on the cross guards, waiting, trying to exude a sense of implacability.

Never mind the pain smoldering across her back. The doubts that tore at her confidence. The hollow ache in her gut, the longing for Asho to stand by her side. She closed her eyes and sensed the cord of white fire that extended from her heart and disappeared through the buildings behind her to the Portal that led to Starkadr. This, more than anything else, gave her strength.

A roar tore through the army. Her eyes snapped open, and she saw a mass of kragh charging through the Gates.

Not just the Aletheian and Bythian Gates, Kethe saw, but *all* of them.

There was a moment of silence, of hushed expectation, and then the kragh were there, emerging from the white fire of the five Gates, twenty abreast and carrying massive shields of wood – no – bridges!

Orders were barked across every rooftop. Arrows were loosed by the thousands, and they hissed down like the most vicious rain, *thock-ing* into the underbelly of the bridge or disappearing into the Portals. The kragh raised the bridges vertically, a few of their numbers on the flanks falling, and then toppled the bridges forward so that they fell with a jarring crash across the trenches, flattening the wooden spikes that emerged from the yard-high walls built behind each one.

Another hail of arrows fell upon the kragh, who stumbled and fell, massacred. No matter; more were coming through, a second wave carrying a second set of bridges. These had greater difficulty. Sergeants were ordering their archers to fire above the kragh bridge crews closest to them and into the backs of those emerging from the farther Gates.

The kragh were having difficulty. The awkward manner in which the first bridges had fallen over the trenches, knocked askew by the stakes and the small walls, not to mention the bodies underfoot, made traversing them treacherous.

But the bridges were massive, and the kragh fought their way across their sloping decks till, with a cry, they raised the second set of bridges and let those crash down over the next set of trenches.

The men behind her were ready to attack, ready to fight. She could feel their bloodlust and terror, but they could do nothing but watch as the third set of bridges came through the Portals. They could do nothing but watch and wait as the archers took their toll.

The kragh were chanting a work song, or perhaps a dirge, fighting to traverse the first, then the second set of bridges, slipping and falling, dropping the bridges only to have reinforcements from behind pick them back up. With supreme effort, they laid the third set of bridges over the next set of trenches, and in doing so reached a set of stakes tied off at the top with red ribbons.

"Here we go," whispered Kethe.

The fourth set of bridges were nearly laid over the second when fire arrows came raining down upon the kragh, their flaming tips brilliant in the dawn. Some of the arrows pierced the bridges themselves, but most of them were aimed into the bottoms of the trenches. Almost simultaneously, the first twelve furrows lit up with an almighty *WHOOMPH* as the oil that had been pooled thickly along their bases caught.

Tongues of flame billowed up into the sky. The kragh's shrieks were matched by a shuddering roar of victory from the humans. The bridges seemed impervious to the flames at first, but then they blackened and caught.

The kragh dropped the fourth set of bridges and charged, maddened by the flames. They hurled themselves over the first open trench and swung at the stakes as they fell upon them. Some of the kragh managed to knock them askew, while others were impaled, but whoever climbed up over the yard-high wall was immediately knocked back by arrows.

The kragh kept coming. They weren't carrying any more bridges — perhaps they had thought four sets would be enough, or had been told to abandon them by their commanders, but on they came, hundreds of them pouring through the Portals every few seconds, apparently impervious to the terrors of death and the flames.

They'd not poured as much oil into the trenches that lay before the Noussian, Sigean, and Zoeian Gates, Kethe realized. Those bridges were burning but maintaining their structural integrity. While the attacks from Bythos and Aletheia were foundering, the kragh staggering over collapsing bridges and forced to fight their way through the burning trenches, the other lines of attack were making far better progress. Some of them were even reaching the middle trenches before being shot down.

The flames were dying, the oil now expended. On came the kragh with their tusks fully displayed, weapons held before them with both hands, running till ten or twelve arrows had perforated their hides, and then they collapsed.

The bridges were ruined. The kragh ceased trying to use them, and instead fought their way down into the trenches, stepping on the bodies of their brothers, then struggled through gaps in the retaining walls.

There was no longer any order to the loosing of the arrows. They came down in a continuous rain. Everywhere, kragh were screaming, throwing up their arms as they fell, bleeding, shoving their fellows aside, fighting for one more foot of ground before they died.

"On my mark!" shouted Elon. He held aloft a white flag. He'd been ordered to wait until a critical mass of kragh had come through. He'd deemed that moment to have come. "Ready! Loose!"

The ballista men arranged around the square might not have heard his yell, but they certainly saw his flag drop. Ten triggers were pulled. Eight of the ballistae were huge, weapons designed to be operated by teams of six or eight, but two of them were the monsters from the castle. These had crews of twelve each, and the sheer violence of their release, the way they leaped and bucked back against their restraints, caused Kethe to flinch and step away.

Their effect was devastating. Eight spears six feet long and as thick as her arm shot through the kragh, punching through chests, heads, shoulders, arms. Massive furrows were dug into the mass of kragh, killing dozens.

But that was nothing compared to the damage the castle monsters wrought. They each fired a spear ten feet long and eight inches thick, topped by special heads that Elon had had hammered out through the night on forges across the city. Each head was a full foot long and eight inches wide, and had a broadsword's blade attached to each side so that they swept out like flanges.

Kethe stared, horrified, at the carnage they caused. They plowed through the kragh with terrible, unstoppable power, clearing a line right through to the Portal and then disappearing into the white flame. Thirty, maybe forty kragh were killed by each of them.

Ragged cheers arose from the soldiers, and fists were pumped into the air, but Elon was already hard at work reloading the ballistae.

Still, the kragh came. The trenches were filled with corpses now, and the stakes were smothered by bodies. Thousands lay dead, but still they came. The arrows flew, darkening the skies, but for how much longer? How many full quivers remained?

"Crossbow men, advance!" Kethe cried, and led them to the last retaining wall. "Kneel!" The first line dropped, resting their huge crossbows on the wall's top. Behind them, a second line formed, crossbows held at shoulder height. A third line behind them held loaded crossbows at the ready.

The kragh had nearly reached a line of stakes that had been painted black. It was mesmerizing, how they came: their tenacity, pushing on despite wounds that would have killed a man three times over. Falling, and rising, only to fall again. It was like watching a rockslide in slow motion.

There was a sense of inevitability to their approach, of certain doom. No matter how many kragh her people killed, on they came. The reek of blood was thick in the air, mingling with the rising bitter tang of terror as her men began to panic. "Death," moaned one man. "Death's a'comin'. Death's here, boys. It's coming our way!"

"Silence!" barked a sergeant, but the crossbow men were starting to fray at the seams. From somewhere came the acrid stink of urine.

Shuddering, Kethe watched the front of the wave of kragh plunge at the black-painted stakes. Some took them in the chest or the thigh, only to tear themselves free, lacerating their flesh, and she guessed that the pain was driving them on. Others put their shoulders to the angled stakes and heaved them up, knocking them back, forcing them aside.

"On my mark," she whispered.

Nobody heard her.

"On my mark!"

Men shook out their shoulders, steadied themselves, sighted down the lengths of their crossbows.

The kragh threw themselves over the black-painted wall, tumbled down, fell by the dozens, then rose.

"Fire!"

The crossbows snapped their quarrels out, and the kragh began to fall. The second rank of men handed their loaded crossbows to the kneeling first, then to replacements from the third rank, who set to reloading.

"Fire!"

All around the square, crossbow men were loosing their quarrels, but again, the greatest number of them was concentrated before the Aletheian and Bythian Gates, where the kragh approach had been slowest.

"Third rank!" Kethe cried. "Move to reinforce the Sigean crossbow men to the left! Go!"

That would greatly slow their reload rate, but their kragh were much farther back than the Sigean line, which was about ready to pull their crossbowmen back and unleash their soldiers.

The ballistae roared their mighty song. Droves died.

How many had they slaughtered? Kethe wondered. Thousands, surely. The piles of the dead now buried the trenches and covered the walls. She couldn't see the kragh emerging from the Portals beyond all the dead.

The crossbows were having a terrible effect on the kragh; for now, they were unable to advance beyond the black stakes, falling over and over again before the quarrels' ruinous power.

"We're holding them!" cried someone to Kethe's right. "We're doing it!"

And they were. The terrain had become too treacherous for the kragh to proceed, and Kethe allowed herself to feel a brief spark of hope. "Fire!" she screamed. More kragh fell, but this time the line was farther back. "Fire!" The ballistae snapped their huge bolts forward, mowing down dozens. "Fire!"

The kragh were falling back, stumbling over a field of their own dead. The retreat turned into a rout. The kragh pushed against those behind them, and the numbers coming through the Portals reversed.

The kragh were fleeing.

The punishment had been too much.

A cheer echoed around the huge square as Kethe's men waved their weapons and hugged their fellows. Thousands of kragh had been slaughtered, but not a single human had been killed.

Kethe fought not to smile. It couldn't be over, but the emotion in the air was too much to ignore, all this riotous celebration. She climbed up onto the retaining wall between her crossbow men and raised her sword, willing it to catch fire. It blazed in the dawn and drew a cry of joy from every throat, every man, woman and child.

Tears filled Kethe's eyes. They'd done it. They'd repelled the kragh.

Chapter 33

Confusion reigned at the base of the Portal. Kragh were stumbling back into Bythos, shoving their fellows aside as they fought and fell. Perhaps half their number had passed through into Ennoia. The war drums faltered, then fell silent. Curses shouts took their place, but the kragh would not continue the attack.

With a roar of his own, Tharok leaped down from his platform and strode through the milling warriors at the front, knocking aside kragh who didn't have the wits to see him coming.

The number fleeing back through the Portal dwindled and came to a stop. Some hundred or so had made it back.

Tharok seized a lowlander by the throat and lifted him off the ground. "What happened?"

Silence spread out around him as the others waited for the answer.

"Death," gasped the lowlander. "We couldn't reach the humans for all the bodies in our way. Death came from the skies! Arrows everywhere. Huge machines throwing arrows larger than a kragh, carving us apart. Crossbows at the front. Fire everywhere! Everywhere dead kragh, piles of them."

Tharok lowered the kragh and looked around. Messengers were creeping back in through the Portals to the other cities. Judging by their lowered heads and hunched shoulders, they had similar news to report.

His army had been defeated.

The fact galled him. He'd scorned the circlet's advice and *failed*. Doing so had cost him, what, about five thousand of his kragh? Nearly half his army.

He had to act. To give orders. But nothing came to him.

Fool!

They were all watching him. Warlords. Chieftains. The medusa-Kissed and his warriors, all of them waiting even as the Portals continued to burn with their inner white fire, even as the humans on the other side celebrated their victory.

"Fall back," he said. "Return to your columns. Send word to the other armies to hold."

His chieftains immediately set to lashing and shoving at the kragh and ordering that the gravely wounded be hauled away. Tharok climbed back up onto his platform and stared down at the Portals. He knew what he had to do – what he should have done from the beginning – but he fought it.

This was my one chance to free myself and my people, he thought. *My one chance. And I ruined it.*

He closed his eyes, knowing he presented a tempting target for any kragh with a spear or bow but not caring. He searched for and found that single, quavering tone that had been the voice of hope

You misled me, he snarled. *You made me think I could do this alone.*

The song did not answer. Did not change in the slightest.

Anger born of despair welled up within him. Had he really thought that he, Tharok, could lead this great army alone? That he was worthy of this challenge?

He was nothing. Just a miserable highlander kragh who had been blessed with an opportunity far beyond his ken. What could he do? Unleash a second attack? No, his kragh wouldn't charge through again. Wait out the humans? His kragh would revolt.

Tharok lowered a shaking hand to where the circlet was hanging from his belt and jerked it free, snapping the leather thong. He raised the circlet, staring in terror and fury at its perfect form.

Curse you, he thought. *Curse you, and I curse myself a thousand times over.*

He lowered the circlet over his brow.

Instantly, clarity wiped away all doubt and confusion. His mistakes were glaringly obvious. He'd done well, in fact; there was much to his plan to be commended, but he'd ignored key resources, had not spent enough time researching and scouting out the enemy in his haste. He had thrown his troops into battle before they were completely prepared.

Tharok shook his head. This had been a promising attempt, but nothing worthy of the world stage. But it wasn't too late. Even now, victory could be wrested from defeat.

"Chieftains!"

His bellow silenced the kragh below. The medusa-Kissed commanders raised their faces to him, eyes narrowed.

"Execute every kragh who fled the battlefield. We suffer no cowards in our ranks."

Those who had fled immediately set to crying out their protest, shoving at the arms that sought to grab them, drawing their own weapons. The wounded howled their protest as axes descended, but their howls were quickly silenced.

Many of the kragh looked to Tharok for reassurance that this was right; in answer to that, he stood with his hands on his hips, exuding confidence. To let the cowards live would be to allow poison into his army – to allow his warriors to think they could choose when to retreat, when to abandon his plan. It was unfortunate that they had been sent to their deaths needlessly, but theirs was not the right to decide when they should die.

That was his prerogative alone.

"Send word to the other armies to do the same!" he shouted as the last of the kragh were cut down. "Go!"

He cast around until he saw the black-robed shaman who had addressed him before. The shaman was standing, hunched, off to one side. His eyes glittered from under the cowl of his hood.

"Tell your mistress that I desire her assistance," Tharok told him. "Tell her to bring it forth now."

The shaman bowed low and hurried out of sight behind a column of rocks.

"My warriors!" Tharok's voice cut through the tumult. "You are my finest. I have saved you for the killing blow. Those who went before you were weak. They were disloyal. I wished to cleanse them from our ranks and purify our army so that only the greatest of us remain. The humans have done exactly as I wished."

He gave them a low, cunning smile and swept the horde with his gaze. His words, he knew, were being passed back to those too far away to hear him.

"Now, we crush them. Now, during their moment of triumph, we will shatter their resolve. Is it not amusing to cut an enemy down while he celebrates a false victory? To let him relax and enjoy a moment of cheer before showing him that he never had a chance?"

It was a weak speech, but it was having some effect; the kragh were nodding, some of them grinning foolishly, eager to show their loyalty. The edge of panic was beginning to wear off. Watching those who had fled the field be slaughtered had shaken their anger, weakened their defiance. Tharok's confidence was soothing them.

"Now is our hour. Now is our time. Their doom is upon them!"

There was a moment of silence, then the remains of his army issued a half-hearted roar. That annoyed him, but he understood. His kragh had just suffered their greatest defeat and were having trouble sharing his confidence. Only their faith in him was holding them in place, but it would be enough.

Turning, he stared out over the badlands, past the remnants of his army to the distant Abythian arch that marked the ramp into the labyrinth. Overhead, the agony vultures were wheeling.

The aurora flickered.

He waited.

The name *kchack'ick'ill* had meant nothing to him before. Now, the circlet provided a wealth of information, and a dark, malevolent sense of expectation suffused him. No matter what price Kyrra exacted later, this gift of hers would end the war decisively in his favor.

His kragh slowly settled, some of them hunkering down, others crouching, others setting to sharpening their weapons or chewing on cured meat.

He caught a glimpse of movement.

Shadows were crawling about the arch.

Then the first broke free of the gloom and began to course toward him. It was massive and serpentine, flanked by rippling insectile legs. Even at this distance, he could make out its stony carapace. It was alien and terrifying, and as more of the same streamed after it – at first a trickle and then a flood – he grinned.

The end of humanity was as hand.

Chapter 34

Asho felt the world disappear from around him, felt his bones harrowed by a freezing cold, and then, with a gasp, he was through and out the other side.

Haugabrjótr.

He reflexively placed a hand on the hilt of his sword as he looked around the stone chamber. Audsley was at his side, hesitating, looking at a cadaverous man in black clothing with a hard, almost distasteful expression.

The man was standing alongside a large table of black rock, waiting patiently, it seemed, as if he'd been expecting their arrival. His gray hair was cut close, and his face was long and desiccated, deep cracks carved into his cheeks and framing his mouth. There was a rigidity to him, a sublime self-control, that made Asho feel as if the man disdained his own body – as if he saw it as an instrument, and a weak one, at that.

Two tunnels extended from the back of the room into darkness, and a staircase led up to a walkway with its own iron door. Everything was clearly lit. Cabinets lined the walls, with broad counters beneath them on which a number of metal tools had been laid out on clean white cloths.

"Magister," said the man, inclining his head. "You are timely."

Audsley matched the gesture. "Athanasius, may I present Ser Asho. He has agreed to assist me in killing Tharok. But he is... weakened. He recently exerted himself greatly in defending the Ascendant's life."

"How noble, I'm sure," said the man with something of a sneer. "Come. I am uniquely suited to help you regain your strength." He gestured at the black table.

Every instinct told Asho to refuse the man's invitation, to insist that Audsley remove them from this stark, barren room. It was clean but very cold, and it had the look of frequent usage; there were manacles on the stone table, and Asho thought he heard a low moan filter through the gloom of one of the corridors, as if it had been exhaled by the darkness itself.

"I won't be bound," he said.

"You are here of your own free will, are you not?" Athanasius smiled without warmth. "Thus, we will not need the restraints."

"And who does?" Asho's hand remained on the hilt of his sword. "What do you do here?"

Audsley was looking increasingly discomfited. "This is, ah, well, an unspoken-of aspect of the Ascendant's Empire. But a critical element. It is here that the black potions which fuel the Virtues are made. It's unsavory, and I don't like it, but now it serves our purposes."

"The black potion," Asho said softly. "The one the previous Grace drank on the battlefield."

"Yes," said Audsley. "Quite so. But, please, Asho. We haven't much time. All will be answered to your satisfaction after our deed is done. I swear it. Will you lie down?"

Asho considered the magister. The haunted look in his face changed him greatly. Gone was the effusive, charming, bumbling man Asho had known all his life. Audsley had lost weight, and his cheeks sagged ever so slightly. His skin was nearly gray with exhaustion, but it was in his eyes that the change was most evident: they were without light, without the gleam of humor and good will.

"If you think it best, Audsley," Asho said, moving to sit on the table's edge. The stone was even colder than the rest of the room, and it seemed to suck the vitality from him.

"Unfortunately, I do. It's for the good of the people. I swear it."

Asho nodded and, without unbuckling his sword, lay down in the slight groove in the surface of the table that was clearly meant to accommodate his body. Then he stared up at the rock ceiling. There, patterns of light from the candles flowed and ebbed into each other, creating subtle gradations of gold upon the stone.

"Now," said Athanasius. "You are a Flame Walker. You derive your power from the Black Gate, which is, as we all know, shut. Hence your need for gate stone to work your magic."

"Not just gate stone," said Asho. "I can drain power directly from demons, killing them in the process."

Audsley and Athanasius both froze.

"P-p-pardon, Asho?" said Audsley. "Drain? Demons?"

"Yes," said Asho, feeling quite matter-of-fact about it. "If they are within a human host or object. I've done it three times now."

"Really?" Athanasius exhaled, betraying emotion for the first time. "That is most fascinating. And how is this effected?"

"I thought we were in such a rush that we had to skip the explanations," said Asho. "Is that no longer the case?"

"After, then," said Athanasius. "You will come and visit? Stay for a while?"

Asho laughed humorlessly. "I think not."

Athanasius and Audsley exchanged a look, and then Athanasius continued. "Your exceptional abilities aside, most Flame Walkers are reliant on gate stone. Simply chewing it, however, is of limited benefit. We have discovered a means to deliver its benefits in a concentrated manner."

Asho listened, his uneasiness growing. "Oh?"

"Yes," said Athanasius. "We have perfected a means of refining gate stone into these." He drew forth a foot-long spike of black stone. "Once driven through your body, it will release magic into your system in great quantities but at a steady rate. This is, of course, a great advantage when compared to our potions; drinking one such would overload you with an immediate boost of power that might not only overwhelm you but also expend itself in a matter of minutes. "

Asho sat up. "You're going to punch a spike of stone into my body."

Athanasius nodded. "It isn't as ghastly as you think. The magic will heal you even as it does you damage; you will be able to pull the spike free when you are done, leaving behind only a minimum of scarification."

"Audsley?" Asho looked to his friend. "Is he telling me the truth?"

"Yes," said Audsley, his voice tight. "He is."

Asho stared at the spike of stone. "And why were these 'perfected'? To what end? Are the Virtues prone to hammering these into themselves?"

"No," said Athanasius. "They are not. And, as you remarked earlier, we are out of time. The procedure is a simple one. Shall we begin?"

Asho forced himself to breathe steadily. "Audsley?"

"Yes," Audsley said once more. "Trust me, Asho. This is necessary if we are to accomplish our mission."

Asho held the magister's gaze. His every instinct bade him hop down from the table. Up until this moment, he would have trusted Audsley with his life. But this other man standing beside him...?

Asho gave a tight nod and lay back down. "Be done with it, then."

Athanasius smiled and spent a few moments tapping at Asho's chest, feeling between his ribs just above his heart and below his clavicle. Then he raised the spike and placed its point against Asho's flesh.

It took all of Asho's self-control to lie still. He felt sick. The prospect of having twelve inches of black rock plunged into his body elicited a visceral desire to twist away.

Instead, he forced himself to watch as Athanasius raised a mallet high overhead. Asho was breathing quickly, his whole body fighting the waves of nausea that the tension was stirring up from his core. His skin crawled, his stomach clenched.

Athanasius brought the mallet down hard.

The spike plunged into Asho, and every muscle in his body clenched and spasmed. He sat bolt upright, rigid as a board, and couldn't scream, couldn't even breathe. He stared straight ahead, his hands locked into claws, his heart swelling as if it were about to burst.

Pain flooded through him. It was as if his body had been covered in a single giant scab and, with one swift movement, Athanasius had torn it right off. He felt raw, wounded, exposed, every part of him throbbing and aching as if he'd been thrown into a cauldron of boiling water.

Hands pressed him back to the table.

"Asho! Asho? Asho, can you hear me? Asho!" The voice came from far away.

He was falling into an abyss without end. His lungs were burning. His heart had yet to beat. His head felt as if it were swelling, about to rupture. He saw nothing but dancing motes of purple, blue and crimson.

A drum was being pounded within his depths, something ancient and terrible, summoning the world to war. It grew louder with each new beat, as if some fell herald were approaching through the darkness, its appearance presaged only by the sound of its drum. Closer and closer, louder and louder, till Asho's mind was shaking with the power of the cadence. The beat grew faster, racing toward a crescendo, and he thought he could hear wailing, could hear the cries of all the people who had been left bereaved across all the years by war.

Just as Asho thought he could take no more, a final almighty beat of the drum caused his heart to unlock, to stutter back into life, and he inhaled with a raw, wounded gasp, filling his parched lungs with air.

Wheezing, he rolled over to his side, then crawled off the table and fell to his knees. He didn't know where he was going, but he was impelled to move. Pain drove him with furious lashes. He kept crawling, but there was no escaping the white star burning inside his breast, a star that poured an endless flood of power into his core and threatened to overwhelm him.

Asho climbed to his feet, swaying, and let out a cry from the depths of his soul. It raged out of him as if he were giving birth to a storm, growing louder and louder, and when he could scream no more, he fell back to his knees and hung his head.

All he could focus on was breathing, on one ragged inhalation after another. Finally, with that dread star still burning in the fabric of his being, he lifted his head, his hair cascading over his face, and looked around.

The walls, ceiling, and floor of the chamber had ben riven by cracks. It looked as if each surface was a pane of glass that had been dropped flat onto the ground. The ponderous table had collapsed into five huge chunks. The cabinets hung askew from the walls.

Athanasius was slowly climbing to his feet, his eyes badly bloodshot, blood running from his nose and ears. But Audsley was standing still, eyes closed, arms crossed before his face, apparently unhurt.

Asho looked down. Two inches of black spike emerged from just below his clavicle. There was no blood. It felt like the terminus of a towering waterfall, pouring and pounding into his body without surcease. Carefully, Asho raised his left arm and worked it around. His muscles tugged and tore around the spike, but immediately healed.

Audsley opened his eyes. "That was... unexpected."

"It worked," said Asho.

He felt febrile. It wasn't the incipient madness that he'd nearly succumbed to before the Black Gate, or the overwhelming rush of intoxicating power he'd derived from the demons he'd absorbed; it was, instead, an ongoing burn, an endless smolder that he yearned to extinguish by draining the spike of its power.

"Asho," said Audsley, taking a step forward. "Are you...?"

Asho flexed his hands and hunched his shoulders. "Hurry. Now, while this power sustains me. Take me to Tharok."

Audsley nodded. "Very well. Come. Take my hand."

Asho did so with his left hand as he drew his blade with his right. Without thought, without effort, it burst into black flame.

"We don't know where he is," said Audsley. "We're going to have to hunt him down."

Impatience tore at Asho. It was all he could do to stand still. "Then, begin."

Athanasius was panting, leaning against the ruins of the table. Asho raised his blade and pointed it at the man. Athanasius blanched and stumbled back, and then the world was gone.

A moment later, they were high above an ocean. The sky was a limitless blue, the air around them warm, and spires and towers of salt-crusted white rose beneath them. Slender bridges connected the the towers, and a fleet of boats was bobbing on the waves half a mile out. Nous.

The Solar Portals rose in great arches on the central column, which was a hive of activity. Kragh were massed there in such numbers that they spilled over onto all the ramps and bridges that led to the Portals. Their attention was focused on the Portal to Ennoia. A half-dozen black-skinned kragh were directing their forces, bellowing out orders, but Asho could tell that none of them was Tharok. None of them was big enough.

"To Bythos!" he cried over the winds.

"I've never been!" replied Audsley. "We have to use the Gates!"

Asho released Audsley's hand. It felt beyond divine to burn his energy, to work at breaking the fever. He dove down toward the Portals, his sword streaming black flames behind him. Oh, how tempting it was to unleash his vengeance upon these kragh, to lay about him with flame, to burn their ranks to cinders.

But no. This wasn't the time.

Asho gritted his teeth and held back his magic. Instead, he swooped down over the heads of the kragh, moving so quickly that even as they roared and pointed at him, he was gone. The great Portal to Bythos was looming above him, and then he punched through its center at full speed, and the world fell away once more.

A blink, a wretched spasm of the void, and he was home. He burst out through the Portal into the great cavern of Bythos and out over the kragh army. It spread before him over the badlands, a huge gathering that dwarfed his imagination. So many. So many! Surely, the Empire could never stand against such a mass?

They were parting, however. Hurrying away to the sides, opening great passages through their center, down which monsters were undulating.

Asho recognized them at once.

Cavekillers.

Once, as a boy, he'd actually heard the rattling thrum of a cavekiller moving through the walls of a cavern. He'd taken Shaya's hand, and they'd fled for their lives. The sighting of just one of these monsters had always become the subject of legends, the cause for great hunts, a source of tales for decades.

But here, now, spilling forth from the distant archway above the Abythian Labyrinth, flowed scores of them. Their legs were scythes that rippled as they swarmed forward, their stone carapaces gleaming dully under the light of the *aurora infernalis*. Their maws were flanked by huge, curved blades that functioned as mandibles. They varied in size from some that were only the length of a couple of horses to truly monstrous elders that were dozens of yards long.

"By the Ascendant," Audsley whispered, hovering beside Asho. "What has he done?"

"If they get through the Portal into Ennoia," said Asho, "it's over. It's all over."

"We have to kill him," said Audsley. "Break his control over their minds."

The fevered power coursing through him snapped Asho back into action. He searched the kragh, ignoring the closest ones who were sounding the alarm, pointing at him with their weapons and talons.

There.

Tharok was standing amidst his commanders and warlords. A head taller than even the biggest of the other kragh, he was staring at Asho and Audsley. The light of the aurora was glimmering on his circlet and gleaming down the length of his vast blade.

Asho grinned. Nothing would help Tharok now. Nothing would save him from the Black Gate's purifying fire. With a great cry of rage, he flew forward, summoning his power, stoking it till it was screaming for release.

He dimly sensed Audsley flying just behind him, straining to keep up.

Tharok roared, and his commanders scattered. He then unclasped his great cloak and threw it aside, took hold of War Breaker in both hands and charged toward Asho, his huge strides eating up the ground.

Asho put on a burst of speed, skimming five yards above the ground.

This was the moment the war would end. This was the moment the kragh would be rebuffed. The cavekillers would turn upon the kragh the second Tharok was killed. This was Asho's chance to save Kethe and everyone else he loved.

Tharok let out a deep roar and leaped. He soared up with impossible power, his huge black scimitar raised over his head.

Asho yelled and brought his blade around, channeling black fire down its length. A plume of ebon fire boiled forth, engulfing the kragh warlord.

Tharok brought his scimitar down and cut the flames in half, and they peeled away on either side of him.

That same down stroke was about to cut Asho in twain.

Asho threw himself aside. Such was his speed that his loss of control sent him tumbling through the air. He lost control, fell, and plowed a furrow through the dirt and rocks, pain lancing through him as he came to a sprawling stop.

But the white star burning in his heart wasn't done with him yet. Power flooded through him, healing his wounds, mending his bones. With a cry, he forced himself to sit up, levering himself out of the rubble.

Audsley was flitting around Tharok, who was turning where he stood, batting aside bolts of black fire with his blade. The scholar was too high up for Tharok to attack.

Groaning, Asho flew up. He had to press the attack. If the two of them could flank the kragh, one of them would be able to incinerate him.

Asho flew forward, but Tharok saw him coming.

The kragh whipped around, spinning in a complete circle, and then hurled his scimitar up through the air at Audsley. It flew so fast that the magister had no time to react. The scimitar cleaved into his side, going deep, and Audsley screamed and fell from the sky.

"Audsley!"

Asho flew at Tharok, who turned now to await him, head lowered, tusks bared.

"Damn you!" Hatred tore through Asho, a black desire to negate everything this kragh had done, to undo all the pain and misery and loss. He raised both hands before him and channeled that raw fury through his arms, unleashing a final, cleansing torrent that would leave nothing of this kragh behind but ash.

Tharok closed his eyes.

A moment before the flames would have washed over him, he extended his hand, palm outward, and a white candleflame flickered into being before it. Then his eyes snapped open wide, and the light flared out in all directions, curving back and around him to form a sphere that rebuffed Asho's attack.

Asho's mind reeled. *What? Impossible!* He drank deep of the spike's power, siphoning more and more from its burning core, and unleashed it in a continuous roar of flame that swirled and poured around the kragh warlord.

Asho felt his palms beginning to burn, saw the rock around the kragh's feet glisten and begin to run.

"Die!" Asho's scream was barely audible over the crackle of the flames. "Die!"

The black flames weren't touching the warlord, and each passing second drained Asho further. With a cry of frustration, Asho cut off his attack. They flickered in a final wreath around Tharok's white sphere and then were gone.

Tharok straightened, and the sphere disappeared. The kragh gazed down at his palms, then up at Asho, grinning.

"Fuck you," said Asho, lowering himself to the ground. "I'll do this the old-fashioned way."

Tharok spoke, his voice as deep as the caverns. "You are worthy, Bythian. But I am greater. Your mind is mine."

Asho didn't try to make sense of the kragh's words. A true knight might allow the kragh to fetch a weapon, but Asho was long past caring about such niceties. Wielding his blade with both hands, he closed in on the kragh, who again extended his palm toward Asho.

Asho slowed, unsure, half-expecting a bolt of white flame, but instead he felt as if a massive hand had closed around him, as if a great, invisible fist were seeking to crush him.

Asho came to a stop. He gritted his teeth, but he couldn't take another step forward.

Then, abruptly, he was not alone within his own mind. Another presence manifested itself. Something was fumbling to get a grip on his thoughts, to connect with him. Like a burglar trying an endless set of keys, searching for the correct one with which to unlock Asho's very being.

Human, he heard the strange presence muse. *Complex, irate, furious, passionate. Weak. Multitudes, vast, teeming multitudes in hive-like cities, ruled by their intelligence as much as their passions. A spectrum of capacities, an endless array of capabilities and potential. The desire for power, for sex, for fine objects, rich clothing, land, castles, dominion over others... but tempered by compassion — no, a love that extends only to their immediate clan. Their inner circle. Brutal like trolls, tender like lovers, geniuses with no appreciation for anything beyond their own cravings...*

Claws were being driven into his mind, were tearing his very essence open. Into those gaps flowed an entity that seemed very much like himself, seeking to slip into his body like a hand into a glove.

Asho strained against it. Terror beat at the walls of his mind. The voice was growing ever more specific as it examined him and read his nuances.

...Furious and bitter from a lifetime of mistreatment, of abuse. A former slave, a pretend-knight, an outsider who hated himself for wishing so strongly to be like his own oppressors... A shaman — no, a magic wielder, a Flame Walker, whose own powers set him farther apart... Asho. His name, his identity, his love twined with bitterness... for another, a female, his mate. Her name, her name...

Asho cried out and forced himself to take a step forward. Tharok was but six yards away and unarmed. Asho's blade was held tight in his right hand. Six yards, and he could cut the warlord down. But that voice was insinuating itself ever deeper.

Sweat dripped from his brow and ran between his shoulder blades. His muscles were burning from strain. To his horror, Asho saw his sword arm rise of its own accord, his wrist twisting so that the length of the blade was angled to cut into his thigh.

NO! His own voice was a visceral cry. *I will not be controlled! I will be nobody's slave, not now, not ever again!*

With a cry of agony, he straightened his sword and took a step, then a second, toward Tharok.

Impressive force of will. Yet he calls on rage for power, a source we can bend to our own use. Asho, it has been too long since a mortal has contended with me in such manner. I salute you.

That wasn't the kragh speaking, Asho thought desperately. Its tone was cold and horrifying, as if the darkness between the stars had been given voice. He watched his blade turn toward him again, clutched in a trembling hand, but this time it was parallel with his throat.

Audsley appeared right behind Tharok, hovering in mid-air, his front drenched in blood where the scimitar was still embedded, and stabbed a dagger into the side of Tharok's neck.

Tharok roared, and his grip on Asho's mind broke.

Asho nearly collapsed, caught himself, and threw himself forward to attack.

Tharok had the presence of mind to grip the hilt of his blade and tear it free as he leaped up and back. Asho's blade cut through where the kragh had been standing a second too late.

Audsley collapsed to the ground with a groan.

Tharok landed a dozen yards away. He reached up and pulled the dagger free, and blood flowed from the wound. Audsley hadn't severed or punctured anything vital; instead, he'd stabbed into one of the mighty muscles that corded the kragh's neck.

"Audsley!" Asho knelt by the magister, eyes on the kragh.

"Go," said Audsley. He coughed up a fistful of blood. "I'm quite well, I assure you. Healing. Even. As I speak."

Asho nodded and rose to his feet. He leveled his blade at Tharok. "Time to die, warlord."

They were ringed in by hundreds of kragh, all of them standing a good thirty yards away as if they were afraid of being immolated by stray flames. None of them made any move to interfere.

Asho stalked forward, Tharok warily giving ground, the huge Solar Portals rising behind him.

The cavekillers, Asho saw, had reached the Bythian Portal. As he watched, the first of them poured into the white flames and disappeared.

Chapter 35

The he cheers had died away. The ranks of soldiers, archers, crossbow men and ballista operators now stood in silence. The caws of the ravens and crows were growing louder as the birds descended upon the mounds of kragh dead. The beating of their wings as they landed and hopped from limb to chest to head was such that the kragh themselves seemed to move, restless in death.

Nobody spoke, because the premonition had been shared by all. The ebullience of their victory had given way to the grim realization that the kragh would not give up so easily. That they had yet to see Tharok's master stroke.

Kethe had waved her arbalists back to their original positions, and they now were flanking Elon's monster ballistae. Sergeants were repositioning soldiers to cover attacks from all the Gates. Young boys were moving down the lines, buckets of water hanging from straps around their shoulders, offering leather cups to the men.

The sun had cleared the eastern roofs and now lit the killing field with sickening clarity. Smoke was rising from the fired trenches, along with the sickening scent of burnt flesh.

Kethe's blade was at her side. She had allowed the white fire to extinguish itself. She felt light on the balls of her feet, restless, impatient, hollowed out by a growing fear. The longer she and her forces watched the burning Portals, the greater grew her dread. Surely, they hadn't won? It couldn't have been this easy. This neat. This painless.

Distantly, she wondered how long they should wait before they sent scouts out to collect the arrows.

"Steady," called Elon. "Ease those fingers off the release. I don't want you firing at shadows."

Suddenly, shouts of alarm came from the rooftops. Kethe tensed, but she couldn't see the base of the Portal beyond the mounds of dead that lay before it. Arrows sliced down from above, but something was wrong.

The shouts weren't ones of alarm. They were shouts of fear. No — terror.

The arrows continued to rain down, but no screams sounded from their targets. Fierce impatience coursed through Kethe. She ran forward ten steps and leaped up onto the first retaining wall, craning her neck to see what was happening.

The largest mound of the kragh dead was nearly six yards high. She'd thought that that was the most horrific thing she might ever see in time of war, but when the whole mound shifted and trembled, she revised her opinion. The mound seemed to rise and writhe at the same time, blackbirds lifting with angry caws.

Then the front slope burst outward, and *something* emerged from beneath. Kragh corpses tumbled or were flung aside by the eruption of a massive snake — no, some hellish, demonic insect. Men around her cried out in shock and horror as the monster reared up for a moment, dozens of scissor-sharp legs feeling at the air, mandibles as big as long swords flexing.

A monstrous centipede, as wide as a cart and who knew how long, most of its body still hidden beneath the dead kragh.

"Release!" shouted Elon.

The monstrous ballista kicked back furiously as it unleashed its huge spear. The bolt punched into the monster's underbelly with such force that it was knocked onto its back, legs flailing frantically as it writhed around the bolt, slicing the haft into splinters.

But the damage was terrible, the sweeping guards having nearly severed the monster in half. It spasmed, then slowed and stopped and, with a twisted, unnatural cracking sound, it turned into gray stone and sank heavily onto the pile of dead beneath it.

Kethe forced herself to exhale and looked behind her. Most of her men were stunned. Elon, however, was shoving at his operators, forcing them to begin loading the next bolt.

"They can be killed!" she shouted at them. "They can die! Don't lose hope!"

The sickening sound of bodies being sheared through caused her to spin around. A second monster had erupted from beneath the dead, only to dive back down, its segments blurring as it dug through the corpses and into the very ground itself. Someone cried out, arrows fell upon its stone carapace and bounced off, and one of the smaller ballistae fired a second bolt which missed, disappearing between the Portals.

"Prepare yourselves!" cried Kethe, watching the bulge that signaled the monster's approach as it seemed to swim beneath the ground, dislodging corpses and punching through trenches. "Crossbows, aim for its stomach!"

A third monster scuttled over the dead, its legs churning and chopping the flesh of the corpses beneath it, only to dive down a moment later and disappear.

Three, thought Kethe. *Let there be no more!*

The bulge burst only ten feet before her, and a man in the ranks let out a shrill scream of fear: "Cavekiller!"

Kethe saw a forest of sword-blade legs, an articulated, creamy white underside crisscrossed with slender tubing just beneath a thick skin, the edges of a stone carapace, and then the creature's mandibles opened wide as it fell upon her.

Kethe threw herself to the right in a dive, hit the ground with her shoulder and came up staggering as the retaining wall exploded. Crossbow quarrels ricocheted off the monster's dull gray carapace and its helmeted head. It moved with terrible speed, swarming forward even as the men broke ranks to get away from it.

They weren't fast enough. The cavekiller overran some five or six men, not bothering to attack them but simply shredding them with its passage, legs cutting through bone as easily as flesh.

Elon was shouting and hauling on the ballista as he sought to swivel it around on its stand. Half his team was scattering, jumping down off the platform, but the others were putting their shoulders to the mechanism, bringing the ballista around — but it was too slow.

"Elon!" screamed Kethe, running toward the beast. She could feel the panic enveloping the ranks around her as more of the cavekillers came through the Bythian Portal. "Elon, get out of there!"

The blacksmith released the ballista and instead hauled up its huge spear, balancing it on his shoulder, then turned clumsily to face the cavekiller.

The cavekiller reared up once more, its stone segments sliding smoothly over each other's edges as it lifted five yards off the ground to face the ballista's side.

Kethe leaped. Desperation and fear gave her strength, and she soared up to land on its back to find its carapace strangely slippery, like a wet marble floor. But her balance was exquisite. She ran up its shifting spine, blazing sword in hand, as Elon bellowed his defiance and hurled the ballista spear from overhead with both hands.

Its massive, leaf-shaped head plunged into the cavekiller's maw, and the monster's body shuddered from the impact. Then it fell like a collapsing wave onto the blacksmith and was gone from sight.

Kethe screamed, imagining the worst, and shoved the tip of her sword into the cavekiller's back, cutting through its stony hide with ease. Still running, she dragged her blade up the length of its spine, parting it as she went, going faster and faster till she reached its head, where she flicked her sword through the first foot of its skull, then leaped, spinning, to land in a crouc h, having cut through its head all the way from back to front.

She almost fell, caught herself, turned, and saw the cavekiller turning to stone. Its head was nearly split in two, the huge shaft of wood reduced to fragments, the spearhead embedded in the monster's petrified face.

Kethe let out a cry of victory that immediately died in her throat.

More cavekillers were coming through the Portal. The killing field was trembling with subterranean passage. The soldiers manning the ballistae fired huge bolts whenever the cavekillers emerged from below, and Kethe saw one slam into a monster's side, knocking it over, legs flickering as it fought to right itself only to turn to stone a moment later.

But, oh, by the Seven Virtues and the White Gate, there were too many of them to defeat.

The soldiers and crossbow men were being massacred. They had nowhere to flee; the streets were barricaded. Instead, they surged around the perimeter of the square, shoving at each other and screaming as the cavekillers dove through their ranks, leaving furrows of the mangled and dying behind them.

"Stand and fight!" she screamed, running forward, blade raised.

The sight of her white flame caused some of the men to rally and run toward her, but not enough of them heard her call. Here and there, she saw other Consecrated trying to repel the cavekillers, but they were too few, and their skills were unequal to the task.

A cavekiller punched into the side of a building, clawing its way through the wall, and crawled inside. Kethe stumbled to a halt, unable to tear her eyes away. It wormed its way up from floor to floor, sending out plumes of dust and shattering windows as it went, and a few seconds later it emerged onto the roof, floundering as the floor gave way beneath it but still surging forward to dive amongst the archers.

Men screamed and leaped off the building; others turned to fire point-blank at the monster, to little effect. In a matter of moments, nearly a hundred archers had been killed.

They'd lost, Kethe realized with despair. Tharok had unleashed a weapon against which they had no defense. Men were gathering about her, crying out questions, huddling in close, but she didn't know what to tell them, how to direct them.

More cavekillers were coming through the Portal. They were undulating and burrowing through the breadth of the square, what had to be a dozen of them now. Her soldiers were being torn apart, their plate armor as little defense against those wicked blades as cloth. Their screams were hideous.

"The Empire has fallen," she whispered.

"What, my lady?" A man stepped up alongside her. He was wearing the insignia of a captain; his face was broad and ugly, and he looked like nothing so much as a frog.

She regarded him, unsure how to respond, and then saw Elon climbing back up onto his ballista. The blacksmith's left leg was strangely twisted, but he wasn't letting that stop him.

"To the ballista!" she yelled. "Help Elon turn that bastard around and load it up!"

"Aye, that's more like it," said the frog-faced man with a grin. "Come on, lads! Let's ram a bolt home for old time's sake!"

He led some twenty of the soldiers running toward Elon, leaving Kethe to face the battlefield alone.

She had to act. She had to impose her will upon the chaos and bloodshed around her. She was the last Virtue.

"My soul to the White Gate," she murmured, then, taking a deep breath, thinking of all the friends and companions who had fallen along the way, she cried out, "My soul to the White Gate!"

And, sighting the largest cavekiller as it came surging through the dead straight toward her, she raised her burning blade and charged.

Chapter 36

The Bythian warrior rose to his feet, burning blade held before him. Tharok felt a swelling emotion that he could only call pleasure; in this, he could lose himself – in this contest of might, of the will to live, to win. Let all the complexities of circlet and identity fall away. Let the doubts and fears, the rage and impotence, become as naught. There was in this fight a purity that simplified him to one thing, and one thing only: a warrior.

World Breaker was light in his hand. It pumped strength into him, allowing him to ignore the wound the dark-skinned human had inflicted on his neck. It made him feel invincible, made him want to charge the Bythian and tear him asunder with his claws. But Tharok was wise now to the dangers of the blade: it granted strength, but not immortality, and so he waited, watching the slender human as he came charging.

The circlet urged him to do otherwise: to retreat amongst his warriors, to summon Kyrra's shamans, to tilt the odds in his favor so as to defeat this human as quickly and safely as possible. But something within Tharok relished the danger. Wanted him to risk himself. He'd tried to break free of the circlet's influence and had failed. Perhaps this was another way.

The Bythian leaped at the last moment. He soared high into the air and then fell upon Tharok with lightning speed, his blade scything down with wicked strength. Tharok swung World Breaker up from the hips with both hands, striking at the Bythian's weapon. Black sparks flew in every direction, and the sheer force of Tharok's parry sent the human crashing to the ground, off-balance.

Tharok was instantly upon him, wielding World Breaker with impossible finesse, attacking the human from all angles. Yet, somehow, the Bythian regained his feet, deflecting left, right, above and below, dancing faster than Tharok could follow.

A line of fire opened up on Tharok's thigh. He hadn't seen the blade slip past his defenses, but it cut deep even as the Bythian spun away.

Tharok fell back with a growl as the wound began to seal. He bared his tusks, waiting to see the Bythian's dismay, but, instead, the man lifted his palm and blasted Tharok with black fire.

Tharok grunted and threw up his white shield, summoning the alien song from his depths, allowing it to envelop him, but a split second later, the fire was gone and the Bythian was again upon him.

A feint.

Tharok laughed in pleasure, stumbling back as the man alternated his attacks with quick bursts of fire.

He was skilled; Tharok would give him that much. But in the end, he was still just a human.

Tharok waited, biding his time, and the next time the human unleashed a blast of fire, Tharok slammed his fist right through the conflagration, burning his hand and arm but catching the human in the face.

The Bythian's features crunched beneath Tharok's knuckles, and the force of the blow knocked the man off his feet. But the warrior had the presence of mind to turn his fall into flight, lifting up before he hit the ground.

Tharok roared and leaped before the Bythian could rise out of reach. He smashed World Breaker down with a two-handed blow. The human blocked it, but the force of the attack sent him crashing back down to the ground.

Tharok landed heavily beyond him, turned, and sensed the dark-skinned human materializing behind him just in time. With a grunt, he ducked, expecting a second dagger blow. Instead, flames washed over him, scorching his back and torching his leather armor. When he wheeled, World Breaker screaming around to take the human's head off, the man was already gone.

The Bythian climbed back to his feet. Tharok caught his balance and saw the man's features knitting themselves back into shape. *Damn.* The Bythian could heal too. Tharok's chagrin turned to grim satisfaction. *Good.* This would make the battle more interesting.

With a battle cry, Tharok attacked. Their blades shot up heated flashes of fire whenever they met. The Bythian wasn't strong enough to go toe-to-toe for long; Tharok could feel him weakening, could sense his blade beginning to bend beneath World Breaker's assault.

Tharok drove him on, blow by bloody blow. The Bythian's face was drawn into a mask of determination and pain, but he refused to give up.

The dark-skinned human appeared in the air above Tharok and immediately unleashed a wave of fire upon him.

Tharok cursed and threw up his left hand, releasing his double hold on World Breaker, summoning his shield of white light even as he continued to attack the Bythian.

But the dark-skinned human didn't let up. If anything, he doubled the might of his attack, the heat of his black fire so intense that the rocks around Tharok's feet began to glisten and Tharok's hide began to scorch despite the shield's protection.

The Bythian screamed, "Now! Everything you have!" and leaped forward.

Tharok was forced to give ground, his entire left hemisphere bathed in flame, blocking and parrying with World Breaker as best he could as the Bythian's attacks grew faster and faster.

This had to end. Summoning his reserves, Tharok hacked with all his strength at the Bythian's blade. He sheared right through it. Its black fire went out.

But instead of giving ground, the Bythian flew straight at Tharok and caught him around the waist. Such was the force of his attack that he lifted Tharok clear off the ground, his shoulder colliding with Tharok's stomach with tremendous force.

The Bythian carried him through the air, and before Tharok could react and bring down World Breaker, they both passed through the Portal to Ennoia.

The darkness screamed all around them, seeking to pour into the very marrow of Tharok's bones, and then they were through, into the light of the morning sun.

They flew in a straight line, right into a pile of corpses. Tharok grunted, slammed the pommel of World Breaker into the side of the Bythian's head, grasped him by the belt and hurled him away.

Groggy, he gained his feet on the treacherous slope and clambered to the top of the hill of dead. Ennoia. He gazed out over the great square and saw little but destruction and death. He could sense the alien minds of the cavekillers as they tore through the humans all around him, obeying the circlet's will instead of their own primal instincts.

He bent down and picked up an ax. The humans' setup was impressive, but it hadn't been enough. Nothing could have resisted the cavekillers.

Tharok grinned. The easiest way to win a battle was to deploy a weapon the enemy couldn't counter, and the cavekillers were so utterly lethal that no force in the world could stop them.

The dark-skinned human appeared above him, arms extended to unleash more flame, but Tharok was ready. He hurled the ax. The human's eyes widened for a moment before he vanished.

The Bythian climbed into view. He looked haggard, lines of pain carved into his pale face, but there was no give in the man's expression. He'd die here if he had to.

"I salute you," said Tharok in the human language. "You are a warrior born. A pity I must destroy you."

The human had picked up a kragh ax, and, with visible effort, he bathed its twin moon faces with fire.

"Come," said Tharok. "Die with your Empire."

A massive object appeared in the sky above him. It was a vast machine, easily the size of a small house, a huge curved bow mounted across its front. The dark-skinned human was touching it with one hand and supporting a broad-shouldered human with the other.

The sheer implausibility of the sight gave Tharok pause. A monstrous ballista, twenty yards up in the sky. Aimed directly at him. The powerful human, clearly terrified, pulled the catch and loosed the bolt.

From directly above, it shot down right at him, a good three yards long, its head flaring out with twin blades of lethal sharpness.

Tharok threw himself aside. The bolt sank into the corpses where he'd been standing moments before, crashing all the way to the ground, rupturing and snapping into great pieces of wood, the two humans who had fired it already gone.

Tharok hit the ground, but before he could stand, the Bythian was there. Time seemed to slow. The head of the man's ax came inching around. Tharok screamed and tried to pull away, but it was too late. He was going to take the hit.

The blade connected with the side of his face, shearing through the corner of his jaw and cheekbone. His head snapped around, and, with a wrenching sense of loss, he felt the circlet fly from his brow.

Tharok fell onto the corpses, then rolled down a few feet to collapse to the dirt. Pain engulfed the side of his head even as World Breaker and his medusa-Kissed constitution fought to repair the damage. But worse, the circlet was gone. Panic seized Tharok. He couldn't sense the cavekillers.

Nauseated by the pain, reeling in shock, he forced himself to rise to his knees. The Bythian was marching toward him with grim finality on his face.

The dark-skinned human appeared to one side. He was mostly healed, the grievous wound that World Breaker had dealt him almost gone. He crouched on the ground and took up the circlet.

"No!" screamed Tharok, extending his hand. "No!"

The dark-skinned human stared down at the circlet. The Bythian had stopped his approach and was looking at his companion in confusion.

"Audsley?" the Bythian asked.

The dark-skinned man stood. He seemed unable to meet the Bythian's eyes. "I'm sorry, Asho," he said, and then he disappeared.

Chapter 37

Tiron and his dragon appeared in a bank of swirling colors. They were surrounded by a soft, velvety blue that darkened quickly into a lustrous purple, only for a large swath to their left to burn away into a deep forest green even as the right lightened into rosy flame.

Tiron tightened his grip on the dragon's horn. Some new part of the spirit world? An interstitial space between worlds? At this point, he was open to any possibility, but the dragon tilted its wings and they veered down, passing through the bright colors and then swooping down and out into clear air below.

Bythos.

The aurora was swirling just above their heads. Tiron saw the other three dragons gliding ahead of him, their tails undulating like vast ribbons, their wings extended, membranes bulging like ships' sails in a full wind.

His heart beat wildly with exultation. Never in his wildest dreams as a young knight had he imagined that one day he might experience such as this. The badlands of Bythos were spread out below them. They had to be hundreds of yards up in the air, skimming just below the aurora.

It was a breathtaking view. The blade towers speared up before them, their rusted spires cutting into the aurora. Down to the left lay the spread of tumbled white cubes of the Bythian slaves, a complex morass of narrow alleys and winding streets, the whole of it larger than Tiron would have ever suspected. Trails crisscrossed the badlands like old scars, while down to the right rose the Solar Portals, surrounded by a great mass of kragh.

Tharok's army.

Yet it was greatly diminished; Tiron leaned forward and with a seasoned eye estimated that only a little over a thousand of the kragh were standing below. Nor were they on the move; instead, they were standing to the sides, opening great channels between them to the Portals, and along these channels rippled insects of staggering size – monstrous centipedes of some kind that seemed to have crawled right out of a horrific nightmare.

KCHACK'ICK'ILL, said Draumronin, its voice carrying easily over the rush of the wind. **ROUSED BY THE MEDUSA. LET US DRIVE THEM BACK INTO THEIR BURROWS.**

The dragon dove. Tiron bit back a cry of alarm and grabbed the great beast's horn, clenching his thighs around the dragon's neck as he felt himself grow weightless, his body lifting as the dragon swooped down faster than Tiron could fall.

The other three were executing a similar maneuver. All four of them dove down toward the plain, which rushed up with dizzying speed; down and around the backs of the Solar Portals, leveling out at the last so that they were perhaps but fifteen yards above the ground. They spread out into a line, their wings beating powerfully to arrest their descent, sending huge clouds of dust billowing out over the gathered kragh.

Shaya's white dragon was the first to breathe its flame, issuing a virulent stream over the first cavekiller, which immediately curled into a tight sphere, its many legs hidden away within its stony carapace, its face hidden under the fan of its tail.

Ramswold's dragon followed right after, and its fiery breath caused the monster to sunder apart, its edges glowing white hot, only for the chunks to petrify where they lay.

Draumronin flew off almost lazily to sweep along the right flank of the approaching monsters. Looking ahead, Tiron guessed that some thirty or forty of them were scuttling forward from the Abythian labyrinth, moving with ease over the tortured rocks of the badlands.

He heard a great whistling indraft as his dragon opened its maw, felt the scales beneath him heat up, and then Draumronin blew forth a sizzling stream of fire which enveloped one of the monsters completely.

Tiron twisted about to look behind them as they flew over their prey - the ground about the monster was polished like smooth marble, while the monster was melted down the center as if it had been made of candle wax.

Tiron looked over at where Ramswold was riding Skandengraur and let out a whoop of victory, pumping his fist into the air. Ramswold did the same, and for a while they simply scoured the badlands, swooping down on the monsters and either immolating them or driving them to burrow deep into the rocky ground.

"Where is the medusa?" cried Tiron when the last of the monsters had been killed. "Can you sense it?"

YES, said Draumronin. It fought for altitude, its wide wings thrusting them up in spurts with each downbeat. The other three were also turning, Shaya's Rauda gaining height the quickest. They turned as one toward the blade towers.

There had to be about a dozen of them. They looked like a collection of wicked swords that had been left at the mercy of the elements for too long; pitted with rust, their black surfaces bubbled and cracked, they conveyed nothing so much as ruin and decay. Narrow windows pierced their sides, devoid of glass or shutters, and in one of these Tiron saw a burning ember of color.

THERE, said his dragon. **AVERT YOUR EYES.**

Tiron tried to, but the sight mesmerized him. Even as he turned his face away, he saw smoldering yellows and crimsons, a nude female torso with full breasts, an alien visage and writhing hair. Her eyes flared open, and Tiron screamed. He wrenched his head aside and threw up an arm to protect his face.

Tiron felt the dragon beneath him shudder, wings beating furiously as it arrested its momentum to hang with its body lifting and falling rapidly before the tower. He could hear the thunderous flapping of the other dragons close by, and then a voice cried out from the tower, powerful but tinged with fear.

"Stay your fire! This is another age, another time! I do not seek dominion as of old, but rather to serve the kragh, to empower them. I have followed Tharok's every command; why should I be punished for my obedience?"

It was Maur who responded, her voice rich with hatred and scorn, her words harsh in the language of the kragh. She spoke but four or five sentences, but in them Tiron heard a condemnation that transcended all language barriers.

THE KRAGH SPEAKS TRUE, said Skandengraur. **YOU ARE A BLIGHT UPON THEIR PEOPLE. YOUR VERY PRESENCE CORRUPTS. YOUR WORDS CANNOT ALLAY YOUR FATE.**

Tiron felt the scales beneath his legs heat up once more, and as a scream of denial rang from the window, all four dragons unleashed their flame upon the tower. Tiron gritted his teeth and squeezed his eyes shut, wanting desperately to look. The flames roared on and on, and finally he peeked through his fingers.

The ebon metal of the tower was glowing white hot. Huge dollops were running down its facade, the window itself having eaten away at its borders and expanded into a great, smooth-edged hole. Within that aperture stood the medusa, limned in fire, her scales incandescing as if the dragon fire were charging their hues with impossible brightness. Her eyes were beyond gold or silver, a reflective, mercurial gleam that caused shimmers to ripple up and down in front of her, forming a barrier against which the dragon fire was breaking.

Yet the concerted streams of dragon flame were overwhelming her resistance. With a shriek of rage, she slithered forward and dove from the window. Tiron gasped and leaned forward, staring down past his dragon's neck to watch as she fell. Her form changed as she did so, hardening, growing a dull gray, her arms melding together, her tail straightening out, her entire body smoothing over so that she was but a spike of stone when she hit the ground.

The sound of that impact was tremendous. A third of her form stabbed its way into the rock, opening a deep crack into which she lodged herself, then stilled. Tiron waited, expecting further change, but nothing happened. She remained in that form, lodged deep, frozen into a great sliver of rock.

"Is she dead?"

NO, said Draumronin. **SHE HAS ENTERED HER DEEP SLEEP FORM, RENDERING HERSELF NIGH INVUL-NERABLE TO DAMAGE. IN SUCH MANNER WILL SHE WHILE AWAY THE MILLENIA UNTIL SHE AWAKENS ONCE MORE.**

The four dragons were slowly gliding down, swirling almost playfully about each other, circling the spike until at last they landed. Tiron rose to his feet, balancing carefully, and then crouched and slid down the dragon's extended wing to the ground.

They gathered about the spike. A cold mist was oozing out of its surface. Although it was lightly scaled, Tiron could make out no distinguishing features. The medusa had encased herself in stone.

Maur spat on the spike, but, despite the ferocity of the gesture, her joy was unmistakable. Her lower jaw trembled, and tears flooded her eyes only to be dashed angrily as she proceeded to cover her face.

Shaya spoke to her cautiously in kragh.

Maur lowered her hands. Eyes wounded and raw, she replied, her voice firm once more. "She says that too many have suffered to achieve this victory. Too many died. Her heart is filled with sorrow over the faces she will never see again."

Tiron could well understand the sentiment. He'd experienced it himself too many times to count. Ramswold was nodding somberly, the elation of the dragon ride passing and leaving in its place the memory of those who had fallen.

"I know what you're feeling," Tiron said softly to him. "I used to feel it myself after a bad fight, one in which, by all rights, I should have died along with the rest. Many a time, I've stood after the battle was won and gazed out over the dead and dying, numb and sick, thinking: It's not bloody fair. By what right do I stand while better men were cut down?"

Ramswold nodded slowly. "Yes. You have the right of it."

"I wish I had some great and deep wisdom to share," said Tiron. "Some explanation as to why we were spared, a reason that might bring sense to this bloody folly. But, lad, there is none, and that's the worst of it. No justification. No reason why one man takes an arrow while a second is spared. Don't let your sorrow be tainted by guilt. Grieve for the fallen, but don't wish yourself amongst their number."

Ramswold looked up at the dragons that were positioned around them, who seemed to be listening with interest. "Yes. Perhaps. But even in this moment of greatest victory, I find myself sure that my Order of the Star is no more. Ulein. Isentrud. Siffrid. Pex. Petran. Stephke. Blasius. Vridel. Fickuld. Jocuf. Zeydl. Rudolf. All followed me into this quest. All lie dead, their bodies strewn from Abythos to the very shores of the Dragon's Tear."

Tiron went to interrupt, but Ramswold raised a hand, forestalling him. "I swore to Ulein that we were part of a greater quest, that our actions would save the Empire. And – they have. But at what cost? In the tales, the brave win through. They do not all die. My friends, my boon companions – slain and fallen." His face was riven by grief. "My victory has been a pyrrhic one. The Order is no more."

Tiron moved forward and lowered himself to one knee before the young lord. "That need not be so. I scoffed at your notions of knighthood when we first met. I was hard on you all this time. But would we be here now if it weren't for your ideals? Your bloody faith in something greater? No."

He looked down at his hands. It was all too easy to remember how they had been drenched in spirit blood, to recall lifting his blade under the shaman's compulsion.

"You're a good man, Ramswold." It took real effort to drag the words out. "You see the good in others, and inspire them to goodness in turn. I lost that somewhere along the way. Perhaps it was beaten out of me during my stay with the Black Wolves. But your ideals carried you and your men onward when others would have failed. The Order of the Star is a brave order, a noble one, and we cannot allow it to fade from this world. If you would have me, I would join it, though I once foreswore ever doing such a thing again."

Ramswold did not react at first, but then he drew his blade and lightly touched it to each of Tiron's shoulders. "I welcome you into the Order of the Star, Ser Tiron. I abjure thee to always fight for a righteous cause, to treat your fellow knights and the peoples of the Empire with courtesy, honesty, and fairness. To wield your blade only in service of justice, and to strive ever and always to uphold the highest ideals of an Ennoian knight."

Tiron felt a strange wrenching in his chest. He was becoming a soft in his old age. Or perhaps it was the fact that he was being knighted once more while four dragons looked on. Or that they had brought justice to the monster that had slain thousands at Abythos. Or that, after believing that the Empire was lost, he now could see how they would win.

"Thank you," he said, his voice gruff with emotion. "I swear to uphold the highest ideals of the Order with my life."

Tears filled his eyes, and he wiped them away in annoyance. But when he rose to his feet, both knees popping, he felt lighter, buoyed by a new conviction, a clear and simple certainty that he'd thought he'd never feel again. He'd continue to serve justice, but now he'd do it as a member of Ramswold's Order.

Shaya had been translating all the while to Maur, who now moved up to Flamska. The dragon lowered its head a fraction, emerald eyes glittering, and listened as Maur asked it a question.

"She wants to know if they will stay with us a little longer," said Shaya. "If they'll help us find Tharok and show him the error of his ways."

THE MEDUSA IS CONQUERED, said Flamska, and though its words seemed to echo in the center of Tiron's chest, there was in its voice a hint of humor, of kindness, that was lacking in his own black dragon's tone. **BUT WE SHALL ESCORT YOU WHERE**

YOU WISH TO GO, AND SERVE AS LIVING REMINDERS OF YOUR KIND'S TRUE SPIRIT.

Maur inclined her head and spoke again.

"She says there's one object that she would ask that they destroy," said Shaya. "The magic circlet that has guided Tharok. That if they could melt it down, she knows Tharok will come back to his old self and lead the kragh home, ending this war."

IT IS MORE PERILOUS THAN EVEN THE MEDUSAS, said Draumronin. **WITH IT, OGRI STOLE AWAY OUR BROTHER JAERMUNGDR. WE SHOULD BE GLAD TO SEE IT DESTROYED.**

Maur bowed this time and turned to the three of them.

"Tell her we would be honored to see this quest through," said Ramswold, his voice growing in strength. "And if the dragons will carry us, we shall ride them to Tharok and the Empire's relief."

Shaya did so, and Maur stepped forward and reached out to clasp Ramswold by the forearm in a warrior's grip. She said no words, but there was such a depth of emotion in her gaze that none were needed.

"Come," said Tiron, clapping on Ramswold on the shoulder as he stepped up to complete the square. A sharp, rich joy flooded through him, and he smiled openly at the others. "Let us find our warlord and put an end to this war."

Chapter 38

With a gasp, Audsley appeared on a balcony. The frenetic madness of war was cut away so dramatically that it was as if a guillotine had fallen, leaving only a sudden and vivid silence. For a long moment, he simply crouched, the fingers of one hand splayed on the black stone floor, the other clutching the iron circlet that Asho had knocked from Tharok's brow.

It was such a simple thing to look at. Unadorned in any fashion, it was plain and leaden-hued, yet surprisingly heavy. It gleamed sullenly in his hand, as if he was seeing it through darkness. Was it truly an artifact of such power?

"Magister Audsley," called the Minister of Perfection from below. "Have you accomplished your task?"

Audsley rose to his feet and stepped forward to the balcony's intricately wrought railing. He looked out over the vast hall at the apex of Starkadr, taking note of the ceiling, composed for the most part of large expanses of clear glass encased within organic curves of slender iron. Late afternoon light was pouring down through the thin cloud cover to illuminate the expanse of the room some thirty yards below.

It was exactly as he had seen it last, though it felt like a lifetime had passed since he'd walked here with Tiron and their guards. Pools of shallow water reflected the sunlight down the center of the hall, flanked on one side by a semicircular amphitheater, while on the other side sat a severe table of black stone long enough to seat fifty.

Corpses still lay strewn where they had fallen centuries ago, but Audsley's eye was drawn past them to the far end of the chamber, where broad steps rose and narrowed until they came to a point almost at the same height as his balcony. There, they culminated in a small space surrounded by windows, a bubble thrust out into the sky. The minister was rising from the stone throne that faced outwards, while Zephyr remained standing alongside the pedestal that rose before it.

"I have," said Audsley, too softly to be heard, so he called out once more, "I have!"

The last time he was here, he had descended the spiraling steps that led directly down to the floor; this time, he willed himself afloat and drifted forward into the air.

He could have teleported directly to the minister, but something within him recoiled at the idea. Instead, he floated slowly toward the man, circlet clasped in one hand, his jaw clenching and relaxing, clenching and relaxing.

The minister waited with barely concealed impatience. Zephyr was a shadow just behind him, her head lowered, eyes gleaming through her messy hair.

The Black Gate must be opened, thought Audsley. *Only then will the balance be returned to the world. Only then will creative energy once again suffuse the air, allowing Flame Walkers to partner with White Adepts, bringing wonder and equality back to the land.*

But no matter how fervently Audsley said these words to himself, he couldn't dispel his fear and unease.

"Come, Magister. My family has waited centuries for this opportunity," said the minister as Audsley drew close. "Do not test my patience by dawdling at the threshold of greatness."

Audsley alighted at the edge of the platform. All around them, the clouds floated, their majestic forms towering like anvils made of the softest cotton. The glass was iridescent and shimmered with subtle colors as the stonecloud flew forward.

Audsley wanted to lose himself in that abstract beauty, to not have to deal with the matter at hand.

Instead, he raised the circlet. "This," he said, "will help you open the Black Gate?"

"Yes, assuredly," said the minister. "Now, give it to me."

There was an eagerness to the man's voice, a hunger that caused Audsley to hang back. "And you will use its power only for the betterment of all?"

"Yes, Audsley. Does equality not suit you? You test my patience. Don't tell me you grow irresolute?"

Audsley looked past the old man to Zephyr. She stood as if she had been frozen, one hand extended to rest on the curved hemisphere atop the pedestal, a finger tracing the circular lip that ran around the hemisphere's base. Her face was expressionless, but her eyes gleamed as if she were fevered.

"What is it?" asked Audsley, his throat so dry he almost croaked. "This circlet. How will it open the Gate?"

"It is a key," said the minister.

"And what is the lock?"

"Everything. On the brow of the correct person, it can open all doors. Even one that was supposedly closed by a miracle, such as the Black Gate. Now, give it to me."

Audsley stared at the circlet. What if he were to slip it on himself? He raised it up with trembling hands, then hesitated.

The minister extended his hand.

Still, Audsley demurred. Did he trust this man? No. But what choice did he have? He was no longer living in a world of niceties and comfort. His innate trust in the goodness of the universe had been shattered. Everything the minister had said seemed irrefutable.

The fear drained from him, the doubt. He felt a leaden indifference settle onto his shoulders. He was but a tool, a means to a greater end. It was not the role of a cog to question the machine.

Do as you are bid, whispered the demon. **Give the minister the circlet.**

Audsley gave a jerky nod and stepped forward, extending the circlet, about to lay it on the minister's palm.

Then, from the shadows, came a flurry of wings. A small, bony shape with faded feathers darted forth, calling out with a *mhhrkao!* that shook Audsley to his core.

Aedelbert landed on the minister's outstretched arm and bit into the meat of his thumb. With a cry of rage, the minister backhanded Aedelbert and sent the firecat tumbling to the floor.

"Aedelbert," whispered Audsley. The indifference that had lain over him like a cloak shivered and broke.

No! screamed the demon. **Do as you are bid! You are mine!**

Audsley's body stilled as if it had been gripped by a mighty vice. He lost all control of his limbs and felt the demon swim forward and infest him like a hand might slip into a glove. Even as the demon forced his arm up, however, palm facing his firecat, Audsley heard a single indelible word echo up from the depths of his being.

No.

From his core swam up a bubble of independence, and, like a sunset bursting over the horizon, Audsley recalled the Ritual of Spiritual Recusal that Zephyr had taught him in that secluded glade in Aletheia. He had buried his own self-mastery so deep that not even his demons, not even he himself would recall that he was still in control until the very moment in which it was needed.

Mine! snapped the demon. **You are mine!**

"I am my own man," Audsley whispered, and his body was his own once more.

The minister let out a curse of frustration and snatched at the circlet in Audsley's hand even as the magister went to pull it away.

Audsley gripped tight and yanked back, then realized a simple truth: Ainos was not present. Both he and minister raised their free hands and engulfed each other in infernos.

With a cry, Audsley fell to the floor, his chest and stomach awash in searing pain. He felt his demons set to healing him, but it was all he could do not to scream in agony as he lay on his side, nearly tumbling off the top step to the hall below.

The minister lay still, his face reduced to charred bone. The circlet was spinning in place where they had dropped it, rotating in ever-quicker circles as it tipped down to the floor. Before it could settle and stop, Zephyr bent down and picked it up.

"Zephyr," groaned Audsley. "Don't. Don't put it on."

She turned it about in her hands, apparently mesmerized by the circlet's dull perfection. "Of course not," she whispered. "Oh, that this should come to me."

There was in her voice such a thrill that Audsley moaned again in terror.

Aedelbert crawled over to where he was lying. His firecat was almost skeletally thin, and his once glorious feathers were tattered and dull, but when he leaned forward to lick Audsley's cheek with a raspy tongue, the magister felt a surge of such love and strength that he levered himself up onto his elbow. "Zephyr. Please. Whatever you are thinking, don't do it."

She moved as if she were part of a dream to sit on the high-backed throne. Audsley could only see her profile from where he was lying as she sank gracefully onto its hard seat, the circlet held before her still.

"How many centuries has it been since this circlet was lost? Stolen by Ogri during the Order's attack, leaving it rudderless and bereft, doomed to float lost in the heavens for eternity. For it to return now, to me, here in the Hall of Guidance - ah, it is almost enough to make one believe in miracles."

Audsley's strength was recovering. He could hear his demons cursing him as they labored to undo the damage, to knit his flesh whole. "Zephyr!" He had to distract her. "Listen to me!"

But she paid him no heed. "To think that it should fall to me to activate the Apotheosis." She covered her mouth as a high-pitched giggle burst forth. "Me! Oh, glory, glory, glory. This is a far better fate. Oh, yes. Oh."

So saying, she extended her arms and lowered the circlet over the top of the pedestal, sliding it down till it was resting perfectly on the circular lip that girded the hemisphere's base.

Starkadr thrummed.

Audsley felt the stone beneath him shiver. The circlet blazed with a corona of black light that spiked and circled. Geometric patterns incandesced down the pedestal's length and shot out across the floor so that, briefly, the entirety of the hall was covered in bewildering lines of white flame which then faded away, leaving only the bare black stone.

Aedelbert scooted in close to Audsley, who placed his arm around the poor firecat's emaciated body. "Don't fear," he whispered, voice shaking. "I'm here, dear Aedelbert. I'm here."

Zephyr extended her hand so that it lay above the circling corona of flame, and then lowered it so that she was palming the top of the pedestal. Her hair immediately flared up as if she had been caught in a powerful wind, and her eyes blazed with light.

"Yes," she whispered, and her voice seemed to echo through the walls. "Let us go where my theatrics will find a fitting audience."

The thrum running through the walls and floor deepened with sudden violence, and Audsley felt a wrenching sense of dislocation as the void stole through his senses. Everything spun away into nothingness and then sprang back into being; now, the light coming through the glass ceiling overhead was different, and the anvil clouds had been replaced by wispy cirrus streaks across a new sky.

"Yes," whispered Zephyr. "Starkadr has stepped back onto the world stage for its final act."

"Zephyr," croaked Audsley, forcing himself to sit upright. "What are you doing? Stop, please!" But he knew that his pleas were falling on deaf ears.

He lifted his hand, willing black flame to spit forth, but nothing happened.

"Now," said Zephyr, her voice deepening with an almost sexual desire, "let us unleash chaos upon the world."

What is she doing? Why won't you do as I command?

She is undoing the world, said the demon within him. He couldn't tell which one had spoken.

Then – I grant you my soul! Take it, all of it! It's yours! Just help me slay her!

411

Fool, said the demon with withering scorn. **What value has your soul now in comparison to the miracle she is about to birth?**

Starkadr's thrum grew high-pitched, a whine akin to that of metal being wrenched out of form.

Aedelbert huddled back into the crook of Audsley's elbow. Together, they watched as black and white flame speared out in all directions from the hemisphere beneath Zephyr's hand.

Do you wish to see the wonder she has wrought?

I - yes.

Zephyr, the hall, the glass bubble and ceiling - all of it disappeared in a flash. In its place appeared a chamber so vast, it seemed more akin to Bythos' great cavern than any manmade space. A mile long? Perhaps more. All of Kyferin Castle could have been housed within its expanse. Its iron walls were carved with strange patterns incised deep into the metal, and its walls were segmented by the protrusion of huge columns whose bases extended out into the room like the buttresses of a cathedral.

Cubes of stone the size of houses emerged from the cavern's floor in the space between those extensions: blocks of stone without windows, doors, or features.

Audsley knew where he was. The basement of Starkadr, the prison of countless demons, the source of the stonecloud's power and flight.

"No," Audsley whispered, hugging Aedelbert tightly to his chest.

The moaning hum that he'd heard before was a dirge here, rising ever higher as if into a scream. The sides of the massive buttresses began to crawl with lines of fire. Encased within each side were fifty demons, Audsley recalled. Fifty plugs of lead inserted into the heart of terrible runes of warding and control.

There were twenty columns running down each side of the chamber, a hundred demons per column. Before Audsley's eyes, four thousand demons were emerging into the world.

Aedelbert chirped in fear and snuggled back into Audsley's arms, but Audsley had no comfort to offer, no solace to extend.

The first of the plugs cracked and fell free, hitting the ground seconds later with a resounding crash. A slender, grey-skinned figure floated out in a column of mist. A tail was wrapped around its thighs, and its wings were unfurling as gently as a newborn butterfly's.

Another crash, and a second plug fell, then a third. Soon, the great chamber was echoing with continuous destruction as thousands upon thousands of ancient cells were split open to disgorge their demonic occupants.

"Oh, Aedelbert," whispered Audsley. "Oh, my."

The larger cubes that ran down the length of the chamber were beginning to light up. These were fifty yards on a side, their surfaces rough with deeply carved runes, with a single vast plug placed in the center of their upper surfaces.

Mal'orem, whispered the demon, its voice turgid with ecstasy. **The dukes of our kind.**

Mal'orem, demons more powerful even than the dread lord that had assailed Mythgraefen during the Black Shriving.

There were twenty such cubes running down the center of the cavernous hall, each subtly larger than the previous one. Audsley saw at last the final cube at the very end of the hall, on which so long ago he had fought a demon and died.

"The *ur-destraas*," he whispered. Terror clawed at the foundations of his mind. "There has to be a way to stop this."

It is too late, gloated the demon. **The command has been given, and Starkadr obeys. Even the greatest of the seals will be torn asunder.**

With a reverberating crash, the first of the giant cubes fell asunder, huge chunks of stone like the innards of a three-dimensional puzzle falling mightily to the ground. Mist was exhaled from its center, where a being ten yards tall was floating up, arms crossed over a muscled chest of purest night, black flame cascading down from its shoulders like an infernal waterfall. It was foul to gaze upon. Its visage was twisted and hog-like, with small eyes that were still closed and twin bull horns emerging from its temples to spear wickedly forth. Its hands and feet were taloned, and even where Audsley was standing in the hexagonal passageway that led back to the airshaft, he could feel the heat washing off its body.

More cubes fell apart, the white lines spreading like wildfire from one to the next. Thousands of demons were coming to their senses along the sides of the room, where they hovered in front of buttresses that were now honeycombed with empty cells.

Their eyes were burning with inner fires, and, slowly, they all turned to stare at Audsley.

Aedelbert leaped up onto Audsley's shoulder, claws sinking through his burnt black robe, and hissed at the demons in defiance.

Audsley took a step back, but he couldn't leave. Not yet. He watched as the first lines of white fire appeared on the great cube at the very back of the room.

Demons were floating toward him, demons by the thousands.

The lines of fire were rising up the sides of the vast cube, blazing with unhallowed brightness.

Aedelbert beat his wings frantically, pulling at Audsley's shoulder, tenting the fabric of Audsley's robe as he sought to turn Audsley around.

Some morbid, horrified fascination was compelling Audsley to stand there, to see what would emerge from the depths of that final, dreaded cube. But Aedelbert's frantic *mrhaos* finally brought him to his senses.

Please. Transport me away from here.

Too late, said the demon. **You are to be their first taste of the new world. Release us, or we will multiply the torment you are about to experience from without a thousand-fold from within.**

The demons were drawing ever closer: a wall of wings and hungry, burning eyes, so many of them that he couldn't take them in without turning his head from side to side.

Release you? he asked, and sensed the demon's hesitation. What had Asho said about being able to kill demons while they were within a host? Were they vulnerable within him? *No.*

Release us! Your death is assured. Release us, and we will be the first to kill you. We will make your death a merciful one.

No, Audsley said, taking another step back.

The vast cube at the back of the room was now burning so brightly that the rear third of the chamber was lit up as if by the sun itself.

Release us, foolish mortal! Now!

I thought you were immortal, said Audsley. *But why spare you my fate? Die with me.*

The demons were flooding the entrance to the tunnel, blocking his view of the chamber beyond. Audsley gave way, hurrying back. They came on toward him, some of them crawling on each of the hexagonal tunnel's walls, others floating in the center. They could kill him in an instant, he knew, but they were fascinated by him, their lips drawing into caricatures of grins. They were experiencing consciousness again for the first time in millennia.

Very well! We will transport you to safety if you swear on all that you yet hold holy to release us immediately thereafter!

They could read his intentions, he reminded himself.

Yes, he thought. *Transport Aedelbert and myself to Iskra Kyferin, and I shall let you go free.*

Through the thick crowd of demons, he saw the *ur-destraas* cube start to fall apart in a blinding glory of light, but before he could make out what was emerging, the world swam in darkness, fell away into the void, and he was gone.

Chapter 39

The ground shivered. Iskra, exhausted, sat up straight, and the messenger standing in front of her desk faltered. For a moment, the iron braziers within her tent had danced, but now they settled and their flames began to burn calmly once more.

"What was that?" Iskra looked to Orishin, who shrugged.

Nobody spoke. Tóki the Hrething had half-drawn his ax from its loop at his hip, but after a moment he opened his hand, and it slid home.

"Weather, perhaps," said Orishin. "Perhaps we are sailing through a storm."

"Perhaps," Iskra said uneasily. In all her time in Starkadr, she'd never felt it stir. She gestured to the messenger and sat back. "Continue."

"I – yes. My apologies. Let me see where I was. *And thus... with greatest respect... unfortunate...* here." The gangly messenger cleared his throat almost violently and assumed a dramatic pose. "Lord Melchior concludes, *It is thus with tragic condolences that I, humble outcast that I am –*"

The ground shivered once more. Iskra's desk trembled, the braziers rocked, and from all across the refugee camp, she heard cries of surprise.

Iskra rose to her feet. Everyone had tensed and were looking warily about as if they were searching for the first hint of a great predator.

"That one was worse," said Orishin quietly. "I dare say -"

And again, the ground shook, this time with such violence that Iskra lurched forward onto her desk, her honeycombed scroll case toppled onto the floor with a crash, and a brazier rocked wildly back and forth before being caught by Tóki.

"To the Ascendant," said Iskra. Her heart was racing, and her body felt suddenly light, almost hollowed out by apprehension. "Commander Patash, begin an evacuation to Mythgraefen." But no one moved. "Now!"

Tóki rushed ahead of her, opening the tent flap. From all around, she could hear men crying out prayers, questions, oaths. Someone laughed.

She emerged into Starkadr's great gloom and strode to the Ascendant's new tent, surrounded by her Hrething and Agerastian honor guard.

Cerulean guards had been placed before the Ascendant's tent, and they stepped aside as she approached, bowing low. She'd almost reached the tent when the ground bucked, then listed down to the left.

The slick floor was their undoing.

Iskra's feet slid, then she went down to one knee. Her guards staggeredand fell. The tent before her swayed violently, its flexible poles adjusting under the weight of the heavy canvas.

Iskra had no purchase. One of the Hundred Snakes slid past her on his rear, cursing and trying to dig the point of his dagger into the rock. Tóki smacked his palms flat on the floor, gaining some traction and arresting his slide. Others attempted to do the same, gliding slowly past where she was balancing precariously, the fabric of her dress beneath her knee affording her a little purchase.

One of the tents that now rose above them upslope gave way. Its side bulged, then split, as barrels toppled over and came bouncing with sharp cracks in their direction. It happened so quickly that Iskra could only gape. Tóki let out a bellow and drew his ax. With supreme effort, he leaped up and batted aside a barrel that was coming right at her before he hit the ground hard on his shoulder. He slid away on his back, unable to stop.

Everywhere, the camp was descending into chaos. Tents collapsed. Men slid, yelling and cursing. Supplies broke free, horses reared and fell. The slope wasn't sharp, but the ground was so perilously smooth that the slightness of the incline didn't matter.

"We have to evacuate!" she cried. "Your Holiness!"

Her yell turned into a cry as the ground dropped out from underneath her, a sudden drop of some three or four feet that caused her weight to rise up, and her stomach floated with an awful sensation before the ground solidified beneath her once more. She sprawled, lost her balance, and fell.

Orishin, who had been at the front of their delegation, had managed to catch hold of one of the tent's guy lines. A piton had been driven with great effort into the rock, and this held him in place. With a lurch, he threw out his hand, and Iskra clasped it.

Her slide slowed, then stopped, and, following Tóki's example, she used her palms to give her a grip on the floor.

Orishin was staring down at her, tiny beads of sweat peppering his brow. "Iskra," he whispered. "Are we falling?"

"We have to get to the Gates," she said, struggling to keep her voice level. "We have to get the Ascendant out."

A slow chaos had enveloped the camp. Men, crates, carts, and supplies were rolling down the slope with the inevitability of a glacier's creep. Iskra thanked the White Gate that most of their forces had been sent to Ennoia, that only a minimal force had remained to run the logistics, maintain the camp, and secure the personage of the Ascendant. She shuddered to think what this scene might have looked like with several thousand additional soldiers.

"Look!"

She didn't know whose cry that was, but she whipped her gaze from side to side, unsure what she was looking for until she saw it: one of the Portals embedded in a twisting pillar was emitting smoke, a black mist from the center of which a figure was coalescing.

Hovering in the air.

"By the Seven Virtues," whispered one of the Cerulean Guards, who was lying on his side, clutching a tent pole. "What is that?"

The figure in the mist was growing more defined by the moment, and the runes over the doorway were glowing a fiery incardinine before fading away. Slender wings unfurled from around the naked being's ashen body. She couldn't determine its sex, but its glowing eyes killed all possible notions of its being human.

"A demon," said Iskra.

"The Portal's demon," said Orishin.

More runes were burning brightly over their Portals, up and down the pillar's twisted length. Iskra turned and saw a second pillar not too far away, saw its burning runes.

"Oh, no," she whispered.

The demon blinked, seeming to come to life by slow degrees, then focused its gaze on the camp below. Iskra saw it smile, an expression that chilled her to the core, and then it darted down amongst the tents. A scream of agony immediately sounded.

"What do we do?" one of her guards asked, his voice raw with panic. "How do we get out if the Portals are turning into fucking demons?"

"We have to get to His Holiness!" Iskra clasped Orishin's hand with both of her own and began to climb up his arm.

A demon touched down on the incline in front of the tent's entrance, sinking into a crouch with exquisite balance, unaffected by the slope. It was slender, built like a young woman without breasts; the space between its legs was smooth and without feature, and its skull was hairless and warped so that it spiked up into two horns. Its nose was a simple pair of slits, and its mouth was lipless and revealed milk-white fangs as it licked an obscenely long tongue over its chin.

One of the Hundred Serpents sacrificed his balance to hurl a dagger at it, then immediately fell over and slid down to the left. The dagger missed the demon by a hair's breadth but drew its attention; with the spiteful energy of a pouncing cat, it was upon him, tearing great gobbets of flesh from the man's stomach that quickly became glistening ropes of intestine.

The guard didn't scream. Instead, he drew his blade, shaking and convulsing, and struck the demon across the shoulder.

The wound was shallow, but the demon hissed in fury, seized the man by the hip and shoulder, and hurled him away. It turned, blinking, seeking a new target, and its eyes locked on Iskra.

Pearlescent white light emanated from the Ascendant's tent, lighting up its interior and pouring out through the tent flaps. The Ascendant stepped out and stood perfectly vertically on the incline, unconcerned by the treacherous surface.

The demon recoiled, then lifted up as the ground fell away from beneath them all.

Oh, sweet terror. It gripped Iskra by the throat and prevented her from screaming. With her heart in her throat, she clenched Orishin's hand with frantic strength as they floated up a few inches off the ground.

This time, they didn't just fall a few feet. They fell for what started to feel like forever and then lurched to a stop. She slammed back against the floor, the wind driven out of her, but before she could react, the floor fell away again.

The demon floated up into the darkness, carried aloft by its wings. Guards, crates, weapons – all of it lifted up around Iskra, hanging and turning in the air as Starkadr plummeted.

The Ascendant rose off the ground along with the rest of them, but he did not lose his composure. One knee bent, the other leg straight, he extended his arms out to the side as if for balance, and then drew his hands together to a form the holy symbol of the triangle.

Yells of growing terror pullulated all around them, accompanied by the shrill screams of the horses. Iskra's hair streamed past her face. It was the strangest experience of her life, to fall continuously just inches above the gleaming stone floor.

More demons were emerging from the pillars, but the speed of Starkadr's descent kept them aloft.

Iskra turned her gaze toward the Ascendant. A slight frown marred his expression, and his eyes were closed. The radiance from between his hands was growing, pushing outward in a visible sphere. Warmth spread through Iskra as the sphere enveloped her. It bathed every-thing in the softest gold, reaching out perhaps fifteen or twenty yards.

But, still, they fell. How high had they been? How long did they have left? What had happened?

Suddenly, Audsley appeared beside her, only to immediately flail as he too began to fall. There was a firecat latched onto his shoulder, and Audsley let out a yell and scrabbled as the firecat beat its wings frantically, . Then, as if he had remembered himself, he floated up in a controlled manner – only to turn, stare at the Ascendant, and scream.

It was a horrific sound. He crossed his arms over his face, and his skin began to blister in the golden light. Then, with a sob, he threw his arms wide, embracing the light, and shadows of virulent darkness fled from behind him: three distinct but distorted shapes that evanesced in the Ascendant's light.

Audsley hovered in the air, staring in wonder and fear at the Ascendant, tears running down his cheeks.

"Audsley!" Iskra shouted. Though there was no rushing wind to yell over, she pitched her voice to carry as if they were within the center of a storm. "What's happening?"

"It's over, dearest Iskra," he said, closing his eyes. "The demons that support Starkadr - they've been freed. All of them! We fall to our deaths!"

"Can you work a Portal? Get us out?"

"No," said Audsley, and she could barely hear his voice. "No, Iskra. It's too late."

Iskra bit her lip. Some primal instinct told her that their fall was about to come to its terrifying end; that, any second now, their world would explode, the perfect fastness of Starkadr's Portal chamber shat-tering like a glass sphere dashed against the floor.

All she could do was turn back to the Ascendant to stare at that young man and watch the golden light flood out from his core.

All she could so was watch as the demons flew down to hover just outside his radiance.

Helpless.

Waiting as they fell.

Chapter 40

A great tower squeezed between two buildings at the edge of the square collapsed, sinking into itself in a welter of dust, roaring like a dying demon. Kethe caught glimpses of a cavekiller's coils thrashing within the cascade of stone and support beams and heard the terrified screams of the soldiers as they fell from the rooftop.

Her right arm was slick to the shoulder with cavekiller ichor. Her body had become a living weapon, but there were too many of them and only one of her. She stood, panting, atop the petrified head of her sixth kill, lungs burning, the White Song keening within her soul. Despite the sense of illimitable power that suffused her, she knew only despair.

The proud army that had gathered to die for the Ascendant was being clawed to ribbons. Men were turning upon each other like rabid dogs, hacking and shoving their way through their own ranks in panic. The cavekillers were rearing and diving amongst them, their appearance as unpredictable as it was destructive. The ground of the great square was a horror, a ghastly ruin of fresh earthen mounds shot through with kragh corpses, riddled with tunnels and slick with blood.

Never had Kethe dreamed that such hell could be visited upon the earth. Wherever she looked, she saw critical need of her presence;

each moment saw more soldiers crushed and eviscerated, saw chaos stalking bloody-handed through the battlefield. If this was the crucible of their Empire, then they had been found wanting.

Another building collapsed, off to her left. She didn't even flinch, but turned instead to watch as it toppled forward over the regiment that had taken shelter at its base. Fifty killed in one go, not counting the archers who had leaped to their deaths at the onset.

Killing these insectile horrors was useless. There were too many. She had to think laterally. What could she do? What was the single most effective strategy she could adopt to change the outset of this battle?

Kethe turned to stare at the Solar Gates. She could only see their tops over the mounds of the dead. The screams that seemed to want to drown her barely registered. This battle was lost, but the war could still be won.

She had to quit her friends, her people, and find Tharok. She had to cut her way into Bythos and cleave his head in twain.

Kethe leaped down silently, falling the six yards to the torn earth with ease, and then ran forward. She leaped over corpses and sink-holes and around stone columns that had once been cavekillers, ever deeper into the maelstrom.

The ground was made muddy by gore. A cavekiller burst out of a tunnel before her, arcing overhead, but she didn't pause. Raising her blade, she sheared through its legs, letting them fall like perilous icicles behind her, and was past and out the other side even as the beast skewed, unbalanced, and fell thrashing onto its side.

The tenor of the cries changed. At the peak of one mound, she turned and saw that the screams of despair had given way to surprise.

She staggered to a stop and looked around the square.

The cavekillers had, without warning, ceased their attacks.

Kethe saw them dive into the ground, one after the other, tunneling out of sight, down into the depths of the earth.

They were quitting the battlefield?

Men were standing about in shock and horror. They were staring at the tunnel mouths as if each of them were a Black Gate in miniature, waiting for them to spew forth fresh nightmares.

None came.

Kethe waited, watching. But for the cries of the wounded, silence lay across the square. Hope dared stir in her breast.

A squat, bandy-legged warrior with a wicked ax leaped atop a ballista and raised the ax. "We did it, you sorry bastards! We drove them off!"

Hesitation and doubt held on for a moment, then ragged cheers swept across the square. Each passing second was proof of the man's words. Somehow, something had changed.

The cavekillers had been driven from the field of battle.

Kethe almost decided to return, to gather their forces and regroup. But they hadn't truly won. Not while Tharok was alive. She still had to see her goal through to the end.

The dips between the mounds of earth and flesh were almost chasms here, and she leaped from one peak to the other, soaring out into the air, her blade rivalling the morning sun. The Portals rose before her, eternally distant, until she climbed a final, tottering mound of the dead and from there saw Tharok facing off against Asho just below.

The kragh warlord's face had been butchered down one side, yet he stood tall, with his black scimitar in hand. His shoulders were heaving. For the first time, he looked less than immortal.

Asho was holding his charge. He was standing some ten paces away, black blade burning.

"Asho!"

Kethe leaped down to land beside him. She reached out for him, opening their channel, and almost vomited. The taint that came howling through was virulently nauseating, a concentrated lethality that made her vision swim. The White Song guttered beneath that awful onslaught, then slowly reasserted itself, burning away the evil so that, with a gasping heave, she managed to inhale and steady herself.

"Audsley," said Asho. "He stole Tharok's circlet and abandoned the fight." Then, startling, he cut off the flow of his taint to her. "No! You can't. Not this time."

Tharok was watching them, gathering himself, eyes narrowing and widening as if he were being besieged by a cavalcade of conflicting thoughts.

"What are you doing here?" Kethe spat in a vain attempt to clear the oily taste from her mouth. "How are you even standing?"

"Audsley," said Asho, and he touched a shard of black stone that had been punched into his chest. "His doing. He gave me this. It powers me, lets me fight, but the price - I don't want to think about it. He teleported me to Tharok, and we fought him. But he abandoned me. He took the circlet and disappeared."

"We'll deal with that later," said Kethe. "First, Tharok dies."

"Agreed," said Asho.

They split up, circling the kragh from opposite directions. He backed away a few steps, then stopped. Apparently realizing the impossibility of keeping them both in view, he instead stared off into the middle distance, his heaving shoulders relaxing. He held his scimitar with both hands, and the smoldering crimson tints that burned beneath his skin seemed to intensify.

Kethe waited till Asho was in position, then, knowing what his movements would be, feeling his intent as if it were her own, she ran straight at Tharok as Asho leaped.

The kragh immediately burst forward, sprinted ten steps and leaped. Kethe changed the trajectory of her attack to blast into him, his dodge having saved him perhaps a second's grace. Her blade flashed at him in a storm of blows that he blocked with nimble precision, wielding his great scimitar as if it were a dueling blade.

Asho touched down on the ground near her and immediately leaped again, somersaulting over them both and unleashing a blast of black flame at the kragh as he did so – flame that Kethe drank in deep, immune to its ire as she pressed her attack.

Tharok raised his fist, and white light pulsed from his hand, forming a shield that curved a yard across, nullifying the flames and disappearing as it did so.

Kethe nearly stumbled, so extreme was her shock. A shield of white flame? But that was the province of the Virtues, of the Empire's most holy. How…?

Tharok's fist crunched into her face.

She staggered back and nearly fell, but deflected a series of blows on instinct. Then the pressure was gone, and Tharok's attention turned to Asho.

Kethe's mind was reeling. Tharok? A Virtue? Dissonance threatened her mind. She wiped the blood from her upper lip, ignored the sharp pain of her shattered nose, and threw herself forward with a scream.

Tharok's back was turned to her. Perhaps he hadn't expected her to recover so quickly. She carved a deep gash diagonally from his shoulder to the opposite hip, then slammed the point of her blade home through his back.

With a roar, Tharok leaped forward, escaping Asho's attacks, and Kethe's blade was torn from her fingers. She saw the deep diagonal cut healing as he flew. The kragh landed awkwardly, high up on a slope of riven earth; then he turned, gasping, sweat and blood dripping from his jaw, and faced them.

Her blade was searing his flesh, its point emerging just below his rib cage. He reached behind his back, clasped the hilt of her blade, and pulled it out. Carefully, as if he were holding a venomous snake, he brought her sword around.

Its flame didn't go out.

He stared down at it. White fire burned and dripped from its length.

"Why isn't it extinguishing?" Asho demanded.

"I don't know," Kethe said, feeling helpless.

Tharok transferred his gaze to his scimitar. He narrowed his eyes, and, with a *whoomph*, black flames ran down its length.

Two blades, black and white. He raised them before his face and then drew Kethe's blade down the length of his scimitar, scraping metal against metal, white fire on black. Where they touched, a gout of sparks burst free, incandescing and searingly bright.

"Kethe," said Asho. "What the fuck."

"I don't know," she all but wailed. "How is he wielding the white fire?"

Tharok stretched and shook out his shoulders. The wound above his hip that should have killed him had sealed over and scarred. He rolled his head on his neck, eliciting a series of sharp pops. Then he hunched over, his musculature tensing, opened his maw, bared his prodigious tusks, and roared.

"Get a blade!" said Asho. "Hurry!"

Tharok leaped down at them, the force of his jump such that he moved in a straight line down from his vantage point. Kethe threw herself aside into a roll and came up scrambling and covered in bloody mud.

A blade! Something, anything - where - there! A kragh ax. She ran and scooped it up only to find that it had only a foot of wooden haft below the double ax heads. Frantic, clutching it in her left hand, she saw another ax a few yards away. She ran and grabbed it, and then, on impulse, broke the shaft off at the same length. Double ax heads in each hand, clutched almost like daggers, she ran back into the fray.

Asho was being battered back onto his heels like a ship caught in a furious storm, stumbling and dodging over the treacherous terrain. Tharok had become an elemental force, both blades shrieking as they fell upon the Bythian repeatedly, without surcease.

Kethe launched herself at Tharok's back, but he heard her coming. He turned, and they engaged in close-quarters combat, her ax heads catching fire as she parried his first blow. The shortness of their hafts and her own unnatural strength allowed her to use them almost like mailed fists: she punched them at him, blocked the sweep of his swords, dueling with only two feet of space between them, a mad, impossible flurry of blows that was only broken off when Asho charged back in.

Tharok didn't give ground. He briefly fought them both, Kethe's old blade wielded against her ax heads, Tharok's scimitar against Asho's ebon sword. Then, with complete confidence, Tharok stepped back and swapped the blades from one hand to the other by tossing them over/under, and returned right back to the fight.

Impossible. She and Asho were fighting with everything they had, and he was holding them off simultaneously. Despite her white flame, she could see her ax heads being battered and notched into oblivion by the power of his blocks, while Asho was unable to find a chink in Tharok's defenses, her old sword rebuffing his attacks at every angle.

"Asho!" she screamed. "Open to me!"

"No!" His voice was a ragged cry. "It'll kill you!"

Tharok dropped to a spinning crouch, and Kethe and Asho leaped to avoid having their legs cut out from under them. Tharok immediately launched himself up and punched Asho under the chin, knocking him flying backwards.

While Tharok was mid-jump, Kethe hit him in the side, wrapped her ax blades around him as she hugged him tight, then dragged them into his chest.

He roared in pain as they fell to the ground and fell apart, but she gave him no surcease. She was upon him in a trice, slicing at him as he whipped his blade back and forth, blocking her with his scimitar, having lost her old blade in the fall.

His free arm whipped around, and dirt flew into her face. She cut through the spray of gravel in a futile fury but was forced to close her eyes immediately thereafter. She leaped back to avoid the incoming attack, but it was too late. On instinct, she parried his blow, but the force sent her tumbling down the hill to lie still at the muddy bottom.

Grunting with pain, Kethe levered herself back to her feet. Asho and Tharok did the same, and they all eyed each other warily.

"Asho," said Kethe. "Now."

The spike in Asho's chest was greatly diminished. Was it the source of his power? Some form of gatestone? Either way, she could tell that he was suffering; he was dripping sweat and shaking as if in the grips of a fierce fever.

"Asho!" she screamed at him. "Open!"

He hesitated – and then he did. The channel roared wide, and his taint came rushing through, a deluge of darkness and filth. This time, she was ready. She summoned the White Song and met the flow with everything she had, consuming it faster than it could overwhelm her.

Kethe rocked back on her heels, lost her balance, then caught it. "Now," she croaked. "Attack!"

Calling on her reserves, she ran forward. Asho lifted his hand, palm directed at Tharok, and from ten yards away, unleashed his flame.

It was different this time. Kethe culled the taint from its casting even as it left his body, leaving nothing but superheated fury. Tharok had regained her old blade, and, with a grunt, he crossed both swords before him and took the flames full-on.

Their impact rocked him. He stumbled, black fire lashing all around him, and into this madness Kethe dove, her ax heads scoring deep wounds in the kragh's shoulders and side.

Tharok was forced to ignore her, to focus completely on defending himself from Asho. He twisted, swayed away, then broke and ran. Asho trailed him with fire.

Her vision swimming, Kethe hurled first one ax head, then the second at Tharok's fleeing form. They both hit him with punishing strength.

Tharok fell.

Asho kept the flames roaring around the kragh, torching the earth, incinerating the corpses. Tharok was hidden within the maelstrom.

Finally, Asho let off with a cry and sank to his knees. The spike in his chest was gone. Kethe stood still, desperately seeking to cleanse him as she felt the ravages of his power undoing the fabric of his body.

But her gaze remained locked on Tharok. His skin cracked and burned, the ax heads sunk deep into his thigh and side, he lay breathing shallowly. Smoke was rising all around him.

He should be dead.

But with something that sounded like a curse, he began to climb slowly and laboriously to his feet.

"No," whispered Kethe. "It can't be."

Tharok stood, swaying. The flames were gone from his blades, which hung at his sides. His flesh was horrifically burned, but slowly, surely, it was healing, the raw, crimson cracks scarring over.

She had to finish him. Had to cut him down before he could fully heal.

But it was all she could do to continue to cleanse Asho, to keep him from sinking beneath the recoil of his powers.

Then, as they stared at each other, the sky was blotted out by stone.

A mountain appeared in the sky above them, a huge and ponderous impossibility, and they were plunged into shadow. Looking up, Kethe felt something akin to vertigo. Her knees went weak, and she fought the instinct to drop to one knee and put a hand out to steady herself.

The mountain's base was rough and unworked, as if it had been torn out of the earth by the roots. It was riven with deep cracks and textured by ragged protrusions, all of it gleaming darkly, as if the black rock were slick with moisture.

She'd seen that kind of rock before, had walked on it: that impossible obsidian expanse that had stretched out under her feet in Starkadr's Portal chamber.

"How is this possible?" whispered Asho.

Tharok was also staring straight up, his jaw clenched shut, swaying with pain.

"Starkadr?" asked Kethe. "Here? How?"

Its base was perhaps a mile across. They were directly beneath it.

"Perhaps - perhaps this is Audsley's doing?" Asho slowly sank to his knees. "Perhaps he's brought it here to help us?"

Kethe could only gape. It was too close for her to take it all in at once; she had to continuously sweep her gaze from one side to the other.

Tharok grunted and pointed at one part of the mountain's base. Rocks were falling from it as something broke free and tunneled down and out into the sunlit air.

A big man with wings of fire.

Kethe's mind was sluggish with shock, but she managed to mutter, "Demon."

"Look," said Asho. "More of them."

Chunks of rock were continuing to fall from different parts of the stonecloud's underside, looking like pebbles or dust relative to the mountain's enormous bulk. Each signaled the appearance of a new hole, and from that dark mouth, a winged figure emerged.

They kept coming. Dozens, then hundreds of them, pouring out like smoke, some of them larger than the others.

"Asho," said Kethe. "Please. What's happening?"

"I don't know," he said. "By the Black Gate, I don't know."

"Do you see that?" Kethe looked past the massing demons at the stonecloud itself. It was listing. "Oh, no," she groaned.

"The demons are free," Asho said, sounding dazed by his sudden realization. "Which means they're not powering Starkadr's flight."

The stonecloud continued to list to one side, and then, with ponderous lethargy, it began to fall.

"We've got to get out!" cried Asho. He cast about wildly. "Through the Solar Portals. It's our only chance!"

Kethe hurried to his side. "They'll be crushed by the stonecloud - we won't be able to come back through!"

"Better than dying," Asho said grimly as he gripped her hand and hauled himself to his feet.

"But my mother! The Ascendant! They're inside Starkadr!"

The stonecloud's fall was gathering speed, and Kethe could feel an awful pressure building up around her. Hoarse shouts and screams of newfound panic echoed all around her – coming from the hundreds of thousands of people of Ennoia.

"Go!" Tharok barked, and he began to stride with great pain toward the Bythian Gate.

"We have to go," said Asho. "We won't help them by staying."

Kethe thought of the men and women who were about to be crushed beneath the falling stonecloud – of her mother and the remnants of the refugee camp inside Starkadr. A great and terrible wail tore itself free from her depths. It was too much to bear.

Above them, the demons were still emerging, massing in their thousands.

"Come!" Asho tugged on her hand. With extreme effort, he hobbled after Tharok, pulling Kethe after him.

Tears streamed down Kethe's face. Tripping and stumbling, unable to tear her eyes from the stonecloud, she followed Asho toward the Portal.

Starkadr was dropping faster with every passing second. The darkness around them was growing more absolute, the gloom turning to deep shadow, then sinking into deepest night.

"Run!" Asho screamed, grimacing with pain and exhaustion as he charged through the bloody mire. "Run, Kethe, run!"

Kethe tore her eyes free from the mountain and forced herself forward, passing Asho and hauling him behind her.

They weren't going to make it. The stonecloud was falling too quickly.

"Leave me," gasped Asho. "Run!"

She didn't bother to answer. She clutched his hand and hauled him after her.

A fierce wind was picking up, streaming past them in all directions. The screams from around the square were continuous, an ongoing cacophony of distress that assailed the depths of Kethe's mind.

Asho tripped and fell.

Kethe let out a scream of anguish as she was dragged to her knees. No time. No time! But she refused to let go of his hand. Reaching down, she gripped him by the arm. "Get up! Asho, get up!"

He looked up at her from where he was lying, his pale face luminous in the gathering dark. "I love you, Kethe Kyferin."

There was a peace in his voice, a resignation, that chilled her to the bone.

The stonecloud was a hundred yards above them, maybe less, falling ever faster. She heard the crashing, rolling roar as it impacted the roofs and spires of Ennoia, the wind a hurricane blast now, giving them mere seconds left to live - and then a huge hand gripped the back of her shirt.

Tharok.

A final attack? Kethe let out a cry of fury that he should seek revenge in this last awful moment - and then he and bounded forward , carrying her and Asho into the Gate's rippling fire.

The void welcomed them, drowned them in its icy blackness, twisted and inverted them, then spat them out onto the broad ramp that led up to the Ennoian Portal in Bythos.

They tumbled, rolled, came to a stop.

Kethe lay there stunned, unable to move. The screams, the wails, the shrieking of the wind that carried the demons' laughter on its edges, the crushing pressure, that falling doom - all of it was gone.

But somewhere in the world, wherever Ennoia might be, Starkadr had just fallen. Tens of thousands of lives had been snuffed out.

Somewhere, a plague of demons was coalescing.

Kethe couldn't move. Couldn't find any reason to move. At her side, Asho was laughing weakly.

Tharok grunted and released her, then slowly set about climbing to his feet. A dozen kragh rushed up and assisted him. Others snatched up Kethe and Asho, lifting them to their feet, hands closed around their arms.

A black-skinned kragh swept a cloak over Tharok's shoulders. The warlord slowly straightened, grimacing as his burnt skin parted to reveal red gashes, only to heal tenuously once more.

He stared at Kethe and Asho, his bestial face inscrutable, then gave a simple command in kragh.

Kethe didn't even struggle. She had nothing left to struggle for.

Instead of cutting her open, the kragh let go of Kethe. She almost sagged down to her knees, but then she thought of Asho and stepped up next to him, slipping under his arm as he nearly collapsed in turn.

Turning to Tharok, she shook her head in dismayed wonder and asked him, "Why?"

Tharok looked past her at the Ennoian Portal. Kethe followed his gaze and felt a dull thump of surprise. The burning fire was gone. The Gate was dead.

Of course. She felt a wave of scorn for herself. Of course.

"That is why," rumbled Tharok. "Everything has changed. We are no longer enemies. Now, we are allies."

He took a moment to look around at what was left of his army, then returned his attention to Kethe.

"Now," he said, "we must fight together – if we are to survive what is to come."

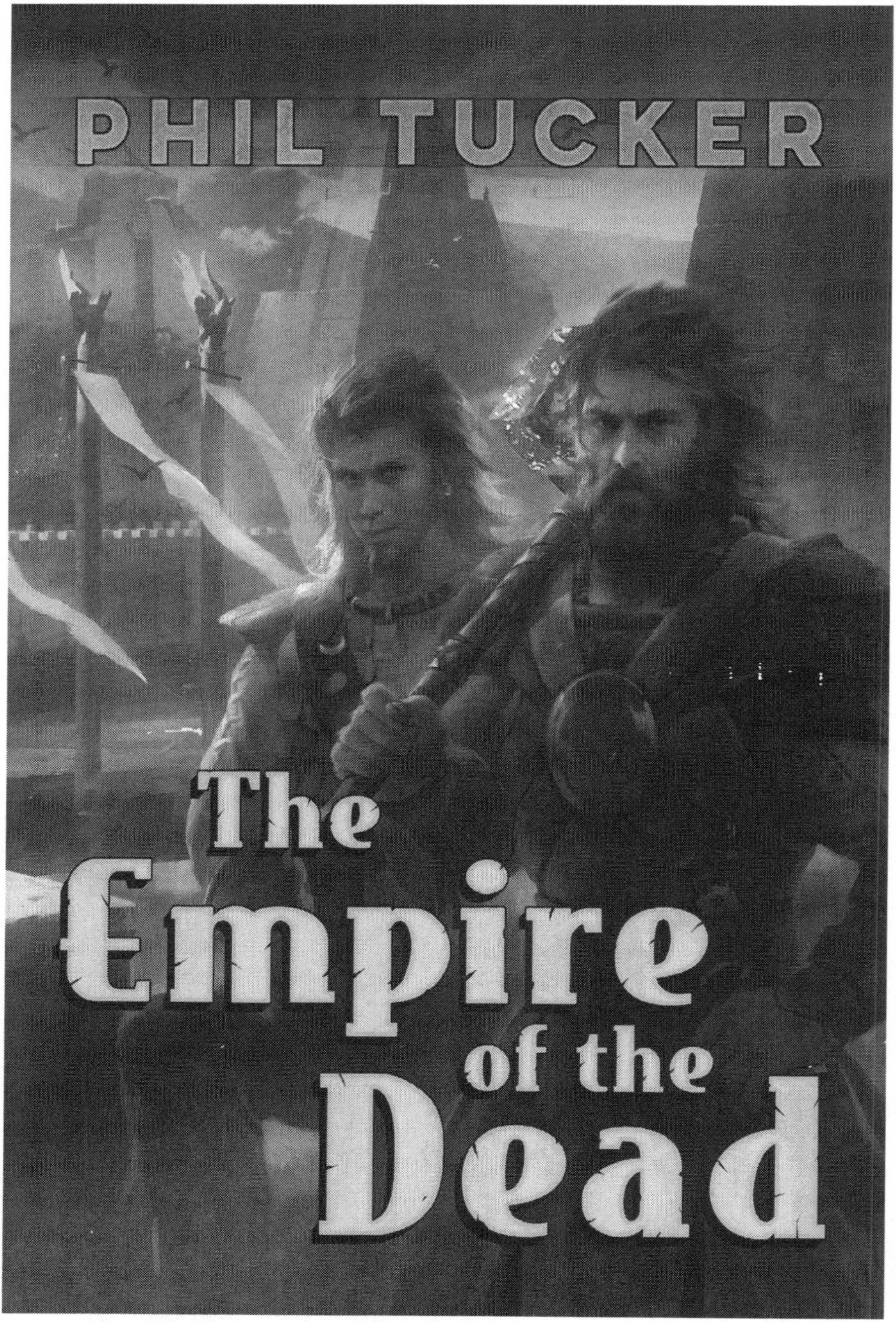
PHIL TUCKER
The Empire of the Dead

The

EMPIRE

of the

DEAD

———— ·⫯⟫⟨●⟩●⟨⟪⫯· ———— ——

Book 1 of the Godsblood Trilogy

I t has been two decades since the daughter of the death goddess enacted her cruel betrayal. Two decades since the other nine gods were slain, their semi-divine progeny murdered, and the disparate peoples of the empire forced to bend knee to their new empress and her armies of the dead.

But when bandits kidnap a youth at the edges of the empire, two aged and broken heroes emerge from obscurity to attempt an unlikely rescue. Neither man relishes confronting the forces of their dread empress, but when they learn that their quarry is being held for sacrifice in the imperial city of Rekkidu, they reluctantly begin gathering a crew of uniquely talented criminals to attempt an impossible rescue.

A rescue whose failure could have shattering consequences. For they are Jarek and Acharsis, the last of the demigods, long thought dead and whose return could shake the very foundations of the empire.

Join Phil Tucker

Thank you for beginning this journey with me. I've always wanted to write the kind of sprawling epic fantasy that I enjoyed in my youth, and I truly appreciate your reading my tale and hope that you've enjoyed it thus far. Please consider signing up for my mailing list. I'll send you a copy of Escape from Bythos, the Path of Flames prequel. You'll find out how Asho ended up a squire in the Black Wolves, and the strange and harrowing events that caused Lord Kyferin to break with all traditions and lift him out of the city of slaves.

If you already have a copy, you can still sign up for my mailing list so as to be notified when future books are released:

EEPURL.COM/B4HLHF